"Jump!"

The word was  apparently greatly

Immediately C ward, heedless of t of tiny figures standing in the snow below.

"Jump!" shouted one of them, and this time all three bent over from the force of their fulsome guffaws. "We'll catch you!" he hollered, spreading his great arms in an expansive, ludicrous gesture.

"Thanoi," muttered the elf, recognizing the tusked faces and the powerful and hulking bodies of the walrus men. His memories of the crude race were bad, dating back to his first quest on this glacier—a search for an orb of dragonkind that had brought him here more than forty years ago.

"Go away," he shouted in reply. "Or perhaps you'd care to catch one of my arrows!"

He tried the bluff, hoping that the creatures hadn't seen that he wasn't armed with a bow. He was disappointed when they only laughed harder.

Explore Further Adventures in the Dragonlance® Saga!

DRAGONLANCE: FIFTH AGE® Dramatic Adventure Game: Everything you need to play in the world of the bestselling DRAGONLANCE Saga. (ISBN 0-7869-0535-2)

DRAGONLANCE Fate Deck: Give the SAGA® game system a try with this complete roleplaying game starter set! (ISBN 0-7869-1145-X)

DRAGONLANCE Classics 15th Anniversary Edition: This special collection of classic products invites fans old and new to play the adventures that launched the DRAGONLANCE Saga phenomenon! This anniversary edition includes both the classic adventures as well as new information and rules for using both AD&D® and SAGA game rules. (ISBN 0-7869-1350-9)

The Bestiary: This beautifully illustrated resource provides readers with an ultimate guide to the animals and creatures of the DRAGONLANCE Saga—beasts from the classic tales set during the War of the Lance, as well as newer monsters from the Fifth Age of Krynn. (ISBN 0-7869-0795-9)

Palanthas: DRAGONLANCE readers and gamers alike can explore the history and sites of the bustling city of Palanthas.

Citadel of Light: In a world shadowed by dragonwing, the Citadel of Light is both a beacon of hope and a valuable weapon in the struggle against the Great Dragons of the Fifth Age. This product includes both source material and an adventure. (ISBN 0-7869-0748-7)

Reader's Companion
The Odyssey of Gilthanas

Douglas Niles, Steve Miller, and Stan!

©1999 TSR, Inc.
All Rights Reserved.

Editors: Joe Gillespie, Miranda Horner, and Pat McGilligan
Cover Artist: Jeff Easley ♦ Interior Artist: Dennis Cramer
Cartographer: Mark Painter ♦ Typesetter: Angelika Lokotz
Graphic Designers: Dawn Murin and Tanya Matson
Creative Directors: Sue Weinlein Cook and Stan!
Art Director: Dawn Murin
Original DRAGON WARS™ Design: Ed Stark and Stan!

Based on the original DUNGEONS & DRAGONS® rules
created by E. Gary Gygax and Dave Arneson.

Based on the SAGA® rules created by William W. Connors.

First Printing: August 1999
Library of Congress Catalog Card Number: 99-62255

9 8 7 6 5 4 3 2 1

ISBN: 0-7869-1446-7

T11446-620

U.S., CANADA, ASIA,
PACIFIC, & LATIN AMERICA
Wizards of the Coast, Inc.
P.O. Box 707
Renton, WA 98057-0707
+1-800-324-6496

EUROPEAN HEADQUARTERS
Wizards of the Coast, Belgium
P.B. 2031
2600 Berchem
Belgium
+32-70-23-32-77

Visit our website at **www.tsr.com**

D. CRAMER

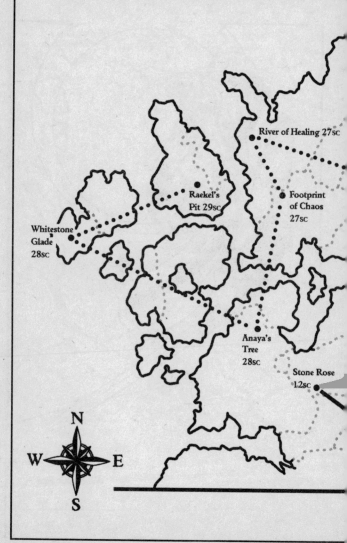

THE ODYSSEY OF GILTHANA

River of Healing 27sc

Raekel's
Pit 29sc

Footprint
of Chaos
27sc

Whitestone
Glade
28sc

Anaya's
Tree
28sc

Stone Rose
12sc

N
W   E
S

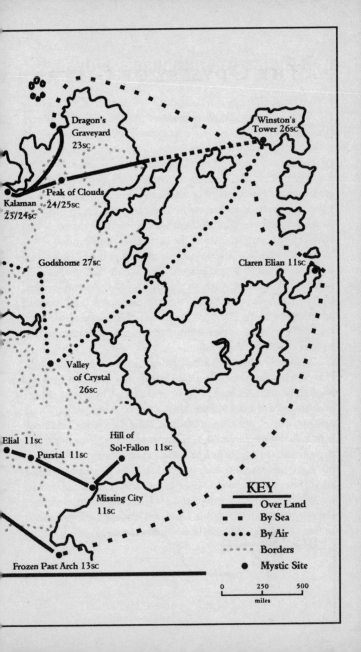

A Guide to Gilthanas's Odyssey

From the beginning, the DRAGONLANCE Saga has belonged to two different worlds: the worlds of literature and of adventure gaming. While novels and game products have always relied on one another to tell parts of the Saga, and while the two have often worked hand-in-hand to delve into tales with a greater depth than either medium could do alone, games and books have remained distinct from one another. Role-playing gamers read the novels, readers used game products as reference material, but there was never a single book that served both communities at the same time—until now.

The Odyssey of Gilthanas was originally going to be a game resource titled "Mystic Places," but when the opportunity arose to try this new format, the DRAGONLANCE team jumped at it. After all, what better way to celebrate the fifteenth anniversary of the DRAGONLANCE Saga, the first world created for both fiction and roleplaying, than to take that natural link to the next stage of evolution.

This book addresses two distinct needs. First, it tells the tale of what happened to Prince Gilthanas between his final appearance in Kalaman near the end of the Chronicles trilogy and his release from Khellendros's prison camp in the Dragons of a New Age trilogy by Jean Rabe. Secondly, this book provides source material in the appendix for several intriguing sites that have existed on DRAGONLANCE maps for years but have never made their way into a book or game product. As it turns out, these sites are places Gilthanas visited during his odyssey. For players of the DRAGONLANCE: FIFTH AGE or the ADVANCED DUNGEONS & DRAGONS games, the information in this appendix applies directly to their campaigns.

SOTHI NUINQUA TSALARIOTH

Off the Coast of Solamnia, 28sc

The water dripped down the surface of dank timbers in a regular cadence, approximately in time to the beating of the prisoner's heart. He had no idea how many heartbeats, how many hours or even days had passed since that persistent plopping had formed the framework of his existence, but he took comfort in it, for the very act of counting, of feeling his heart beat, confirmed that he was indeed alive.

And while he lived, he should feel hope . . . shouldn't he?

He tried to resist the part of him that answered: perhaps not, perhaps hope was over. After years of wandering, after escapes and fruitless quests, after deceit and betrayal, he was back where he had begun. A prisoner, locked in the darkness, left alone to rot.

This time his cell was a ship—a vessel of the Dark Knights bearing him to an unknown destination. He felt the gentle rocking of the hull and heard the straining of the timbers as the swells rose and fell. He had thought that it was utterly dark, but when the throbbing in his skull subsided slightly, he recognized that his eyes were too swollen to open. Either that, or a beating at the hands of the guards had blinded him, and he had been mercifully unconscious at the time.

Yet he gradually became aware that, in this damp and chilly hold, he was not alone. He examined his surroundings by smell and by sound. The air was musty, stained with the ordure of mold and urine, and underlaid by the more vile stenches of feces and rotten flesh. No breeze caressed his skin, and the sense of dampness came from more than the steady dripping—it permeated him in the chill of the stagnant air, in the lack of any suggestion of warmth from the sun or any source of Krynn-bound fire.

Cruel shackles bound his wrists to a wall, holding him spread-eagled in a sitting position. His arms and hands, suspended to the sides, felt numb, and his buttocks and legs were stiff from bearing his weight on cold, unforgiving timbers. When he fully understood his position, he took heart from the fact of his iron manacles: the shackles served as a confirmation of time. It had not been weeks or months since he had been placed in this hold. In fact, he had not changed posture to eat, nor even to drink, so he knew that he had not been like this for very many days—else he would be dead by now.

He was below decks on a large ship that was bound for he knew not where. But he could take some minimal comfort from the knowledge that others were in this place with him. He heard hushed whispers—people's voices scarcely daring to make a sound. He heard someone shuffle close to him with bare feet gliding almost soundlessly across the smooth boards.

And then he heard words, and his life began to return to him.

"My Prince . . . O Royal Master—can you ever forgive me?"

The voice was a groan and was followed by emphatic shushing; obviously other prisoners wanted the speaker to keep his voice down to spare them the risk of punishment by the stern Dark Knights who guarded them.

"Please," whispered the prince. "Try to be silent . . . and know that I have forgiven you. You but acted upon the impulse of your heart—and if I had not done the same, we neither of us would be here today."

"I . . . I'm sorry," replied the one the prince remembered as Lethagas. Leth was a young elf, but he had served faithfully and well. Now his guilt, and his grief, were burdens that the prisoner neither needed nor deserved.

For a time the hold was silent save for the gradual creaking of the ship. He tried to let his mind drift away, to recall an image of silver beauty, a laugh like the music of the cosmos . . . gods, how he missed her. He had crossed a world to find her, sought for years, for decades . . . only to come to this. And still he would not acknowledge defeat.

The swelling around the prince's eyes gradually lessened, and he could at last get a blurred look at his surroundings. Six other prisoners shared the hold with him, though only he was so rudely chained to the wall. He recognized Lethagas among them. The others, like Leth and himself, were male elves. To a man ragged garments barely covered their filthy skin, and they bore unkempt golden hair. Pale skin suggested that the prisoners had languished below decks for quite some time.

Eventually, a hunchbacked turnkey silently brought a bowl of food and a pail of water under the watchful eyes of a pair of Dark Knights. These guards, cloaked from head to foot in black, observed like very dangerous statues as the grotesque servant unlocked the door in the iron bars at the front of the cell. He opened the portal only wide enough to push the bowl and bucket into the hold. A single grimy ladle floated in the brownish water.

When the guards left, the elven prisoners took turns scooping out bites of vile chowder and drinking putrid water. The prince was pleased to see none of the bickering, even fighting, erupt as it would among humans or dwarves entrusted with a similar regimen. The others even allowed Lethagas to offer the prince the first serving, though he declined and supped in turn with the rest.

The eating ended before the hunger. Afterward, the prisoners gathered around him—the elf with the long scar on his face who wore leggings of silver and a tunic of burnished leather. Apparently they knew that the guards would stay for a while because one, an elder who was missing one eye and limped awkwardly on a withered leg, at last spoke up.

"He called you prince, noble elf. What is your name?"

"I am Gilthanas Solostaran, prince of Qualinesti," he replied simply.

"We know of you, O Prince," said the crippled elf. "And we hail your family's name. But tell me: How do you come to be the prisoner of the Dark Knights, hauled in this ship of death?"

"That is a story that I, myself, don't even understand," replied the elf with a wry chuckle. "And it would take a very long time to tell."

"Then we are indeed fortunate," declared the elder. "For there is only one thing in which we are wealthy, and that is time."

Gilthanas looked at the group, all of whom regarded him with attentive eyes. Truly, he didn't know how his road had brought him here, but perhaps it would help him to understand if he were to put the story into words. . . .

🗡 🗡 🗡 🗡 🗡

"Once I had a great deal more than mere time," Gilthanas began. His thoughts drifted back, and it seemed as though he might have been looking at an earlier life—an existence before dungeons and quests and wanderings had given shape to his days. Indeed, he might have been considering the life of someone else for all the similarities he could bring to his present circumstances.

"I had power and wealth . . . I had a reputation known far and wide, status as a hero in the greatest cause of the world . . . and yet, I could not find happiness."

"I remember," said the elder prisoner. "You were lord of some city in the north . . . Kalaman, was it not?"

"Indeed, good friend. But pray, tell me your name."

"I am called Banatharl, of Qualinesti Vale." The elf's voice was soft, distant, and Gilthanas knew that he, too, was trying to reconstruct a well-removed past. "I was a follower of your brother Porthios, until the Dark Knights made me their pet."

"Ah, Porthios . . . he has a place in my tale, though our stories are not as intertwined as many brothers might be."

"To Kalaman, then?" prodded a younger elf, who introduced himself as Carranias, also of Qualinesti. "Was that not your fiefdom after the War of the Lance?"

"Indeed. I came to that city at the culmination of the Vingaard Campaign, the spring season of battles resulting in the defeat of Highlord Ariakas, the Dragon Emperor of Ansalon."

"You came at the head of the liberating army, did you not?" prodded Lethagas.

"As a part of that army . . . my sister Laurana was the Golden General, appointed by the Knights of Solamnia to lead them in the triumphant campaign. I flew upon Silvara . . . greatest, wisest, most beautiful silver dragon in all the world. Together we battled the wyrms of Takhisis, Queen of Darkness. We slew many powerful serpents of blue. And when the Dark Queen's armies fled Kalaman, Silvara and I came to rest in the city's great plaza. It was soon after our ultimate victory at Neraka that the people of Kalaman sent for me and asked me to be their Lord Mayor."

"But were you not a prince of Qualinesti?" asked Banatharl.

"Indeed, but that realm was the fiefdom of my brother Porthios. His rulership seemed secured, and it even bore splendid portents for the future. You will remember that shortly after the War of the Lance, he married Alhana Starbreeze, who was herself heir to the other elven realm, Silvanesti."

"She was a queen to Qualinesti as well," nodded the elder. "And the people held out great hope that she would bear a child to the king and queen—an elf who would bring the promise of the unification of our ancient race."

"True. And with my homeland thus in good hands, I had cause to use my talents elsewhere, to go where I was needed."

"And you were needed in Kalaman?"

"So it seemed . . . but still, it was not as easy as that." Gilthanas fell silent as the rest of the story unfolded in his memory. He could not speak of his love for Silvara, of the beautiful silver-haired elfmaid who had torched his heart into fire as if kindling it from chilly coal. She was his perfect lifemate. She should have been his bride and borne him children. . . .

But then he had learned the truth: Though she could choose to look like a woman, with beauty so deep that it tore his heart, she was not an elf. In her heart and soul and true flesh she was a silver dragon. Silvara had lived for more years even than the decades-old elven prince. She was a creature of ancient might and nearly immortal wisdom. He had loved her, and he thought she had loved him, but their differences were too great. It had seemed to both of them that their lives had been ordained to be stories in separate books.

It had not been the silver dragon who had made the initial, fateful decision. Instead, the elf had turned his back . . . Gilthanas had sent Silvara away and turned his life to helping the humans who needed him.

For many years, he almost convinced himself that he had done the right thing.

The other elves in the cell maintained a respectful silence, obviously aware that Gilthanas was reliving memories he did not wish to share. But the prince was conscious of his audience, of the tale he had started to tell, and so he drew a deep breath.

"Let me just say that my years in Kalaman went by in a blur . . . that I was effective there, I even dare to say popular. But I wasn't really needed. Nor did I find in the work the kind of usefulness that let me know I was doing the right thing. Instead, I grew more and more restless, and as the years turned to decades, I knew that I would have to leave."

"Did you know where you wanted to go?" asked Banatharl.

Gilthanas laughed ruefully, shaking his head. "It was only that fact that kept me in the city for as long as I remained . . . thirty full years after the War of the Lance. But as time passed I became increasingly restless, longing for . . . for someone I had lost.

"History passed in the rest of Krynn, of course. I learned that my brother Porthios was in Silvanesti, working hard to drive corruption from that land, to clean the detritus left in the wake of the war—which war, as every elf knows, was particularly cruel to that land of our hallowed ancestors."

"It is said that the late Silvanesti king's nightmares became real," whispered the younger elf, Carranias.

"It is said truthfully," whispered another ancient elf.

"And when the realm's own regent, Konnal, failed to conquer the corruption, Porthios arrived. It was he who led the Silvanesti to victory in their own realm." Carranias asserted his knowledge of elven history, while the other listeners nodded in mute agreement.

"And as reward for his service," Banatharl said bitterly, "Konnal had him arrested, thrown into a prison cell and sentenced to death. I know this, for I flew with those who would have rescued him in Silvanasti . . . but even then, our lord took care to see that war was avoided between the two elven nations."

"Aye. But I knew none of this as I decided to visit my brother. I merely wished to see the hallowed kingdom he had restored and to learn from him about the lives of the rest of our family. It was with a sense of freedom, even exhilaration, that I departed Kalaman. I traveled by sea to Sanction, and then overland until I had reached the border of Silvanesti."

"Did you tell your brother you were coming?" This question came from Carranias, whose eyes had widened with his imaginings about these royal doings.

"No . . . fool that I was, I wanted to surprise him. Of course, if I had gotten in touch with him, he might have warned me away, or I might have been able to help him. As it was, Konnal's agents seized me before I had ridden many miles down the peaceful forest trails.

"Despite that bitter assault—or perhaps because of it—I still remember the wondrous sensations of my entrance into the elven kingdom: Silvanesti spread like a garden around me, with fragrant blooms drooping heavily from lush branches, trees sculpted into such perfection that they formed arches overhead, and a natural canopy that extended for miles. I came to a pond—a still pool that reflected the sky with mirrored perfection—and here I dismounted to enjoy an afternoon's rest beneath the shade of a lush evergreen.

"And this is where Konnal's agents took me . . . they rushed from all sides, threw nets, and beat me with clubs. Before I knew what was happening, they had made me a prisoner."

"Did they take you to the palace or to some prison in Silvanost?" Banatharl wondered, speaking of the capital of the realm and one of the oldest cities in the world.

"Would that they had . . . but instead I was taken to a mere hole in the ground, a dirt-walled dungeon where I was the only prisoner, and my guards were picked from Konnal's personal agents."

"Where was that place?"

"I did not learn until much later . . . but I languished there for a long time. It turned out to be a dozen years, while so many things passed in the world beyond. My guards gleefully related the events I was missing: of Porthios shamed before the ruling Sinthal-Elish, of his arrest and imprisonment in the Tower of Stars." The prince's voice tightened. "They joked about the irony, boasted of how the two princes of Qualinesti were the prisoners of Silvanesti because they foolishly tried to bring the Qualinesti and Silvanesti nations together. My own fate, I was assured, remained a secret from the outside world. . ."

"While Porthios made his escape," Banatharl interjected.

"Aye . . . Tanis Half-Elven and two loyal griffins, plucking Porthios from the high tower and bearing him to safety. My guards were infuriated by his escape—they beat me bloody in their vexation—but the cruel fellows gloated about the fact that my brother had gone away, and he didn't even know that he was leaving me behind. They also mentioned how Alhana, the rightful ruler of Silvanesti, had also been exiled."

Gilthanas drew a breath. In the silent prison, his elven listeners remained rapt.

"Of course, it was not long after that the Chaos War wracked Krynn—the summer of heat that marked the departure of the old gods, the vanishing of magic. That fact I encountered even in my cell, where the tiny incantations I had performed to make my imprisonment more tolerable—a glimmer of flame, a small cloak of warmth or coals for drying—all ceased to function.

"I tell you, good elves, that was the beginning of years when I felt utterly bereft. I longed for my homeland and convinced myself that I would die in that hole—that I would never see Qualinesti, nor the one I missed above all others, again. . . ."

SOTHI NUINQUA TSALARIOTH

The Hill of Sol-Fallon, 11sc

The key turned in the lock with a harsher sound than usual, perhaps because this time it was twisted with anger, or perhaps gloating delight. Whatever the emotion of the person who unlocked the door, Gilthanas knew that this was not his usual jailor come with his repast of stale bread or vile stew.

Scrambling to his feet, the elven prince stood erect and glared at the shadowed hallway beyond. Years of confinement had paled his skin and, no doubt, weakened his muscles, but they had done nothing to break his spirit. And when he saw the one who had opened his door, that spirit compelled him into a furious rush—a wild attack of swinging fists and inarticulate curses.

Naturally, Konnal had not come alone. The two guards of

Silvanesti's military governor stepped forward with upraised staffs. Gilthanas paid no heed, desiring only to get his fingers around Konnal's throat. But while he saw only the sneering face of his enemy, the guards did their efficient work, one knocking his hands aside with a sweep of the pole, the other cracking the prisoner across the skull with a blow that dazed the prince, sent him stumbling against the door and then slowly slumping to the floor.

"Your brother never displayed such rash immaturity," said the self-appointed leader of Silvanesti in a tone of gentle rebuke. "He had the grace to accept his imprisonment with dignity intact."

"I know that he escaped!" growled Gilthanas, dismayed by his own weakness and trying with bluster to cover up his frailty.

"You believe that old tale? In truth, I set him free . . . I had no more use for him here. And perhaps you also know that I compelled him to return to Qualinesti, where he was treated as an outlaw—a traitor to elvenkind. Since then there have been rumors that he was killed during the Chaos War. I choose to believe them."

Qualinesti! Even the name of his homeland brought longing to the heart of Gilthanas. When he pictured the broad swaths of forest, the crystalline towers of his nation's capital, and the serene and beautiful elves who were his people, he needed all of his willpower not to allow his grief to show in his face and eyes.

"But now," Konnal's tone was lofty, gloating, "it is time to turn our attention to more immediate concerns. You will come with me."

The haughty Silvanesti stepped back from the door. Gilthanas didn't want to go with him, but the prospect of even a few minutes outside the constricting cell was enough to overcome his loathing for the one who had imprisoned him. He ignored Konnal and held his head high as he passed through the door, and past the dirt-walled jailroom beyond.

One of the guards preceded him and the other followed as the little procession advanced up the stairs and through a narrow doorway that emerged onto a sloping field beneath the open, sunlit sky. Gilthanas was blinded by the brilliance, squeezing his eyes shut because of the mind-numbing brightness that overloaded his senses and threatened to shut down his brain. At the same time, he exhilarated in the vastness of his surroundings, by drawing fresh air through his nostrils and delighting in the odors of trees and grass, of fresh air and a warm, dry breeze.

"Move!" One of the guards pushed him roughly from behind, and by opening his eyes to slits he could see at least the ground beneath his feet. He sensed that they were moving uphill, and by the time they had gone a hundred paces, his eyes had become attuned enough that he could open them and look around.

Together with Konnal and the two staff-wielding elven warriors, he stood atop a high, rounded hill. The sculpted forests of Silvanesti spread to the far horizons, though the elevation itself was smooth and grassy. Around him were several columns of white marble, and the crest was paved in similar alabaster stones.

"Do you recognize this place?" asked Konnal.

"No."

"I'm not surprised. You Qualinesti are indeed ignorant savages, with little knowledge of our race's proud heritage. This is the Hill of Sol-Fallon."

"The place where the first Sinthal-Elish met and formed the pact of elves that created Silvanesti." Gilthanas felt a perverse pleasure in demonstrating some awareness of elven history.

"Precisely. Your cell is a small cave that has been excavated into the hillside below."

"Perhaps it is fitting that, in your hate and prejudice, you have imprisoned an elf from a different realm here. How like you, Konnal, to debase a place that should be hallowed."

The military governor of Silvanesti just laughed. "Enjoy your chances for bluster, 'Prince.' This will be your last opportunity to speak such words, or any others."

"You're going to kill me." Gilthanas stated the fact, unsurprised—but also, with a tingle of energy, unaccepting. He tried to think, to imagine some means of escape, resolving that his life would not end easily.

"Yes. Right here, in honor of the sacrifices made by our ancestor Silvanos and his fellows, who left us such a legacy—"

"Legacy of hatred and blindness!" snapped the prince of Qualinesti. "Yes, I suppose my blood will be a fitting offering to your dark furies."

Konnal's eyes narrowed and his hand went to the long-sword at his waist. Then he shrugged. "I can't expect a fool such as yourself to understand."

"Why kill me now?" Gilthanas asked. "I have been a prisoner for . . . how long? Ten years?"

"Twelve. They have been years of dramatic changes across Krynn, though you might not know about that."

In truth, the prince didn't, except for one case. Shortly after his capture, he had noticed the failure of his magical abilities. It was as though during the familiar ritual of spell-casting he had been trying to drink from an empty vessel— his words, his arcane gestures, had called forth nothing at all. The practice of magic might as well have been the gibbering discourse of an infant, for all the effect it had produced.

He didn't want to admit his ignorance, yet he had to do something, if only to stall for time. "What are these changes of which you speak?"

"Our world has entered a new age . . . an Age of Mortals. The gods have abandoned us and taken their powers with them, leaving elves and dwarves and humans to make their way on their own. But Krynn is beset by new threats, as well . . . creatures of chaos that would destroy our lands from within. There are stories, too, of great dragons—massive creatures, beyond the ken of previous knowledge—who threaten to claim all the world from without."

"And so you decided to kill me?" Gilthanas retorted wryly. "I'm not sure I follow your logic."

"The only reason I have kept you alive this long is that I wondered if, at some point in the future, your life might be useful to us . . . a bargaining chip, so to speak, in such interactions as the Qualinesti forced upon us. But now, as of tomorrow, to be precise, there will be no interactions between Silvanesti and Qualinesti—or, indeed, between Silvanesti and the rest of the world."

The prince was curious in spite of himself. "How are you going to achieve this?"

Konnal laughed, and there was a hint of madness in the sound. Even the two guards, Gilthanas noticed, looked warily at their leader.

"Tomorrow we will raise a barrier around our land—a fence of magic that will sever all ties between Silvanesti and the rest of the world. The Qualinesti will never learn of your fate, because after the barrier is raised neither they, nor anyone else, will know anything that happens within our realm."

"You're insane!" Gilthanas spat out, reacting by reflex. "You would cut yourself off from everything else in the world? Think of the cost, of the loss to yourselves!"

Konnal sneered. "We have everything we need. Indeed, we have much that is coveted by others. The barrier will see that our possessions remain intact and that none may interfere with the hallowed lives within this forest."

"This 'forest' is a tamed garden! Think of it, you fool—all your children will grow up knowing nothing more of life!"

"All they need to know they will find right here," Konnal shot back. The pure conviction rang in his voice, and Gilthanas was aware that this deranged elf actually thought he might convince his prisoner of the rightness of his actions. "We have the world's highest levels of art, and a true sense of our own history—of our own rightful dominance in the story of Krynn. And with the barrier, we will ensure that this status remains unchanged and secure throughout the rest of time."

As he listened to Konnal, Gilthanas had been looking around, wondering about his chances for escape. He might get away from Konnal and these two guards with a quick dash, but he saw more elves in the red tunics of House Protector gathered in knots about the base of the hill. And he had no illusions about his stamina after twelve years of languishing in prison. Perhaps he could take the governor hostage, use him to compel the guards to stay back. . . .

Even as Gilthanas had the thought, Konnal stepped back and his two attendants moved to block the prince's path. Staffs raised, they stood ready to prevent him from attacking Konnal.

It was then that Gilthanas caught the first glimpse of wings overhead—of proud creatures gliding lazily through the skies. He looked up to see griffins, a dozen or more of them, circling over the top of the hill. The mighty fliers had long served as aerial mounts for elven warriors, and for just a moment he longed for the speed that might carry him away.

"You see that even the griffins await your execution," Konnal declared with a laugh. "They know of our plans for the barrier, and you might be surprised to learn that they fully support it."

The shadow of wings grew broader across the hilltop, and the governor raised his arms to the sky, crying out in glee. "Come, my feathered allies . . . watch the demise of our enemy!" With a flourish he drew his sword, while the two guards advanced to flank Gilthanas.

The first griffin flew over, and with a contemptuous flick of his taloned foreclaws, it knocked Konnal to the ground, drawing a startled oath. Gilthanas saw that two more had pushed the guards away, while another grasped his shoulders firmly. He felt his feet rise from the ground, and though the claws supporting him pressed painfully into his skin, he laughed aloud at the fury on his former captor's face. Konnal brandished his weapon wildly, but already the griffins were twenty feet overhead, gliding away from the hilltop.

Another of the graceful fliers glided underneath him, and the griffin supporting Gilthanas let go, dropping the elf onto the broad back. He looked at the white-feathered wings stroking the air, carrying him westward, and watched as the Hill of Sol-Fallon and the gardened forest of Silvanesti surrounding it receded below.

"Perhaps not all of your clan wants to stay within the new fence of Silvanesti?" the prince murmured, looking into the wise, yellow eye of griffin flying beside him.

The creature merely nodded his head, and then the flight spread through the skies, angling toward the border of the ancient elven realm, and to all the world beyond.

D. CRAMER

Shadow of the Mind:
The Missing City, 11sc

Her name is Mala—well, that's what I call her, anyway. She's never corrected me, so I guess it doesn't bother her. But then nothing I do seems to bother her in the slightest. I walk with Mala to the well every morning as she fetches water for her family. We never talk. I'm not even sure she knows I'm there—I usually stay a few yards behind her, or I run ahead and just watch her pass by. It's a comfort just to be near her.

I've never seen such a beautiful woman in all my life. Not just physical beauty either (though I've never met anyone else whose merest smile caused my heart to ache); her spirit is just as beautiful as her face. Mala has rejected a handful of suitors because she can't leave her parents all alone.

Sometimes her sisters come to visit in their husbands' carriages; servants drive them down from the Garden District. They bring extravagances like fruit from Silvanesti, and they coddle and fawn over their aging parents, but they never do any real work around the house. And before night falls (usually long before), they climb into their carriages and ride back to their mansions, leaving behind the squalid home they escaped by finding rich merchants to marry. They leave Mala to do all the chores, to sit up with their mother when the cold night makes her joints ache, and to help their father do nearly everything—a brain seizure has left the poor old man unable to walk or take care of himself (though he's still quite practiced at berating Mala when he doesn't get his way quickly enough).

So life just passes Mala by. Her future days will be nothing but the same routine of chores until the work bends her back and the worry wrinkles her face. She'll wake up one morning to find herself transformed from a fair maiden to a venerable spinster virtually overnight. Her youth will disappear. Her looks will disappear, too. But she will still have me. Mala always will have me.

The trouble is, she'll never know.

I think about this as I follow her on the morning trip to the well. We live in two different worlds. There is no future for us, no hope that the passion in my heart, my love for Mala, will overcome the boundaries that keep us apart—they are too great. I can only walk along in the periphery of her world and take what joy I can from watching her and silently sharing her days and nights.

You'd think such thoughts would sour my disposition and lead me to despair. But Mala is smiling that hopeful grin she sometimes gets, and that wipes away all the sadness from my heart. What is she thinking? What makes her hum happily as she walks to the well? Something has happened. In the time between now and when I last saw her, just before I blew out my candle last night, something has occurred—some news has been delivered, or a revelation has been reached. Mala has hope, and I am delirious.

As we round the corner, Mala's gait speeds up. She fairly skips to the water, but I come to a dead stop. There's something lying at the foot of the well. At first it seems to be a bundle of rags, but then I notice a hand and a strand of hair.

It's a person!

Mala walks right by, taking as little notice of the prone form as she does me. While she lowers her bucket into the well, I run up to the body. Where did it come from? Who is it? Perhaps one of the Legionnaires from the port? Or a seaman from that trading ship that put in last night? Put enough rum in one of those sailors and he'll wander halfway to Icewall before passing out. This one is lucky to have staggered only this far.

As I near the body, though, I realize this is no sailor sleeping off too much drink. His clothes are too threadbare, his skin too fair (though he's severely sunburned). Rolling him over, the stranger's hair falls away from his face revealing finely chiseled features and slender tapering ears. An elf!

We've seen a few elves passing in the weeks since Military Governor Konnal sent word that all loyal Silvanesti elves should return to their homeland, and the ones we have seen were all headed toward the forest as quickly as possible (though I hear that even they can't get through the invisible barrier that's gone up around the elf lands). This one looks like he's crossed the desert alone and unsupplied. I can only guess that he's coming from Silvanesti, that he somehow got out before the shield was raised and fled across the sands. It's not terribly far, but without the proper clothing and a sufficient supply of water, the trip still can be deadly.

While I check to see that the elf is indeed still among the living, Mala retrieves her full bucket, grips the handle with both hands, and carries it off. Completely oblivious to the elf's plight or my ministrations, she rounds the corner, heading for her house—a good idea.

There is nothing I can do for the elf here. I have to get him out of the sun and find a healer to tend to his wounds. I'll leave him at Mala's house. He'll be safe there while I go down to the port. Falaius Taneek and his Legionnaires are always looking for ways to help folks. I can't think of anyone who needs help more than this poor fellow.

🪶 🪶 🪶 🪶 🪶

The healer was right, after a few days of rest and lots of water, the elf is looking much better. He still hasn't awakened—well, not fully. He's opened his eyes a few times and mumbled all sorts of crazy things in his sleep. He's talked quite a bit about "the war" (though with the long lives that elves lead, I can't really be sure which war he's talking about) and silver dragons, and he even looked me square in the eye and called me "Tanis." I'm sure that when he wakes up, he'll have some interesting tales to tell.

But wait—his eyelids are fluttering. I think my guest is finally conscious. Yes. Yes, I can see this is no waking dream he's having. He rubs his eyes as the world swims into focus. Look at him, gazing around the room unsure of where he is, not even certain whether or not this is a dream. I should speak to him instead of sitting back in the shadows, but this is the best way to determine his intentions. You can't be too careful these days.

The elf stands and walks slowly across the room, staring at everything with undisguised wonder. He clearly doesn't even know what city he's in. Reaching out, his hand passes straight through the chair standing in the middle of the room.

This is cruel. I shouldn't torture him so. But it is fascinating to watch him try to puzzle it out. Is he a ghost? Why can't he touch the chair? He's an educated and well-trained one, this elf. Despite the peculiar (some would say unnatural) surroundings, he doesn't panic. Instead, he tries to think of an explanation for the phenomenon he sees. I'll just watch another moment before I—no! Mala enters the room, that same hopeful smile on her face.

The elf sees her. "What manner of place is this?" he asks and reaches out to grab her shoulders. First his hands, then arms, and finally the whole of his body passes straight through her. And she goes about her business, taking no notice of him in the least.

"She cannot see you," I say from the corner, finally stepping out of the shadows and into the candlelight.

"Am . . . am I dead?" the elf asks.

"No." I laugh. "And before you ask, neither is Mala. She's just somewhere else. Don't ask me to explain it. That's simply how things are here in Gal Tra'kalas. Get used to it."

He stares at Mala as she bustles out of the room with an armful of towels, clearly amazed at what he sees. She's full of life and beauty, but as Mala passes between us, he still can see me through her body; she's more real than a phantom, but not fully of this world.

"Gal Tra'kalas? The Missing City! How did I get here?"

"If you don't know, then I'm not sure anyone does, friend." I try to calm him. The first few hours in Gal Tra'kalas can be very disorienting. "Sit down. The bed is quite real, I assure you. You slept soundly on it these past few days."

"This is your home, then?" The elf tries to act casual, but he's obviously still disoriented and more than a little distracted by what he sees.

"Yes, mine. But hers as well. It's a little difficult to explain."

A knock on the front door breaks the awkward moment. The elf turns to me as if to ask if that's a real knock or a phantom one.

"That's for me—or more likely for you." I get up and move to the door in the front room. "You can't hear anything that goes on in Mala's world."

When I open the door, the frame is filled with a giant of a man. This is Falaius Taneek, leader of the local Legion of Steel cell. They maintain the port and govern the Missing City (though they have no influence on the spectral happenings in Gal Tra'kalas). After the healer finished with the elf, he told me Falaius likely would check on things when the elf was up and around. Apparently Falaius deserves his reputation for always being in the right place at the right time. Either that or the healer has an uncommon gift for judging recuperative powers.

"Good day, Aman Daun" Falaius rumbles with his usual terse formality. For a barbarian, he's terribly well-mannered, but it never comes off naturally; he always seems to be forcing civility into his voice, and, in the end, it makes him seem all the more imposing (quite a trick for a man whose shoulders spread wider than the broadest oak tree). "Is your house guest feeling better?"

"Very much so," I answer and invite the Legionnaire into my home with a flourish of my arm. I always feel the need to respond to his stiff courtesy with my best interpretation of courtly grace. "In fact, he just awakened. Mala put quite a scare into him, and I've been trying to explain the situation."

"No explanation is necessary." The elf has gathered his wits and comes to meet us at the door. My sham of courtly behavior is evident by his every move—this elf is used to moving in the company of kings. "I know the tale of Gal Tra'kalas. The city was destroyed in the first Cataclysm, yet somehow clung to spectral life. Phantom buildings rose from the rubble, and ghosts continued walk its streets in an unnatural mockery of life."

Ah, I forgot how deeply elves detest the undead. Of course, such feelings are only natural for a people whose culture is so closely tied to life. Restless spirits foul any area they touch, leaching the beauty and life from the most verdant site.

"You do not know the tale well enough, my friend" I say, trying to put the elf at ease.

"True," adds Falaius in his soothingly deep voice. "The people of Gal Tra'kalas may be ghostly, but they are not ghosts. None of the scholars, mystics, or sages who've passed this way can tell me what they are, but they are clearly not undead monsters."

"Bah! I've told you time and again what they are—who they are." I always lose my patience when we have this conversation. No one wants to believe the truth of the matter.

"Yes, Aman, you have. Forgive me for being so thick-headed that I cannot see the truth, but I am just a simple warrior. The workings of the magical world confuse me." Falaius tries to placate me. He doesn't really accept the truth, but for my sake, he pretends. I believe he thinks I'm on the brink of madness and it's best to humor my "delusions."

Just then, Mala strides through the room (and through both Falaius's and the elf's bodies) carrying a bundle of neatly folded shirts. What's she doing? Perhaps she's going to donate old clothing to the poor. That would be just like her. They barely can afford to put food on the table, yet she still wants to give to the needy.

"I must say, I know some small bit about magic, but even the little I've seen today is beyond my ken." The elf again passes his hand through a piece of furniture, then shakes his head wryly.

"Yes." Falaius uses the word to clear his throat. He's not one to waste time in idle conversation. "Forgive my lack of manners, friend, but now that Aman has brought you back to health, I have some questions that need answering, most of them concerning who you are and how you arrived in the Missing City."

"Of course. My name is Gilthanas Solostaran, and I am at your service." With this, he bows deeply and is overcome by a wave of dizziness, nearly collapsing in a heap at our feet. "If it is not too much of an imposition," he asks after regaining his composure, "may we continue in the other room? I believe I have not yet recovered fully from my ordeal."

We return to the bedroom where Gilthanas sits on the corner of the cot—only after making sure there truly was a solid object under the hazy blanket and sheets. Apart from occasional bouts of fatigue, he seems to be fine. Falaius sits cross-legged against the wall, his left shoulder and knee swallowed up by a phantom dressing table, and I return to my accustomed spot in the dark corner.

As Gilthanas tells his tale, filled with intrigue and adventure befitting a Hero of the Lance, Mala continues to flit around the house bundling more and more of her family's worldly goods into towels, sacks, and even a small crate. I find that my attention to Gilthanas's story wavers, then disappears entirely. What is she up to?

Finally, while Gilthanas describes a harrowing escape from certain death, Mala enters and strips the bed on which he sits (something both he and Falaius find particularly distracting). However, she doesn't lay fresh sheets on the bed, as she does every week when changing the linen. When she merely gathers up the bedding and carries it into the other room, I can take no more. I leave behind the elf's account of a harrowing, headlong flight into the desert and follow Mala into the main room.

Practically everything the family owns is packed and stacked near the doorway. Mala's mother ties a knot in a towel containing the few pieces of jewelry she owns, then cinches the towel around her waist like a belt. Her father sits on a barrel, his familiar scowl much less severe than usual. Meanwhile, Mala runs about making sure that all the packages are sealed tight. Her lips never rest all the while; she obviously is bubbling happily about the reason for all this activity—whatever that is. Obviously, they are going somewhere, but where? This is more than a short excursion—they're taking everything they can carry.

They must be moving!

Perhaps one of Mala's sisters finally has offered to bring their parents to live in her husband's mansion. More likely, the husband has decided that it is too embarrassing to have his wife visit this dilapidated section of town and so has paid for his in-laws to relocate. They'll finally get the comfort and care that they deserve. I knew Mala's hard work would be rewarded.

But will Mala move with them? Surely neither of her sisters would want to have to tend the parents herself. They will have to bring Mala with them to continue to act as their caretaker.

After I built my home literally within hers, just so that we can be close to one another, is Mala going to leave me? Certainly, I can visit her wherever in Gal Tra'kalas she goes, but it will take me months, possibly even years to rebuild. And just think how expensive it will be, since the new home is sure to be much more opulent that this one.

But what if someone else already has built a home in that part of the Missing City? The Garden District is one of the most popular locales for merchants and Legion officers to live. What if the sister's home already has been claimed by that foul-smelling Khurrish trapper? Or worse, that gray-haired Legion scout? That lecherous old ruffian will spend his idle time watching Mala bathe, or taking target practice at her mother hobbling around the house! I will not stand for such things!

Whoever lives there now simply will have to move. There are plenty of Gal Tra'kalan homes that have not yet been reconstructed. I'll do the work for them myself, but Mala and I must stay together! I cannot bear for us to be apart.

Look at her. Flitting around so happily, completely unaware of the agony this causes me. Oh, Mala, if only I could talk to you. If only you could tell me what's happening. But wait! She takes a piece of paper out of her apron pocket and opens it up. As she reads it, her face flushes with joy and anticipation. What does it say?

I rush to look over her shoulder, but she dances out of the room and into the kitchen. Following her, I find that it's too dark to read anything in there, but Mala doesn't put the paper away; she gazes at it even in the dark. The words are so joyous, she can read them with her eyes closed.

What could be on that paper? It looked like a letter. Why would her sister send a letter with the news? Perhaps they aren't moving in with one of Mala's sisters. But why else would they be moving? And why would Mala be so happy?

I follow close on her heels as she goes back into the bedroom where Gilthanas's story is reaching its conclusion. He recalls seeing the city after a day and night in the desert.

"After so long in a Silvanesti prison, the crossing nearly killed me. I was half-crazed with thirst when I saw that well. And when I could see the water, even watch people drink it, but found that it was all ephemeral as a dream, I fell unconscious. The next thing I knew . . ."

Gilthanas's voice trails off as I rush hurriedly past him over to the dresser. Mala laid the paper down in order to gather another bundle of towels. Now I can read . . .

✦ ✦ ✦ ✦ ✦

I can hear the comforting drone of hushed conversation long before the words become clear. It's Gilthanas and Falaius. They're not in this room, but they are nearby.

"I must say, I still don't understand the nature of this place," I hear Gilthanas say. He still isn't certain that the spectral people he sees aren't undead spirits; you can hear it in his voice. He expects for Mala and her family to suddenly give up their charade and reveal themselves to be life-draining fiends.

"I'm not sure anyone does" Falaius answers.

"My host seems to think he has an insight others cannot perceive."

"You must forgive, Aman" the Legionnaire says. "His sense of perspective is, shall we say, impaired when it comes to the woman he calls Mala." Yes. He would say that. Falaius has spent many years living here, but he has never truly accepted Gal Tra'kalas for what it is.

"Though you were half-blind with dehydration, your reaction to the Missing City was quite normal. Most people see the towers and walls waving in the desert heat and assume they are seeing a mirage. However, when they get here and see the amazing detail in the buildings and even the ghostly inhabitants, people change their minds, believing instead that the city is all one tremendous illusion cast by a long dead sorcerer, or perhaps even by the gods themselves."

"Yes," Gilthanas adds with authority. "I came to that conclusion myself, though I know no sorcerer of any robes who could create such an effect."

"But the truth is even more fantastic. The mirage really is Gal Tra'kalas." Falaius has a sense of wonder in his voice that I've never heard before. Perhaps he does understand the grandeur around him. "As near as I can tell, the city belongs to a world where the first Cataclysm didn't happen. I don't pretend to understand how it is possible, but the people we see are real. They are far too complex to be simple illusions. They are born, grow, fall in love, and die just like anyone you know. The city is alive too . . . well, as alive as any city is. Buildings are built, others are razed. Businesses open and prosper. Animals run the back alleys looking for scraps of food. If you make it your business to pay attention to a particular building or person or family, you'll see the unmistakable rhythm of life unfold before you. Make no mistake about it, Gal Tra'kalas is real."

"If that is true," Gilthanas wonders aloud, "then how can anyone bear to live here?" The elf has faced many strange things in his life, but I dare say that other than the return of the gods, this must be the most bizarre.

"Well, we didn't know. When the Legion first came here, there was only the mirage and a city's worth of ruins—crumbled walls, and mountains of brick and mortar debris half-hidden by the mirage, which we too mistook for a magical reconstruction of Gal Tra'kalas. My tribe has always called this spot the Missing City, and it seemed like an ideal place to build an outpost. If we built exactly behind the illusion, doing our best to recreate the facades of the buildings, only the closest inspection would reveal our presence. We'd have a town that no one could find—truly a Missing City."

Even though I know the story backward and forward, I lie here listening to Falaius. The cot is comfortable, and I feel a little light-headed. Odd. I don't remember going to bed.

"It was only after we'd been here several months that anyone began to suspect the truth. And by the time we were certain, our outpost had grown into a town. Most people stopped building in the 'occupied' sections of town. When you feel well enough to come down to the pier, you'll see that the newest buildings all stand just past the end of Gal Tra'kalas's city limits."

Gilthanas considers what he's heard. "And the people who already built their homes in the shadow city?"

"Each made a choice" the Legionnaire says noncommittally. "Many of them relocated, but the Legion maintained their original building. After all, the 'phantom folk,' as some of my men call them, can't see, hear, or touch anything of ours.

"Of course, most of the civilians chose to move. The wealthy merchants in particular were uncomfortable with the notion of sharing their homes with others, even if those others are not of this Krynn."

"But there are others who chose to stay?"

"Obviously. Most of them simply refuse to accept the people of Gal Tra'kalas as anything other than illusions. They take pride in the fact that they maintained their homes while their neighbors were run off by mere tricks of the light. But others, like your benefactor, Aman, consider them wholly real. They build their lives around people from both worlds, neither more or less important than the other. My men call these folks 'shadow walkers,' because they tread the edge of two worlds. Most others just call them crazy."

"So the people in this house—Mala and her parents—are real to Aman?"

"They're more than real. They are his family. And Mala . . . well, let's just say that I don't think I've ever felt as strongly about anyone as he does for that ghostly woman."

I'm shocked. Not only does Falaius understand the city, but he also understands me. I always thought he snickered behind my back like the rest of them, mocking my feelings for Mala. I have to apologize to him.

I sit up on the bed, and the room spins. I have a lump on the back of my head the size of a dagger's pommel. What happened?

"Yes," Gilthanas sighs, "I understand. His life is very similar to the one I've led these past years. The only things that matter to him are untouchable. For me, they were memories—shadows of the mind—but no less real because I too could not touch them. At times, it was easier to believe they were reality and my cell was a recurring nightmare. Silvanesti is full of those memories."

"But the people of Gal Tra'kalas are not memories," Falaius replies. "They are here, as much a part of the Missing City as we are."

"And how much the worse for our friend if he cannot separate his dream from his waking world?" the elf pauses. "We ought to awaken him for this."

Falaius clicks his tongue, as he always does when wrestling with a difficult question. "I think it may be kinder to let him sleep. There's nothing he can do. Watching this would be too painful."

What's wrong? Did Mala's father have another seizure? Did he die? We all knew it was coming, but no one is ever prepared for such a thing.

"If Aman must lose the one he loves, it's best that we afford him the opportunity to bid her farewell. In the years to come, he will draw solace from the closure. Otherwise, this will be a wound that never heals."

Mala? Has something happened to Mala? By all the departed gods, no!

I stand on uncertain legs.

If she's dying I must go to her. I have to be there for her, with her—even if she doesn't know it.

"What will happen when they leave the city?" Gilthanas asks.

Another tongue click announces that Falaius doesn't have a definite answer. "People leave Gal Tra'kalas all the time. They just disappear as the pass through the gates. Who can say where they go after that? The merchants come and go on a regular schedule, and they always return with carts full of goods from Silvanesti or Nordmaar. Do they really go to those places? Who can say? Maybe there's a whole other Ansalon for our ghostly neighbors to explore. For Mala's sake, I hope so, though that will be no real comfort to Aman."

Leave the city?

Now I remember!

The note that had Mala so excited was an invitation for the family to come live with her aunt in Shoole. They are leaving the city. That realization must have been too much for me. I think I blacked out. That must be how I got this lump on my skull. How long have I been unconscious? What does it matter? What matters is that Mala is leaving!

I've got to stop her!

My legs already are moving. I stumble out the door of my house—our house. Gilthanas and Falaius stare like I'm a wild beast. Perhaps I am. My heart beats with the same desperation as a rabbit's when the scent of the fox is in the air. The wagon rounds the corner pulled, I'm sure, by the horse Mala's sisters have given them—a cheap price to have their embarrassing relatives leave the city for good.

Gilthanas catches my gaze. I can see he knows the panic that sweeps through me. "Do what you can," his eyes seem to say. "In the end, it will do no good."

Meanwhile, Falaius walks toward me with a sad expression on his face. He holds out his massive hand, obviously meaning to lay it sympathetically on my shoulder. As heartfelt as that consolation might be, I know his true thought is to keep me here until it is too late.

Before Falaius can clasp my shoulder, I dash down the street. If Mala's going to Shoole, she'll take the wagon out the North Gate, and that's only a few blocks away. On the streets, I'll never catch the horses, but I have an advantage: I don't live in Gal Tra'kalas—I'm in the Missing City!

In the middle of the block, I turn right and run straight through the front wall of the candle-maker's shop. Leaping over the pile of rocky debris that used to be the kiln, I pass out the back and into the alley that cuts across the Northern District. Gilthanas can't possibly keep up with me; he's still too weak from his ordeal. In most instances, Falaius would have no trouble overtaking and subduing me, but he doesn't know this section of the Missing City as well as I do. He doesn't know which spectral buildings can be passed easily through and which hide dangerous piles of rubble, or even open pits. No, my well-meaning friends will have to take the streets just like Mala.

Through the Tan Griffin Inn and around the livery stable (it's been impassable since that merchant rebuilt the colossal barn), I see the North Gate ahead. I run heedlessly through the Gal Tra'kalans on the street. Usually I treat them with the same courtesy I do the more solid citizens of the Missing City, but right now I'd run straight through anyone who stood in my way.

At the gate, I stop and look back down the street. Nothing. No carriage. No Mala. Just the usual spectral pedestrian traffic. Did I read the note wrong? Is she heading for the West Gate instead? I can't possibly get there in time.

Before my fear sharpens to panic, a flat wagon pulled by two horses rounds the corner. Driving the team at a slow trot is my own Mala, a smile of breathless anticipation painted on her face.

"No!" I shout, waving my arms back and forth wildly. "Mala, stop! Don't go! Don't leave me!"

I know she can't hear me, but I have to take the chance. I yell like the madman everyone already thinks I am.

Now Falaius and Gilthanas round the corner. I can see them through the wagon, racing toward me, afraid that I'll do myself some harm (though what I could do, I can't imagine).

Despite my shouting and arm-waving, Mala drives her horses straight through me. Of course she does. What else could she do?

I sink to my knees in the dusty, haunted road.

As my companions reach me, I look over my shoulder to watch as Mala, my one true love, is about to dissipate into nothingness.

She stops the wagon, lays down the reins, and turns around for one last look at her home. A smile full of hope and the promise of a happier future plays across Mala's face, and she waves good-bye.

I wave back, too stunned to speak. I know she doesn't see me, but it doesn't matter.

Picking up the reins, she urges the horses on. One step, two, three . . . she fades into the swirling sand. Mala is gone. I throw back my head and howl to the cloudless sky.

There is no one left in this world. I'm all alone. If only the desert could swallow me up the way it has Mala. "I have nothing," I whisper to the wind. But the only answer I get is a hand laid gently on my shoulder.

Gilthanas bends down on one knee behind me, a look of painful memory on his face. Falaius stands back, giving us a sense of privacy while still being close enough to intervene should it become necessary.

"You have your memories, friend Aman. That is all any of us truly carry through this life."

"Memories? Memories of what? She was never real! I spent all these years chasing after a woman who is nothing more than a wisp of smoke. Gilthanas, you may have walked in the company of the gods themselves, but you have no idea how I feel."

"Don't I?" He takes his hand from my shoulder and stands, looking down at me the way a parent looks at a petulant child. "You've just lost the one you love, a pain everyone sooner or later must face. It matters not one whit whether you had a few months or a lifetime together, or whether you ever were ever actually together at all. Do not confuse yourself by finding the faults in your past—they have no bearing on the emotional chasm before you.

"A hole has been torn in your heart. It will heal, but the process takes time. Will you spend that time wisely? Will you savor the sweet moments and release the rest? If you do, the scar your heart bears will be light."

I whirl on the elf. None of this is his fault, but he makes a convenient target for my rage.

"What if I don't want it to heal?" I growl.

Gilthanas looks at me ruefully.

"Then you have two choices. You can stay here and wallow in the memories, see all the things you used to see, do all the things you used to do. This is a tried and true method to keep your heart from healing, though as many before you have discovered, the pain will never cease. Or, you can devote yourself to finding the missing piece of your heart and returning it to its rightful place."

I sneer derisively.

"That's impossible, and you know it."

"Perhaps," Gilthanas smiles. "But no more impossible than finding a silver dragon who wishes to remain hidden."

Laughing I say, "And you've told us how well that worked out. How many years were you in that Silvanesti prison?"

"Enough," the elf points out, "to reconcile my past and put it behind me. There were days when the only thing that kept me alive were my memories. Now that I'm free, I live for the future. What will you live for, Aman, the future or the past?"

"The future," I say uncertainly. He's right; whatever happened before doesn't matter. Mala is gone, and nothing I do will change that. But if I take the love we had and build upon it, then that is the best way to honor the past. As long as I remain true to my inspiration, Mala will still be with me. "Do your memories no longer haunt you?"

Gilthanas pauses. I think he's unsure how to answer the question. "Perhaps they haunt me still, but they no longer rule me. I have more pressing matters to attend. I am a prince of Qualinesti. I have a duty to my people."

"When your duty is done," I ask, "then what will you live for?"

Falaius, sensing our conversation is nearing its end, steps forward and helps me to my feet.

"My duty will never end." The elf stiffens. He looks into the dirt, unwilling to meet my gaze. "This is my life."

"Then you are an even sadder creature than I."

❧ ❧ ❧ ❧ ❧

A week later, Gilthanas was well enough to resume his trip back to Qualinesti. Falaius Taneek brought him a pack of supplies, and a map of the easiest route to Purstal. From there, he planned to follow the merchant trails across the Plains of Dust.

I sit on a mound of rocks amid the ancient ruins of Shoole. Unlike those in the Missing City, no ghostly buildings rise from this site. The sea wind constantly blows through this place, sounding mournful.

He was right, I have to live for the future.

This part of the city seems roughly equivalent to the Garden District in Gal Tra'kalas. I imagine that the stones I sit on form the wall of the home where Mala lives now.

I'm heading up to the north—to the Isle of Schallsea, in fact. I hear that Gilthanas's old companion, Goldmoon, has founded a "Citadel of Light" there, and that she teaches people to speak with spirits. Now, I realize you're not a spirit, Mala, but this is the best place I know to start. Who knows what this new magic is capable of?

I hop down and gather my supplies. The road, and my future, lay in front of me. But before I head off, I turn and take one last look at the ruins. There's nothing there to see, but I smile and wave a fond good-bye.

Wherever she is, Mala waves back.

SOTHI NUINQUA TSALARIOTH

The Ancient City of Purstal, 11sc

For days Gilthanas walked across the dry wastes. Each morning he awakened to the same vista: flat, brown land stretching to the far horizons. And each day he wondered if he might not have been smarter to stay in the city and wait—the gods only knew how long—for some ship that might carry him all the way to Qualinesti.

But he had also learned things, disturbing things, about developments in his homeland. Most significantly, the Knights of Takhisis, dark warriors who served the five-headed queen of Evil dragonkind, had conquered the elven realm during the Summer of Chaos. The elven Speaker, the prince's nephew Gilthas, was serving as a puppet on the throne, manipulated by his Dark Knight masters. Waiting for a ship had become too aggravating when the memories and fears about his homeland had so filled his thoughts, and so he had set out on foot.

At least he had begun to banish the memories of Silvara and convince himself that his life must run its course without her. Somehow he believed that when he reached his homeland, everything would make sense and his life would have fulfillment and purpose. At night, sometimes, this hope seemed translucent and intangible, but with the coming of dawn he once again seized it like the bottom rung of a solid ladder.

He knew little of the lands he passed through, but with his vigor and strength regained and the protection offered by a cheap iron sword he had purchased for the wages of a week's hard labor, he felt capable of overcoming any obstacle fate might lay in his path. In the city he had learned that he could walk to the Torath River and follow that watercourse until it eventually reached Elial. There, he would strike out along the Duntollik Run and continue west until he made it to Qualinesti. He had been warned about dragons and bizarre creatures of chaos that might lie along the way, which would destroy him if he was so much as noticed.

The elf had reached the riverbank some ten days ago, now, and had failed to see any sign of a rivercraft—or any kind of habitation or village. He found the river clean enough to refresh his water supply every day, and sometimes he caught fish. Though there were clumps of brush along these waterways—the only vegetation other than grass he encountered here—he endured the chill of the near arctic clime rather than risk a fire. His supply of elven hardbread was sufficient for more than a month of travel, so he didn't particularly worry when, most days, that was the only food he could provide for himself.

As to hideous creatures waiting to prey upon him, he saw no sign. True, he occasionally heard rumbles of supernatural storms beyond the horizon to the south or west, but he maintained his vigilance and never observed any immediate threat. If a dragon appeared, the elf had a simple plan: He would lie down on the dry ground and cover himself with as much dusty dirt as he could quickly gather. Then he would simply wait, eyes on the sky, confident that the serpent would never notice him—even should it fly directly overhead.

It was on the eleventh day after he had reached the river that he first noticed an irregularity in the horizon. The river had grown to a wide, sluggish expanse to his left. The sun was beginning to set, reflecting off the broad flowage when before him he observed a series of shapes scattered across the flat ground. They stood perhaps a mile away from the water, and as he walked closer he got the unmistakable impression that these were ruins. That was a wall, here before him, and beyond he saw the tattered remnants of great stone houses surrounded by tangles of bramble.

Below his feet the dust had scattered away from some patches of ground to reveal smooth, interlocking paving stones—a wide avenue leading from a crumbled gate, between the buildings. A stone basin, cracked and dry, indicated where a splendid fountain or wading pool must once have gathered cool waters. A gust of wind carried dry powder through the air, stinging his eyes and irritating his nostrils.

Before him rose the greatest edifice in this ancient city of the dead. Surely it must once have been a palace—the gaunt outline of an ancient doorway gaped like a hungry mouth in the broken facade of a wall. His eyes widened with wonder as he slowly climbed the marble stairs leading to the doorway. The roof had long since collapsed, but within, outlined by fading sunlight, Gilthanas saw the remnants of corridors and columns, and of a sweeping expanse that might have been a throne room or a chamber suitable for hosting a great ball.

He passed beneath the still-intact arch of the doorway and kicked through the rubble on the floor. These were mostly loose tiles of slate, obviously scattered here when the roof had caved in. He crossed the hallway and passed into the entryway of the great room.

Something scuttled through the shadows at the base of the wall beside him, a little shape scurrying through the hall. Reflexively he placed his hand on his sword, even as he heard more noises to the rear. Gilthanas spun, but he saw nothing save thickening shadows as the sun continued its relentless descent.

He passed into the great room and saw that columns had once stood around the entire periphery of the place. Now many of these had fallen, but enough remained—some splintered at knee or head height, others rising more than a dozen feet toward a vanished ceiling—to provide a glimpse into the splendor of the past. He advanced across a floor of mosaic tiles and was vaguely surprised to see the colored stone at his feet. With a sense of eeriness he realized that something, or somebody, had cleaned off this surface, tending it with more care than anyplace else in these ruins.

Once again saw movement in the corner of his vision and he turned, the heavy iron blade drawn from its sheath and waving in the cool air.

"Who's there?" he asked.

"Just us."

The reply came from behind and he spun about again, then burst out laughing at the sight of the short, pudgy, and unkempt figure regarding him from a dozen paces away.

That fellow immediately twisted to look anxiously over his own shoulder, then turned back to glare at Gilthanas. "What so funny?" he demanded.

"Just . . . nothing," replied the elf, mastering his amusement to render a deep and acceptably formal bow. "It is a pleasure to meet you . . . one of the Aghar, I am assuming."

The gully dwarf's chest puffed out nearly as far as his bulging belly. "And yes so it is to I myself . . . I am ass . . . ass . . . ass-you-ming," he parroted, insofar as he could remember what Gilthanas had said.

"I am Gilthanas of Qualinesti," said the wanderer, still maintaining the air of dignity.

"Me too!" cried the gully dwarf. "That is, me got name too . . ." If the little creature remembered his cognomen, he apparently had no desire to share it.

"Is this your city?" inquired the elf.

"Me . . . my clan . . . we build this place!" boasted the other.

"I see." Gilthanas forced himself to keep a straight face. The Aghar, after all, were known across Krynn as the ultimate scavengers, moving into any dwelling or ruin that had become viewed as uninhabitable by its original owners. "And what is the name of your great metropolis?"

"This Purstal . . . Great Capital of the Aghar. This is, and Elial is too! That our other great capital, many days that way from here." He pointed in a vaguely northwestern direction.

Gilthanas was suddenly struck by a sense of melancholy. He wondered about the folk, humans most likely, who had built these once-splendid edifices. What had happened to them, that they left their cities to fall into ruin and be claimed by the lowest of the low. Would this happen to Qualinesti one day? The pang of homesickness grew, quickened by a more urgent question: Was it happening already?

"I . . . I have to go," he said, suddenly wanting to be out of this place, to be on the way to his homeland.

At that moment another gust of wind snaked between the ruined walls and more dust wafted past Gilthanas's face. He felt that irritation in his nose and then, before he knew what was happening, he exploded with a convulsive sneeze.

"I'm sorry," he apologized, shaking his head to clear the water from his eyes. He noticed with some surprise that the gully dwarf was staring up at him with an expression bordering on awe.

"It . . . it is you. The Sneezer has come!" proclaimed the Aghar. He shouted, waving his hands, dancing a shambling jig around the stunned Gilthanas. "The Sneezer comes! The Sneezer comes!"

"I don't understand," the elf tried to interject, beginning to worry. "And I really have to move—"

"But wait . . . you sleep here, sleep good. My tribe cook you one really fine feast tonight! We wait alla time for the Sneezer . . . now you come, now you get big party! And then you sleep . . . and we give you stuff, gifts we make for you. Only then you be on your way!"

"I don't think. . . ." Gilthanas's voice trailed off. He was mystified, but admittedly intrigued.

"Where you go in such hurry, anyplace? I mean, 'anyway?'" demanded the rotund dwarf, glowering suspiciously. "You not like our stuff?"

"No, it's just that. . . ." For a moment Gilthanas felt his thoughts run away with him. He remembered a dragon of silver, supple, curves and a graceful neck. She was an elf maid, and his beloved, and at that instant his longing for her was an emotion more powerful than he thought he could survive. But he shook his head—she was gone, and he had his life before him. "I'm going home," he said quietly, almost sadly.

"Well, go home—but not before you have our feast, take our stuff. You da Sneezer, right? We been waitin' for you. Now you come, see our stuff!"

Gilthanas didn't have the strength to resist.

$$\text{🐾 🐾 🐾 🐾 🐾}$$

Aghar hospitality proved to be as insanely frenetic as the gully dwarves themselves, but Gilthanas was surprised to find himself enjoying the attention and the friendship of the filthy runts. He learned that the legend of "The Sneezer" had been handed down from generation to generation . . . that the Aghar here in Purstal, and in the nearby sister city—or sister ruin—of Elial, both had been living their days waiting for the arrival of the one who would sneeze.

Of course, the gully dwarves had no real understanding of what the Sneeze meant to them, which was just as well, from

Gilthanas's point of view. He drank their wine, which was not bad, and ate their food, which was bad. He listened to their tales, enjoying one old would-be mystic who loudly sang of an arch on the glacier to the south.

"The Frozen Past Arch!" screeched the Aghar, in a quasi-sing-song. "It is the place where true hearts can seek their desire!" With a few questions, Gilthanas learned that the arch was reputedly a relic from a very ancient civilization, and that its powers were real, but difficult to unlock.

Finally, the Aghar brought forth gifts for their honored Sneezer. Gilthanas was agreeable and prepared himself to accept some moldy rat-skin cloak or perhaps a backpack with no straps. He was stunned when his humble hosts instead gave him real treasures, including a cloak and boots that would keep him warm in all weather, a decanter that would always pour fresh beverage, a scroll that mapped out for him the Plains of Dust and the adjacent Icewall Glacier, and finally a fine sword, a blade of elven steel that had been forged more than two thousand years ago.

Touched and more than a little drunk, he embraced many of the gully dwarves, danced with them, and fell asleep on a heap of rags in the same room with a hundred Aghar. When he awakened, his hosts were still sleeping. Despite his thick tongue and pounding headache, Gilthanas gathered his new treasures, gave his hosts a whispered farewell, and once again started on the road toward his home.

D. CRAMER

Reflections on a Rose of Stone:
Stone Rose, 12sc

Welcome to the garden!

Oh, my friends, I didn't mean to frighten you. It's just that so few people come here anymore that I am terribly glad for the company. Here, I've a skin full of mulled wine—allow me to make amends for spoiling your solitude by sharing it with you.

No, no, no . . . I insist. What kind of caretaker would I be if I scared away my only guests? A poor one, let me assure you!

No. It is my job to make sure you enjoy your visit. Hopefully, you'll have such a good time that you'll tell all your friends and relations to also make the journey. So pass around the skin and drink your fill. Today, you are the guests of Tam Granger, the keeper of the garden—an uninspired name, but when your entire town is named Stone Rose, there's really no reason to think of a fancy title for the main attraction.

Just about the only people who come through here these days are merchants and mercenaries, and neither of them have time to stop and smell the roses—so to speak. Pilgrims and explorers rarely make the trip to Stone Rose anymore. I can't say I blame them for staying home, what with the Knights of Takhisis holding Qualinesti in their iron grip, and Sable the Black Dragon turning all the New Coast into a bloody swamp! But those who make the trip see something so amazing—I'm not fibbing one bit when I tell you it's unique on all of Krynn.

Walk with me a ways, and I'll show you what I mean.

Pardon my saying so, but by the look of your tattered clothing and that haunted tint to your eyes, I'd hazard to guess that you're refugees from Qualinesti. I thought so! The way you flinched when I mentioned the Dark Knights was a dead giveaway.

It's a sad, sad time, I tell you. "Age of Mortals" indeed! If it was our age, would half the land be ruled by dragons the size of small castles? No, sir! But you take your beauty where you can—and I don't know of anywhere more beautiful than the garden in Stone Rose.

Look out there. It takes your breath away, doesn't it? Over an acre of rosebushes in all shapes and sizes. Those over there are trimmed in the shapes of dragons, a griffin, and a pegasus. Off to the north, you can see lattices covered with vines and flowers the size of your fist. But the centerpiece, literally, is the maze. Now, it's not much of a maze—you can see the hedges are only about waist high—but that circle at the center sits under the shade of a rosebush grown and pruned into the shape of a miniature vallenwood. It's the best place in the whole town to sit and quietly sip your mulled wine.

(Why do you think we're heading there, eh?)

Yes, all this would be marvel enough, considering the fact that we're on the edge of a desert! But it's even more fantastic than you think. You see, all the roses, every bush, vine, and tree, are made of stone. And not some crumbled granite either. The stone is smooth and polished, and shines like the marble statues you'll find in Solamnian noble homes.

Look at them!

The detail is so fine that you can hardly tell the difference between these and the real thing—well, except for the color . . . and the smell. If these were live flowers, the air would be thick with perfume. Our roses don't smell so nice as the normal kind, but you never have to sweep up the petals in the fall! As the groundskeeper, let me tell you, that makes me very happy. We also don't have to deal with bees and other nuisance bugs, so all in all, I'd say we get the best of both worlds.

Careful, though. Those thorns are just as sharp as they look, and they're sturdy enough to do some real damage. I remember one little kender who got curious about whether the bushes were made of stone on the inside as well as the out. He stuck his whole arm in through a gap in the branches. Not the brightest thing I've ever seen done, but you know how kender are when they get a notion in their heads.

Well, he got his arm wedged in there as far as it would go and grabbed onto the first branch he found. Sure enough, it was made of stone—and covered in thorns. He yelped like a dog that had stuck its nose up a beehive. The kender then tried to pull his arm out as quick as can be. That was his second mistake.

Instead of just having a few holes in his hand, he snagged his arm on just about every thorn on the way out. He yanked the arm a ways, yelped again, yanked some more, yelped even louder, until finally, he got himself free. It wasn't a pretty sight, let me tell you. Luckily, Sondra Softtouch, the mayor's daughter, heard the commotion and came running.

Sondra spent a year studying up there with Goldmoon and her mystics on Schallsea and came back quite the little healer. She patched the kender up quick enough. And though he was still very curious about the flowers, that kender kept his hands in his deep little pockets the rest of his stay.

Yes, I've got a whole lot of stories about the garden. I suppose that's what comes from spending my whole life tending the place.

What? You don't think stone roses need tending?

Weeds grow here just as well as they do anywhere else. They may not be a threat to these bushes, but they still look a mess. And who wants to visit a messy garden? Then there's the mess that people make. You wouldn't believe the kind of things folks will just up and leave behind if they don't actually live in a place. I've found everything from torn clothing to rotten eggs just sitting in the garden. And you'd faint dead away if I told you how often I find daggers and short swords with their blades chipped (and sometimes broken clean off) by someone who got it into his fool head to try to take a genuine stone rose home with him. Do you know I've even seen a minotaur battle-ax with a goodly chunk missing thanks to one of these stems? Even I'm amazed.

Are the roses magic?

Well, that's hard to say. Magic would explain why they stand up so well to normal blades. But then again, I'd think the same thing if you started taking swings at a boulder—no sword was meant to strike a rock over and over again.

Some folks say the garden is a cursed site.

The story goes that a long time ago, back before the gods rained fire down on ancient Istar, back when this part of the land was green and fertile, a great castle stood where our little town is now. In that castle, they say, lived a very wise king and his only son, Prince Dottaard.

As the fingers of age tightened on the king, he began to worry about the fate of his kingdom, for his son was yet unmarried. In order to remedy this situation, the king sent his four swiftest riders, one in each direction, to make this proclamation known throughout the land: Whatever woman Prince Dottaard married would not only become princess (and eventually queen) of the realm, but also would receive all the lands south of the castle and half of the kingdom's treasury to do with as she pleased. The prince, he thought, would never choose to marry a woman who would abuse such a gift.

The next day, hundreds of young ladies visited the palace, each more beautiful and elegant than the next. The only one the prince had eyes for, though, was Rosella. Rosella wore a cape of deepest black, and though she kept the hood pulled low (hiding her eyes in constant shadow), the flowing red locks that spilled over her shoulders and her ruby lips said this was a woman of exquisite beauty.

By midday, Prince Dottaard dismissed all the ladies except Rosella, and by sundown, he was sure no other woman matched him so perfectly. The wedding, it was decided, would take place one month hence.

The king was beside himself with joy. His son would have a wife, his kingdom would have a princess, and he could die a happy man.

That evening, however, as the king passed Rosella's chamber, he heard a strange, ancient voice coming from within. Peeking through the cracked door, he saw Rosella remove her hood to reveal that she was not a youthful maiden at all, but rather an ancient sorceress. The cloak she wore was really her wizards robes—black robes—and she cast a spell so that when it was pulled tight about her, she would have the visage of a princess.

"I have cast a spell," Rosella cackled to herself, "to make that fool prince fall in love with me. In one month, we will marry and half the kingdom will be mine!"

The king ran off to tell his son the terrible news, but Rosella's spell was so powerful that the prince did not believe a word of it. He was going to marry Rosella, and his father could do nothing about it. As the wedding day grew closer, the king plotted and planned, but he could find no way to save his son and his kingdom from this terrible woman.

Then, one week before the wedding, a palace maid overheard Rosella talking to the captain of the guard. "I am terribly allergic to roses," she said, "so you must not allow any guests to bring them to my wedding. Not even the tiniest rosebud may be woven into a lady's headdress, is that clear?"

It certainly was clear to the maid, and she hurried to tell the king what she had heard. It gave him a clever plan.

On the day of the wedding, the king came to his son and apologized for his rude behavior toward the bride-to-be. "In order to make amends," the king said, "I have arranged the most glorious event ever. The wedding will take place in our own courtyard, and everyone in the kingdom will be there." This pleased the spellbound prince, and he went to tell Rosella the wonderful news.

As the bride and groom walked out arm-in-arm, Rosella gasped, then drew back in horror. The entire courtyard had been transformed into a rose garden with trees, bushes, and shrubs of all varieties, each at the height of bloom.

While the entire kingdom watched, Rosella sneezed so hard that her hood flew off, revealing her true form. As panic swept through the crowd, Rosella sneezed again and again. Finally, her concentration was so shattered that she could no longer maintain the spell that bewitched Prince Dottaard.

Freed from Rosella's control, the prince immediately announced that the wedding was off and called for the palace guard. Though they were no match for the sorceress, the guards drove Rosella off. Before she left, she turned to the king and said, "Your roses have beaten me, but they will never do so again!"

With that, she waved her hands in the air and every bush, tree, and shrub turned to stone. Then she repeated the motion and disappeared in a puff of smoke.

When the king explained what had happened, Prince Dottaard went to thank the palace maid. In the end, though, the two fell in love, and one month later, they married.

The wedding was held in the garden of stone roses, which bride, groom, and king all agreed was the loveliest place in all the kingdom.

Quite a story, eh? It was my daughter's favorite when she was a wee girl. Most folk don't take it as truth, but it's the one we usually tell visitors.

The story we like to believe is about a sculptor and a princess. (Funny how they all seem to be about royalty, eh?)

In the Age of Might, shortly after the Kingpriest of Istar made his Proclamation of Manifest Virtue, there lived Princess Kojen, a beautiful and mighty warrior of the House of Kharolis. She railed against the doctrines of the Kingpriest, who declared that any woman who engaged in battle or other "manly duties" was a follower of Evil and should be put immediately to death.

Princess Kojen, as was the fashion for ladies in the kingdom of Kharolis, was a strong leader—a position the Proclamation strictly forbade her to hold—and often enjoyed the pleasures of archery, fencing, and horseback riding. In fact, just about the only thing she did which would have met remotely with the Kingpriest's approval was the time she spent with her lover, a sculptor by the name of Serran.

Though Serran would beg Kojen not to flaunt the Proclamation so boldly, she just laughed at him. "It is who I am," she told him. "You would not want me to ask you to give up your chisel and mallet, would you? No. Then how can you ask me to give up all of the things my blood aches to do? And how can anyone who forces me to do so possibly be the living embodiment of all that is Good?"

Serran blanched at the question. "That is heresy, Kojen! Do not ever say that again!"

The princess merely laughed at her lover. Her will was too strong to allow her to do anything other than speak her mind at all times, no matter what the consequences. And when word of Kojen's unrepentant ways reached the Kingpriest, he sent a force of one hundred soldiers to arrest the princess.

When the soldiers approached Serran's workshop, Princess Kojen met them with cold steel. The battle raged for three days and three nights, and when the sun rose on the fourth day, Princess Kojen was the only one left standing.

"This is not the end of this, Serran," she said as he tended her wounds. "More soldiers will come—perhaps a thousand or more. And I will not be their only target. In order to get to me, they will strike at you, and I cannot have that. Tomorrow morning, I must leave so that you will be safe."

Though it broke his heart, the sculptor knew it must be so.

"I have a present for you," Serran whispered as he held Kojen in his arms for the last time before she left. He held out his hand, and in it was a sculpture of a rose, delicate and perfect in every detail. "As this flower will never fade and wilt, neither will my love for you, dear Kojen. For every day that we are apart, I will carve another rose so that when we are reunited, we will have a monument worthy of our love."

The princess left the next morning at dawn.

A week later, a thousand soldiers arrived at Serran's home looking for Kojen. And though a hundred different officers questioned him as to the princess's whereabouts, the only answer he ever gave was, "She has gone." And all the while, he never looked up from the perfect blooming rose he carved from a block of solid marble. When the soldiers left, Serran carried the rose out to his garden and placed it in a wooden lattice alongside six other perfect stone roses.

From time to time, the sculptor would hear rumors of his princess. If they were all to be believed, Kojen traveled from one end of Ansalon to the other and back. She may have even visited the fabled Dragon Isles. But the one place her wanderings never took her was back to Serran's side.

Before he died, Serran sculpted more than twenty thousand individual roses as well as every leaf, limb, and lattice that you find in the garden today.

❦ ❦ ❦ ❦ ❦

Who wouldn't face an entire army to defend a love as true as Kojen and Serran's?

If that story is even partly true, then it's no wonder the garden is such an inspirational site. In the forty years that I've tended it, I've seen all manner of man, woman, and beast come into the garden and leave changed to the core.

There was a man who traveled here all the way from the Estwilde, where he ran a grist mill. Seems that all his life he had heard of the garden at Stone Rose and felt an unexplainable urge to see it. He sold his mill, packed the few things that mattered most to him in this world, and hiked across mountain, desert, and dragon realm to get here. Let me tell you, I could see every mile he'd crossed caked onto his face or frayed off his shirt, but a happier man I'd never met. That is, until he sat on the bench under the shade tree.

You see, sitting on that bench was a woman who had taken every last copper from her dowry to pay for a similar trek, all the way from a farm in Tanith.

They took one look at each other, and it was as if they'd known one another all their lives. They sat under that tree and talked deep into the night. When I came back the next day, I found them curled in one another's arms, asleep beneath a stone hedge.

Well, the mayor performed their marriage ceremony that evening. They live on a farm just down the road. See, even those of us who visit the garden every day still get swept up in the emotions it brings out.

One morning, I arrived at work to hear a piteous yowling coming from somewhere in the hedge maze. After searching around for a while, I came across a black kitten—it couldn't have been more than four weeks old—whose matted fur had become caught on a stone thorn. I haven't a clue what happened to the mother or the rest of the litter, but it was plain to see this little fellow was all alone in the world and in need of some looking after. So I brought him home in spite of the fact that my nose clogs up and my eyes tear every time I so much as touch an animal. And don't you know it, that cat loves to be petted.

Yes, the beauty of the place will make a body do some awful strange things, like this elf that passed through here the other day. He was a strange one, a Qualinesti just like you folks. But instead of running away from the Dark Knights and their minions, he was headed straight back into the forest. Still, in the end, I think the garden helped him find the right path to walk.

🏹 🏹 🏹 🏹 🏹

When I came into the garden that morning, the elf was already there, standing in front of that bush over there, staring hard at that rose—the one that is partly open and faces almost due west.

His clothing marked him as a vagabond, but his bearing made me look twice. Now, to us humans, all elves look more or less proud. The way you carry yourselves, tall and thin and straight, makes you seem as though you expect to be congratulated for just walking into the room. I don't mean this as an insult, just as a comparison to us humans. Because the elf I saw that morning had an air that made him seem . . . well . . . haughty is the only word I can think of to capture it.

Being as how I leave people alone unless they look like they need help or a friendly ear, I went about my business and let the elf go about his. When I finished my weeding, though, I noticed the elf was still staring at the same rose.

Coincidence, I told myself. I just happened to catch him at the same place I saw him earlier. A lot of visitors wander the garden for hours, stopping and gazing at the same three or four sculptures that appeal to them most.

When I came back from my noon meal, though, the elf was still there. So I decided to make sure that he was all right. I walked up next to him, yet he didn't even know I was there!

I cleared my throat. "Good afternoon." I said and waited for a response. When he didn't give one, I continued, "There are plenty of pretty roses here in the garden. Mind if I ask what makes that one so interesting to you?"

He finally turned to look at me, and I could see a single tear welled up in his eye.

"Nothing. It is just the first one that caught my eye." His voice was dry and distant. "It is . . . they are all so . . . perfect."

"Yes, they sure are. Beautiful, too."

"And terribly, terribly sad" he added.

"What?"

"The roses. They are very sad. Can you not see that?"

I really had no idea what he was talking about, but I thought it best to listen a while longer. I couldn't figure out if he was the wisest elf to ever visit the garden or just the plumb craziest.

"No," I told him. "Why are the roses sad?"

"Because they cannot be what they were meant to be."

I told him that I still didn't understand and offered him a sip of water. I was sure that he was heat-mad.

"The rose," he began, speaking very patiently—the way you do when you're explaining something very important, "wants to bloom. That is what all roses want: to grow from tiny buds full of promise to exquisite flowers that please the eye and the nose, and finally to move on, for beauty in this world is merely transitory."

"But these roses are always beautiful," I said.

He looked at me as if I was speaking in the goblin tongue.

"The roses don't want to be beautiful—that's just what they are, they can't help it. No matter what they do, they always will be beautiful. What they want is to grow. And that is the one thing these roses may never do. They have a duty."

"A duty?" He was heat-mad for sure. If I was lucky, he'd just pass out and I could get Sondra to heal him.

"Yes, a duty—like me. My duty is to return to Qualinost, to help my people, to lead them out from oppression. That is a beautiful thing—a proud and noble destiny."

"But it's not what you want?"

"No! With all my heart I want to follow another path. My heart, my past, and my love all call out for me to go to the frozen lands to the south, but my duty calls me westward."

His madness was beginning to make more sense.

"And don't you ever follow your heart?" I asked. "Is duty always your master?"

"Always," the elf replied. "It is all I've ever known. I am truly like the flowers in this garden. Their stone skin prevents them from blooming, from ever reaching their potential. They are trapped in a state halfway between their beginning and their end. I too am trapped. For if I go to perform my duty now, then as surely as I stand before you, duty will keep me trapped the rest of my days. There will never be a day when I am free to follow my heart's desire."

I didn't know what to say.

"Well, you're here now, and you have a choice. Why don't you follow your heart?"

The elf stood completely still for a very long time. So long that I thought the heat finally had cooked his brain.

"I don't know if I have the strength to. I've followed duty my whole life. Can I ignore it now?" He looked at me, his eyes aflame with confusion. "Can the rose ever break through its stone skin and truly bloom?"

I hadn't a clue how to answer him. Truth be told, I wasn't even really sure what the question meant. So we just stared at one another for a very long few moments. And when we looked back at the stone roses, we saw something remarkable.

A slight wind blew through the garden, and from amid the very stone rose bush we stared at, a red shape bobbed back and forth. It was a rose—a real living rose. Now, I'll often find small rosebushes sprouting around the garden. I take care to dig them up and bring them to my own garden at home. They somehow seem to detract from the beauty of the statues. But I hadn't seen any plant budding in this particular stone hedge all year—yet there one was.

The elf smiled.

"I have my answer," he said, then turned to me and bowed deeply. "Thank you for your time and thoughts. They have been most enlightening."

With that, he turned and left the garden.

🍂 🍂 🍂 🍂 🍂

I'm not sure what answer the elf received, and I surely don't know whether he headed home to Qualinesti or south to the frozen plains (though what he expected to find there, I haven't a clue). But I do know that I let that little rose stay in the garden—there it is, poking out from the top of the stone hedge. It seems important somehow.

Oh, but storytelling is a thirsty job—even more thirsty than gardening.

Pass me the wine, and when I'm done, I'll tell you the tale of how we cured the mayor of sleepwalking through the garden on the nights of the full moon!

D. CRAMER.

SOTHI NUINQUA TSALARIOTH

The Frozen Past Arch, 13sc

The farther across the ice he went, the more Gilthanas convinced himself that the huldrefolk portal would prove the key to his journey. He trudged steadily, day after day, across a wilderness of unrelieved frost and snow. The Courrain Ocean was somewhere off to his left, but he would worry about that later—for now, it was just important to keep making progress south.

Fortunately, the enchanted cloak the gully dwarves had given him kept him warm even in the most harsh arctic conditions. He slept directly on the snow but never felt a chill underneath him so long as he kept the scarlet fabric between himself and the glacier. Also, no matter how harsh the wind that tore across the flat swath of ice blew, it could not penetrate the tight weave of the cape that he kept wrapped around him.

Fondly he recalled the simple generosity of the gully dwarf clans in Purstal and Elial. On this cold expanse he actually found himself missing the companionship of his hosts in those ruined cities.

Eventually he arrived at the great precipice, the Icewall, and here at last he turned his course toward the east. For many more days he plodded, always looking up at the sun-dazzled face of blue-white cliff. He began to ration his food, though—thanks to the magical decanter of Purstal—he had no worries about drink. Alternately he poured sweet nectar of squeezed citrus fruit to invigorate his limbs, or tart red wine to warm his torso, and with the singleminded purpose that had driven him since the garden of Stone Rose he continued on.

And then he saw it.

The arch was so tall that it rose from beyond the horizon, even though it towered a mile or more past the crest of the Icewell. As Gilthanas walked closer, the arch seemed to sink from his view behind the nearer skyline, until at last he stood at the foot of the great cliff and could see no sign of the massive stone shape rising into the sky above. Darkness settled around him as he was studying the sheer surface, though the ice seemed to glow even in the pale light shed by a crescent moon.

After an hour of study, the elf conceded that he could not climb this cliff anywhere along here. Of course, in the days before the Summer of Chaos, he could have cast a spell, using his training and talent to control the arcane powers he had mastered for most of his adult life. A spell of levitation would have carried him easily up the cliff, or—if he was really in a hurry—he could simply have teleported himself and his possessions up the precipice, or even into the very shadow of the arch, for that matter.

However, that magic had departed with the gods who had

abandoned the world to its mortal masters. And so Gilthanas found himself faced with the prospect of an impossible climb.

Instead, he resolved to find another way. For the next day he marched across the glacier, now following the foot of the cliff until, at sunset, he reached the sharp dividing line between ice and sea. Here the glacier ended in broken shards and spires—a treacherous landscape that shifted and surged with tempest and tide. However, Gilthanas was not interested in going further.

Instead, he saw where the cliff of the Icewall ended and where the vast shelf of bedrock became a tumble of boulders and rubble spilling into the harsh, cold sea. Icicles draped many of the large stones, and here and there great swaths of loose snow had swept avalanche channels through the slope. At least the surface was irregular, though, allowing Gilthanas to climb it.

He began ascending at dawn, using his sword as an icepick and counting on the grip of his boots to cling even to the slipperiest of surfaces. He avoided the worst of the avalanche chutes, and when forced to cross a lesser ravine, he hastened with reckless abandon. Once he leaped out of a gully seconds before a tumble of icy snow roared from the precipice down to the sea.

By nightfall he found that he was only halfway up, but he rested in a windswept crevasse between two boulders. Even the protective ability of the cloak was taxed, causing Gilthanas to move out before the dawn. To remain still any longer meant he'd risk freezing to death.

Thus it was that the first rays of the sun fell across him as he pulled himself over the ultimate crest of the Icewall. Before him, ten miles or more away but rising in crystalline relief against the azure sky, the Frozen Past Arch crested in glorious perfection.

It must have taken hours for Gilthanas to cross that distance, but he was not aware of time passing. Instead, he had eyes only for the massive semicircle of stone—the portal that swept into the sky and then curled back down to the ground. It seemed to the elf that this course must be symbolic of the promise for his life and future. He had a destiny—a path to follow—and its course was before him!

Finally he stood beneath the stone surface. It might have risen a thousand feet over his head, but he had no way to make an objective reckoning. He sniffed the air, he listened and tasted and touched, seeking for some sign of the portal's power. But he wasn't surprised to find no glimmer of a magical aura.

He did not take this as evidence of failure. Instead, he had anticipated this—surely the power of such an ancient and hallowed place would not be focused so directly that any dumb brute that wandered beneath it would be affected. No, to reach the center of the arch's power, Gilthanas knew he would have to do more.

He would have to climb.

For the first time he took stock of the arch's surroundings. He realized that other unnatural shapes softened and masked by a permanent snow cover stood around him. In one place a great dome mounded out of the icepack's surface, appearing too smooth and symmetrical to be anything but a designed structure. Of course any outer surface it may have displayed was buried beneath millennia worth of glacial accumulation.

Beyond the dome was the suggestion of a crooked wall, also smooth and icy on its exterior. Other structures that might have been elaborate towers or giant statues were now buried beneath the ice, though they still jutted upward enough to suggest imaginative design and incredible workmanship.

Gilthanas walked a circle around the base of the arch—a span with a diameter of nearly a thousand paces. The body of the structure seemed to be a curving shaft of solid stone. Each footing was only twenty or thirty feet across, and no broader than the trunk of a full-grown vallenwood tree. Yet these pillars swept upward and in, somehow bearing the weight of a span that seemed to deny possibility. The prince knew that no one in the world, not even the most skilled of dwarven stonemasons, could have built anything resembling this in the modern era. He needed no further proof of the arch's origins—this was clearly an artifact of a long-vanished race, boasting workmanship of a quality lost to the world.

At the foot of one of the stone legs he saw that narrow steps had been carved into the surface. The climb, especially at the beginning, looked to be treacherous and steep. Still, Gilthanas wasted no time in dropping his satchel of treasures given to him by the gully dwarves. He wrapped his cloak around the bundle and, wearing his sword in its sheath and using the soft boots on his feet, he started up the stone stairway.

For its lower course this was more accurately a ladder, since the arch started out rising nearly straight up into the air. The steps were only wide enough for his toes, but his fingers could cling to the higher notches in the stone surface, and he made his way without a great deal of difficulty. Soon the wind began to whip at him, and he felt the chill through his wool tunic, but he clung tightly to his handholds and made sure that each foot was firmly planted before he advanced to the next step.

By the time he had risen a hundred feet above the surface of the glacier, the angle of incline had decreased enough that Gilthanas could climb without the use of his hands. Even so, he remained hunched forward, and as the wind rose to howling force, he frequently grabbed at the stone surface to steady himself. He began to take note of the irregularities in the surface of the ice below—the shrouded structures of the ancient huldrefolk city.

This was not a ruin in the same sense as Purstal, where it was possible to guess at the nature of the structures and clearly perceive their purposes. Here, any purposes eluded his understanding—except, perhaps, for one great bowl that might have served as some kind of amphitheater. Otherwise the walls, domes, irregular shapes, and icy spires that extended for miles inland made no sense in the context of any city Gilthanas had ever seen.

Finally he stood at the top of the arch, where he found a smooth platform no larger than the main table in a typical inn. Like the rest of the arch, this flat expanse was clear of snow and ice—a fact which, for the first time, struck him as unusual. With a steady stride he walked to the center of the platform and turned to face the sun. He spread his arms wide, braced himself against the wind buffeting him, and raised his voice to the heavens.

"Silvara!" he cried. "I seek you! May the power of the arch fulfill my quest!"

He waited, feeling the chill of frostbite on his cheek, seeking some sensation of ancient power—some magic that would sweep him away from here. But he sensed no indication—no smell or taste of an aura. He listened, but the sound that reached his ear evoked a much earthier company.

"Jump!"

The word was followed by a hearty laugh—the speaker apparently greatly enjoying his suggestion.

Immediately Gilthanas opened his eyes. Stepping forward, heedless of the long drop, he looked down to see a trio of tiny figures standing in the snow below.

"Jump!" shouted one of them, and this time all three bent over from the force of their fulsome guffaws. "We'll catch you!" he hollered, spreading his great arms in an expansive, ludicrous gesture.

"Thanoi," muttered the elf, recognizing the tusked faces and the powerful and hulking bodies of the walrus-men. His memories of the crude race were bad, dating back to his first quest on this glacier—a search for an orb of dragonkind that had brought him here more than forty years ago.

"Go away," he shouted in reply. "Or perhaps you'd care to catch one of my arrows!"

He tried the bluff, hoping that the creatures hadn't seen

that he wasn't armed with a bow. He was disappointed when they only laughed harder. "Are you going to throw them down? Perhaps we can catch them in your pretty cloak!"

Now he saw that the largest of the walrus-men, the speaker and presumed leader, was holding out a scarlet bundle. The other two pawed through the robe, howling as they picked up the elf's treasured belongings.

Gilthanas flushed with rage. Not for the first time did he truly miss his magic, knowing that in years past he could have unleashed his power on these insolent wretches to punish them thoroughly—while barely batting his own eyes from the effort. Gritting his teeth, he checked that his sword was loose in its scabbard and started back down the stairs he had ascended

Only then did he stop and reflect. He had felt no power—no arcane effect atop the arch—but he had been so sure he could find Silvara by using it somehow. Purposefully he stepped back across the platform, this time turning his face to the east. Again he beseeched the ancient power of the huldre, calling Silvara by name, straining his mind for some sensation, some suggestion of an image, of his silver dragon maid.

But there was nothing beyond the howling of the wind and the increasingly mocking laughter from below. He squinted in the distance, following his tracks back across the snow, and then he saw it:

A brown shape, clearly the hull of a sleek boat, lay in a notch on the icy shoreline. Had the thanoi come here in that craft? Certainly he hadn't seen any sign of them in the ruined city beforehand. Yet, though his tracks were clearly visible, there was no spoor leading from the boat, or anything suggesting that the walrus-men had come from other than the snow right below.

Once more Gilthanas started down the arch. On the lower, steepest stretch, he was forced to face the steps and thus turn his back to the thanoi, who had gathered in a loose ring below him. The elf startled the hulking bullies by spinning when he was twenty feet off the ground and leaping to the snow to land beyond the ring of walrus-men. By the time they had recovered from their surprise, turning to face him, he was standing with his sword drawn.

"It has been years since I have killed one of your clan," Gilthanas declared coldly. "But it is not a knack I have lost."

"Hoark, hoark!" laughed the largest thanoi. "A big sting for a little fellow." The creature hefted his formidable weapon, which was a wooden shaft with a vast sheet of clear ice forming an ax-blade at one end. Gilthanas didn't let the crude appearance of the weapon fool him; he knew that the frostreaver was a weapon as deadly as any razor-edged blade of steel.

"Give me my things, and I will go," the elf declared boldly. "Unless you choose to fight."

"We give your things back—but only if you go that way," grunted the thanoi, pointing inland.

Immediately Gilthanas remembered the boat. Did they want to keep him away from the craft? Or did they merely intend to follow him across the glacier and kill him at their leisure?

"I have a mind to go there," he replied, indicating the coast. "But I will take my things, regardless."

"No! Go away!" bellowed the greatest of the walrus men.

"Are you thieves?" the elf scoffed. "You wouldn't know what to do with those things if you kept them!"

"Do?" The thanoi's voice dropped to a menacing growl. "Do this!"

Gilthanas was startled when one of the thanoi hoisted the decanter of Purstal and smashed the glass against the stone arch. Another tore asunder the scroll—the precious map that had brought him to this point. And the third rent his cloak into small pieces with savage, grunting tears.

The elf lost his temper and charged in to attack. His steel sword shattered one frostreaver, then cut down two of the lumbering thanoi. He stabbed the last one in the back, furi-

ously twisting the blade, then kicking the corpse as his trembling rage lingered long after his enemies were dead. Most of his magical treasures were gone, destroyed uselessly, mindlessly . . . and for what?

Finally, cold and thirsty, he plodded across the ice, seeking the wooden hull he had seen from so far above. Darkness fell, but now he couldn't stop, for to sleep was to die. The cold wind tore through his tunic, and he longed for the cloak. If the boat proved useless, or even barren of provisions, he would undoubtedly perish from exposure to frost or sea. But now it was his only chance.

He discovered the craft and was astonished to see that it appeared new—at least, it showed no signs of weathering. It floated in a natural slip between two jutting prongs of ice. The planks were smooth, and the hull was polished to a high sheen. There was no snow in it, nor were there tracks in the fresh powder around it. He scrambled over the gunwale, estimating the vessel at a good twenty-five feet long. More to his delight, he found a cask of water—somehow, miraculously unfrozen—and a crate containing many fresh loaves of elven warbread. The provisions should last for a month or more. Furthermore, he looked under the foredeck and found clean blankets and several plush furs. However, the boat held no oars, and he could not find any sign that a mast had ever been mounted.

Most curious was an elaborate scrollwork of words carved into the transom. He recognized the structure of verse, though the letters themselves were arcane and utterly foreign to him. Nevertheless, he ran his fingers over the words, whispering to himself. He decided to camp here and warm himself in the furs while he made his plan.

He dozed off, and the last thing he did was mumble the words "Elian Wilds," with the vague notion that he could get supplies there.

Suddenly, the boat began to move.

A Moment in Time:
Elian Wilds

Time is a strange thing.

Years. Months. Days. Hours. Minutes. Seconds. Even the briefest of moments. They can all drag on for what seems like eternity, or they can fly by in a split second. No matter how long one spends with a lover, it is never long enough, but the time spent with a reviled commander seems twice as long than it actually was.

Some say that the moment of a man's death lasts forever and that he has enough time to relive his entire life and even experience how things might have been. As Gilthanas and I both dropped our guard and lunged at each other in all-out attacks, it was clear to me that only one of us would be trapped in that eternal final moment while the other's life would proceed forward in fits and starts, with each day, hour, and minute seeming to vary in length.

The Meeting, 18SE

I never thought it would come to this when I first met Gilthanas. He was the most wondrous thing to have entered my life up to that point.

I had just survived the Test the month before, and the Superior Master said that he had been impressed with my performance. One of the foes I had bested was actually of a rank far higher than I thought I would ever be skilled enough to attain—in fact, to this very moment, all these years later, I feel that it was more luck than skill that allowed me to succeed.

When I received the message that the Superior Master wanted me to meet him on the docks of the Forbidden City, my heart filled with both elation and dread. I felt elated because an audience with the Superior Master is something that he reserves only for the greatest of the ranks, the Red's Emissary, or those who had earned a special mission from which they do not return. It would be the greatest of honors for the Superior Master to select one as young as I am for such a mission, but it would also mean that I would not have an opportunity to take a woman and carry on my family line. Although I would be counted among the honored dead, it would be a death without meaning for I would have no children to recite the achievements of my life.

I hurried through the streets of the Forbidden City, trying to ignore the strange sounds that occasionally came from within the buildings and staying well clear of the bloodsucking vines that had helped me defeat one of my foes during the Test. Even though my peers considered me strong enough to walk in the Forbidden City, the crystal buildings still seemed like places from which unfathomable horrors could spill forth at any moment. Several times during the Test, I had thought I had caught sight of the golden-skinned dwarves that had forced my forebears into a state of slavery through their powerful magic. But whenever I stared in that direction, I discovered that the image was a mirage—just the light reflecting off a crystal doorway or a spot where the crystalline building had healed itself of some damage it had incurred. The combination of the crystal and dried blood—for all the crystal buildings bled when damaged—often caused men of higher rank than I am to make mistakes. I took it as a sign that my courage and steadiness were increasing when my imagination played only one such trick on me that day.

When I reached the dock, I found the Superior Master standing on the outermost point of the pier, gazing upon the turbulent waters beyond our island. As I moved closer, I noticed that a thick fog was rolling in, obscuring the sea.

Before I announced my presence or spoke my name, he said, "Welcome, young one. I brought you here because I had a dream that made me believe that you will find your destiny here. Behold."

From within the fogbank, a wondrous vessel emerged. Intricate carvings covered its transom. A single passenger sat within the boat, and as the vessel drew swiftly toward the docks, I saw that the passenger appeared human yet somehow did not. I first thought that it was a child, but when the boat drew close enough, I saw the curious bone structure of his face, as well as the large, slanted eyes, and the ears that ended in points.

He moved with a grace that was unlike any I had ever seen, as he leapt from the boat onto the dock. He said a few words in a language I did not understand, eyeing us carefully, his hand resting near the sword by his side. He was trying to appear nonthreatening, but it was clear to me that he was ready to defend himself if we should have hostile intentions.

The Superior Master spoke to him, saying something in what sounded like a different language than what the stranger had spoken, but the strange one then responded in that same tongue. They bowed to each other and the Superior Master said something and indicated me. All I understood was my name.

The stranger then turned to me and spoke in heavily accented Elian, "I am Gilthanas of Qualinesti. It is a pleasure to make your acquaintance, Master of Rank Solov."

"What manner of person are you?" I asked. "You are unlike any man we have here on the Elian."

"I am Qualinesti," he replied, a momentary look of confusion upon his face. Then he suddenly gained understanding. "You have never seen an elf before? Is that what you mean?"

I looked at the Superior Master, feeling my cheeks flush with embarrassment. Gilthanas sounded so surprised that I felt as though I may have missed something in my education. The Superior Master said, "We rarely leave our island, Your Highness," the Superior Master told him. "The young one has never been to the mainland. I think he would find it very illuminating if you were to tell him of your race, yourself, and whatever undertaking has brought you here."

We retired to the Superior Master's dwelling and Gilthanas told me of wonders such as I never knew existed and made it clear that he was a wonder himself. He was a prince of his people, the Qualinesti elves and had already lived as long as two human lifetimes and would live at least seven more if he did not die through misadventure. All of his people lived such long lifespans, he said. He also told me of dragons that were not destructive like the Great Red who was our Mistress but were instead kind and gentle. He was in love with one, and he was currently attempting to reach her. He had put into port in Claren Elian, hoping to find supplies here, but his trip had been much shorter than he had anticipated. "The magical boat I travel in apparently journeys much swifter than any other craft."

"Yes and no," the Superior Master said. "I have read of craft such as the one you travel within in one of the libraries here in Claren Elian, Your Highness, and it may seem faster to you but in fact it travels much more slowly. You are trading safety and comfort for time."

Gilthanas frowned at him. "I'm not sure I understand."

"This magical craft has the ability to take you unerringly where you want to go," the Superior Master began, "yet, no matter what destination you seek, five years will pass while you travel."

"It didn't seem like five years, though," Gilthanas refuted, still frowning slightly.

"Ah, that's the magic of the vessel at work. Though you may spend what seems like hours on the boat, five years will pass in the lives of others not onboard the craft with you. You can go wherever you wish, and no one can detain you," he finished.

Gilthanas sat quietly for a long while, his handsome face wearing a thoughtful expression. Then he said, "Silvara and I both have many centuries ahead of us. It is better that I travel unerringly to where I think my search can start than to just wander aimlessly."

The two moved onto other topics, such as the world beyond our island. At first their conversation revolved mostly around the Superior Master espousing the glory of our Red Mistress and warning him of her might. Gilthanas learned much about the terrible dragons who now controlled lands that once belonged to others, such as humans and elves. I myself found out more about the world outside our island home, including the fact that these dragons of colors blue, red, white, and black could twist the lands they controlled into terrain that favored their natures.

The Superior Master and Gilthanas also discussed the silver dragons—who could change their shape at will, more miracles!—and many other beings that I could barely conceive of. Gilthanas even showed me some combat techniques his people commonly employed and congratulated me on how swiftly I mastered what he considered very complex dueling maneuvers. I told him that it was only natural that I should, as I was a Master of Rank, one of the greatest fighting men on all of Krynn. He agreed and said earnestly that for a human as young as I, I was truly an amazing warrior. His words filled me with pride, for he was a brilliant swordsman himself, and he was also a being with far more life experience than I could ever accumulate.

After sharing a meal with him, I walked with Gilthanas to the docks. Here, he boarded the boat, and it headed out to sea. He turned and waved as the fog rolled in and swallowed him.

I told the Superior Master that I was grateful for the opportunity to meet Gilthanas, but that I failed to see how this would affect my destiny.

Still watching the elf fade in the fog, he said, "It will become clear shortly, young one."

Suddenly, I heard the silky voice of the Emissary behind us. I whirled swiftly and fell to my knees, daring not to look at the slender, robe-wrapped form of the one who spoke for our Mistress. "What are you doing here?" she demanded. "I have been waiting in your chambers, Superior Master. Have you forgotten your place?"

The Superior Master did not kneel before the Emissary. I am told the Superior Master did not kneel before her even when she bested him in battle but instead merely admitted that she was his better. With this admission, the Ranks of the Masters started to do the Red's bidding until such time as a member of the Ranks proved their better. I, however, was no Superior Master, and I had seen the Emissary destroy men greater than I for lesser offenses than failing to kneel.

The Superior Master stood his ground and replied, "We have had a visitor. The young Master and I were attending to him and seeing him back on his way."

"You should have just killed the fool," the Emissary stated. "Who was this person?"

The Superior Master responded by relating Gilthanas's tale. I glanced up at the Emissary, who was listening in silence, her mottled gray robes swirling around her in the wind. The hood fluttered, affording me a brief glimpse of the blue-black metal mask that hid her face. I quickly dropped my eyes again.

When the Superior Master revealed that Gilthanas was searching for a silver dragon, the Emissary interrupted with a shriek, "A silver dragon?! I will brook no mention of silver dragons! Our Mistress will not tolerate such creatures anywhere near her domains, save those that she intends to slay to power her totem! I want you to pursue and slay this elf immediately!"

I looked toward the fogbank where Gilthanas had vanished moments before, my blood running cold. We could not pursue the elf, nor did we have any way of discovering where he may have gone. As the Superior Master explained this to the Emissary, I noticed her delicate, glove-clad hands clenching and unclenching. When he was done, she said, "You have five years to prepare then. You will find him and kill him. His silver dragon too, if you fail to kill him first. There will be no solace for silver dragons or their human companions, so says our Mistress. Prepare your Ranks. I will report to our Mistress in person." With a swirl of her billowing cloaks, she was gone.

The Superior Master told me to rise. He asked me what I thought of the elf and his dragon lover. I said he seemed like a good man, and that he and his lady seemed as though they deserved happiness. The Superior Master nodded in agreement and then asked me if I could kill the elf and the silver dragon if so charged.

I said, "I am one of the Masters. I do whatever you bid, Superior Master."

He said, "I am charging you with a very important mission. You will have time to find a woman and to start a family, but at the end of four years from this day, you and nine others—whom I will allow you to handpick from the Ranks—will venture forth into the world beyond Elian and learn what you can about Gilthanas and Silvara so that you may destroy them both."

❦ ❦ ❦ ❦ ❦

Four years passed as though they were seconds. I was known as a favorite of the Superior Master, so many fine women wanted to become mine. I chose a spouse quickly, and we had two strong sons and one daughter before the end of the fourth year. When my fourth year ended, I had finished training six others in the combat techniques that Gilthanas had shown me. In addition, the Superior Master and others who had returned from the mainland spent many hours telling us what it was like there, and I narrowed down Gilthanas's potential destinations. One of us would travel toward the city of Flotsam on the Blood Bay, one to Kurmost on the shores of an elven forest, two would travel to the distant city of Palanthas, and six of us would journey to city of Kalaman, for it was there that Gilthanas and his love once lived. Maybe the silver dragon was still there, and maybe we would need great numbers to slay her.

Some dark nights, as I lay in my woman's arms, I wondered if it was right to kill Gilthanas, particularly since he had succeeded in opening my mind to an entire world beyond Elian and showed me some of the combat arts of his people. While I had shown him some of our martial arts in return, he will not have had years to practice countermeasures to them as we had done.

In the end, it came down to my duty to the Superior Master, the safety of my people, and the future tales of my sacrifice that my children would tell. However, did I really want glory so badly that I was willing to kill a wonderful being such as Gilthanas for it?

The Eternal Moment, 28SC

I eventually arrived at the only decision I could. As the light flashed off the steel of our blades, a thought about whether he had ever found even a hint of his lost love flashed into my mind.

I would never know. At the end of this moment, the blood of one or both of us would be spilled upon the dusty ground. This moment that could barely be qualified as an instant, yet which could possibly last forever for one or both us, would be one of finality one way or the other.

SOTHI NUINQUA TSALARIOTH

Dragon's Graveyard, 23sc

The mist parted and Gilthanas found himself under a moon-lit sky, looking up at a rim of dark, forbidding cliffs. The boat was nosing into a small cove, and gentle waves broke upon a fringe of sugar-white sand.

Though his mind tried to accept the facts as explained by the Superior Master on Claren Elian, his emotions found it impossible to believe that five years had passed since he had embarked from that eastern realm with Silvara's name on his lips. It had been a full ten years since he had discovered this boat on Icewall Glacier and had first set sail in pursuit of his beloved Silvara.

But now, perhaps, that quest was coming to an end. He had set the boat on a search for Silvara as he left the Elian

Wilds. Now the elf stood in the hull, watching the beach as the boat glided forward, nudging gently into the soft sand. He climbed over the prow and took a moment to ensure that the craft was firmly beached—though he reminded himself that, whatever happened here, he was finished with it.

Then he looked to the land, taking in the lofty semicircle of cliff that rose directly from the fringe of sand to soar high into the night sky. The face of the stone was smooth and, in the darkness, almost featureless. If a path, ravine, or sloping ledge led upward, he could see no sign of such a route. Perhaps daylight would reveal something useful.

Until then, he decided he would examine the length of the beach. In fact, the night sky was very bright, with a full moon casting brilliant moonlight. That white orb now appeared to be at zenith.

He paused, turning his eyes skyward and studying the white circle with fresh curiosity. It struck him as a very odd coincidence that, after a journey of hundreds of miles, coursing around the long coast of a continent, he should arrive at his destination underneath a full moon—and with that moon apparently at the summit of its climb through the skies. His interest quickened as, beyond the white, he saw a slender crescent of shadow pass across the face. The moon was being eclipsed by Krynn.

This alignment confirmed his guess: His presence here, now, could not possibly be a coincidence.

"The Dragon's Graveyard appears only when the moon is eclipsed by the world."

Gilthanas, startled by the deep voice behind him, looked in the direction of the sound. He saw a narrow gap in the face of the cliff, but the rock walls closed in overhead and concealed the niche in full shadow. Then he gasped as a brown metallic head emerged, followed by a serpentine neck of the same bronzed color.

"A dragon!" he gasped, his head pounding. "Then it's

true—this is a place hallowed by your kind, by the clans of Good dragons."

"Indeed it is," murmured the serpent, slithering forward so that much of its gleaming body emerged from the narrow crack. This was a bronze dragon now scowling unhappily before Gilthanas. The wyrm crouched, catlike, with its head looming directly over the prone elf. "So much so that we resent the intrusions of other, lesser folk. Explain yourself, elf . . . tell me why I should not kill you right now."

"I am not your enemy." Gilthanas slowly rose to his feet, gratified that the dragon pulled its jaws back slightly to give him room to stand. The serpent regarded him with dark, slitted eyes, and he couldn't help but remember Silvara. *She is a metallic dragon too, a silver cousin to this bronze.*

Yet there were differences, even more than similarities, between the two serpents. This was a male, with the thick brow ridge and broad snout of his gender. His voice was deep and menacing, utterly lacking the softness Gilthanas remembered in the speech of his beloved. And his manner, despite his slight withdrawal, remained menacing.

"I have come here seeking a silver dragon," Gilthanas said. "I want to know if she still lives . . . and if not, to mourn her."

"Perhaps a worthy quest," mused the serpent. "Though presumptuous of you to assume that you are a worthy mourner for one of my kin-dragons. Why do you seek to do this?"

"She and I. . . ." Gilthanas suddenly realized that he couldn't tell this bronze serpent the truth, at least not the whole truth. "We fought together during in the War of the Lance," he blurted. "She was a bold and beautiful flier, and together we slew many of the Dark Queen's wyrms."

"A great hero, you must be," said the wyrm mockingly. Yet for the first time Gilthanas heard uncertainty in that voice. It occurred to him that this was a much younger dragon than Silvara—though his tail remained out of sight, he was no more than half as long as his former consort.

"Is this beach the Dragon's Graveyard," Gilthanas asked. He saw no sign of tombs, or any other monuments or remains. "Have I come to the right place?"

"The graveyard lies not on the beach itself; however, you are at the right place, at the right time," replied the wyrm. "You will not be allowed within . . . the graveyard lies beneath the sea, and only a Good dragon may go there."

Gilthanas shook his head, more and more frustrated. "Do you know Silvara, Sister of Heart?" he asked boldly. "Can you tell me if her bones lie in the graveyard?"

"Silvara!" replied the serpent, all but gasping. His eyes narrowed, and he lowered the crocodilian jaws to regard the elf coldly. The next words tumbled forth in a sneer. "She is indeed a heroine of our metallic clans . . . and she has not been here. So far as I know, she has vanished."

Gilthanas felt the hope flowing from his body and forced himself to resist the urge to slump in dejection. He would not reveal weakness in front of this wyrm. "How . . . how do you know?" he demanded. "How can you be sure?"

"Because I am Sterellus, guardian of the graveyard. And I have been posted here these many years, holding this place proof against the monster dragons that have recently claimed lands to the north and south of here."

"Monster wyrms?" Gilthanas remembered the stories of the great red dragon, Malystryx, who had menaced the eastern portion of Ansalon, and of the other Evil dragons that had started taking other territories. He shuddered at the thought that, during the years of his voyage, even more of these horrendous overlords had claimed parts of the land. "What dragons? Where are they?" he pressed.

"There is Red Fenalysten in the deserts to the south . . . and Black Mohrlex, who makes his home in Nordmaar's swamp. And finally, closest to us here, there is the mighty Green Lorrinar, who has sought to remake the Woods of Lahue. Any one of them would seize the treasures here, if he could but discover this place and best our guardian."

"That is, you?" asked Gilthanas. "Forgive me, Sterellus, but I have heard of these overlords . . . that they are true monsters, greater by far than any mortal dragon. How is it that you could stop one of them, should he come here?"

The bronze snorted, and for a moment Gilthanas wondered if he had gone too far. Still, he held firm, masking his misgivings with an expression of bland curiosity.

"I would meet them in ambush," snarled the dragon, though not without that tremor in his voice. "Now, go away from here! I have never seen Silvara, not here, not anywhere! And I do not want to see you any more!"

The serpent backed into the notch in the cave, and Gilthanas strolled along, staying close to those metallic jaws. The nervousness in Sterellus was uncharacteristic of a dragon, and the elf's suspicions had been fanned into flame.

"Leave! Do you hear?" demanded the wyrm, lifting his head up high. Now the whole dragon, including the serpentine neck, had withdrawn into the crack in the cliff face.

Gilthanas drew his sword in a lightning gesture. He cracked the flat of the blade against those jaws, then stepped forward to hold the enchanted weapon against the joint where the neck met the bronze breast.

"I think you're lying," he said conversationally. "And I will leave—but not until you tell me the truth."

"Ouch!" cried the dragon, trying to twist away. But the cave was too narrow, and the sharp blade held him pressed against a cold stone wall, with no room to wiggle.

"You're right . . . I'm not here to guard this place! I'm too young, too small, too weak!"

"You are!" agreed Gilthanas, pressing harder. "Tell me more!"

"I'm dying!" squawked the bronze, with such passion that the elf eased up his pressure and stared at the slitted eyes in shock. There was a misty film over those pupils, a rasp to the breath that came from the great nostrils.

"I can see that . . . I'm sorry," said the elf.

"It is a pernicious disease resistant to magic . . . it has been eating away my insides for too long, now. Some of the elders claim that I was born with this illness and that it's a part of me. I have been waiting here, for the right time."

"And while you were waiting here you saw Silvara, didn't you?" Gilthanas demanded. "Was she here?" He lowered his blade, but kept his gaze on those huge eyes.

"Yes, yes she was! I tried to keep her here, to have her keep me company until I died . . . but said she had a place to go, and she flew away!"

"Then she lives?" Gilthanas pressed, his heart soaring even as his weapon pressed forward aggressively. "How long ago was this?"

"Years, many winters!" blurted Sterellus. "I don't know how long ago!"

"Where did she go?"

"She told me that she wanted to see a friend . . . a creature she knew who lived on a lofty mountaintop."

"Who? Where was this?"

"I don't know!" insisted the bronze dragon.

Abruptly Sterellus stiffened, his eyelids closing as if he had entered some sort of trance. Gilthanas pressed the blade harder into the supple neck, but this time he drew no further reaction. The bronze dragon's attention was directed elsewhere. A low, tuneless sound emerged from the great jaws, and the prince realized that the creature was singing a mournful song.

Slowly, carefully, the elf backed away. He cast a glance over his shoulder and was astonished to see the waters slowly receding to left and right, revealing a shimmering pathway along the floor of the bay. In the distance, half concealed by foaming froth, he saw objects of bright silver and long skeletons of white bone.

Then Sterellus was moving. The bronze dragon padded out of his crack and crossed the beach, starting along the pathway that led to the Dragon's Graveyard. Gilthanas took a step after, but water spilled toward him in gentle waves that lapped with enough menace that he knew this place wasn't for him.

The dragon moved farther along the road toward his grave, and Gilthanas looked along the shore. Silvara had been here and had left to go to a high mountain. Where?

He couldn't know, but he did know something about this coast. Kalaman was not far from here—Kalaman, the city where he had been honored as lord, had been revered as governor for so many years. He had friends there, and they were wise people, with access to maps and libraries.

In that instant he made up his mind. He would go there, seek what help he could find and try to discern where this mountain might be. He cast one look at the enchanted boat and knew that he would leave it here. It might take him months to reach Kalaman, but that was all . . . and with Silvara before him his quest had taken on new urgency. No longer could he afford a five-year interval while he traveled with magical ease.

He looked again along the path leading into the sea. Those were bones there, white skeletal remains of mighty creatures. Silver and gold glittered among the remains, and here and there he saw signs of other objects—a marble statue here, there an array of chalices adorned with glittering diamonds. That was a magical place—a sacred place. And Sterellus was right, Gilthanas knew . . . it was a place of dragons. He had no business there and could feel only relief at the knowledge that his beloved Silvara had not ventured into it.

He slid his sword back into its scabbard and took a last look at the shimmering roadway. Sterellus was in there, his life waning, ultimately finished. Gilthanas turned his back and started to walk, no longer willing to waste time.

He had a treasured love to reclaim.

They Also Serve:
Kalaman 23sc

From the journal of Sir Migel Aurrafil,
Chief Advisor to Tierrel Rychner, Lord of Kalaman

23rd day of Fleurgreen, 23sc—Spring is nearly over. That has never meant much here in Kalaman—our climate varies so little from season to season—but it does mark the passage of time. Summer once brought joy and festivities to the city. The common folk were apt to gambol across the commons simply for the joy of being alive. But no longer.

Now, the spineless fools are afraid to walk the streets at midday. Ships still sail into our harbor, and commerce still pumps life-sustaining steel into our economy, but only just barely. The sailors remain aboard their ships, not daring to wander into the heart of town (not that it would do them any good to do so, anyway). The city is but a shadow of its once great self.

A shadow? Even in my despair, a hint of my renowned humor shows through.

The cause of all this misery is the shadow that has fallen over Kalaman—indeed across all of Nightlund. Who feels safe in a city thrown into perpetual twilight? No one! The sun never sets on Kalaman—but neither does it ever rise. It simply hangs there, just below the horizon, painting the sky blood red. From the moment the gods left, we have been the butt of their final joke. They may have deemed this the "Age of Mortals," but the gods made sure to leave their mark indelibly on all our lives.

And yet the rabble is so starved for someone to look to in their hour of need that the people continue to pray to Paladine, Mishakal, and the other departed gods—the very gods who inflicted this curse upon them. What the people need is a hero—a flesh-and-blood figure—who can banish the fear from their minds. If Lord Rychner had a greater rapport with the masses, we would have turned the fortunes of the city around by now.

Sadly, though he is a man of impeccable taste and breeding, Lord Rychner will never be a man of the people. This puts the people in a very delicate situation. We need a leader—a hero to the bedraggled commoners—but it must be someone who poses no threat to Lord Rychner's position—and my own job. For months, I have struggled with this issue.

Today, the neatest solution possible walked right up to the palace and knocked on the front doors.

Imagine our surprise when the royal trumpets blared to herald the arrival of the former governor of Kalaman, Gilthanas of Qualinesti! Here is a man the people loved! The brother of the Golden General who freed the city from the

Blue Dragonarmy, he led the defense against further attacks and stood as a symbol of freedom. I wager that if, for some reason, you were to walk into ten different pubs throughout the city, you'd find that nine of them either have a tapestry bearing Gilthanas's image, a favorite song of his exploits, or a traditional toast to his health wherever he may be.

Gilthanas led Kalaman out of its worst years and into a golden age. If anyone can rouse the imagination and enthusiasm of the simple folk, it is he. As an elf, Gilthanas does not appear to have aged a day, unlike the people of the city. Gilthanas is a walking symbol of all that once was great about Kalaman and yet may be great again. All I have to discover is whether or not he desires to return to his former post—and if he does, whether he has an opening for a senior advisor. I owe Lord Rychner a great deal, but I owe myself even more.

From the diary of Lady Jennetta Aurrafil

10 Holmswelt 23sc—Migel is such a boor. I haven't the faintest clue why I married him. No, that's not true. I really had no choice. When you're the last daughter of the last daughter in a long line of last daughters, you cannot afford to reject a proposal from the likes of Migel Aurrafil. Still, when he courted me, he was a completely different man, throwing money at the most frivolous things just to make me smile. People still talk about how he convinced Lord Rychner to hold a special ball just so that he could propose to me in front of the city's finest families. I fancied that he was the most wonderfully romantic man in all the world.

After ten years of marriage, though, and after an endless series of coteries and galas, I have discovered this truth: A man possessing money and influence can also possess a complete lack of wit, grace, and tenderness. I can think of no better proof of this than my own Migel.

All those extravagances and the public courtship were merely to increase his own reputation. The fact I was the benefactor of them held practically no weight in his eyes. That he wooed the daughter of a peasant and successfully introduced her to polite society only proved he was a man who knew the hearts of "the common folk," cementing his position as Lord Rychner's chief advisor. I am merely one of the cobblestones used to pave his path to power.

Tonight, I suffered through yet another tedious formal affair, one carefully calculated, no doubt, to provide my dear husband with more influence in the affairs of state. Still, there was a distinct difference in the air tonight, and it manifested itself with the arrival of the guest of honor—ex-Governor Gilthanas. The room practically silenced as all present bent an ear to eavesdrop on his conversation.

Gilthanas is a well-spoken man and very pleasing to the eye. I remember my mother telling me about seeing him address the populace after the forces of Evil were driven from the city once and for all. Her recollections did not half-capture the feeling of facing him in person. I'm certain that every man in the room was piqued with envy as the women nattered about his style and grace.

Every man, that is, but Migel. He stayed so close to Gilthanas that one might think them joined at the hip. I'm not sure what my husband has in mind, except that whatever it is will increase his stature in the palace. I do know that Gilthanas cannot discern the whole of it; a man as noble as that would have no part in Migel's petty power plays.

I hope Gilthanas decides to remain in Kalaman for a time. The city would be a significantly better place if he could bestow even a smattering of his integrity and honor upon our so-called leaders.

Sir Migel's Journal

17th day of Paleswelt, 23sc—Things could not proceed more perfectly. In the three months since Gilthanas's return, we have seen a marked and continued increase in the morale of commoner and gentry alike. And once it became clear

Gilthanas had no intention of remaining in Kalaman very long (thus posing no threat to the political status quo), his natural charm beguiled even the nobles. When I asked him about his family in Qualinesti, he mentioned briefly that he intended to see them again, but when pressed, also stated that he had no intention of taking his nephew's place on the throne. Although this hadn't been a fear of mine, I find it heartening to know that he doesn't wish to rule elsewhere when we need him so much here.

However, I, for one, am saddened by his disinterest in regaining his post. Just think of what I could do as chief advisor to this great man! Still, it is important I take advantage of his presence now, for Gilthanas seems eager to depart.

Just this afternoon, I found him poring over maps and charts in the palace library. As I asked him where he planned to go next, hoping to glean some insight into his motives, I noticed he had drawings of several far-flung regions sitting open before him. He made some polite, noncommittal reply, but I discerned he did not know where his travels would take him. Something, or someone, was leading him on a merry chase and so far has eluded even his keen senses.

If I am right, and his quarry, whoever or whatever it may be, is beyond his sight, then I may have a trump card to play. But does Gilthanas chase a person or a treasure? Whatever it is must be incalculably valuable, for he refuses to discuss it with anyone in the palace. In order to know how best to handle the situation, though, I must have a better understanding of his circumstances.

I believe I have just taken steps that will provide me the information I require.

As Gilthanas asked me questions regarding the maps in the library, I feigned complete ignorance (after all, why furnish him with answers when he is not forthcoming to my own inquiries?). I did, however, tell him of Jennetta's passion for cartography. He will, no doubt, seek her counsel and, in the process, open his heart to her (she seems to breed that sort of confidence in everyone she meets). In an effort to aid him, she certainly will pass information to her husband that Gilthanas might never entrust to me.

As always, my wife proves useful in ways that a more genteel woman never would. Her coarser talents provide me with resources and insights that any other man in my position couldn't possibly match. Her common heritage is at once a blessing on my reputation and an excuse for any breach of protocol I am forced to make. The ultimate irony lies in the fact that Jennetta feels she needs me more than I do her. She would, I believe, leave me in an instant if she perceived how heavily I rely upon her; my reputation and career would shatter were that to happen. Thankfully, she cannot see beyond her own fears of poverty.

On another subject, I must admit that I find it troublesome that some agency out there wishes to destroy our hopes for a brighter future. This very day some fellows in dark, loose-fitting garb confronted Gilthanas within the palace. Thankfully, his skill with his blade and the support of the palace guards prevented him from falling to these unknown men. Gilthanas himself hasn't the least idea of who these fellows are or why they would want to kill him. I fully intend to find out who is behind this.

Lady Jennetta's Diary

12 *Reapember* 23sc—Gilthanas sought me out again today. (I have finally grown used to referring to him by name rather than "Your Grace" or some other formal title.) He is quite exhilarated by the plans he and Migel have drawn up. And to think, they never would have arrived at this solution were it not for me.

When Gilthanas first came to me, I was almost overawed by being alone with him. After all, it is not every day that a simple cartographer's daughter gets a private audience with a man of legend. It was only when he explained that he came to me because of my family's occupation that I calmed enough to enjoy his company. If any good came from growing up in that cramped shop, being able to aid Gilthanas is certainly it.

He began by questioning me about faraway places like the Isle of Sancrist, the hills surrounding Palanthas, and even the fabled Dragon Isles. At first, I could discern no rhyme or reason to his interests, but slowly it dawned on me—they were all places that have mountains where silver dragons have been known to congregate. I further surmised that he must be looking for his former lieutenant (and, if palace rumors are to be believed, paramour), Silvara. Although she most often appeared in the from of a wild elf, whenever the dragonarmies attempted to retake the city, she resumed her natural shape—that of a silver dragon. Shortly after the war, the Artist's Guild decorated their hall with a grand mosaic of Gilthanas riding into battle on Silvara's back.

Though I was loath to pry into his personal matters, once it became obvious that I suspected the truth, Gilthanas insisted on telling me the tale of how he and Silvara parted. A tear still comes to my eye as I reflect on it. Why is it that we can only recognize the important moments in our lives when we view them in memory? Gilthanas's heart will not be whole again until he finds Silvara—yet he has only the vaguest clue where to search.

Together, we have fixed upon a dozen sites that seem likely places Silvara might have gone. They are spread across the entire continent and beyond. It would obviously take Gilthanas years to visit them all. Meanwhile, Silvara might move along to anywhere else she pleases—perhaps even across one of the great seas. The matter seemed hopeless.

One night, I could bear the sorrow no longer. In wretched tears, I came to Migel, the only source of solace available, and surprisingly, he actually comforted me and attentively listened to all I had to say.

When I finished, instead of berating me for being an emotional fool, he held me close and soothed me. Stroking my head with his palm. "Everything will be all right," he promised. And so, it seems, it will be.

Migel spoke with Gilthanas the next day. He convinced him that such a quest would take a lifetime (even for an elf) and still might bear no fruit. Instead, my husband offered to speak to Lord Rychner on Gilthanas's behalf. Kalaman was in a state of peace. Surely the lord would spare a half-dozen of his swiftest riders to scour the land to search for news of Lady Silvara. They could cover the entire continent in less than a year, and should their efforts prove fruitless, more riders could embark immediately to cover six more paths. If they met with success, Gilthanas would know exactly where to go without wasting years on futile journeys.

I have never been more proud of my husband than the day he convinced Lord Rychner to support this plan. And I have never seen a happier soul than Gilthanas when he heard the news.

For the past several weeks, Gilthanas and I have pored over my grandfather's maps daily, plotting out the six best courses for the riders to follow. I believe we are nearly through.

Paladine, if you can yet hear our prayers, I beg you to grant whatever blessings you can to this endeavor. No soul I have ever met deserves happiness more than Gilthanas.

Sir Migel's Journal

8th day of Gildember, 23SC—If ever there has been a more perfect plan than this, I know nothing of it. I not only have secured an increase in the prosperity of the city as a whole, but I also have made myself indispensable to both Lord Rychner and Governor Gilthanas. My Lord cannot do without me, for I am the one who knows how to keep Gilthanas from leaving the city. The governor, on the other hand, relies upon me to keep him updated on the progress of our continent-wide search for his former consort.

Gilthanas has agreed to accept his former title for as long as he remains in Kalaman. We told him, not untruthfully, that it would elate the masses to hear about the decision. After all, in every appearance his return brings back the golden years. Gilthanas may not be able to dispel the eternal twilight that grips the city, but he has worked every other sort of miracle the people could hope for.

At the governor's behest, the open-air market once again fills the streets with produce, baked goods, and all manner of handicrafts. Market days are only three times a week (as opposed to the daily affair they were in years past), but before Gilthanas's return, there hadn't been a market day in nearly five years.

The governor himself wanders the market each day, greeting everyone he meets with a firm handshake and a civil nod of his head. And he always makes it a point to buy one or two items from the stalls, even if the palace larders are full. "The only way to raise confidence is to act confident," he has told me on several occasions. At his insistence all members of the palace staff must spend at least an hour a week walking the market, and he strongly encourages us to make at least one purchase.

As a result of the market days, other shops in the town square have not only reopened, but also are doing business unlike any they've known for years. More and more trade ships consider Kalaman a necessary stop, and their sailors come into the city rather than staying on their ships at night. Inns throughout town again have more full rooms than empty ones, and the Vingaard Brewery cannot produce its dark, viscous ale fast enough to meet demand.

Kalaman very well may soon regain its position as the trade port second only to Palanthas. And given the fact that Palanthas is now under the sway of both the Knights of Takhisis and the Great Blue, Skie, many traders may find it more profitable to move their cargo through our fair city. And it is all thanks to me.

Would it be too much to think that one day I might hold an office of my own? Lord Mayor, perhaps? That is not too much to ask for bringing life and prosperity back to an entire city. All I have to do to ensure my success is keep Gilthanas in Kalaman, and that is accomplished easily enough. Additionally, although no progress has been made on discovering who would send assassins after him, I feel that since no further attempts have been made on his life, Gilthanas no longer has anything to fear from that unknown aggressor.

Keeping him here is easily enough done. After all, I have kept him this long on nothing more than a promise and a prayer. I see no reason why this situation cannot be maintained indefinitely.

Lady Jennetta's Diary

3 Frostkolt 24sc—What a false friend I am! Gilthanas came to me today, and though he is as stoic as anyone I've ever met, he confided in me that his heart begins to despair of ever seeing Silvara again. I listened with rapt attention, cooed where I ought, and advised him to be patient. "These things take time," I said. "She has had nearly two decades to sequester herself. You can't expect to locate her in just a few short months."

He smiled and patted my hand. "Of course you are correct" he said and smiled gamely. It was all I could do to smile back. How can I live with this terrible secret? And what kind of friend am I if I do not share it with Gilthanas?

Last night, I came to Migel's study to inquire as to any items he might require from next week's first market day. When I arrived, though, he was engaged in conversation with Rika, that detestable toady he calls a clerk. Rather than barge in on their discussion, I resolved to wait silently by the door and enter only when there came a break in the discourse. It was never my intention to eavesdrop, but when I heard Gilthanas's name mentioned, my curiosity got the better of me. To my utter dismay, they were talking about what lies they could fabricate to make Gilthanas believe that the search for Silvara was proceeding smoothly.

"We must give him something solid—a sighting or a merchant who met Silvara along his travels," Rika intoned as he paced back and forth across the library. Migel, seated behind his reading desk, watched him with a scowl.

"Sit down!" my husband ordered, then returned to the issue at hand. "It must not be solid enough to cause him to leave. If the elf thought that someone had recently seen his dragon wench, he would be on his way there before the words finished echoing in the grand hall. No." And here he stroked his chin in a manner that sent a chill through my entire body. "If it must be a rumor, then it must be an old one. An innkeeper who saw Silvara three years ago."

"Yes!" Rika said fidgeting in the seat he'd taken. "She stopped in Palanthas on her way to who-knows-where."

Migel waved his hand dismissively. "Palanthas is too large a city. I think Throtl would be a more useful locale. A person could be going anywhere from that goblin-infested hole, particularly if that person was really a silver dragon."

With that, both Migel and Rika began to laugh in the most malicious manner. I was quite taken aback and must have gasped out loud, for my husband rushed to the library door and threw it open, catching me in the bright light of the reading lamps.

"How long were you standing here?" he demanded, holding me firmly by the wrist. "How much did you hear?"

"Enough to know that you are a detestable villain." I'd never spoken to Migel in such a tone. He released his grip on my arm. "Enough so that when I share it with Gilthanas, he will see you for the liar that you are. He will leave Kalaman as quickly as he can, and you will be left to explain why."

My husband smiled cruelly at me.

"And what happens then?" He turned and strolled casually back to his seat at the desk. "When Gilthanas leaves what will happen to our city? Do you think the market will remain open without our great governor here to instill the simple folk with confidence? Of course not. Kalaman will plunge immediately back into the dark and frightened times we faced until six months ago. Gilthanas is the only one holding this renaissance together."

"What of it?" I asked. "He owes us nothing. Rather, it is we who owe everything to Gilthanas. Is this how we show our thanks? By lying to him about his one true love? By making a mockery of the only thing that matters to him?"

"All we are doing, my dear wife, is creating hope in his breast so that he will remain patient while we find his love. It does no one any good to have our much beloved governor running off to chase shadows and rumors across the countryside. No, all we are doing is giving him faith that he and Silvara will one day be reunited. As long as they end up together, does it really matter that Gilthanas's faith is placed in a lie?"

I couldn't tell right from wrong anymore. Damn Migel and his artful words.

"Is it kinder to keep Gilthanas in Kalaman, where he can ease the suffering of the entire population, than to let him run hither and yon on a search that might never end?"

I could not answer.

"I suggest you think about that, my dear, before you condemn both the governor and the entire city to what is likely to be decades more of darkness and confusion."

So I held my tongue when Gilthanas and I met. And though I still cannot answer whether telling him the truth is the correct course of action, I'm not certain how long I can perpetuate Migel's half-truths.

Sir Migel's Journal

28th day of Brookgreen, 24SC—I am surrounded by buffoons! Sailors already provide Gilthanas with too many rumors of places Silvara may be without my own incompetent staff presenting him with ones of their own creation. I swear, I would kill Rika this very instant if I did not think that any replacement I found would be twice as inept.

This morning, I found my fool clerk regaling the governor with a preposterous tale about a silver dragon protecting Goldmoon and her mystics on the Isle of Schallsea. Thankfully, the dragon in the story was a male, and so Gilthanas paid it no heed.

To make matters worse, one of my riders returned to Kalaman today. He and the others have been living high on the hog in Ohme for the past six months, toasting every sunrise and sunset. It seems they have run through the satchel of steel I gave them quicker than anticipated. There are coins to spare in the treasury these days, so that is no obstacle.

My problem is that word has gotten about that my man has arrived. Gilthanas already has demanded an audience with the rider, and it was all I could do to convince him to delay until the man had time to rest. Now I have spent the entire afternoon coaching the sod on what to say—exactly which lies we have told the governor and what specific answers to give to specific questions. I can only pray this simple man does not fall to pieces in the presence of "the hero of the people." (If I had known how troublesome that title would be, I'd never have suggested it. Gilthanas now seems to have an almost arcane power over the common folk—they can hardly speak clearly in his presence, let alone think.)

To make matters worse, the rider brings with him news of a sighting of the governor's dragon maid. Apparently, Silvara has been seen flying around a particular spire in the Astivar Mountains. The rider says the place is called the Peak of Clouds, and legend tells that it is home to a wise and benevolent kyrie hermit. Whether or not such a bird-man lives there does not concern me at all. However, it is imperative Gilthanas not find out about this rumor.

Matters here in Kalaman are at a critical juncture. If we can increase outgoing trade by another four ships a week, we can add another pier to our waterfront. And that will in turn bring more merchant ships to the harbor. We stand at the verge of fulfilling all my dreams for our city. I cannot allow the governor's romantic interests to jeopardize Kalaman's future—my future!

Lady Jennetta's Diary

1 Yurthgreen 24sc—I am a cowardly, faithless woman, and I deserve all the shame I've brought upon myself. For the past ten months, I have done nothing but lie to a man with a heart as noble and a spirit as pure as any I've ever encountered. I believed my husband, a man I know to be of scandalous honor, and accepted his word that when actual news of Silvara arrived, he would pass it immediately on to Governor Gilthanas. Somehow, I trusted that when a choice was to be made between personal comfort and moral responsibility, my own Migel would choose the righteous path.

What a fool I am.

I have made a point of staying within a discreet distance of my husband whenever he entertains members of his staff. Oh, I played the dutiful hostess and feigned bored disinterest, but in truth, I listened carefully to every word searching for some hint of deception. That hint came last night.

The tedious Rika, after one glass of wine more than his usual limit, made a passing comment about the rider who visited the palace last week. That toady said something to the effect of, "He took his truth back to Ohme."

Migel cast upon the toady such a withering gaze that Rika immediately commented on how late the evening had gotten and showed himself to the door. For my part, I, pretending to notice nothing amiss, bid Rika's vanishing form a fond good evening, then commented on how odd my husband's clerk was behaving. This seemed to satisfy Migel that Rika's slip of the tongue had eluded me.

The next day, while Migel was in court advising Lord Rychner on the matter of proposed construction along the waterfront, I re-entered his library and found his personal journal. Oh, what a fetid tangle of intrigue and lies I found therein, the very worst of which was the matter concerning Governor Gilthanas.

Migel finds this matter too important to leave to chance, and so do I. I have no doubt that Gilthanas saw through my husband's courtly politics, but I fear he did not know how rotten Migel is at the core—that is, until I brought the journal to the governor's quarters.

I was unsure as to how Gilthanas would react. Would he throw down the tome, quickly gather his belongings, and leave the city by the most opportune method available? Perhaps he would grab his sword and stalk over to the council chambers to exact revenge on Migel. (I was likewise uncertain as to whether or not I would perform my wifely duty of begging the governor to spare my husband's life.)

What he did, however, took me completely by surprise.

Governor Gilthanas, upon reading that his own true love, Silvara, had been spotted at the Peak of Clouds, kissed my hand in a most elegant manner.

"Dear Jennetta, you have saved me. While others in Kalaman only muddied the waters of my mind, you have been a spring of truth, light, and honor. I have not the words to thank you, but I hope that you will find some measure of satisfaction that it was your kindness that allowed me to find my heart. Do not let the scoundrels in this palace ever question your integrity or sincerity."

And with that, he was gone.

Despite the governor's words, though, I know that I have been an unfaithful wife. I've broken every rule of conduct Migel taught me when he took me from my family and brought me into this world of courtly delight. I no longer deserve this life of privilege.

And so I too have packed my belongings and prepare to leave the city. I've not touched one of the jewel-encrusted necklaces or golden earrings. Those belong to Migel, and even before I was a lady, I was never a thief. No, I take only the clothes on my back (a cotton shirt and tweed trousers that

Migel never allowed me to wear) and my grandfather's maps. Perhaps I'll walk some of the roads he sketched, presuming they're still passable.

This diary, as well as Migel's journal, I will leave with a bookseller I know in the market. I fear my husband was right when he said that without Gilthanas, Kalaman will return to the days of cowering in the twilight, fearing what may lurk in the shadows. If that is the city's future, so be it. The citizens cannot rely on some shining hero to banish the darkness from their lives. Most heroes, I've come to suspect, are more like Migel than Gilthanas. And the more power we give them over our lives, the more there truly is to fear in the gathering darkness.

SOTHI NUINQUA TSALARIOTH

The Peak of Clouds, 25sc

"Now, working with the element of rock . . . that's the next lesson . . . at least I think it is . . . isn't it? What is that form of magic called, anyway?"

"Geomancy?" Gilthanas answered helpfully, as he always did when his teacher's mind wandered.

"Precisely!" Keelak nodded his feathered head, bobbing his full body forward and back on his skinny legs. The kyrie puffed out his chest and stretched tall. "I see that I have taught you well."

"Of course you have," Gilthanas replied. "Have I not absorbed every lesson you have imparted to me?"

"I remember when you first climbed up here—twenty years ago, it was—and we started with lessons on aeromancy.

It took you most of that time just to learn a spell that would move a little gust of wind."

Gilthanas cleared his throat in embarrassment, then spoke. "Actually, it was only a little more than a year ago when I first climbed to your peak." The prince couldn't help but make the correction. Certainly he was prepared for most of his pedagogue's little imaginings, but he would not allow himself to be remembered as a fool.

Even if, when he had first started his studies of the new magic, he had been as helpless as a babe trying to swim up a raging stream.

He recalled his arrival here at the Peak of Clouds . . . of the sheer, obviously unclimbable mountain that had risen before him from the tangled heart of the Astivar Mountains. It had taken him two weeks to find the hidden passage near the base of the mountain, and even that had not been an easy route to the summit. Chilly and lightless, the secret way had wound through a maze of corridors and ascending shafts within the massif. He had wandered for many days, seeking only to work his way upward.

Dwarves lived there, and he had spent tense moments in a confrontation with the mountain dwellers. He learned that they were masters of the undermountain, but cared little for the upper reaches—and nothing at all for the exterior of the summit. At length they had given him leave to pass.

And finally he had emerged here, on the cloud-wrapped summit. Keelak had greeted him as though he had been expecting him—later, the elf realized that the absent-minded kyrie had simply thought that he recognized Gilthanas from a series of lessons he'd been conducting in his mind.

But within that mind, which sometimes seemed as fog-shrouded as the mountaintop, there lurked a brilliant sense of intuition and an instinctive understanding of the changes that had been wrought in the world with the arrival of the Age of Mortals. Keelak had longed to share this knowledge, and so he had demanded that Gilthanas become his pupil.

At first the elven wanderer had refused, intending only to learn what the ancient kyrie knew of Silvara before continuing on his way. The creature revealed that he had in fact known Silvara and that she had departed from here for a destination she had made known to the kyrie. But Keelak, despite his apparent senility, had been shrewd enough to negotiate a deal: Only after Gilthanas studied his teachings, and learned enough of the new magic to master three schools of sorcery would he impart this information.

Now, thirteen months later, Gilthanas willingly admitted that the kyrie had proven to be an adept teacher. While he might not have remembered what he ate for breakfast, he seemed to understand the way that stone and air, fire and water were linked to the powers lurking within a mortal heart. He had shown the elf how to harness those forces and use the power in a way that was much like the magic of old.

During that time, it seemed to Gilthanas as though the world had shrunk around him. Nine days out of ten the aptly named Peak of Clouds was encased in murk so thick that the kyrie and the elf might have been enclosed in a walled room. They conducted their studies and their lives on the flat plateau of the mountaintop—a circle the size of a large playing field. A narrow passageway descended to a series of caverns where the two sought refuge during the rare intervals of bad weather, but for the most part Gilthanas and Keelak had lived outside.

On the rare days when the clouds blew away and the extent of the Astivar Mountains was revealed as a dazzling vista, Gilthanas never tired of drinking in the view. The mountain range was green and lush, vibrant with water and life, and often draped with decorative tendrils of mist that swathed the lower valleys.

To east and west were more dire panoramas, however. In the direction of the rising sun he could see as far as the fetid swamp of the black dragon overlord called Mohrlex. Several times the elf had seen that monstrous form, like a great shadow of impossible proportions, sweep through the sky over his realm, or wallow and cavort in one of the shallow ponds. In the other direction lay the sprawling, thick forest enhanced for the reclusive dragon, Lorrinar. He had never observed the great green master of that realm, but Keelak assured him that the serpent existed and that he was a ruthless overlord.

Though the kyrie lived simply, these were days of comfort and pleasure for the elven prince. He found the challenge of using his mind a refreshing process, and he showed a remarkable adeptness in learning the ways of the new magic. He could mold air into a variety of shapes, call up—or tame—the wind, and even weave spells or gain information merely by concentrating his efforts. He had mastered three schools—divination, enchantment, and aeromancy—but lately he had been growing restless, and he knew that soon it would be time to ask the kyrie to fulfill his end of the bargain.

That chance was propelled by outside circumstances, as Gilthanas was attempting to convince Keelak that he had, in fact, only been here for little more than year.

The first of the black-clad figures appeared on their plateau with a suddenness that froze Gilthanas in place. Two more of the masked intruders quickly popped into view, while the first launched himself across the mountaintop with a rush. All were fully concealed but wore loose clothes that gave them freedom of movement. Each wielded a longsword in one hand and a short, narrow dagger in the other.

Fortunately, Gilthanas had never abandoned the habit of wearing his sword when he was thus exposed. He drew the weapon and met the other's slashing attack with a quick parry. Cold, dark eyes glared at him through a slit in the mask, and then the mysterious attacker spun away and, in the same gesture, threw a sharp dagger straight at Gilthanas's heart.

The steel sword whipped past and the knife clattered away—and now the elf knew the tactics, recognized that these intruders were trained assassins similar to the ones that had attacked him in Kalaman. Who they were and who had sent them were questions he forced aside for the moment. Abandoning any thought of mercy, he charged and stabbed the knife-thrower through the chest.

But the other two were rushing forward. His gangly, feathered arms flapping, Keelak hopped forward, screeching at the assassins to halt. Gilthanas groaned as one of the figures slashed the gentle kyrie across his face and chest. Keelak tumbled to the ground.

Another attacker whirled closer, and the elf struck him down. But his own thrust left him vulnerable, and he recoiled suddenly with a sensation of burning pain across his cheek.

He was cut! His first thought was that he had lost an eye, and his vision swam with red. He struck unerringly, however, and the last of the assassins bled his life onto the stone cold mountaintop. Gilthanas clapped a hand to his face, feeling the bloody cut, but finding that his eye remained whole.

In moments Gilthanas was kneeling beside the stricken Keelak. The elf shuddered in horror as he saw the deep gash and the blood welling into a wide pool. He thought that the kyrie was already dead, but then the wounded face twitched and one eye cracking open.

"Good pupil, you were . . ." croaked the dying creature. "You deserve your True Heart . . . your silver one. Seek her among the gnomes . . . in their tower by the sea . . ."

And the kyrie said no more.

A Moment in Time:
The Assassin's Path

A sharp, well-forged blade in the hands of an expert swordsman can cut the flesh without the person feeling anything—until the blood starts spilling over the skin. It was just such a blow I struck against Gilthanas, the first elf I had ever met.

Or did I?

We had lunged at each other, each of us deflecting each other's blow at the last moment, our swords ringing. We both kept our balance and whirled away from each other, slashing as we went.

But did I strike him?

It would take a moment for the brain to realize the body was dying. And some moments can last forever.

Following the Path, 25SC

Some days seem like years. That is how the days felt while I was traveling with a white-haired elf who called herself Stalker. I rarely saw her face—she kept the hood of her cloak drawn at all times, much like the Emissary did back on Elian. Also like the Emissary, she kept herself wrapped in layers of cloth that kept her sex and race ambiguous—and her array of poisoned blades hidden—to all but the keenest of observers. Her expert talent at voice mimicry made it even more difficult to discern what sex she was when first dealing with her. It wasn't until she disrobed in an effort to seduce me on our second night traveling together that I was even certain she was female.

I ended up traveling with Stalker after becoming an unwilling guest of Khellendros, the mighty blue dragon who rules the sandy lands of Ansalon's northwest. After explaining to the Dark Knights who detained me in Palanthas that I was an Elian agent of the Red, I was taken to a cave not far from the city. Here, I met their fearsome master. It was the first time I had been in the presence of a dragon, and it took all my strength of will not to just whirl and flee even before he spoke, so strong was the sense of menace and dread that surrounded him.

When Khellendros spoke, it was with a deep voice that was surprisingly rich and comforting, not at all the hissing, reptilian sound that I would have expected. Further, his Elian was as perfect as that spoken by any native of my island. He said that he had an interest in Gilthanas as well; he cared naught for the silver dragon, but he wanted the elf captured and imprisoned within his dungeons. When I restated that my mission, and that of my brethren, was to slay Gilthanas, Khellendros asked, "Does it matter to Malystryx whether Gilthanas is dead or imprisoned?"

I replied that it probably didn't. The Emissary's main concern seemed to be the silver dragon. There was no question that we were to slay the silver dragon, should we encounter her. The Emissary had made that clear during the years we waited for Gilthanas to emerge from his magical passage.

The dragon responded, "My main concern is that Gilthanas and his old comrades in arms caused me many difficulties half a century ago. I do not want to see those difficulties arise again, so I want him neutralized—unlike the others, he is not old and feeble. If the Golden General wasn't preoccupied in her homeland, I would be taking similar steps to have her dealt with as well."

I pointed out that if he was dead, Gilthanas would never pose a problem again. Although the dragon agreed that I made a compelling case, he asked that I trust in his experience with Gilthanas and in the wisdom of the ages that he—both the elf and the dragon—represented. "We are both far wiser and cunning than you could ever hope to become Solov, despite the fact that you are highly intelligent."

We discussed the matter further, and we eventually agreed to imprison Gilthanas in Khellendros's dungeons since this option was just as good as having him dead. I made it clear, however, that I was not skilled at subterfuge nor was I at all talented in taking foes alive. The dragon bared his fangs in what I suppose passes for a smile among his kind and said, "I suspected as much. That is why I have chosen to provide you with an ally."

Stalker stepped from the deepest shadow in the cave already wrapped in her many cloaks. She did not speak Elian, but she spoke the tongue of elves and of the Solamnians—languages I had mastered to some extent with the aid of the Superior Master.

"If you find yourself incapable of taking Gilthanas alive," Khellendros said, "Stalker can do so. None in my service are as adept as Stalker in directing victims into traps . . . even if the traps are somewhat overmuch at times."

"But they work," came the soft voice from within the shadows of the hood.

Khellendros had a report that Gilthanas was in Kalaman. When I mentioned that some of my brethren had traveled to that region, he stated that the local lords were supporting Gilthanas and that my fellow Masters had been killed in battle with palace guards. He restated the need for more elaborate tactics like those practiced by Stalker. I considered the wisdom of his words and took Stalker as my temporary ally.

If anyone demonstrates why women should not be warriors, it is Stalker. Never mind their duty to their men and society at large to bear children so that someone can carry on the bloodline and retell the tales of their fathers' deeds, but they act entirely too capriciously for their own good. First, after I rejected her on our second night together and explained that I was devoted to the woman I had at home, she laughed at me for not taking advantages when they were offered to me. "Life's supposed to be fun," she said. "Besides, women are more than brood mares for you men. When you start seeing what is truly around you, you'll find that we have a lot more to offer than just children."

As we journeyed, her behavior grew even more tiresome than it had been when we started. She would take care to point out other women who bore weapons, sometimes urging me to spar with them. I always refused. No woman could stand up to my expert combat maneuvers. Stalker always shrugged and said that my "overweening pride and ability to underestimate possible foes" would prove to be my downfall or that my "blindness" would lead me to an early grave.

When we had the luxury of an inn to stay in, she would often find an engaging companion and leave me to my own devices. Usually I sat in front of the common room's fire and watched its dancing flames, thinking of home or of the mission. Sometimes I went up to my private room and practiced combat maneuvers in an attempt to keep from thinking of what I'd left behind. One thing I noted, though, was that when we left the inn, Stalker's companion was discreet enough not to make an appearance. I silently thanked these men for not bowing to her own "overweening pride."

During one of her trysts at a campsite, however, curiosity got the best of me. I crept after her and a companion who she'd found traveling on the road that day, following them to the edge of a stream, where I discovered the depths of depravity that makes up Stalker's soul. As both she and her companion seemed lost in the passion of the moment, she grabbed a dagger from their discarded clothing and drove it into his eye without warning. I retreated from this scene after that, for she didn't stop with his death. I had to wonder what kind of monster the dragon had saddled me with.

As our travels continued, I kept a careful eye on Stalker, trying to determine if she used any pattern to select her victims. I came to realize that she killed only the ones who responded crassly to her advances; she merely robbed the others and left them tied to a nearby tree . . . although the ropes were usually so poorly tied that I suspect the victim worked himself free within a few hours. I admit that on one level I feel as though she was doing the world a favor. Any man too weak to resist her temptations would probably just spawn another weakling.

When I asked her about it, Stalker defined these acts as keeping life "fun" and keeping her spirits high, and she became very annoyed when I expressed disapproval. I have to admit that I found her to be a far more palatable companion after a night of "fun," as she seemed cheerful after it and would appear quite interested in intellectual pursuits. For hours, she would engage me in philosophical discourse about the definitions of "fun" and "honor" and "right" and "wrong."

All of these irritations seem like nothing compared to the last one, however. We had entered Nightlund several days before, crossing the Vingaard River and moving into the unnatural pall that hung over all of this country. It rained steadily as we traveled eastward. The roads turned into streams of mud, slowing our progress.

As we trudged along the road, she became very aggressive in her assertion that murdering men was perfectly acceptable because it made her happy—especially in these dreary surroundings. Although I felt an urge to argue this point with my weapons instead of words, I reminded myself that she was the servant of one of the Red's allies and restrained myself.

As we started to get tired, we were lucky enough to come within view of a run-down inn. Stalker suggested that we spend the "night" in dry and comfortable surroundings. "Clean sheets will go a long way to making me more cheerful about life in general, even if there's never a sun in the sky around here."

I made Stalker promise that if we stayed at the inn, she would not kill any of the other patrons or staff. She swore that she wouldn't.

The name of the inn was "A Knight's Rest." It was run by a family who all had big ears and looked as sickly as the vegetation of the shadow-drenched landscape around us. Few guests had arrived, so securing rooms was easy.

Stalker insisted that we enjoy a decent meal together after stowing our gear and changing into dry clothes. While we sat in the common room eating the bland food that I had found typical of most regions I'd visited across Ansalon, the word "Gilthanas" drifted toward us from the bar-counter. We looked in that direction as one and saw a human woman in mud-spattered boots and trousers. The innkeeper's wife was hanging her sodden cloak next to the fireplace, while the woman pulled maps from a leather satchel and opened them on the counter. Stalker rose to her feet and sauntered toward her, pulling back her hood. I followed. As Stalker walked, her posture seemed to change—as it always did when she was about to fool a victim into trusting her. I found the way she could change her bearing and personality in the space of a moment remarkable.

The woman pointed to one of her maps, saying, "This road and that road are wiped out, Will. And that one . . . that one you can pretty much write off as well. From what I've heard, there's some sort of nest of walking dead near the bridge."

The innkeeper cursed. "Between the dragons, the undead, and the damn shadow that's been hanging over the land, there's not going to be any travelers left anymore!"

Stalker said, "Pardon me for interrupting, but we overheard you mention the name 'Gilthanas.' We happen to be looking for an elf-prince named Gilthanas. We were led to believe at the last inn that he is currently residing in Kalaman. If you know of him, can you tell us whether he is still in the city?"

She regarded us with suspicion. "Are you friends of his?"

"My friend here is a former adventuring companion of Gilthanas's. And me . . . well, many years ago, I gave my heart to him, and he gave me his. We'd given him up for dead, so naturally I—"

"Are you Silvara?" The woman suddenly looked very excited. Stalker didn't laugh, but I have no doubt that she was having a difficult time containing herself when she leaned closer to the woman and answered in the affirmative. The woman started to excitedly dig through her maps. "Oh, to think I would meet both you and Gilthanas! My husband treated him most ill, your ladyship, he—"

"Please," Stalker said softly, brushing her white hair from her eyes. "We Good dragons do not stand on ceremony. Just call me Silvara."

"Us meeting here makes me wonder if the gods of Good might not be watching over us after all."

Stalker took her hands into hers, looked into her eyes, and said in an earnest tone, "They do, my friend. The gods aren't gone. They are just testing us. And if we remain strong, they will return."

Stalker made many other soothing noises and told many other lies, and when she was done, not only did we have a complete account of Gilthanas's activities during his year in Kalaman but we also had news of his destination. Further, she gave us the only map she possessed of the area around the Woods of Lahue for our journey to the Peak of Clouds. When she left, she seemed to walk on air. I told Stalker that she had been cruel to the poor woman.

Stalker replied with a grin, "I gave her hope. How can that be cruel?"

I said that they were all lies.

"Those 'lies' got us what we needed," she noted impatiently. "Now get off your moral high horse and start thinking about what we should do next." Without waiting, she continued, "I'm now wondering if those reports we heard of a silver dragon heading west out of Nightlund might have been true. If Gilthanas is looking for Silvara, she's probably also looking for him, hoping for the kind of sappy, lovey-dovey reunion that makes right-thinking people sick to their stomachs. I think this woman might be wrong in her belief that Gilthanas was going east. After all, he came from the east."

I pointed out that her logic was flawed, as he had arrived by boat and may have disembarked at any point along the coast, which puts his direction of travel in question. She scowled at me and said, "I don't believe in logic. Logic has never done me any good. I think we should head west."

I said I had no intention of going back in the direction we just came from.

"Look, even if Gilthanas is still in this area, if we go back west, we can set a trap for him, nice and close to Khellendros's strongholds. Along the way, I can drop some references that might make him think Silvara went that way . . . after all, if I could make that silly woman think I was Silvara without even trying, just imagine what I could do if I made a serious go at impersonating her? I could lead him right into our arms!"

I told her that I didn't think the kind of cat-and-mouse games that she so enjoyed were appropriate when hunting one such as Gilthanas. I said I wanted to confront him in an honorable fashion and then give him the chance to surrender to her or be killed by me.

"Where's the fun in that?" she asked. "Don't you get any pleasure out of toying with your prey? If you ask me, that's half the fun . . . letting your prey come to you, and then letting it 'escape,' if there's time for that."

"No," I replied. "That is not how we conduct ourselves. Masters of Ranks kill our quarries, swiftly and as simply as possible. Death is no game."

"Everything's a game, my too-serious friend. If you don't learn to play, you'll find yourself regretting all the fun you passed up." She sighed and stretched. "You know, I think I'm starting to realize that you and I don't exactly make a good team. Our masters may have common interests, but we just aren't working out. Why don't we try it this way: I'll head back westward in case that woman was wrong, and you go east through the green dragon's domain to see if he really did go looking for that magical mountain."

I pointed out that she was supposed to help capture Gilthanas in case I found him. I also pointed out that she was supposed to work with me if she found him first.

"Yeah, yeah, yeah," she said. She searched through the many layers of her clothing. She drew forth a golden ring with a bright red stone and threw it on the table. In rattled across the boards and came to rest between my hands. "This ring's part of a matched set. They'll let us summon each other. You'll wear one, I'll wear the other, and whichever of us finds Gilthanas first rubs the stone. The other stone will then turn bright blue. That person then twists the stone, and he or she will be transported to the vicinity of where the other one knows Gilthanas to be. All you or I have to do is concentrate on wanting to find him . . . and then the one who got the message will be where the sender was thinking about!"

She couldn't explain anything else about how the rings worked—"It's magic! What do you want from me?!"—and so I took the ring and we parted ways.

At least I was rid of her. And even if she found Gilthanas first, I believed she would be honorable enough to contact me via the rings. Similarly, I believed her honorable enough not to betray me by giving me a cursed magical item. I believed that our service to masters who were allies would be enough to keep her madness in check.

I would then be there in a moment, and then the quest would be over.

SOTHI NUINQUA TSALARIOTH

Winston's Tower, 26sc

How long had he been wandering the wilds of Ansalon?
Gilthanas no longer knew, nor cared. Instead, he allowed himself a moment of elation as he craned his neck and studied the
lofty expanse of the tall, narrow structure rising from the coast.
The ship pitched and rolled beneath his feet as the captain
worked her into the rough waters along the Karthay shore, but
the elf had eyes only for his destination. He was fascinated by
the elaborate image atop the spire, like shining glass facets that
formed a sort of rosebud. The ship's captain informed him that
the object had once been a lighthouse beacon, but that it had
not worked during the man's lifetime on the sea.

A dozen clues had brought the elven prince to this tower
built as a fortress to ancient Istar, and now, a monument to

gnome technology. His latest information had suggested that Silvara had come here, and he had doggedly followed her trail, even to the point of booking passage from the mainland. As payment, he had used the platinum coins he had found on the bodies of the assassins who had slain Keelak and attempted to kill Gilthanas himself. Unfortunately, his search of the bodies hadn't yielded any information regarding the source of their mission. That was a mystery that the elf had vowed to address eventually.

A stone wharf extended into the sea from the base of the cliff below the tower. The captain ordered a boat lowered, and the crew rowed close enough that Gilthanas could leap to the dock. With a few surreptitious glances, the sailors rowed back to their ship, which hastened to put on canvas and get away from this place. The elf could only chuckle as he made his way up the stairs carved into the cliff face. He was here, and perhaps he would find answers within this towering edifice.

His elation passed quickly as he began to consider the problem of entering and searching the tower. The dark face that he had first assumed was stone now looked to be smooth metal, without even the joints that might have made scaling a stone wall at least a possibility. A ramp curled around the base of the tower, leading past several open, beckoning door-ways, but the prince decided to make a little more cautious approach.

Halfway around the tower he found another irregularity in the wall: a series of stone steps rising to a small platform against the base of the structure. They looked like the stairs leading to a typical entryway, except he could see no door. He climbed to the space and examined the wall closely for any sign of a seam or break. The only thing he could discover was a small silver button extending perhaps a finger's width from the wall. Otherwise, he found no sign of any break or any mark in the metal plate that would have indicated a door.

Gilthanas, like most inhabitants of Krynn, knew a little of gnomes. "Tinkers," they were called, and they had a legendary fascination with invention. The development of a complicated machine was the typical life's goal of any gnome worth his or her weight in salt. Occasionally these machines worked, usually in some way not anticipated by the inventor. Quite often, the machine proved deadly to its designer and to anyone else who happened to come within reach of its claws, gears, levers, wheels, and so forth.

Thus, Gilthanas regarded that silver button in the wall with a certain amount of trepidation. He knocked on the wall, determining from the sound that it was in fact metal, and it seemed to be quite thick. He pushed and prodded along the surface as far as he could reach, even drawing his sword and tapping over his head, to no avail. In the end, his lack of patience led him to the inescapable conclusion: He had to press the button.

He placed his thumb on the silver circle and pushed. The button glided into the wall with smooth ease, though he felt some sort of mechanism engage on the other side. For two long, long heartbeats, nothing happened.

And then Gilthanas was pressed flat, crumpling against the surface under his feet. In a split second he realized that the platform was rising at tremendous speed—that acceleration pressed him down. He was lifted dozens of feet up the face of the tower and then, abruptly, the platform snapped to a halt.

The elf, of course, kept rising, catapulted high into the air by the forceful lift. His stomach lurched and his senses whirled, but he had the presence of mind to look upward. At the top of the tower, he saw a platform extend, and he immediately deduced that this was a landing that should have caught him on his way down, after he had been lifted past it. However, it had clearly emerged too early, and the elf smashed into the bottom of the platform's surface with numbing force.

Only his quick wits saved his life. Anticipating the impact, he had lifted his arms over his head to cushion the blow to his skull and kicked his legs out to either side. One foot flailed through a gap in the girder supporting the platform, and then he was hanging upside down, his knee crooked through the opening while the world spun dizzily more than a hundred feet below.

Immediately some sort of machine cranked into motion, pulling the platform back toward the rim of the tower. The girders folded, and Gilthanas perceived that, in a few seconds, his leg would be pinched or perhaps even severed at the knee between massive steel beams. With a desperate lurch, he pulled himself around, catching the edge of the metal rod with his hands and extricating his foot from the rapidly shrinking gap. As the girders folded together, he flung himself forward and sprawled onto the top of the tower, watching in amazement as the platform settled to become merely a part of the flat floor.

"That went well," he murmured to himself, rising to his feet, dusting himself off, and checking for broken bones. His head hurt, his leg was chafed, and his fingers were cramped from the strain of supporting his weight, but nothing seemed permanently damaged. The great light loomed above him, and he passed several deadly looking devices that might have been weapons of bombardment. He didn't touch any of them.

He found a trapdoor leading through the top of the tower and gingerly lifted it, relieved to find that no machines were involved. A short ladder led him to the metallic floor of a round room, which seemed to occupy the full circle of the tower's diameter. Bright light emerged from several panels along the walls, fully illuminating the place.

Immediately he caught the scent of death. Looking around, he saw several doors and a few dead gnomes sprawled on the floor before one of them. There were various tables and shelves with strange mechanisms upon them in here. One in particular caught his eye: It was a massive assemblage of gears and pulleys attached to a spear. It had apparently worked, for impaled on the spear was the body of another dead gnome—no doubt the intrepid inventor himself.

The elf felt his spirits sinking. How was he going to learn anything here if all the gnomes were dead? Still, he had only started to explore the tower.

He went to one of the doors unblocked by corpses, and opened it to reveal a long shaft with a chain circling over a pulley mounted in the roof. As soon as he had pulled the portal wide, the chain started clinking, and a quick downward look showed him that some sort of compartment was rising toward him. Common sense told him to slam the door and run, but some perverse curiosity held him in place. The approaching cage slowed, finally coming to a gentle stop perfectly in line with the floor of the room.

Within that cage, not surprisingly, were several dead gnomes in various stages of decomposition. Recognizing this as some sort of lift, Gilthanas had seen enough—he would try to find an old-fashioned stairway. When he closed the door, his intuition was rewarded as he heard the chain whip through the pulley with unfettered speed. A second later he heard the cage crash into the floor far, far below.

Further search revealed a dark stairwell behind another door, and the elf slowly began to descend. His eyes were attuned to minimal light, but even so, he found it hard to make out any details in here. Lower and lower he crept, pausing to open an occasional door and carefully explore chambers beyond. He found the remains of many gnomes, as well as odd bits of machinery, but nothing that indicated anyone was alive. Always he went back to the stairs, still making his way downward.

He estimated that he was nearing the bottom of the tower when he heard a faint cry, the sound echoing through the hollow metal.

"Hello?" he called. "Is someone there?"

"Help!" The cry was repeated, urgently. "But be careful."

"I'm coming!"

He moved as quickly as he could, calling out again, hearing the responses in a male voice that, though weak, was clearly invigorated by hope.

Finally, he stood before a silver door, with a series of buttons down the right side of the frame. The voice seemed to be coming from within.

"Who's in there? Are you hurt?" Gilthanas asked.

"My name is Lethagas . . . and I'm not hurt, at least not any more. I've been in here for years—it's been that long since I've heard a living voice! Please, get me out!"

"I'll try," Gilthanas promised, though he looked askance at the array of buttons. "Do you know which button I should push?"

"Don't push any of them!" The voice came back, so shrill with panic that Gilthanas jumped back from the silver door. "That is, can you try just pushing on the door?"

He did, and surprisingly enough the portal swung easily open to reveal a spacious room of metal walls illuminated by the same white brightness he had noticed above. With a sob of joy, the prisoner called Lethagas stumbled forward, hastily interposing his body between the silver door and its frame.

"It wasn't locked?" Gilthanas said in amazement, at the same time seeing the golden hair and slender, pointed ears of a fellow elf.

"No, but it fit so smoothly into the wall that there was no way to pry it open from the inside."

"You've been in there for years? How did you survive?"

Mutely, Lethagas pointed at a series of nozzles along the far wall. As the two elves watched, one of these spewed a narrow stream of water, which splashed on the floor and then flowed through a grate just below. The next nozzle then dropped a few plops of green goo, which also dribbled through the grate.

"Automatic food and water," Leth replied, tautly. "Fiendish, isn't it?"

"More likely accidental," Gilthanas said. "How did you come to be here?" he asked, guiding Lethagas out of the tower.

"I was on an adventure with two friends . . . we were looking for a machine that would help us defend Qualinost. We thought there would be good profit in it, so we flew here on griffins that have always been loyal to my family. One of my friends died atop the tower, pierced by some kind of spear-machine. The other one got tangled in some gears—I saw him mangled before my eyes."

"And you. . . ?"

"I was just looking for a place to rest. I stepped into this room, the door closed behind me, and then I spent several years here until you came along. I owe you my thanks—not to mention my sanit, and my life."

"Glad I could help," Gilthanas said. "But what is it about Qualinesti that it needs defenses?"

"The Dark Knights and the Speaker of the Sun are still at odds, to be sure, but new threats are taking shape. Sooner or later one of the Great Dragons is certain to lay claim to our forests."

Many more questions came to Gilthanas, but he didn't get the chance to ask them.

"But what's your story, friend?" Leth asked. "Not to mention, how did you survive this far?"

He was about to answer when both elves became aware of two voices, clearly bickering, and coming closer.

"Put a lock on the door, I said . . . I said it would work better with a lock, but no! You had to be right, again!" The speaker was a male, but his tone was high-pitched and almost frantic with irritation.

"It would have worked!" insisted the other, in an even higher, apparently female, voice. "But who said they could open it from the outside! That's not even fair!"

A moment later, two gnomes strolled into view, coming up the stairs that Gilthanas had been descending. They were short and plump, barely waist high to the elves. Each was dressed in a gown of blue and had long gray hair. The male also displayed a beard of the same color that descended all the way to the floor.

"I say," remarked the bearded one, ignoring Gilthanas to squint up at Lethagas. "Would you mind stepping back into the Perpetual Prison? Our experiment is far from over."

"I would mind, very much!" snapped the elf, his long-fingered hands curling into fists.

"There's no need to be huffy!" retorted the female gnome sharply. "After all, you've been our guest for five and a half years now. Haven't we fed you every day?"

Leth blanched. "Five and a half years?" he croaked, sagging against the wall.

But the gnomes weren't listening. "Technically, the machine fed him, not us," the male was reminding his partner. "After all, what's the point of a Perpetual Prison if one has to tend the prisoner? Who would still be a prisoner if you would have just let me put a lock on the door!"

"Never mind that! It still worked and will work again—or my name is not Drussilandahooperdaughterasticrellicre—"

"Enough!" snapped Gilthanas, remembering another thing about gnomes: When one started to say his—or her—name, the recitation had to be stopped immediately. Otherwise, it could take several days. "The point is, you have no right to hold this elf prisoner!"

"Why, the very idea!" sniffed Drussi. "Have you no respect for science? For knowledge, or invention, or discovery? You're both ignorant savages!"

"I'll show you savagery," growled Lethagas, stepping forward, clearly ready to wring a gnome's neck. He continued to mutter, "Imprisoning me in a cell for years . . . feeding me with foul slime . . . leaving your fellow gnomes to rot on the floor around us. . . ."

Gilthanas placed a calming hand on the younger elf's shoulder. "Perhaps we can talk a bit," he said to the gnomes. "Are there more of your people here?"

"There were lots," chirped the male. "There've been a few accidents, though."

"And there'll be more, you old fool!" snorted Drussi. "As if you could do anything right, Spudderapakoosongrandson-fatherianricktillation–"

"How about we just call you 'Spudder?'" Gilthanas interjected. "Now, do I take it you are the only two gnomes left here?"

"For now," admitted Spudder.

"I came here on a quest," the elf continued. "I'm seeking a dragon of silver, and I learned that she was coming to help gnomes in a tower. I think she came here. Did you see her?"

"Silvara?" asked Drussi. "Of course we did!"

"How long ago?" Gilthanas's heart quickened, and he scarcely breathed as he waited for her answer.

"Not long . . . a few years, at the most."

"But she was here! Where did she go? Did you talk to her?"

"Only to tell her we didn't need any help. She got kind of huffy, and then she left."

"To where?" cried Gilthanas, feeling his hopes slipping away.

"She wouldn't tell us—or rather, we didn't ask," said Drussi. "Now, if you'll forgive us, we've got work to do . . ."

"Not so fast!" Lethagas declared. "First, you'll see that we can get out of here!"

Gilthanas was sagging with defeat, barely listening to the debate as the other elf finally persuaded the two gnomes to see them out of the tower. Drussi and Spudder led them down the stairs until they reached a cavernous room that was apparently underneath the base of the tower.

"My griffins?" Leth asked. "Have you seen them?"

"They're still out there, flying around. Probably waiting for you," Drussi sniffed.

"How do we get out?" he asked.

Spudder pointed to a large machine: a wheeled mechanism with a studded drill mounted on the front. "This is our digger. It will take you through the wall."

"You have to dig your way out?" Gilthanas asked in disbelief.

"Us? No! You're the ones who want to leave!"

"Do you have any rope?" he pressed. "I think I'd rather take my chances climbing down from the tower or going out the door."

"If you insist," muttered Spudder, adding an epithet for 'coward' under his breath. The elves ignored the taunt and convinced the gnomes to climb with them to the top of the tower. Although both gnomes insisted the lift worked just fine, going up at least, the elves preferred to trust their feet.

Finally, they stood beneath the trapdoor, each elf wrapped in a heavy coil of rope. Remembering that this portal had been the one part of the tower unblemished by any sort of machine, Gilthanas reached upward to push the door open.

"Wait!" gasped Drussi, too late.

A blade slashed out of the ceiling, slicing down to gash Gilthanas's hand as he snapped it back.

He cursed and clapped a hand over the wound. "A second later and I'd have lost my hand."

"We have a trap to protect the door!" insisted Drussi.

"Most traps try to keep people from coming into a place," growled the elf. He looked at the cut, which did not seem very deep. "Still, there was no real harm done."

"Not yet," said Spudder, shaking his head. "But wait until the poison takes effect. . . ."

Opportunities:
Valley of Crystal, 26sc

From Linsha Majere's Personal Journal

9th day of Reapember, 26SC

I am Linsha Majere, Knight of Solamnia. I am the daughter of
Palin Majere, the man who brought sorcery back to the world
when mages thought it lost. I am the granddaughter of Caramon Majere, one of the heroes who prevented the Dark
Queen from claiming dominion over Krynn during the War
of the Lance. I am a Rose Knight, the guardian of two thousand years of tradition. These legacies intimidate me some
days, and in my darkest moments I fear I will never live up to
them, particularly in light of how I have been called to serve

the Orders of the Knighthood.

I serve under Lady Knight Karine Thasally in a clandestine circle in the city of Sanction. Like all other Knights there, I live a lie, but it is a lie I am uncomfortable with. I want to bring honor to my family name as my parents and grandparents did before me. It is not enough to have become the first woman not of Solamnia to be admitted to the Order of the Rose. I want to show I am worthy of my family name, and some days I want it so bad, it hurts. On those days, I am willing to do almost anything and take any chances that don't violate the Measure or endanger the security of my hidden circle. After all, if I spend all my time in service playing the role of a foul-mouthed alley-basher of loose morals named Lynn of Gateway, the chance to live up to the legacy of the Majeres may never present itself. Of course, such a preoccupation with personal glory is in conflict with the Measure, but it's very difficult for me not to succumb to the feeling that serving just isn't enough.

And that's why I've started this journal. It isn't so biographers can someday "get the story right," as my grandfather so frequently says when lamenting that none of his now-famous friends kept consistent journals (and that now hundreds of bards are telling their life stories in as many different ways). No, I am keeping this journal in the hopes that it will find its way into the library of Castle Uth Wistan. But, rather than serving as a record of my great deeds—although I hope to have some of those to record as well, if Lady Karine doesn't find I have violated the Measure so grossly that she casts me out of the Knighthood—the purpose of this journal will be to record my mistakes. It is my hope that as I write of them and reflect upon them, I also will learn from them, and that other young Knights may learn as well. Maybe they will avoid making the same errors I have.

Then again, maybe not. Everyone's been in situations after which they look back and realize they were too cocky or just willfully ignorant of the facts staring them in the face all along. Sometimes we do it because of love, sometimes we do it because of ambition, and sometimes we do it out of inexperience.

I should feel blessed I made it this far and experienced only one such situation. I should feel doubly blessed that I still live so that I can learn from the past and never make the mistake again, whether it was borne of ambition or inexperience. Certainly, love was furthest from any possible motivation I might have had to do what I did, consciously or subconsciously.

It occurs to me that the very purpose of this journal may go against the Measure. Is it too prideful of me to assume that someday a young initiate as I once was might read these words and thus be warned about the folly of overconfidence? No, I don't think so. After all, I got the idea from Gilthanas of Qualinesti, one of the celebrated Heroes of the Lance. Despite what many believe, he was still alive as of the very morning I started this journal. In fact, his words inspired me to start it, and it was his words that made me realize that even when things seem the darkest, there is always hope.

The events that led me to where I am now—sitting by a stream several days' ride north of Sanction while my horse Windcatcher waters herself and I wait for my wounds to heal—started a little over three weeks ago at the Broken Horn, a tavern in the city of Sanction. Unlike many other Sanction taverns, though, the mood at the Broken Horn was generally a friendly one, in some ways not unlike the inn my grandparents run in the Abanasinian tree town of Solace. That night, things were particularly friendly. I was playing dice with several other regulars, and we were exchanging good-natured barbs—mine being the most crude, because that's what everyone expects of Lynn—and I think the general cordial atmosphere probably contributed to my lapse in judgment.

I had just cleared twelve silver off the table when Lonar entered the pub. Ever since I first met him, I'd felt there was something different about Lonar. He was more handsome than the average scum dwelling in Sanction, and I'd seen him conduct himself with honor on more than one occasion. Once, he stepped into a fight involving a minotaur and a boy barely big enough to lift his own sword—and then took the child back to the village he'd come from. Sanction was not the place for kids in search of adventure. Many others would have saved the boy and then sold him into slavery.

I'd enjoyed several conversations with Lonar about topics ranging from which nation produces the best blades to whether there is any link between the arrival of the Great Dragons and the final departure of the gods, and even more esoteric philosophical topics . . . although in the latter type of conversations, I always guarded myself. Lynn isn't exactly known as a scholar, and if I was to start discussing things from the point of view of the ideals held either by the Knights of Solamnia or by Goldmoon's mystics, I feared I would raise suspicions. So, I instead just used a series of bastardized Khurrish arguments about Fate and a chosen champion that would drive Evil from the land. Whenever Lonar would push me on my ideas, I'd resort to insults rather than reason or admitting my theories were unsound. I felt awful having to pass myself off as so unknowledgeable in philosophy and so ignorant of even the basest standards of intellectual discourse, but I had appearances to think about.

Still, I wanted Lonar to like me at least, so I tried not to be too offensive. He seemed like a decent man, and he was well read and knowledgeable. I also thought he had a nice smile. The only fault I could see in him was that he was one of Hogan Bight's top men . . . and I found this a fault only because part of me wanted him to be better than that. His service to the shady, mysterious lord of Sanction also guaranteed that whatever friendship we might forge would be forever based on false pretext. How could I ever reveal that, although I genuinely liked Lonar, I befriended him because my mission in Sanction was to discern the goals and motivations of his master? I had on more than one occasion worried about whether deceiving someone I thought to be an upstanding person for my own ends was against the Measure. When I used the mystic abilities I was taught by Goldmoon to examine the nature of his soul and found that he was only slightly more tainted with Evil than my fellow Knights, those concerns grew even greater. Each time I considered them, though, I concluded that as long as I took steps to protect Lonar from physical harm (should the circle move against Bight on information I'd obtained from him), there was no dishonor in deceiving him.

At least no more dishonor than the lie I live in Sanction.

That night, Lonar had come to the Broken Horn for only one purpose. He paused just inside the doorway, scanning the packed common room. His eyes came to rest on me. He pushed his way through the crowd. "Can we talk, Lynn? Outside?"

"Sure," I replied. The other players scowled at me as I left the table. I gave them a sweet smile. "Sorry boys. I'll let you win your money back some other night."

As Lonar and I walked up the street, he said, "I hear you've been asking around for work that's a bit more respectable than the alley-bashing and gambling you've been doing."

I shrugged. "Maybe. So long as the pay's good."

"The pay's good. The pay comes from Lord Hogan."

My heart skipped a beat and my spirit soared. My effort to be friendly toward Lonar and to seem capable whenever he was around was paying off! I kept a calm facade, though. "Lord Hogan? What would Lord Hogan want with me?"

"Nothing, but I could use an extra sword on an expedition on his behalf. It'll take us through ogre territory. Would that be a problem?"

"I can outrun ogres," I said.

He grinned. "I'll pay you fifty steel coins right now. The balance depends on the outcome of our expedition. I'll provide food and fodder, but you need to provide your own horse. Still interested?"

"Definitely. Windcatcher needs some real exercise," I replied. "Plus, fifty steel is more money than I've gotten this month so far. What's the nature of the expedition?"

"I'll tell you once we're underway." He hesitated, looking me up and down, not lasciviously, but rather in an appraising fashion. "You're probably going to be the only woman in our group."

"You know what I do if someone gets grabby" I replied, patting the dagger on my belt. "But if they keep to themselves, I'll do the same."

Lonar flashed me a brilliant smile, one that made him appear even more handsome. He handed me a pouch of coins. "We leave at dawn. Wait at the mouth of the eastern pass."

After Lonar departed, I went to notify Lady Karine of my good fortune. She was the leader of the circle, so it was only right that I inform her of my imminent departure, but I was also hoping for some advice, for she is far more experienced than I am. She was not in, however, and her squire did not know where to reach her. After what I now know was too little consideration, I thought I could handle the situation without any advice from Lady Karine, and I felt confident that she wouldn't have forbade me to undertake this journey. I could think of no reason for Lonar to believe I was anything but what I appeared to be, and even if some sort of setup was in the making here, I had yet to encounter anyone in Sanction who was my equal with a sword. I felt that as long as I kept my guard up, I would be fine. So, I left a message with the squire and went back to my quarters to prepare and get a few hours sleep.

The following morning, Windcatcher and I were the first to arrive. Shortly, Lonar arrived with four other men, bringing our number to six. He also had two pack mules in tow. I only recognized one of the men, a lecher by the name of

Kresh. Fortunately, as far as I went, Kresh always had been all talk and no action. He had seen what happened to men who tried to force themselves on me.

"Introduce yourselves if you wish," Lonar said. "As far as I'm concerned, all you need to know about each other is that you're all capable fighters who can hold your own in battle."

The four strangers made no attempts at pleasantries. Kresh looked me up and down, as if he could see straight through my armor and cloak. "Lynn and I already know each other," he said. "But who knows? Maybe we'll have a chance to get closer on the road."

"Careful, Kresh," I replied. "If you get closer than a sword's length, you might impale yourself."

One of the strangers, a man of swarthy complexion that revealed a Khurrish heritage, found this more amusing than I would have thought possible. After he finished guffawing, he said in heavily accented Solamnic, "I like a woman with spirit."

After avoiding Dark Knight patrols, we rode all day through the eastern pass from Sanction, stopping only twice to allow our steeds to rest. As we camped that first night, Lonar finally revealed our destination. "Some of you may have heard of the Valley of Crystal. That's where we're headed. We're going to fill the packs we empty of food with crystals and deliver them to Lord Hogan. Any questions?"

"Yeah," I said, "How is our balance going to be calculated?"

"You'll all get an equal share of ten percent of the value of the crystals we bring back, as appraised by Lord Hogan."

I shrugged. "Sounds fine."

The men thought so, too.

The next few days were uneventful, except for lewd comments and verbal sparring between Kresh and me and belly laughs from the Khur. Lonar spent some time quizzing me about my travels beyond Sanction, placing particular emphasis on the area around the New Sea and Schallsea. At the time, I didn't suspect that it was anything but conversation on his part. After all, he originally hailed from Caergoth, and I believed that he was trying to see if we perhaps had visited the same places. Now I know that he was thinking far more sinister thoughts.

We were traveling through a narrow pass two days away from the Valley of Crystal when the ambush occurred. Three Khurrish men stepped out from behind rocks. "Your money or your life!" one called out.

"'Your money or your life?!'" exclaimed the man who found Kresh and me amusing. "What manner of bandits say such foolishness?"

"Serious ones," replied the speaker. He barked a word in Khurrish, and three arrows cut down our jolly companion.

Lonar let out a roar and spurred his horse forward, drawing his sword. The three men in front of us reacted with surprise, having clearly assumed their demonstration would subdue us rather than enrage us. Still, they shot another volley of arrows. While an arrow felled one more of the strangers who had traveled with us, another tore harmlessly through my cloak as I kneed my horse away.

I spurred Windcatcher forward but leaped from her back onto a ledge on the side of the canyon. She was trained to gallop until clear of the battle area, then stop to await my return.

I scaled the wall swiftly, mentally thanking both my grandparents and the mystics at the Citadel of Light who had let me scamper like a monkey first through the trees of Solace and later up and down the cliffs of Schallsea. I reached the top where the archers were, finding that they were still focused on killing my companions down below. I slowly drew my sword and dagger. Then I cleared my throat.

One archer turned and I flung my dagger at him. It lodged in his neck, and he went down with a strangled cry as I closed on his four companions. They dropped their bows and drew the wickedly curved blades the Khurrish warriors are known.

I ducked under a wild swing by the lead warrior and, as we engaged, stabbed him in the belly. I withdrew my weapon swiftly, slashing another foe's leg before retreating out of sword range. He fell to the ground, screaming.

The last two Khurrish bandits attacked together, stabbing at me from the right and the left. I danced away from the swordsmen, drawing my second dagger as I did. I used it to block a swing from the left foe and used my sword to hack his head from his shoulders. The headless body spasmed as it fell.

The final warrior and I circled for a couple of moments. The screams of the man I had hobbled faded to moans and whimpers. My one remaining foe suddenly rushed me. I parried two of his blows, then he overextended himself with a lunge, and I dove toward his open side. My sword punched through his chainmail. He coughed up blood before falling limply to the hard, dusty ground.

The whimpers behind me suddenly went silent. I whirled to see Lonar standing there, his sword deep in the back of the Khur I had wounded. A bow and arrow lay in the Khur's still-twitching hands. "You left this one alive, alley cat. And he almost got you. Lonar to the rescue."

I set my face in a mocking expression and raised my sword in a salute. "Very gallant of you, Sir Knight, but I could have handled it."

He gave me an odd smile that I now know was born of suspicion. He said, "Based on that display, I'd say you're being wasted in Sanction. You should be leading the life of a sell-sword."

"Maybe you can put in a good word with Lord Hogan," I replied, wiping my sword on a dead enemy. He nodded, clapping me on the shoulder.

We climbed down into the canyon. The four strangers were all dead. Kresh saw this as a good thing—more for him and me to split at the end, and more mounts to carry our crystals.

"Only if we don't run into more trouble," I said.

The rest of the trip was uneventful. We spent a day burying the bodies. I struggled to hold my tongue as Kresh looted bodies. I looted one myself to keep up appearances, but as soon as I return to Sanction, I'm going to arrange to have the items sent to the Citadel of Light as a donation.

Late in the second day after the ambush, we spotted rays of colors dancing in the blue sky. I pointed them out, commenting on their beautiful and bizarre nature.

"Seen 'em," Kresh said. "Wasn't impressed the first time. Ain't impressed now."

"Those are reflections from the valley," Lonar said in a more conversational tone. "And while those lights may be pretty, they'd burn your eyes out if you were to enter the valley right now. We're going to camp near the entrance and go in only after sundown."

We reached the valley, and I saw a small sample of what Lonar meant. A narrow canyon led from our campsite to the Valley of Crystal, and in it danced sheets of colored light so bright that I saw spots for minutes after I looked at it. Lonar and Kresh both found that amusing.

The sun set as we established camp. While Kresh built a fire pit, Lonar and I went to the valley to gather the first batch of crystals. We took only saddlebags because, Lonar explained, the crystals were sharper than razors and would slice through less sturdy containers. Even in the moonlight, the valley was awash with colors, making it one of the most beautiful sights I had ever viewed. The crystals stretched for miles, covered in undulating waves of colors.

"This is amazing," I said, my breath stolen by awe.

"People say the Chaos god touched this place," Lonar said. "Lord Hogan wants to gather crystals both for research and to pay the ogres so they don't side with the Dark Knights. Ogre shamans want these things very badly, but they refuse to come in here themselves. Why, we're not certain."

We gathered crystals for about two hours, until each of us had filled two sets of saddlebags. By the end, my leather gloves had been reduced to tatters, and I had several small cuts on my hands.

Back at camp, Kresh had built a large fire pit. I offered to water the horses. Kresh said there wasn't any water within fifty miles of the valley, so the horses would have to do with only a little until we were ready to leave.

"That's no good," I said. "The horses can't go too long without water."

"If we work hard, we may gather enough crystals to be on the way back tomorrow," Lonar said, retrieving a whetstone from his pack. "The horses will be fine for that long."

I agreed with him, but still spent some extra time on Windcatcher, talking to her and thoroughly brushing her down. When I rejoined Lonar and Kresh at the crackling blaze, I suggested that they should tend to their own horses. "It's bad enough we can't water them until we leave the valley. They'll serve you much better if you treat them right."

"Really?" Lonar said, cocking an eyebrow. "And where did an alley cat such as yourself learn that?"

"On the road. One of the men guarding the caravan I traveled with was a Khur. You know how they are with horses. They eat on them, sleep on them, and they know how to get the most out them. A horse that is brushed and rubbed down after a day's ride will outperform a horse that's been treated like a pair of wooden shoes and just left by the door."

Lonar stopped sharpening his sword. "You may be right, little alley cat," he said. He got to his feet and did that interesting little twirl with this sword he usually did just before sheathing it. Only this time he didn't. He just rested the blade against his right shoulder as he walked around the fire and behind me.

"I ain't rubbing down no horse," Kresh said. "That's not a job for a warrior. If you ask me, that's woman's work."

"Good thing I'm an alley cat," I said, taking a piece of dried meat for myself.

Lonar laughed behind me. "Sharp-tongued as ever, Lynn. I think we might have been friends you and I, under different circumstances."

Pain exploded in the back of my neck, as Lonar struck me with what must have been the pommel of his sword. I fell forward as the world seemed to go white. Before my vision cleared, my training as a Knight of Solamnia caused me to instinctively struggle to my knees and start drawing my sword. Then I was kicked hard in the stomach and collapsed again, taking several more blows over the next few minutes. Every instinct was swept away as a haze of pain consumed my mind. All I could do was gasp for air.

As the world swam in and out of focus, I felt strong hands grasping me and throwing me against one of the boulders. As I struggled to recover my breath, I heard my sword being drawn from its sheath. It clattered against the stones somewhere, and the hands grabbed me again and pulled me into a sitting position with my back against the boulder. Then something tore through the haze of pain: The feeling of cold steel against my neck, followed by warm breath on my right ear. "This is where the game ends, alley cat," Lonar whispered.

Everything snapped back into focus. The pain became sharper than before, and as Lonar moved back to lock his brown eyes with mine, I saw his face in far greater detail than I ever had before. I saw his chiseled features, the beard that was coming in strong after our time on the road, the small wrinkles that appeared at the corners of his eyes as he smiled at me, and the coldness in his eyes. I realized that the charm and warmth of his smile had been purely superficial and that it had hidden a dark soul, just as I hid my true nature behind the facade of Lynn. Fighting back both fear and pain, I said, "What's going on, Lonar? Why are you doing this?"

"You might fool the riffraff at the Broken Horn, but you're not good enough to fool Lonar Hiddel."

"I don't know what—"

He silenced me by pressing the blade harder against my throat and shushing me. "No more lies, little alley cat. No more lies. I grant you, you're good. Isn't she, Kresh?"

"That remains to be seen," Kresh said.

"Always thinking with his loins, that Kresh," Lonar said with a sigh. "Suffice it to say, dear Lynn, he thought you were just another sword-wielding wench in britches. It wasn't until we ran into those bandits that he saw what I saw the first time I watched you brawling in Sanction."

"So I can fight. I had to learn how. I—"

"Yes, yes. Spare me the sob story. You were taken away by slavers but escaped and a kindly man taught you how to use a sword . . . or maybe your father never got a son, so he taught you how to fight, but before you could inherit the bandit empire he'd built, Knights of Takhisis wiped it out. Are either of those close?"

"I have no idea what your problem is, Lonar."

He slapped me. I tasted blood in my mouth. His smile widened and his eyes grew colder. "No more meowing. My 'problem' is that you are too good with that sword to be just another wench in britches. You are too good at fighting, period. I've been watching you. And I've been doing a little bit of checking up on you. For a supposed alley-basher, you don't seem to rack up many victims. You gamble, you brawl, but you spend little time lurking in alleys and waiting for drunks. Why is that? It's a lot quicker than dice games.

"And when you brawl. Hmm . . . I think you try to hide it, but you just can't. When it comes to the martial arts, you are simply too good." He grabbed my chin in his hand and leaned closer, putting his face inches from mine. "You're no common rogue, Lynn, no matter how hard you try to pass yourself off as one. But who are you? Certainly, no Knight of Solamnia would be so rude, nor would she ever allow the kind of dishonor to befall her that you engage in nightly. No, there is only one type of person you can possibly be."

His eyes grew even colder as he said, "So, what Order are you a member of? The Lily or the Skull?"

I was so stunned that I barked out a laugh. He didn't understand the nervous reaction and slapped me again. He delivered a knee into my stomach, twice. Each time, I spasmed forward, but Lonar slammed his free hand against my chest, forcing me back against the stone.

"This is not funny, Lady Lynn," he snarled. I vomited forth the bit of dried meat I had eaten, then alternately dry-heaved and tried to catch my breath. "This is your death, and it can be a painful one. What. Order. Are. You. With?"

"Please," I moaned. I'm not ashamed to admit that once the spasms from the blows to my stomach subsided, I started shaking with fear. "I'm not a Knight of Takhisis. You've got it all wrong."

"Have I?" He pushed the tip of his stiletto harder against my neck. I felt the warm trickle of blood as he penetrated the skin.

"Yes," I whispered. "In the name Paladine, I swear I am not a Dark Knight."

"In the name of Paladine? Paladine?! Are you trying to make me think you're a Knight of Solamnia?!" He laughed. "What do you think, Kresh? Could our little alley cat really be a Knight without her shining armor?"

"Too skinny," Kresh said. "And too good-looking. Ain't never been a good-looking woman Knight. That's why they become Knights in the first place.

"I'm a Knight of Solamnia," I said, my words spilling forward swiftly before reason stopped them. Fear of death and the sting of the insults they were heaping upon me had become too much to bear. "I'm a Knight of the Rose! I spit on the memory of Lord Ariakan and I spit on the scaly hide of Takhisis! I came to Sanction on a special assignment from Grand Master Liam Ehrling. My mission is to investigate the activities of your master, Hogan Bight, but I'm not really your enemy as the Dark Knights are. The Orders just want to know what he's up to, but he wouldn't deal with them! I'm not a Dark Knight!"

Revealing my rank with the Orders may be a violation of my vows. I will make sure I emphasize this act when I submit my report to Lady Karine. I did not violate the Measure by leaving Sanction without her permission or knowledge, but revealing myself as a covert Knight to someone who is not a member of the Orders is in all likelihood a grave offense.

It doesn't matter that it didn't do me any good.

Lonar cocked his head, and his eyes still coldly glared. "A Rose Knight? You?! You must take me for an idiot, Lady Lynn! Why didn't you just go ahead and spin a lie about being a personal emissary from the Emperor of Ergoth who wants to take a peek at Lord Hogan's forces from the inside to see if we're worthy of military aid?"

"I'm telling the truth," I said.

He regarded me for a moment, looking thoughtful. The stiletto remained painfully at my throat, still digging past my skin. Suddenly, he said: "What is the sixty-eighth point of the Measure?"

I blinked "What?"

"The 68th point. What is the sixty-eighth point? If you're a Rose Knight, you know it."

"There aren't sixty-eight points in the Measure," I replied, "not anymore. Grand Masters Gunthar and Liam revised it years ago."

"Then we're an impasse. My father was once a Knight. He got thrown out before I was born, but he made me memorize the main points and standards outlined in the Measure because he thought it was a good code to live by. I think he was right to do so. Some of them make a lot of sense. And if you could have told me what the sixty-eighth point was, I might have let you live to present proof of your affiliation. But now, I just think it's a trap.

"At any rate, Rose Knights aren't the type of people who hang out in bars and fraternize with lowlifes. Rose Knights have more honor than that." A new tone had crept into his voice, a tone that struck an even deeper fear in me than before.

Kresh heard it too. Rising to his feet, he asked, "You're not just gonna kill her?"

"That was the general idea," Lonar replied.

"That'd be a waste. Let me have some fun first."

Lonar shrugged and struck me on the forehead with the hilt of his stiletto, causing the back of my head to slam against the rock. I finally lost consciousness. When the world swam back into focus, the stench of Kresh's unwashed body filled my nose. I had been pulled away from the rocks and was flat on my back. The stars swam brightly in the heaven. Someone was tugging at the strings of my breeches. I heard Lonar say, "Don't let her scream. I hate it when women scream."

Kresh laughed, and I realized that he had been struggling with my breeches. "You're awake. Great. I wouldn't want you to miss the last and greatest thrill of your life!" He slapped me hard across the face, and then started struggling with my breeches again.

"Just cut them off," Lonar sighed from somewhere nearby. "She's not going to need them again."

My head suddenly cleared as a different kind of terror flooded my being. Not only was I going to die here, but also they were going to take away every shred of dignity I possessed before they killed me. I had completely misjudged Lonar. I had been taken in by good looks, charm, and the fact that he was less tainted with Evil than many of Sanction's residents.

"I guess you're right," Kresh said. "I can't undo the cursed knot she used."

"Please, Kresh," I whispered. I would not allow these cretins to do this to me. "If I cooperate, will you let me live? I don't want to die. Please."

He grinned at me and ran his tongue over his crooked

teeth. "Sure. Maybe I'll decide you're too valuable to kill," he whispered back, leaning close.

I kissed his unshaven cheek and he returned a putrid kiss on my mouth as I ran my hands down his back and over his side, finding his waist and caressing it.

My right hand found the dagger on his weapons belt. With my left, I started to undo the buckle, hoping he truly always thought with his loins as Lonar said. Kresh didn't disappoint me.

"Yeah," he said. "Undo mine first . . . then take care of that damned knot on yours."

I think Kresh died more startled than in pain. I swiftly drew his dagger from his hilt and slashed his throat. He jerked backward, his hands instinctually going to his neck to stop his life from pumping from his body. Blood poured from between his fingers and spilled upon me as I scrambled out from under him.

Lonar was less surprised than Kresh. He rose to his feet on the far side of the campfire, drawing his sword. "You should have just lain back and taken it, alley cat," he said in an irritated tone. "If Kresh had enjoyed himself, you might have lived a few more days."

"Not a good bargain," I replied, quickly drawing Kresh's sword from its sheath. He was twitching like a fish out of water, not quite dead yet. I kicked his hand aside as he grabbed for me. Lonar and I started to circle around his body. "Why don't I just lay you out next to him and return to Sanction with the crystals and earn Hogan Bight's favor that way?"

"You haven't won yet, Lynn." He twirled his blade as he approached. "I'm going to be hard to kill, particularly since you're using Kresh's inferior weapons. You and I, being real warriors, go for quality in our weapons. Kresh went for what cost the least."

He was right. As we circled, each of us attempting to find just the right moment to strike, I noticed that the sword I was using was horribly unbalanced. I took a chance and scanned the area for my own discarded weapons, but Lonar took that as an opportunity to rush at me.

I parried the swings that came too close, backing away from him. He was very good. I barely held against his blows, as did the weapon I held.

Our battle carried us away from the camp and into the entrance of the Valley of Crystal. The white-blue glow of the crystals beneath the moonlight reflected on Lonar's well-honed blade, making it appear magical. The sword I wielded was so ill-used that it remained a dull gray.

The beating I had suffered at his hand caused me to tire quicker than I normally would, so he managed to knock the sword from my hand with a flurry of blows. However, he left his side open while doing so. I dove forward, intending to punch the dagger through his chainmail. Instead, the blade snapped on the links. Lonar backed away from me as we both looked at the broken weapon in my hand with amazement. He checked his gut for wounds, found none, then swiftly moved between the dropped sword and me.

"Be reasonable, Lynn. Let me know who you really are. That way, I'll know where to send your body."

I backed away from him, my booted feet stumbling across the first few scattered crystals. Several of them shifted loose. I took a couple more steps back. "Yeah. Let's be reasonable. Let's go back to Sanction together. You can bring me before Hogan Bight. Maybe he'll believe me. I promise I'll leave out the part about you standing by while Kresh attempted to rape me. I think Lord Hogan's a bit more honorable than someone who would countenance such a thing."

"First, Lord Hogan would take my word over a Knight of Takhisis—or even a Knight of Solamnia—any day. He knows that I share his concern for keeping Sanction free from oppression by any of your dying religious orders. Lord Hogan is preparing for the future while you keep looking toward the past, at the expense of the people of Krynn. The gods have left the world to the mortals, yet you Knights—on both sides of your little squabble—seem to have missed that entirely."

"The Knights of Solamnia have always been about more than service to the gods," I said.

He continued, ignoring me: "Second, Lord Hogan has made it clear that he doesn't want any members of the so-called 'fighting orders' in his city—last time, you nearly created a massacre when your Dark Knights, the Knights of Solamnia, and the Legion of Steel showed how bad guests can be. You have nothing to say that he would want to hear. You and yours are part of the past."

"I think if your master was to actually talk to a Knight of Solamnia, he'd discover that we've learned from our mistakes in Sanction. I think—"

"You never learn from your mistakes. None of you 'Knights' do. And I think I've given you enough time to come clean and to say your last words."

He advanced toward me. I quickly crouched and blindly scooped up a handful of crystals and dirt and flung them at his face. He screamed in pain as the crystals slashed him, and I moved for my sword. Even partially blinded, however, Lonar managed to swing at me with his sword, catching me across the breast. Although his strike didn't penetrate my armor, it did knock me to the ground. Sharp crystals cut into the back of my legs.

Lonar bellowed wordlessly, blinking as blood from the cuts on his forehead streamed into his left eye. He raised his sword to deliver the killing blow. I fought against my reflexes and kept my eyes open and fixed on the gleaming blade to watch the final strike as it fell. As I stared at Death in the face, I finally beat back my fear. I suddenly felt calmer than I had in years. I whispered, "Paladine, please watch over my soul."

But the killing blow never landed. Instead, Lonar suddenly jerked a half step forward, and the blade of a sword burst from his chest with a crunch of bone and a snapping of chainmail links. He coughed, and blood welled forth from his mouth and the wound on his chest. The sword retreated and he fell to the ground, twitching as life fled from his body.

"Filthy dragonarmy scum," someone said in elven. "You will burn my forest no more."

Standing above Lonar's form, holding my sword, was a figure out of legend. He appeared just as he had in Gramps's tales—an elf with long golden locks, large blue eyes, and a face so handsome that he puts even others of his fair race to shame. Grammy could still make Gramps jealous by describing how her heart had fluttered when she first laid eyes on Gilthanas of Qualinesti. Now that I had seen him myself, I understood why.

"Gilthanas?" I said, still not entirely believing my eyes. He turned his large blue eyes toward me. There was a strange look in them, a look of fury. Then, his expression filled with recognition.

"Tika!" he exclaimed. He helped me to my feet. "Tika, what are you doing here? I thought you were dead!"

That was even more surprising to me than his appearance. My parents and Gramps frequently commented on how much I resembled Grammy about the face, but surely Gilthanas had to know she was much older than I was at this point.

"You're wounded," he continued, noticing the cuts on my legs. "Did that animal do that? And your hair. Did he cut off your beautiful locks?"

From what she told me when I decided to cut mine, Grammy has worn her hair long her entire life, taking advantage of the spectacular curls that nature had gifted her with. Although I had inherited the red color she had when she was young, I had not inherited the curls. I also chose to wear my hair short because it was more comfortable when wearing a great helm.

His question confirmed that he thought I was Grammy, though. I came to question whether this was really Gilthanas. Could he just be a madman? He had a scar down one side of his face, and Grammy had never mentioned a scar. But a long time had passed since she had heard from him, so long, in fact, that she and everyone else thought him dead. As I was trying to decide what to do next, I heard someone calling his name.

"Here, lean on me, Tika," Gilthanas said. "I'm sure Tasslehoff has some bandages in his pack. We'll fix your legs in no time."

"Thank you, Gilthanas." I said. The name felt strange when I said it, somehow false. But, despite his obvious madness, how could he be anyone but Gilthanas?

He helped me back toward the camp. Another elf came into view. "Tasslehoff," Gilthanas cried. "Tika has been attacked by draconians! She needs our help!"

The other elf rushed to our side, and the two of them helped me toward the camp. Once there, the second elf offered me a blanket so I could stay decent while he tended my wounds.

"I will return to the pass," Gilthanas said. "I don't want any of that scum sneaking up on us."

"Don't go too far," the other elf said.

"Your friend seems quite insane," I said as I slowly and painfully slid out of my pants.

"Yes," the elf said, looking in the direction of his fair-haired comrade. "He has been affected by a rare gnome poison. His madness is only going to get worse, and he'll die within a few months if I don't get him a cure. Oh, I'm Lethagas, by the way. His name is Gilthanas."

"I thought I recognized him," I said. "My name is—"

I caught myself. I already had violated my oath of secrecy once that evening, under duress. I wasn't going to do it again out of thoughtlessness.

"—Lynn. I'm from Sanction. We came out here to gather crystals to sell to the lord of the city. My 'partners' decided to take something from me that I was unwilling to part with. So, they died."

"Rest assured, I will attempt no such thing," Lethagas said. "Now, try to relax. This might sting a bit."

"Why are you two here?" I asked through gritted teeth as he poured alcohol on the back of my thighs. "You won't find help in the middle of nowhere."

"I saw your fire. Our griffins need rest, and I hoped that someone here might help us."

"Your mounts can rest, but as for help . . . well, it's just like an elf to look in the wilderness for something that can be found in a city." I ended the comment with a snigger, trying to imitate the sound I had heard from a trapper who frequented the Solace inn while I was a child. He was perhaps the most virulent bigot I have ever met, and Lethagas seemed to pick up on my changed attitude.

"That could be so," he replied. "There is occasionally wisdom to be found in nature. However, we did find you, a citizen of Sanction. Can you tell me of any wise men who live there? Anyone who can help my friend?"

"Fix my legs, then we'll talk. And watch that blanket," I replied, forcing a cold tone into my voice. I sensed Lethagas stiffen, and his ministrations became a bit less gentle.

Even at the time, I felt I should have shown more gratitude. A legend had come to save me at a time when I didn't really deserve saving, and had thus given me a second chance. Yet, as I thought about it, I realized the second chance meant that I had to stay true to my vows and stay in the role of Lynn for as long as I was with these elves. And that meant being as crude as I possibly could, reaching deep back into my memory for the very worst of the racial slurs I had heard from the patrons at the Inn of the Last Home.

Eventually, my behavior became too much for him to bear. "I need to get more bandages from my saddlebags," he said, heading toward the trio of griffins that stood silhouetted against the rising moon. Moments after he left, Gilthanas appeared at my side, having arrived without making even the slightest sound. He looked appraisingly at my injured legs. "Tasslehoff did a good job," he said.

"Gilthanas," I said, his name still sounding false on my tongue. I needed to prove to myself that he wasn't just some lunatic who had fooled both himself and Lethagas . . . I couldn't help but think the gods, even if they had left Krynn behind, would have rewarded Gilthanas with happiness with Silvara instead of insanity for his service during the War of the Lance. I took his hand and concentrated for a moment, focusing upon the pulsing of my heart and drawing forth the mystical powers that Goldmoon had opened up to me during the summers I spent on Schallsea.

When I opened my eyes again, Gilthanas was looking at me expectantly, but now I also could see the bright green and blue life energy that so brightly represented his soul. I had seen a similar pattern when I had looked at Laurana, the one time I met her. I no longer had any doubt. He was Gilthanas.

But where the glow of his sister's soul had been calm and soothing waves, Gilthanas's form was surrounded by a seething and chaotic mass of colors. He was indeed deeply, perhaps irrevocably, insane.

"Tika?" he said, noticing the sorrow that must have registered on my face at that realization. "Are you all right?"

I held his hand tighter. "This is so unfair," I said. "How could this be, Gilthanas? Why aren't you with Silvara? The stories people tell of you and her. . . . Are they all just fantasies? Lies? Is everything ugly and grim? Can't there ever be a happy ending?"

He frowned at me. "Silvara? How do you know about Silvara and me?"

The nimbus of light about him seemed to flicker out as I allowed my spell to end. With it went my last bit of hope. "You and she did a great service for Krynn and the children of Paladine. Why didn't Paladine reward you better?"

"Tika, Tika, Tika," he said in a slightly patronizing tone. "The gods give mortals only the rewards they deserve. Truth is, I didn't deserve Silvara. I didn't know what I had in her.

She tried telling me—showing me—but I was too wrapped up in myself to realize it. Even after I lost her, it took me decades to realize what I had done. Now I'm trying to get her back, to earn my reward. Do you know I drove her away because she lied to me?"

"You did?"

"Yes, she isn't a Kagonesti at all. She is a . . ." He hesitated, looking at me with a slight frown. "Wait. You're not Tika. You look a little like her, but you can't possibly be her. She should be much older."

"Yes!" I shifted excitedly, but the pain shot through my cut legs. Instead, I just clutched his hand. "I'm Tika's grand-daughter. I'm Linsha Majere."

"Linsha? You're how old? Eighteen? Nineteen? You look almost like your grandmother did when I first met her. Does she live still?"

"She's as feisty as ever. Caramon, too. But listen, your friend Lethagas told me that you've been poisoned. What happened?"

"Fate," Gilthanas said. "Fate and pride. I drove Silvara away because I was too proud to admit how deeply I had fallen in love and how much her lie had wounded me. And now I'm going to waste away as a lunatic without ever get-ting back together with her." He looked at me sadly. "At least I got to meet you, Linsha Majere. Are you following in your grandparents' footsteps?"

"A little less successfully, perhaps, but I'm trying," I replied, indicating my wounded legs.

"Draconians will always be a match for a young warrior, no matter how tough she thinks she is." He paused again. "That was a draconian I saved you from back there, was it not?"

I didn't have the heart to tell him the truth. "Yes. A Kapak. But, you seem fine now. Tell Lethagas about Silvara while you can. I'm sure he'll help you."

"I have moments like this one, but they are getting rarer

and shorter with each passing day. And Lethagas already knows about my quest to reunite with Silvara. He has promised to stay with me until I have found her. First, though, he wants to stop the poison from killing me. He is a very sensible and loyal companion, Leth is." He started to stroke my hair with his free hand, an absent-minded look crossing his face. "You should let your hair grow out. Your grandmother had such lovely hair."

"You know what I think? I think that we've both been granted a second chance here tonight. It was Fate that brought us all here . . . Fate, or maybe even the hand of Paladine himself." I shifted again, trying to look into his blue eyes but only wincing with pain. "I think that Lethagas guiding his griffins to our fire was no mistake. You were fated to save me from my attackers, so that I could have the chance to become the Knight I've always wanted to be. And because you saved me, I can give you information on not just one place where you might find a cure, but two! Paladine be praised, Gilthanas, but I think that I can help you and your silver dragon reunite!"

"Silver dragon?"

"Yes, you and Silvara?"

"What are you talking about, silver dragon?" Gilthanas leapt to his feet. "Silvara is not a dragon! How dare you accuse my beloved of being a rampaging monster?!"

I think Gilthanas might have struck me if Leth hadn't returned at that very moment and dragged him away. Gilthanas didn't regain his sanity while I was with him and Leth. Instead, he fought imaginary creatures and set Lonar's body on fire because "zombies will reanimate if you don't!"

It was very difficult for me to maintain the facade of Lynn during that time. I wanted to join their quest, but I knew I couldn't. I had duties to return to. But I still helped Lethagas as best I could. Couched in racist and abusive terms—such as threatening to kill Gilthanas because his insanity was disgusting me even more than elves typically did—I provided them with information on how to reach Godshome (a mystic site my "mother" once visited) and the River of Healing (a place a Knight told me about a few years back). I think Lethagas is a brave and honorable elf, and that Gilthanas did right in placing his trust in him. I just wish I could have left him with a better impression of me. What will he think of my parents if Gilthanas remembers our conversation and tells him who I am?

I continue to attempt to help them on their journey. As I slowly make my way back to Sanction, I offer nightly prayers to Paladine and his two sons, and hope that one of them is listening and is willing to help Gilthanas on his difficult path.

I'd throw a prayer or two in for myself, too, but I'm saving them in case my wounds get infected before I reach Sanction. Hopefully, my infractions against the Measure will be deemed light enough to let me take advantage of the second chance Fate or the gods have given me.

It's my most sincere hope right now. And if you're reading this, it probably came true.

Ashes: Godshome, 27sc

**From the Journal of Lethagas of Qualinesti,
started in the Year 26sc**

Entry 14, In Godshome

I have few actual memories of the evacuation of Qualinesti during the War of the Lance. I was still very young at the time, barely more than a baby, and my father believes that the horrors I experienced caused me to block them from my mind. But sometimes, when sitting at a campfire, memories of screaming, the sound of beating dragon wings, and the sight of a forest aflame all around me flash into my mind, leaving me breathless for a moment.

As I sit here in this desolate valley, a fire raging and a skinned rabbit sizzling on a spit, some of those memory fragments are drifting through my mind, along with the both the joys and hardships I experienced while growing up in Qual-imori, our city of exile.

One memory in particular echoes through my mind.

My mother was very religious. When I asked her why the gods had let the dragons destroy our home in Qualinesti, she responded that E'li had chosen to let the dragonarmy destroy those elves who were weak in spirit and corrupted by the taint of humans. She believed that the gods had given the forest of Southern Ergoth to us, and that there the best of the elven nations would grow strong. She viewed the return of divine powers to the priesthood as evidence that the elves of Southern Ergoth were indeed chosen over all other peoples. The next step, she said, would be the rebirth of the legendary city of Godshome—only it would be reborn under the banner of a united elven kingdom.

Godshome. My mother loved telling and retelling the leg-ends of Godshome, explaining in a dozen different ways how it was both a city where god-fearing people of all races gath-ered to worship and a secluded vale where those whom the gods found worthy were given their direct blessing. The city was supposedly built to appear like a giant wheel when viewed from the air, while the vale contained living statues of all the gods and a pool which could grant mortals the power to reach the stars themselves.

I had only ever heard those stories from my mother, and I hadn't heard about or thought of Godshome for years when suddenly Lynn of Gateway mentioned it.

She was a very strange woman, even for a human. She had every appearance of being a rogue and a scoundrel, yet before we parted ways she had used the map from Gilthanas's pack and indicated not one but two places to which I might take him to find healing. A look of pain crossed her face when Gilthanas started howling apologies at Silvara, Tanis Half-Elven, and several others whom I couldn't place. The way she winced made me think that she might have known some of the people he was seeing in his fevered visions, but when I pressed for details, she became rude.

After lambasting me with slurs that I'd heard only the most black-hearted of villains level against my people, she insisted that she was doing this only to repay us for saving her life when the scum she was traveling with attacked her. She insisted that if she didn't help me find a way to cure Gilthanas, she would have to kill him because he disgusted her so much. Yet, when she didn't think I was watching her, I saw her look at my friend with such pity that I knew she felt heartbreak, not disgust, at his state. But, if she chose to lie about her motivations, that was her decision.

The two places she added to Gilthanas's map were "Godshome" and "River of Healing." She explained that she'd heard of the places from a retired explorer, and from other disparaging remarks it seemed this explorer was a mother whom she had little love for and who had shown little love for her. Still, Lynn was sure that the information on these sites was valid, and that I would find a cure for Gilthanas at either one.

The River of Healing was located in the faraway Vingaard Mountains while Godshome was merely a few days flight from our camp. "If there's anywhere the gods can still be found, it's there," the rogue had assured me. "And the gods can heal pretty much anything that might ail a mortal . . . except lack of faith, I suppose."

That was an interesting statement even if I am still not entirely sure what she meant. After all, how could someone stand in the presence of the gods and not believe? And if the tales my mother told were true, then Godshome would have to be one of the most glorious sites in Ansalon.

But, now that I have arrived at Godshome, I see that it, like so many other places in the world, has lost all magic. I am glad my mother died before the Summer of Chaos, for its end surely would have broken her heart. However, the sight of this vale would have hurt her even more.

I found the ruined city of Godshome first, soaring on griffin back over the arid landscape of Neraka. A large encampment of Dark Knights had established themselves here, although for what reason I do not know; perhaps they were searching for signs of the departed gods as I've heard mystics from the Citadel of Light have done?

Whatever the reason for them being there, it simply added motivation for me to avoid those ruins—to view it simply as the landmark that it is. According to both my mother and Lynn of Gateway, the gods could be reached directly in the vale, not in the city.

So, I flew the griffins into the nearby mountain range, soaring through narrow canyons and circling over valleys that appeared inaccessible to anything but flying creatures. Unlike most other mountain ranges in Ansalon, these did not appear to contain the ruins of ancient ogre cities; perhaps even at the height of their civilization, those Evil beings had shunned this range, sensing that the powers of the divine held sway here. Nor did the range seem to hold any valleys that matched the description my mother had given—bowl-shaped with a circular pool in the middle.

As I searched, I also thought of how my mother had said that the valley could be found only if the gods wished it. I wasn't sure exactly what to expect; if the gods still resided there, they would allow me to find it . . . or not. I decided that I would search for four days. After that, I would head west in search of the River of Healing.

It took me two days to find the valley. During this time, Gilthanas slipped in and out of a half-awake state, often experiencing violent rages during which he thrashed in the saddle. I eventually had to land and tie his arms to make sure he didn't unfasten his harness and fall to his death. I came to fear that he might kill himself before the poison did. But, the stories about Godshome kept coming to my mind, filling me with hope. Gilthanas was the son of Speaker Solostaran, and he had stood against the hordes of the dragonarmies so the

Qualinesti could return to our homeland. Surely, if someone who had sounded as disreputable as Lynn's mother could find Godshome, the gods would extend a welcoming hand to Gilthanas.

My hopes started to wane when I circled above Godshome Vale. It was readily recognizable as the place I sought: a bowl-shaped valley with a lake that formed a perfect circle at its center. The water of the lake seemed strangely black, but something white shone within it. Steeply rising, rocky slopes lined the valley, offering no exits from the valley that I could see from the air. Blackened, toppled stumps covered the area as if the entire valley had been subjected to a fire far greater than even that which had swept through Qualinesti when it fell to the dragonarmy.

I landed the griffins. Gilthanas was unconscious, so I left him bound in the saddle. Nowhere could I see the statues of the gods that supposedly stood within the valley. As I walked toward the curious black lake, the breeze sent a fine gray ash scurrying back and forth across the barren valley floor.

When I reached the edge of the sunken area at the valley's center, instead of seeing dark and polluted water, I found myself gazing down upon a solid glasslike substance. It was cracked, almost as if a giant had struck it dead-center with a fist. Despite the cracks and the ashes that the wind pushed across it, the surface appeared highly polished, allowing me to see reflected in it the pale, scarred moon that had appeared in the heavens on the night following the defeat of the god Chaos. I looked to the clear blue sky. The sun was sinking behind the mountains, and the moon was nowhere in evidence.

I could see no statues of the gods. I could see no lake in which mortals could swim to the stars. Nothing but ash remained, making this place a mockery of what it had once been.

I cursed the gods, then and there. I cursed them for abandoning Ansalon, for giving people like my mother false hope with their brief return after the War of the Lance. I cursed them for leading Lynn of Gateway to give me false hope and waste precious days in my quest to save the man who had saved my life. I dared them to strike us both dead. I dared them to show themselves, to prove to me that they were nothing but cowards who so feared for their own safety that they first shattered the world in response to the Kingpriest of Istar's demands of submission. I taunted them for fleeing in the face of the god of Chaos and then cursed them again for leaving those who worshiped them not even the magic of wizards. I raged at the heavens until my throat grew soar, and until I noticed that Gilthanas had freed himself and was raging right along with me.

I realized the futility of crying out to the gods. They are either deaf or dead. The ashes in this valley, the ashes that will be impossible to keep from clinging to the rabbit that I am roasting, are probably their remains. Whatever the truth is, the gods are gone. I sought their aid, and they could provide none. I will once again restrain Gilthanas in the saddle of one of the griffins and then we will travel toward Solamnia in search of the River of Healing. Or, better yet, a sage who can provide a cure even sooner.

Of Elves and Adventures:
River of Healing, 27sc

Have I got a scheme for you, my friend! A genuine money-maker that can't fail. All we have to do is. . . . Will you look at that? Just like an elf to draw a knife on a guy for doing what comes naturally. If she didn't want menfolk coming onto her, she bloody well should stay out of taverns—or at least she should dress in a more modest fashion!

Have I ever told you how much I hate elves? Gods, it makes my blood boil just to think about those pointy-eared know-it-alls breathing the same air I do.

Why? Because they've made my life a living hell, that's why. Just about every time I had a racket that looked like it would work for the long haul, some damned elf has come along and screwed it up!

When I was a kid, I'd set up this nice little scheme where me and a partner were peddling visions from Takhisis. We'd set up shop in one of the temples in the Old District where we'd found a hollow that would let someone in a secret chamber pose as the "voice of the god." You've no idea how much drunken or stupid Dark Knights would pay to hear their goddess speak once I "channeled her" through my body. Worked like a charm . . . until some damn elf showed up. Didn't know there were elves among the Dark Knights, did you? Well, there are. And this one had been around for the construction of the rooms we were using. I barely escaped with my life, and my partner—who had taught me every-thing I knew—was lynched by the Dark Knights right there on the spot.

But, hey, that's what happens sometimes. That's the risks we take. I could have let it go if it'd been just that one time.

But a few years later, another elf ruined things for me. I'd gotten settled in Caergoth where I was doing a brisk business in selling Kagonesti herbal cures for everything from gout to impotence. Of course, the cures were nothing but applesauce, oatmeal, and thyme, but people were snatching 'em up anyway. Until this holier-than-thou elven wench with feath-ers and flowers in her hair and a leaf tattooed on her cheek showed up, I was doing fantastic business. I guess she came looking for me, thinking I was one of her pointy-eared cousins or something, and when she discovered I wasn't, she first gave me a lecture about truth and honesty . . . and then she started kicking my ass.

Hey, there's nothing funny about this. Between her and the townsfolk I barely escaped!

But that's not it. If that had been the end of it, I might have just chalked it up to bad luck. But two months ago, it hap-pened again! Another damn elf showed up and ruined by life!

After Caergoth, I eventually ended up in Korval. I'd headed north instead of south, because the idea that somehow elves in general were just bad news for me was already starting to form in my head—I had no desire to get any closer to Qualinesti than I'd already been.

At any rate, Korval looked like the perfect place for a completely fresh start. It was a quaint little village with about a dozen citizens that still held regular services to Mishakal and Paladine in a little temple at the heart of the town, and everyone was the perfect stereotype of 'salt of the earth.' Basically, it seemed like the perfect place to take it easy while dusting off some of the old stand-bys like faith healing, spirit channeling, and fortune telling.

For the first four months, Korval was paradise. All I had do was 'read' a few goat entrails and correctly guess that one of the town leaders was sleeping around with another town leader's wife and I had free room and board.

But when I heard the legend of the River of Healing, I knew I had it made. According to a favorite local story there, there was this river in the mountains where Mishakal liked to skinny-dip. A by-product of this was that the waters permanently took on part of her divine essence so that those who bathed in them would be cured of whatever ailed them. Problem is, terrible creatures haunted the only pass leading to the valley where this river could be found.

Being the resident all-around supernatural good guy, I announced that I would brave whatever foes lurked in the pass to bring back bottles filled with the blessed waters. After all, if anyone deserved the benefit of Mishakal's gift, the people of Korval did, and, clearly, it was fate that had sent me to them. The good people said there was no need for me to risk myself—they were doing fine without the healing waters they said—but, being the brave and selfless soul that I am, I put myself on the line for them.

Well, no, not really. All I did was load up on dried fruit and cheese and rough it for a few days in the hills to the east of town. I'd brought a dozen or so bottles along, too, and after three weeks, I filled them from one of the many streams running through the hills and then headed back into town.

Of course I knew that the yokels would eventually catch onto the fact that the bottles had nothing but drinking water in them. Part two of the plan was to tell them that I had discovered a way to put the evil spirits of the pass to rest so that they could safely travel to the River of Healing them-selves . . . all it would take was that platinum holy symbol from their temple and that jewel-encrusted medallion that's been the mayor's symbol of office since the time of the Cata-clysm. You see, the angry spirit in the pass is really a priest of Takhisis and only those two mighty symbols of Good can smite him. Yeah, you can see right through it, but I'm sure the good people of Korval would have swallowed that line with-out hesitation.

I never got a chance to even try it, though. While I was en-joying my hero's welcome and distributing water to the old, infirm, and sufferers of colds, a trio of griffins flew overhead.

Yeah, you're absolutely right. Griffins mean elves. Believe me, my blood ran cold at the sight. I silently prayed that they would just keep going, but no. They circled back and spiraled in for a landing.

There were two of them . . . two males. One of them was a total loon. He thought the mayor's daughter was his sister and mistook me for Sturm Brightblade one moment and a draconian the next. Oh, and he thought Korval was some place in Qualinesti and that we'd assembled a feast in his honor.

At any rate, the sane elf, named Left or some-such, said he'd come looking for a guide to the River of Healing, or at least a map—his raving pal had been poisoned and needed to be dunked in it before it was too late.

First, everyone pointed fingers at me. Then the villagers offered up some of the bottles of water I'd given them. The crazy elf—who at that point in time believed himself to be

Kith-Kanan, founder of Qualinesti—guzzled three bottles of 'sweet wine, the like of which he had never tasted before' and suddenly seemed lucid.

I was the only one who was startled, of course. After the madness went out of his eyes, Left started relating a whole string of very confusing events to the other elf—you know how elves can babble, and babble he did. He spoke of all sorts of nonsense like diamond-filled valleys.

Meanwhile, I did what I could to subtly encourage them to get their scrawny butts out of my town. "There's a storm coming," I said, "and if you don't leave now you may be trapped."

He looked like he was buying it . . . but then the Salt of the Earth decided to pipe up again. "Are you sure, Seer?" asked Old Man Wellbyt. "My knee ain't swollen." And then the Widow Nell started talking about her arthritis. And then they all started talking about wanting to feed the elves before they got on their way. And of course the lighter-blond one had to use his ne-found coherence to say, "It's not that we doubt your abilities, soothsayer, but my experience says that the ailments of the elderly are more accurate in predicting the weather than even most Wizards of High Sorcery could. I think we'll do just fine if we leave tomorrow rather than today. Plus, I'm famished, and I would be honored to share a meal with the good folk of Korval." And, of course, Left agreed with him. Those pointy-ears stick together like glue. Wait . . . was his name Left? Perhaps it was Leapt? Oh well, it doesn't matter.

Naw. It's never a problem to recover from the 'But my knee doesn't hurt!' when doing the weather prediction bit. C'mon, give me more credit than that! Plus, I had the advantage of demurring to "the wisdom of many lifetimes, collected in this one man, in he who is Gilthanas."

Yeah, I laid it on thick, but it worked. If there's one thing I know about elves, it's that they have egos as big as their ears . . . and if you want to distract one, you appeal to his ego.

But, as it turned out, I shouldn't even have bothered. I was still buttering up Blondie and making suggestions for the feast when his face suddenly took on a hateful expression and he said, 'I'm going to tell you something I should have said years ago: I find the whole idea of you and her making love revolting. She's still a child, and she's only going after you because it makes her feel like an adult. If you lay a hand on her, I may just have to kill you.'

I don't know what he meant, and I never found out, because the next thing he did was shriek, "Silvara! Silvara!" and run up to the Widow Nell, run his hands through her white hair and start raving about how he has desperately searched for her and how only she could fill the emptiness in his heart. Flowery elf courting nonsense like that.

Yeah. He'd flipped out again. It was all we could do to keep him from running off with the old bat. Left turned on me angrily, and I thought the gig was up, but then Wellbyt piped up, "The legends of the River of the Healing says that people must bathe in it for its effects to take hold. Wylan will take you there, I'm sure."

Yeah. 'Wylan' is what I told them my name was. Seemed sort of magical-like. I mean, who'd ever buy into a magical-mystical-worker named Pehter?

At any rate, Left started pushing me to show him to the River of Healing, and once again, the Salt of the Earth decided to be helpful. "No, you should go with them. That poor elf needs your help more than we do. Perhaps they can assist in slaying the spirits in the pass?" And of course, Left said "We will help you in any way we can . . . if Gilthanas recovers, I've no doubt he will join your mystic in slaying the Evil spirits that are keeping you from the River of Healing." And then he proceeded to bore us all with the mighty deeds of Gilthanas—who was hiding under a nearby handcart, screaming about blue dragons with the heads of snails.

No, I'd never heard of Gilthanas until that day. Huh. So, he really was some kind of elfking. I never would have guessed.

Not that it would have made a difference one way or other. He still got strapped to the back of one of the griffins like an unruly baby and we took off for the mountains, flying low along the pass that the yokels thought led to the River of Healing.

Here's a bit of advice for you—if someone ever offers you a ride on the back of a griffin, turn it down! Not only is it damn cold—why those pointy ears don't fall off while they're flying around on those beasts I'll never know—but you'd never think that creatures with beaks could have such foul breath! That, and they're damn unruly. As I was mounting mine, it almost bit me in half.

At any rate, we flew low through the pass, the lifeless gray slabs of rock that make up the Vingaard Mountains rising on either side of us. Then Left—who was riding the lead griffin and seemed to be commanding all three of them somehow—lost control of his griffin. It seemed to buck in midair, and if he hadn't been strapped into the saddle, I'm sure he would have been thrown to his death. A split second later, mine did the same and it started screeching and climbing steeply into the air as it thrashed its head back and forth. I found myself flung against the back of the saddle so hard I feared my spine would break

The griffins were screeching and Left was shrieking orders to get them back under his control and the one I was riding suddenly went from a climb to a steep dive, throwing me forward in the saddle . . . and when it did, I saw what was causing the problem. Then I started screaming, too!

Clinging to the griffin's side was the ghostly shape of a strange man-hawk—a creature with a human torso and head but winged arms and the legs of a bird. Its transparent talons were tearing the mount's belly and it was stripping flesh off the griffin's side with its ghostly teeth. When I screamed, it glared at me with red eyes and released my mount. The griffin snapped at the phantom with its beak but the terrible creature was unaffected. Instead, it fixed its eyes on me and shrieked, 'Huuumaaaan! The destroyer of our aerie!' My mount once again jerked upward in a sudden climb, Left pulled his griffin away from his attacker, and the monstrous creatures pursued, swarming all around me.

I'm not ashamed to admit that I wet myself as they came at me. I'm a con artist, not an adventurer, so real ghosts are not my forte—and ghosts of some bizarre flying humanoid are not even on my list of things I knew existed! So I started screaming like a lady-in-waiting confronted with a spider: "Get me down! Get me on the ground!"

The phantoms were swarming all around me. One of them came straight at me, its glowing red eyes locking onto mine and a sensation rushed through me that said that gaze was searing my very soul!

"Huuumaaaaaaan!" the creature shrieked, bearing fangs and preparing to rip into me with its talons.

I squeezed my eyes shut and started whispering a prayer to Reorx. Why? Well, honestly, it was the only god I could think of at the time! I'm not very religious, to be honest, but I found that dwarves part with their cash easily if you convince them that you've got a piece of something that Reorx touched or regurgitated during a drunken binge. So, Reorx came to mind because he's the god I've dealt with the most.

Ha! No, I don't pray regularly. The gods have never really done anything for me, but they haven't done anything *to* me either. Why attract potentially negative attention? Plus, if you can believe those people from Schallsea, the gods aren't listening anymore. Interesting. I never had you pegged for the religious sort. Branchala, huh? Well, you'll have to introduce us some time.

At any rate, I closed my eyes as the ghost rushed toward me and muttered a prayer. My mount changed directions again, once more plunging downward. The air rushed against my face with unprecedented force and the icy chill of the phantom claw as it cleaved the air where my head had been moments before. I huddled in the saddle, keeping my eyes shut as the rush of wind in my ears drowned out the cries of the ghosts. I thought my skin grew so numb that I could no longer feel the wind upon it, and then the rush of wind faded in my ears as well.

And then Left's voice: "It's all right, Wylan. You can open your eyes now."

I looked around and discovered that the griffin had landed; my face hadn't gone numb . . . the wind had just stopped. I looked up and saw that the ghostly bird-men were still circling above. They seemed unable to come closer.

"You saved our lives," Left said. "And I owe you an apology. Back in Korval, I was thinking you were a fraud, but you've proven me wrong. I have some small knowledge of spirits, but even I never would have guessed that their existence is restricted to the air. What kind of spirits are they? They remind me of banshees, but their behavior is different."

I was so stunned that it took me a moment to find my voice. I had impressed an elf! My mind started reeling with the possibilities. Where to begin, I was thinking. How much could I make out of this? So many ideas flooded my mind that I didn't know where to take things from there. So I started talking to stall for time, basically spinning lies about the ghosts. I started explaining how the spirits were slain by Dark Knights during the Summer of Chaos and how the bird-men have been haunting the pass every since.

"Were they aarakocra or kyrie?" Left asked.

"Aarakocra," I told him, not really knowing what either of those things are but, as you know, as long as you sound authoritative, people believe you. No, it's not strange how I remembered those two names when I didn't catch Left's. Just let me tell my story! I told Left, "They were once peaceful, loving creatures . . . look what kind of monsters they have become in the afterlife, all because of those hateful Knights. It's terrible. Terrible." Which, of course, triggered the response I wanted. The Dark Knights have been squatting in Qualinesti for at least thirty years now, and I was pretty sure Left wasn't too happy about it.

Anyhow, I got him ranting about the Dark Knights for a bit, successfully making him forget all about whether those ghosts were aarakocra or kyrie. And when Gilthanas started howling about the slugs that were filling the sky, Left decided that we should get underway. The River of Healing awaited and soon Gilthanas's mind would be restored.

That was one of the moments I wished I was a violent man. I could have bashed Left's head in, right then and there and turned back. Oh yeah, "the danger was over." Don't you know anything, Selin? I thought being a worshiper of a bard god and all you would be familiar with all those stories about adventuring parties that either go up a mountain or climb down a hole. The first monsters met are never as bad as the ones that follow!

But, since I'm not a violent man, and since I couldn't come up with a reason why we shouldn't take the loony up to the top and dunk him in the river, we started out again, walking the griffins along the ground instead of flying on them.

That was a creepy couple of days, let me tell you. It felt like we were being watched the whole time. I didn't dare look up because I knew what was watching us—those ghostly birdmen. They were just waiting for us to take to the sky again so they could rip our hearts out. The only upside was that Gilthanas slipped into a semiconscious state and stopped his howling.

Eventually, the pass opened up into a beautiful lush valley, the kind of place where in those stories I mentioned before you'll find two-headed ogres enslaving unicorns and fair maidens.

No, of course there was nothing like that in the valley. It was just a valley, although a beautiful one. It was shaped a bit like a bowl and from the mouth of the pass we could see a lake of sparkling clear water with a small building by its side. A broken and overgrown road led to the building, and a river that glittered like the lake snaked its way out of view among some evergreens.

I proudly pronounced that this was the River and the Lake of Healing. Left asked what the building was, and as I fumbled for an answer he volunteered one. "Is it a temple of Mishakal?"

I quickly agreed with him and made a lucky guess that it was abandoned based on its run-down appearance. I told him that priests had settled here after the War of the Lance but that the Dark Knights had killed them too. That triggered another round of cursing and condemning of Dark Knights—Left was about the easiest guy to manipulate that I've ever come across and I was starting to wonder if I should just go ahead and join him and his friend. Living off them would no doubt be easy.

But then I remembered that these were elves I was dealing with. I just had to get rid of them before they ruined my sure thing in Korval. So, I reminded Left of his unfortunate buddy.

We walked the griffins down the shore of the lake. Here, we untied Gilthanas and started to undress him. At that point, he started muttering about Silvara again. Hey, that isn't funny. But I can tell you that I let Left deal with undressing him after that.

At any rate, he got stripped and we walked him to the shore of the lake. Left asked me what we were to do. I shrugged and pushed Gilthanas in. Left cursed my name and jumped into the water after his friend. They both emerged moments later—I don't know if you can picture it, but elves look even skinnier when they're wet. And, based on Left's foul mouth, I think they get about as angry as a cat in water as well.

Gilthanas seemed okay, though. For a split second. Then he slugged Left, shouting, "Foul Konnal! You will not imprison me again! Not when I am this close to finding my beloved Silvara!"

Cursing under my breath, I waded into the lake. Gilthanas was trying to drown the stunned Left, still screaming about Konnal and Silvara. I grabbed hold of his shoulder and he whirled on me. "Tanis!," he bellowed when he spotted me. "Tanis, you will pay for robbing my sister of her virtue!" And then he grabbed me by the throat and thrust me under the water.

I have no idea who this Tanis guy is, but I hope for his sake that he never crosses paths with Gilthanas. I don't think he'd walk away from it. Gilthanas would have killed me if not for Left. Left hit Gilthanas upside the head and dragged both of us from the water.

"Why didn't it work?" he demanded as I tried to cough the water out of my lungs. I suggested that maybe there's a reason it's called the "River of Healing." Then I realized that my sarcasm might have tipped my con and I quickly added: "Drinking the water of the lake works for minor ailments, but perhaps only the river itself can cure serious conditions."

Left looked doubtful and distrustful, but he still grabbed the unconscious Gilthanas and tossed him over the back of one of the griffins. He then rode the beast across the lake. I watched as he submerged Gilthanas in the river. The crazy elf regained consciousness and struggled. But Left forced him under the water and held him there for several moments. Then he dragged Gilthanas out and threw him on the shore. He stood over the other elf for a moment, and then Gilthanas stumbled to his feet. They stood across from each other for what seemed like a very long time, and then they embraced. It had worked. The river had cured Gilthanas of his madness. It was a happy ending for everyone but me.

Well, I guess it might have been if Gilthanas hadn't turned out to be such a damn "credit where credit is due" honor freak. First he apologized profusely for attacking me, explaining that he remembered mistaking me for Tanis, his sister Laurana's dead husband.

Really? That Tanis. Huh. I didn't know the Golden General was married to him. That does make sense, though. And I can understand why Gilthanas would be ticked. After all, he wouldn't want human blood contaminating his precious elven bloodline, now would he?

At any rate, we spent the night in the ruins of the Temple of Mishakal—which was quite the place, by the way. There were images of a naked woman bathing in the lake. Gilthanas thought that it was an image of the goddess Mishakal. There were a couple of statues of her in there as well. Selin, let me tell you, if I were to start attending service on a regular basis or worship someone, I think it would have to be Mishakal. If the service gets boring, I'd just sit back and enjoy the scenery.

Okay. You're right. That's being disrespectful to the goddess. I apologize. And I got myself sidetracked again.

As I was saying, after spending the night in the ruins, we headed back to Korval. I tried convincing Gilthanas and Left that I would make it back just fine on my own. And once I got there, I told them, I'd round up a bunch of the young men and we'd come up here and repair the temple and use it as a shelter for the sick who need the healing waters. I think I could have convinced Left to go, but damned Gilthanas wanted to travel to Korval and thank the people there for their kindness. What kindness? All they did was point their fingers at me and say, "He'll take ya to where you want to go!"

But, being that he was the elf prince, he got his way. We walked the griffins back through the pass—Gilthanas was a lot harder to bamboozle as far as the ghosts go than Left was but I nonetheless did it—and we eventually reached Korval. The Salt of the Earth gave Gilthanas his promised feast. They hailed me as the greatest thing to happen to their village since they discovered fire. They offered Left their daughters. No, not really. I'm kidding about that last part. But they did go way over the top. Still, if Left and Gilthanas had just eaten their pork and been on their way, it might still have been a happy parting for me as well as them. But have you ever known an elf to keep his mouth shut where there's a chance to get in front of an audience and impress them? No, of course not. And neither have I. And let me tell you, Gilthanas behaved true to type.

During the feast, the Lord-Grandwhathaveyou of Kalaman and Qualinesti got up and gave a toast and a speech in my honor. He told them all about how I intended to reopen the Temple of Mishakal in the valley and started urging all of them to relocate up there where the ground was fertile and the magical waters would keep them healthy. "You can create an island of tranquility, joy, and health . . . and you have Wylan of Solanthus to thank for it!"

The next morning the elves left. By the end of the week, some of the younger people of Korval were preparing for a mission to explore the pass to the River of Healing. After Gilthanas's little pep talk and grand explanation of how I'd discovered the ghosts were no threat, they were no longer afraid. That Gilthanas. He could probably sell sand to the people of Relgoth. By the end of the month, the young folk had come back and they decided that moving to the valley was the thing to do. Everyone was so excited that I was going to lead them to this wonderful new place, away from illness, bandits, and probably even bad weather.

The following night, I gathered my belongings and left town. Why? What do you mean *why*? I'm not interested in having villagers fawn over me unless there's a take to be had. Helping them move their damn town would have been hard work, and being a real spiritual leader is a lot harder than just pretending to be one. Leadership is for blabbermouths like Gilthanas and Dark Knights. Me, I just want people's money. Once Gilthanas told the people of Korval that the River of Healing was safe, there was no money to be had. There weren't even any free meals, because they were going to expect something of me. Something real. Damn elves. Like I said, they've ruined every good thing I've ever—

No, don't you give me that. Gilthanas and Left didn't leave me the opportunity to do good. They fouled an opportunity to . . . hey, isn't that just the strangest damn thing.

Look at that. That elf woman, the one who threatened Stumpy with a knife . . . isn't that her? Heading up the stairs with Sir Lorannus? Elves are crazy. She'll turn down a perfectly good guy like Stumpy, but is perfectly willing to share her bed with an officious ninny like Lorannus.

Damn Dark Knights. They're almost as bad as elves if you ask me. They deserve each other.

Oh, speaking of Dark Knights and deserving each other, I didn't come here to bore you with stories about elves. I came to recruit you for my latest scam. How does this grab you: Fragments of Sturm Brightblade's sword. I have just the buyer lined up.

SOTHI NUINQUA TSALARIOTH

Hargoth, 278c

The port city of Hargoth was a bustling center of humanity about a day's flight from Korval. The constant movement of people made Gilthanas immediately long for the days of wandering, of solitary living and study, or of the sole companionship of Lethagas.

The younger elf, in contrast, seemed to welcome the surrounding activity and threw himself into the life of the city with boisterous enthusiasm. It was Leth who found them a clean, inexpensive room in an inn where elves were welcomed, but not questioned. Now that they were traversing western Ansalon, Gilthanas had decided to keep his identity a secret. Nearly all the elves they encountered came from Qualinesti, and he wished to avoid attention, as well as the attendant rumors that would arise if the wandering prince was known to be this close to home.

Instead, he waited around the inn or wandered the city as an anonymous vagabond. He let his companion ask the questions, knowing that Leth was getting around Hargoth and seeking any information he could regarding silver dragons. The youngster was subtle and coy, never mentioning Silvara by name as he looked around the busy waterfront and worked his way through the many crowded inns.

Late one evening, after ten days in the city, Leth awakened Gilthanas when he returned to their room. The prince noticed the traces of dawn already brightening the horizon.

"I have found an elf who wants to talk to you . . . who says he has information about silver dragons."

"Where is he?" Gilthanas blinked the sleep from his eyes and shrugged into his tunic. Pulling on his boots and buckling his sword around his waist, he stood, wide awake and ready to go.

"He will meet us near the Sailor's Guildhouse at the wharf," Leth replied. "He's waiting for us now."

In a few minutes, the pair made their way through the nearly empty streets of the town. The sky had brightened to a very pale blue when Gilthanas saw the peaked roof of a large hall. Nearby was the shadowy entrance to a small, stone building.

"There he is." Leth indicated the figure waiting within the dark alcove.

"That's an elf?" The fellow's furtive manner and heavy cloak reminded Gilthanas more of a human scoundrel—some pirate or back-street cutthroat. He couldn't see the elf's face, except for a vague outline of his chin.

"I hear you's looking for silver dragons," said the mysterious fellow in a hoarse voice that did nothing to dispel Gilthanas's earlier impression.

"Who are you?" demanded the prince, immediately suspicious.

"Forgive me, O Great Lord," sneered the fellow in a voice dripping with mockery. He pushed back the deep hood and Gilthanas saw the pointed ears that proved him an elf. His long hair was tied in a narrow tail down his back, which was a style unusual for a fellow elf. "I am but a humble servant unworthy even of being named in your presence."

Gilthanas decided not to press the issue. "What do you know of a dragon of silver?"

"A dragon . . . not just any one of them? Are you going hunting for specific prey, then?"

"The reason I seek this dragon is not your concern."

The elven scoundrel shrugged. "Maybe . . . maybe not. But I'll show you where we can find the answers."

The mysterious informant abruptly pushed open the door behind him. Within, Gilthanas saw a dark corridor, dimly lit by candles. But his eyes immediately fastened on the horrible image rendered on the interior wall.

Five heads gleamed black at him, leering with unblinking stares. Each was the terminus of a serpentine neck, and even before he saw the five colors Gilthanas knew that this was a place of Takhisis, the Queen of Darkness.

"Traitor!" he cried, seizing the elf's cloak and roughly pushing him against the stone wall.

"No!" insisted the other with surprising conviction. "You should know that other elves are aiding the Dark Knights also—they offer the only hope of victory in this dying world. Enter and see for yourself. Listen! You will learn—you will see!"

"I will not!" Gilthanas insisted, furious. He drew his sword and pressed the tip against the elf's throat. "What do you know of silver dragons?"

"Nothing!" wailed the miserable wretch. "Just that the Knights will help you find them and kill them! There is a reward for each Good dragon slain. They will pay you well!"

Gilthanas's arm trembled and he felt a powerful urge to drive the sword home and end the quivering life of this foul creature. Only some vague memory of kindness held his hand, and at last he cast the elf to the ground, drawing back his foot to kick . . .

And abruptly turning away.

He slammed his blade back into the sheath as Leth fell in behind him.

"I'm sorry," said the young elf miserably. "I thought he was . . . that is. . . ."

"Never mind," said Gilthanas, still sickened at the thought of his people turning to the Dark Queen.

"Should I keep looking and asking?" inquired Leth.

"There's nothing for us here," Gilthanas said with a sharp shake of his head. Silvara's trail was cold, lost in the tangle of a vast continent. He fought against a wave of hopelessness, and knew there was only one thing he could do.

"It's time to go home," he said, and his thoughts brightened at the memory of Qualinesti.

The Endless Moment Shatters

I saw Gilthanas's expression shift as he turned toward me again, completing the spin during which one or both of us had delivered the final and fatal cut to the other. The tense look that had appeared on his face as he prepared to fight me softened, and his chest rose and fell rapidly. For some reason, my awareness focused on the scar that now marred his features, which otherwise remained unchanged from the first day I met him. It had been a decade since we had first met and during that time the first wrinkles had appeared on my forehead and the beard of manhood had sprouted on my chin. However, if it hadn't been for that scar upon Gilthanas's face, I might well have thought that we had met each other for the first time only moments ago.

Not only did elves live a very long time, but they did not change in appearance as they aged.

How long would a life such as mine seem to one such as he? Would it be like a moment to him? Does it seem as though we age and die, as he stays young?

He moved away from me, but he didn't move. Magic must be at work again.

In any case, it would be over in a moment.

"Why?" I heard Gilthanas say. He moved closer to me. For some reason, the sun no longer glinted off his sword.

Why? Would there be time to explain? There are those who say that the moment of a man's death lasts forever, but that would only be from the perspective of the dying man. I could not possibly tell Gilthanas what he wanted to know. For in another heartbeat, he would be gone. A killing blow had been struck, and I felt certain that it was mine.

The Footprint of Chaos, 28SC

I lost Gilthanas's trail completely after the Peak of Clouds. The dwarves living at its base knew only that warriors had attacked him while he had been living with a hermit who dwelt on the peak—they knew this because they had tended to his wounds. When I asked about a silver dragon, they reported that such a creature had indeed resided here for a few years, but it was before Gilthanas showed up. The dwarves couldn't agree on when the dragon had departed, although they knew that it had either gone north, east, or northeast. They had told the elf the same thing, and he had headed in one of those directions as well.

The encounter with the dwarves made me realize how badly I wanted to be back on Elian Isle. On Elian, people are honest and straightforward. They tell you what they think when you ask, they offer to help whether you need it or not, and they are all honorable and honest in all things. In the rest of the world, everyone always looked for an angle that they could exploit to get something from you whether they had earned it or not. I left the dwarves, wondering if their confusion about what direction Silvara and Gilthanas had gone in was genuine or because I didn't pay them enough.

The only honest and straightforward people I'd encountered were the kender, who somewhat resembled the elves but exhibited a completely different personality. Kender always told me exactly what they thought and, in contrast with the rest of the peoples of Ansalon, were very refreshing. Predictably, all others despised them for their unassuming ways.

The encounter with the dwarves made me realize how much I had grown to miss my people. As near as I could tell, I was the last surviving Master of Rank who had been charged with the slaying of Gilthanas. It was up to me and me alone to finish the mission. Even if I could fabricate some excuse to return home, I would be returning in failure. That was not an option, for it would stain the honor of my children.

For the next several weeks, as I moved along the borders of a land claimed by a black dragon known to men as Pitch, my children were foremost in my thoughts. So many years had passed since I left. They would not remember or recognize me, for although the years had flown by for me as though they were nothing, they added up to a lifetime for them . . . a lifetime which I had not been part of.

They would not recognize me, nor I them, if we were to meet. My woman had undoubtedly told them of my glorious mission, but I was just a name to them. They would honor this name, but they might never get a chance to know their father. Even if they did, I could never reclaim the joy that I know my father derived from watching me grow from a baby into an adult.

Masters of Rank knew that they might need to pay the price of not seeing their sons grow up. During my lonely trek, this suddenly seemed like an unbearable price. For the first time since I left Elian, I again wondered if I had made the right choice, although the questions no longer revolved around Gilthanas and his honorable heart. No, now the doubts revolved around me. Had the honor of this mission cost me more years than the honor was worth?

I pursued these thoughts no further, for suddenly the magical ring I had received from Stalker seemed to vibrate on my finger. I looked at the stone and found that its color had shifted! She had found him! Now, I would see if the ring truly worked, as she believed that it would

I grabbed the stone between two fingers and twisted it. I felt arcane energies surging through me, and the world around me dissolved into a swirling sea of colors. I closed my eyes as I started to feel dizzy. Within a moment, the air around me went from humid and heavy with the sour smell of rotting vegetation—for I was in the middle of a swamp—to cool and heavy with the acrid smell of something burning. I opened my eyes and found that the world around me had coalesced again but that it was completely different.

It was a barren and brown place, a stark contrast to the lush greenery of the swamp I had come from. Overhead, flourishing trees had obscured the dome of the sky just moments before. Now they didn't. But where was Gilthanas? And where was the fire that caused the smell of burning vegetation?

I scanned my surroundings. I stood on a grassy ridge. To my left was a verdant and pleasant landscape that retreated toward the horizon in a series of hills. To my right was a canyon incongruously shaped like a giant foot. Its sides and the ground around it appeared as though they had been subjected to great heat—as though the canyon had been scoured into the surface of the world itself by huge gouts of fire. The smoke I could smell appeared to be the fire burning at the bottom of the rift, for the canyon was filled with smoke.

But I could see Gilthanas nowhere. Neither was Stalker apparent, nor any other living beings. I was completely alone. Why had I appeared here, at this deserted place?

I inspected the canyon to make sure Gilthanas wasn't within its smoky depths—although I felt that I was not alone as I searched it; no one responded when I called out for the elf and Stalker. It occurred to me that perhaps Gilthanas had already been here and that he had slain Stalker as she attempted to capture him. I could easily picture that—she was playing games, but Gilthanas was too swift and intelligent for her, turning the stalker into the one being stalked.

But since I saw no evidence that any violence had befallen either Stalker or Gilthanas, and since I had no knowledge of where in the world I was, I established camp near the strange canyon and waited until someone arrived who could give me some information. I noticed that the gemstone had returned to its original color, indicating that there was yet magic in the ring, and that I could possibly try calling Stalker to my location should I discover Gilthanas nearby after all.

Around noon the next day, three gigantic birds appeared in the sky. As they drew closer, I realized that they were some curious hybrid between lions and eagles, and that upon two of the beasts' backs were riders. I had never seen such creatures before, but they matched roughly the descriptions of griffins that were detailed in the Forbidden City's storehouses of knowledge.

As they landed on the very ridge I had first appeared on, I saw that both riders were elves—and I saw that one of them was Gilthanas, his golden hair flowing in the breeze as his magnificent mount came in for a landing.

Gilthanas dismounted and waved to me. I waved back. He called out to me in a language I had not yet mastered, but I responded to him in the elven tongue. I had learned it before leaving Elian and had recently practiced it with Stalker. Gilthanas seemed pleasantly surprised by my greeting, which was a formal one that denoted friendship and a willingness to assist the person to whom it was being offered. It was my hope to draw him near while keeping him off-guard so that I could strike quickly.

As he moved closer, Gilthanas said, "You speak Qualinesti very well. "Are you from Abanasinia?"

"No, but I have had an opportunity to learn your tongue," I said, weighing my words as I spoke. I would slay Gilthanas so I could return to my family, but I would not do him the dishonor of lying to him. "For a time, one of your race was a traveling companion of mine. How can I help you?"

"We have heard that a silver dragon has been seen around here. Have you seen one? Or a Kagonesti elf, perhaps?" Gilthanas's eyes suddenly widened as he examined my face. "Solov? Solov, is that you?"

I smiled. "Yes, it is indeed. It has been a long time."

"A very long time! I never thought I would see you here! What brings so far from your homeland?"

"You." Before he had a chance to react, I drew my sword and slashed. He leapt back with reflexes that would have put a cat to shame. I swung again, and again he avoided my blow, sidestepping my attack and drawing his own sword to further deflect mine.

His friend cried out and drew his own weapon, but Gilthanas waved him back. The elf prince backed away and demanded, "Why are you attacking me? We parted friends those many years ago. What has changed?"

My response was to attack again. The sounds of our clashing swords rang across the countryside. As our battle carried us toward the strange, smoke-filled canyon, it soon became apparent that we were evenly matched—while he may have centuries at his disposal, not even elves could exceed the combat skills of a Master of Rank.

Faced with this knowledge, we stepped back. It was clear that our duel would be won by a single sword stroke and that victory would come through luck as much as skill.

We both dropped our guard and lunged at each other in all-out attacks. Sunlight danced along the edge of his well-honed sword. Only one of us would survive the next moment. Still, our skills asserted themselves and our blades clanged against one another once, twice, and then we both did a spinning slash, moving away from each other and then taking stock of the situation.

"Why?" I heard Gilthanas say. His sword no longer glinted in the sunlight.

In the hands of a master, a well-honed sword can kill a man so quickly that he doesn't realize he's dead until several moments later . . . until he feels the blood starting to trickle. It is in that final moment that some people say the dying one relives his life, repeatedly, so that the moment becomes an eternity. Is that what Gilthanas was about to experience?

He moved closer to me, yet he didn't appear to be walking. He moved farther away, but still his legs did not seem to move. His sword no longer shone in the sunlight. Something dark was smeared along its edge.

"Why did you attack me?" His face appeared sorrowful, the face that was unchanged from the day I had first met him, aside from the scar on the right side of his face. I should give him an answer, but he wouldn't have time to hear it. He was about to die, and I was about to go home to my family.

I remembered the day I first met Gilthanas. I never would have thought it would come to this. He was the most wondrous thing to have entered my life up to that point. . . .

❧ ❧ ❧ ❧ ❧

"Why?" Gilthanas asked again, gazing down upon the crumpled form of Solov. There would be no answer. The battle could have ended in only one way, and as it did, the time for answers passed and could never again be reclaimed.

SOTHI NUINQUA TSALARIOTH

Anaya's Tree, 28sc

This place called Qualinesti was not the land that Gilthanas remembered. So many changes had affected it that he found it hard to convince himself that he and Lethagas had in fact returned to their homeland.

The natural forest of the elven kingdom had always been wild and trackless, but now a tangled maze of shrubbery grew so densely that, in most places, it all but blocked travel. Tendrils of moss draped from the loftiest branches, while vines and brambles fought for control around the mighty trunks. There were good, well-maintained roads, but—as the two elves had been warned—Dark Knights patrolled them.

They had heard the stories in Hargoth of the massive green dragon, Beryl, who now claimed this forest as her own.

She tolerated the elven leaders, but only because she had intimidated them to the point of abject slavery. They knew of the Dark Knights, who presumed to walk as lords here since their conquest of the elves during the Summer of Chaos.

And even the Knights ruled only at the sufferance of the mighty green.

The current ruler of his people, inheritor of the Sun Medallion once held by Porthios, was the Speaker of the Sun Gilthas Solostaran. He was the son of Gilthanas's sister Laurana and of Tanis Half-Elven. Gilthanas had learned that his sister now lived with her son in the capital of Qualinost, but he had already decided against going there. Instead, he would seek his brother Porthios, reputed to live as an outlaw in the depths of the tangled forest.

For that quest, Gilthanas could think of only one place to begin.

To reach the grove, the two elves rode their griffins, the original trio of the flyers that had brought the pair from Winston's Tower on Karthay. To avoid discovery by Beryl or the Dark Knights, the creatures flew beneath the towering treetops in the wide canopy of space above the middle branches. Progress was slow, with the griffins and their elven riders gliding from one tree to the next and then perching on stout limbs, searching before them with eyes, ears, and nostrils.

Finally, near nightfall, they came to a place where the gnarled and monstrous trees of the forest came to an abrupt end. Before them was a strip of meadow, beyond which rose a line of stout oak trees. The massive oaks formed a broad ring and grew so closely together that the center of the grove was lost in shadow and tree bark.

"This is the place . . . I know it is," Gilthanas told Leth.

"There'll be guards," whispered the younger elf, peering out through the branches.

Gilthanas nodded. He could smell the presence of men; their sweat and smoky clothes mingled with the taste of fire and steel, marking them as Dark Knights. "Let's leave the griffins here."

The three creatures settled watchfully on stout limbs above the forest floor while the two elves scrambled down to the ground. As night fell, they saw that the Knights, some on foot and others on horseback, made regular rounds about the oak grove. Still, the two stealthy visitors did not find it an insurmountable challenge. After the passage of a quartet of riders, they crept across the strip of open ground and soon entered the cool freshness among the ancient trees.

The scent and ambiance of the familiar forest surrounded Gilthanas like a welcoming cocoon. He remembered when this had been the air of all these woods, and his heart broke at the thought of what his nation had become.

But he would take no time to grieve.

Instead, he led Leth through the thick trees and in between clumps of mushrooms on soft, mossy paths. Though the foliage created a thick canopy overhead, the pair of elves could see clearly. Soon they reached the heart of the grove and stopped before a massive tree.

The trunk of the oak was as big around as a cottage, and the limbs rose, gnarled but mighty, high into the night. A great crack was scored down the face of the tree, and Gilthanas felt a momentary reverence. He knew the history of this place—the legacy not just of his nation but of his family. This was the tree of Anaya, lover of Qualinesti's founder Kith-Kanan. And from that crack had stepped Silveran Green-hands, Kith-Kanan's heir and successor as the Speaker.

Now, Gilthanas could only hope that legacy would lead him to his brother.

"I heard you had come to Qualinesti . . . I thought you might come here."

He whirled in disbelief as the words—as the unmistakable voice of Porthios—reached him from behind a nearby oak.

"My brother! I could only hope to find you here!" Gilthanas started to step forward but was halted by the stern voice.

"Wait! I will let you look at me, but know that I have changed, brother . . . I am scarred by grief and war," Porthios stated in a low voice.

Gilthanas fingered the slash that crossed his eye. "So am I," he replied.

Even so, he was not prepared for the view of his elder brother. Porthios concealed his head with a deep hood, but scars wrinkled his face. His lips merged smoothly into his skin, making his smile seem ghastly, like the leer of some fleshless skull. But his eyes danced with joy, and his arms clasped Gilthanas in an embrace of deepest affection. For long moments the two brothers hugged, without speaking, barely even breathing.

"I dreamed you'd come," Porthios said softly. "I waited for you and knew your travels would bring you here."

"I have wandered far, brother." Gilthanas drew a breath, and talked of his quest, of the madness and deception and despair that had marked his path. "But when I came home, I knew that I had to come here, to Anaya's Tree."

"It is good that you did not go to the city," Porthios said. "The Dark Knights would have taken you in a minute—even if our nephew didn't turn you over to them himself."

"Gilthas . . . he has betrayed his people . . . his family? I've heard the stories, but I can't believe he would do this or that our sister would let him!"

Porthios shrugged with real regret. "Truth to tell, I don't think he has much choice. He is pulled in every direction, and to embrace one master would be to die before another. Suffice to say that Qualinesti is not the land you left."

The elder brother put his hands on Gilthanas's shoulders and looked at him frankly. "Nor is it a place you should plan to stay, my brother."

The younger prince was shocked. "But you live here . . . an outlaw, I know, but you resist the Dark Knights and the green dragon! Are you saying I'm not good enough to fight at your side?"

Porthios shook his head. "Of course you are . . . but I know this about you: You are seeking a treasure, and you will not find it here. Nor should you abandon your quest."

"Silvara? I have lost her, my brother. She is gone to me!"

"Perhaps . . . perhaps not. You know that you are close to her ancient home and to the place where Paladine touched Krynn."

"Whitestone—on Sancrist!" Gilthanas said. He remembered hearing her speak with reverence of Whitestone Glade. Before she left Kalaman many years ago, she had mentioned that she wanted to visit that hallowed site to meditate for several days. "Of course she would seek communion with her god there. I'll visit the Glade first, and if she isn't there still, I can visit Foghaven Vale in Southern Ergoth."

"I cannot say for certain . . . but only suggest that, if I had come as far as you, I would find a way to finish the rest of the journey."

"You are right, brother. I must go."

Leth and Gilthanas left the grove before the dawn, crawling through the meadow to the trees of the forest proper. Above them they could barely make out the white shapes of the three griffins, still perched on their limbs.

They were about to climb the tree when a nearby exclamation startled them.

"Let go! Stop that!" A voice, the musical tones of a female elf, jolted through the night.

"Here, now," growled a deep, unquestionably human response. "You know these woods are off limits—you'll be speaking to the captain, you will."

"No!" Now the elven voice was shrill with terror.

Before Gilthanas could react, Lethagas, sword in hand, bolted through the darkness. The prince heard a sharp oath, followed by a gurgling grunt. He had just risen to follow when Leth came back, leading a disheveled—but very pretty—white-haired elf woman by the hand. She wore leathers cut similarly to that of a Kagonesti elf.

"C'mon!" he whispered. "Get to the griffins!"

"Thank you—you saved my life!" gasped the female. Abruptly she pulled Leth to her, and their lips met in a fierce, crushing kiss.

"We've got to get out of here!" Gilthanas hissed urgently.

Only after another few seconds of taut embrace did the elf woman release Lethagas. She looked at him with pure adoration, while Leth, for his part, seemed unsteady on his feet. He was breathing hard, and his face was locked in a giddy grin.

Somehow, the pair held hands while they climbed the trees to the griffins. They paused for another passionate kiss before mounting the three flyers. The feathered creatures flew away before further sounds of alarm rose from below.

"I am called Alla," said their new companion, addressing Lethagas. "And I owe you my life . . . everything that I have."

"Why were the guards attacking you?" demanded the young elf, his voice tight with rage as he remembered the scene.

"I . . . I was trying to enter the sacred grove and honor my father," Alla replied. "But that is forbidden by the Dark Knights. They would have killed me!"

"You are safe, now, with us," Leth declared gallantly. Riding three abreast, the trio of elves on their griffins flew over the sea toward the Isle of Sancrist.

D. CRAMER

The Abduction:
Whitestone Glade, 28sc

"Do you think they still watch over us?"

I had been waiting for this question ever since I took
on the duties of preparing and then testing Sir Willam for
advancement in the Order of the Sword. As part of my effort
to get to know him, I had assigned myself to share his watch
in the Whitestone Glade, one of the most holy sites in Ansalon. Until just a few years ago, we had believed magic had
fled, but then a young Rose Knight named Linsha Majere
believed that the intervention of the gods themselves saved
her from an attacker in the Glade. This night, the winter wind
blowing through the barren forest seemed particularly harsh,

and the young Knight probably needed the conversation to take his mind off the cold.

"What do you think, Willam?"

His eyes wandered across the Whitestone Glade before us. The massive stone glinted under the light of the pale moon. "I don't know. My father taught me to honor the gods whether they are present or not. Anything less would be a violation of the Measure: Just because the gods are absent doesn't mean we should stop honoring them or obeying their strictures. But do you think they're really gone?"

"Well, you've heard of Lady Linsha's experience in the Glade. She believes it came from the gods, not from within her. I'm inclined to believe her because of two things. First, she was taught to master the Final Gift of the gods at the feet of Goldmoon herself. Second, she is a Rose Knight and I consider her honor to be beyond question."

"I would never question her honor, Sir, nor the truthfulness of her statement. Lady Sheryl beat me soundly on the training field to defend her friend's honor when she suspected I was doing that very thing, and I do not want to repeat the mistake with the Knight who may sponsor me for admittance into the Order of the Sword. I just can't help but wonder. Much changed in the wake of the gods' departure. Can we truly be certain that we guard a holy site?"

"We can't," I said. "All we can be sure of is our own beliefs and the Measure. If you learn to be true to those and to uphold their standards, you will serve effectively as a Knight of the Sword."

"Just once," Willam muttered. "I'd like to see the stars flash as they did for Vinas Solamnus. I'd like to know that there really is something greater than us that isn't a dragon. I would really like to have a sign that they are still out there and that our service to them means something."

"If there is proof, Willam," I said, "then what does belief matter? We cannot pretend we know the minds of gods, nor will we ever be certain that they will again give us proof of their existence beyond life itself and the Final Gift of mystic magic that they bestowed upon the world."

"Takhisis still whispers to the Dark Knights. Or so they claim."

I shrugged. "If you wish to believe the Dark Knights, Willam, then you have your proof that the gods are still active in the world. If you seek hard enough, maybe you'll find your own proof. Or maybe it's right here in this Glade."

He looked back at the stars. "What do you believe, Sir Gavin?"

"What I believe is unimportant. *Your* beliefs are what matter. I will tell you this: I believe in the good of the Knighthoods. I believe that our duty to oppose Evil in all its forms, the duty that Paladine, Kiri-Jolith, and Habbakuk charged Vinas Solamnus with, is still ours. The gods do not need to impress me with priestly parlor tricks for me to know that."

Willam gave me a thoughtful look, then fell silent.

I looked at the Whitestone. I hate thinking about the gods, because it always starts me thinking about the Orders when I was a child. I grew up during an age of revival for the Solamnic Knighthood. The ranks were swelling with new members and the gods were again guiding them forward. I dreamed of being like my father, a Sword Knight, a holy warrior who in his youth had brought the will of Kiri-Jolith to the remnants of the dragonarmies all across Ansalon.

Sadly, I was not to follow his example. Within weeks of my becoming a squire to Lady Riva Silverblade of Castle Eastwatch, the Dark Knights invaded and seized Palanthas. As the Orders rallied to counterattack, Chaos walked the surface of Krynn and we had to unite with the Dark Knights to drive him back to the Abyss from whence he had come.

Blue and silver dragons united as their human allies had, and together the Knights of Solamnia and the Knights of Takhisis plunged into the Abyss. But not squires. Squires remained behind to hold the fortifications along with common warriors and the heads of the Orders. Chaos was defeated, but at the cost of virtually everyone who went to oppose him.

If it hadn't been for Lord Liam Ehrling and Lord Gunthar's revised Measure, the Knighthood would probably have died. The attempt to join with the Dark Knights in rebuilding Ansalon almost led to our own Knighthood's destruction anyway . . . they murdered Lord Gunthar and attempted to seize control of Sancrist and destroy us. This was before Takhisis supposedly started whispering in their ears again, but it clearly demonstrated the fact that they pay lip service to the concept of honor but in fact have none.

Although we've survived, I still feel as though we are but a pale imitation of our forebears. My father's armor glittered in sun. He was like a giant walking among men when he inspected his troops. I have to struggle to keep my armor polished, and I have to struggle to keep focused on the Measure and to keep my actions devoted to furthering the precepts of the gods . . . because in my darkest moments, my faith both in them and in the Solamnic Orders is weak.

"Ho!" Willam cried, his voice and the hiss of his sword leaving its scabbard bringing my attention back to our guard duty. "Who goes there?"

"Stay your hand, Sir Knight," said a dark figure among the trees, his Solamnian tinged with a slight accent. "We are friends who have come in search of information."

The speaker emerged from the trees, stepping into the moonlight-drenched glade. He was a blonde-tressed elf male who was slightly taller than is the average among his kind. Something about him was slightly familiar. When two other elves emerged from the woods, my heart almost stopped. One was a fairly nondescript male, but the other . . .

White hair flowed around her face, which was a vision of beauty, and under her thick winter cloak I caught sight of the buckskin garments traditionally worn by the Kagonesti elves on Southern Ergoth. Because of her, I knew where I'd seen the blond elf before! In Kalaman, in the castle of the lord, there hangs a portrait of the two painted shortly after the War of the Lance! Gilthanas and Silvara had just stepped into my life!

But weren't they both dead? Could the gods have answered my prayers? Could they have come from the past to take me back with them? But these joyous thoughts were swiftly proven as silly as I should have recognized them to be the moment they entered my head.

"I am Gilthanas of Qualinesti," Gilthanas said, "and these are my trusted companions, Leth and Alla. We have come to Sancrist in search of information about the Good dragons."

"You are not Silvara?" I asked the Kagonesti Gilthanas identified as Alla.

She blinked. "By the gods, no!"

Alla and Leth exchanged looks. My first thought was that they were amused at my expense, but then I noticed that she reached out and touched Leth's hand. It was a quick and very brief movement, but enough to make me realize that if she was anyone's love, she was his.

My thoughts must have appeared in my face, for Gilthanas said, "No offense has been given, Sir Knight, let me assure you of that. But we do need your help, if you can grant it."

"I will help in whatever way I can, but first forgive my manners. I am Sir Gavin, Knight of the Sword and this is Sir Willam, Knight of the Crown. Further, a prince such as yourself should have been directed to the castle, Your Highness," I replied. "Which of the men at the docks sent you here instead?"

"None. We arrived on the backs of griffins, but I thought it best to land in the woods and not cause alarm in the castle. I wanted to revisit the Whitestone Glade along the way . . . and, honestly, I was as surprised to see you two here as you must have been to see me."

"How so?" Willam asked.

"I thought the gods gone. Why guard this place?"

"Your commander's absence does not mean that it is appropriate to disrespect him by forgetting to tend to his equipment or accomplish the tasks he set before you," I said. "Besides, we believe that Paladine's power still resides here."

"Is that so?" Gilthanas swept his eyes across the Glade, undoubtedly noting the withered grass and the absence of the eternal spring that once had existed there. He did not comment on that, but instead looked at me with an earnest expression. "Then Silvara must have been here. She honored Paladine above all other gods."

"Is that what you require our assistance with? Finding the Lady Silvara?"

"Yes. We parted ways in Kalaman. I am desperately trying to find her. Has she been here? Has she been assisting the Knighthoods in continuing their service to the gods?"

"Perhaps," I said. "I don't know. If she has visited Sancrist, Lord Liam would know. Come, follow us to the castle. Willam will attend to your beasts."

"No, I believe it's best if we take care of that, Sir Knight," Leth said. "Griffins don't take particularly well to strangers, especially not ones that are barely tamed such as these."

"Understood. If you would be so kind, Leth, we will wait here while you and Alla take care of them then."

"I should go along," Willam said. "There may be gnome creations in the forest."

This took me somewhat aback, but I saw no reason to deny his request. As he followed Leth and Alla from the clearing, I again saw her touch her companion very briefly.

❧ ❧ ❧ ❧ ❧

When we returned the castle, Lord Liam had, naturally, already retired for the night. Gilthanas insisted that he not be disturbed, and so I had Willam contact the seneschal to arrange quarters for them while I contacted the shift after ours to tell them to start their watch in the Glade early.

The following morning, I heard from a page that Gilthanas had asked Lord Liam about Silvara, but that Liam knew not of her whereabouts. My thoughts drifted back to a dispatch from Southern Ergoth dating back a few years. It claimed that a silver dragon had been spotted there. I wondered if I should tell the elf-prince, or if it would just be sending him off on a fruitless chase. But, then I received word through another page that Lord Liam expected my attendance at a feast that evening in Gilthanas's honor. I decided to speak with the elf-prince then. I had Willam's training to think about during the day. Lady Sheryl and I were to drill him in skill with polearms today.

Although hastily arranged, the feast was nonetheless as splendid as protocol required when honoring royal visitors like Gilthanas of Qualinesti. The Grand Master wanted his senior Knights there, so a pair of recent initiates in the Order of the Sword took my next shift in the Glade. I wanted Willam at the feast, as I feel that a mentor should attend to all aspects of his student's training—and learning to sit still for hours on end during feasts can be an important diplomatic skill.

As I looked around the Grand Hall, I noticed that the chamber could accommodate perhaps five times the people that were currently seated here. As Lord Liam rose to his feet and offered a brief speech and a welcome toast to Gilthanas and his companions, I noticed how his voice echoed in the hall. My mind again drifted back to when I was a child. I would sometimes sneak onto the balconies that circled the hall on the second floor and there watch Lord Gunthar and the Knights feast, the light of the torches dancing off their armor. When Lord Gunthar or another Knight would toast the assemblage, his voice would not echo from the walls, because the room was almost full.

I shifted in my seat, allowing my eyes to slide across the Knights, most of whom were watching Lord Liam as he spoke. Of the two who weren't, one was watching Willam—Lady Sheryl, who has been pining for his attentions since she took command of Revered Daughter Crysania's honor guard, at the specific request of the venerable priestess—and Willam himself, who was watching Alla.

Lady Sheryl is a sad case. She isn't very skilled in the courtly arts, having been raised in the less-than-gentile town of Newports, and Willam is a bit too thick skulled to realize that her overtures on the training fields are not to belittle him but instead to get his attention. It's interesting how adults often behave like children in affairs of the heart, as in Sheryl's case, where she relies on jibes and punches when she should just tell him how she feels. She is no shrinking violet in all other matters, so no one would bat an eye if she were to do so. Except perhaps Willam, who would probably be as surprised as can be.

I looked briefly at Alla. She wore a borrowed gown and jewelry and appeared even more stunning than she had earlier in the day. It was clear to me why Willam couldn't keep his eyes off her. Her exotic appearance in the Glade intrigued the boy, and now he appeared to be completely entranced by the image of her as a noble woman of unsurpassed beauty. I found myself hoping that Willam was wise enough to not let his heart become captured by her beauty.

That hope strengthened when I saw Leth's hand wander to her fingers as they lay on the table and gently squeeze them. Alla turned to him, and he smiled warmly. It confirmed to me what I had suspected yesterday: They were a couple, which meant there was no room for the likes of Willam.

As the feast progressed, Gilthanas spent most of his time speaking with Sir Liam. Clearly, he had been out of touch for some time, and much of what he knew of the tumultuous years since the Chaos War was rife with misinformation. On the current state of the Knights of Solamnia, Gilthanas interrupted the Grand Master's explanation of how covert circles are being established in many areas by cursing the name of Sir Aurrafil. He quickly apologized for his outburst, but then explained that Aurrafil had told him a variety of lies during the year he spent in Kalaman, including the "fact" that the Knights limited themselves to Sancrist.

"He might not have been purposefully lying," Lord Liam said. "Few people realize how extensive our rebuilding efforts have been. Most of the attention is being focused on the Legion of Steel, which serves our purpose rather well. We are finding ourselves with capable allies in many cities when we attempt to establish our covert circles, and while the Knights of Takhisis are busy watching the Legionnaires, we can regain the footing we lost in the Chaos War."

"Speaking of the Legion, Lord Liam, have you had a chance to review Lady Karine's latest dispatch from Sanction?" asked Lord Quintayne. "The notion of using a single Knight as the visible contact point between our circle there and the Legion seems like the perfect way to avoid the debacles of years past."

"I agree," Lord Liam replied. "Now, if only Lady Linsha, or any of the other Knights, could discern Hogan Bight's motives in the city, we might actually get somewhere."

The discussion about Sanction continued as kender tumblers rushed onto the floor of the Grand Hall and began performing the classic routine "Lord Toede's Hunt." During this, Gilthanas turned to me and said, "I have been hearing tales of great dragons larger and more powerful than any we ever faced during the War of the Lance that have seized huge swaths of territory. What of the metallic dragons? Surely, they must oppose these beasts?"

"Alas, I wish it was so. I know of two metallic dragons who have survived the Dragon Purge: a brass dragon who has taken up residence along the Silvanesti border in the south, and a silver dragon known as Mirror at the Citadel of Light."

"Yes. I heard of Mirror while in Kalaman." A sudden sadness appeared on his features as his eyes drifted to the kender clowns. "As I told Lord Ehrling, Sir Knight, I came to Sancrist hoping to find a dragon, or at the very least someone who knew where she was last seen . . . and if not her, then maybe one that could tell me where she may have gone."

"I don't know if this means anything, but we recently had word from Castle Eastwatch stating that a silver dragon had settled in the nearby area."

"Any word as to whether it is a male or female?" Gilthanas suddenly straightened in his chair, his face brightening.

"No, I'm afraid not. At any rate, I don't put much stock in the report. This wouldn't be the first time that Lady Riva and her Knights have either misinterpreted or simply imagined something. One can hardly blame them as their assignment is not an enviable one."

Gilthanas frowned. "What do you mean?"

"You haven't heard? About fifteen years ago, the biggest white dragon anyone had ever seen claimed dominion over most of Southern Ergoth. People just call him the White these days. By all reports, the beast has buried Huma's Tomb and much of the Last Gaard Mountains under magically generated ice."

"What of Qualimori? And Silvamori?"

"Most of the citizens fled to the isle of Cristyne. The Kagonesti stayed and attempted to defend their lands from the dragon. As far as we can tell, they were mostly wiped out in the process."

Gilthanas sat stunned for moment, the building excitement I had detected in him dispelled. I noticed that Alla was gripping Leth's hand so hard that her knuckles were white. Her eyes seemed to shimmer with tears. The poor woman must have been witness to some of the atrocities perpetrated against her people by the White Dragon. Chivalry dictated that I end this particular line of conversation.

"With the almost total absence of metallic dragons on Ansalon now, I think that the silver dragon in question is more likely a product of their imaginations rather than your Silvara."

"Still," Gilthanas said, "this is the best lead I have had since I started my quest to reunite with her! And it makes sense—Castle Eastwatch is close to Foghaven Vale where she once made her home! If any dragon were to attempt to drive off that white beast, it would be her. Are you personally acquainted with Lady Riva, Sir Gavin?"

"She was one of my sponsors," I said.

"Excellent. Could I trouble you for a letter of introduction? I would very much like to travel to Castle Eastwatch and speak with her and her Knights about this silver dragon. If it is not Silvara, at least my mind will be at ease. She has no reason to trust me, however, and may not be as hospitable as you are here on Sancrist—I know I would think twice about trusting strangers if I were living in the shadow of a powerful dragon. Even white dragons can be devious if they put their minds to it."

"I'd be happy to write you a letter of introduction, Your Highness. And I feel confident in assuring you, Lady Riva will give you every bit of cooperation she can."

"I am in your debt, Sir Knight."

"Nonsense." I smiled gently. "This is but a trifle, and if you find your beloved, my ability to take joy from it due to the small part I played will place me in your debt."

Gilthanas nodded and smiled, this time with radiant joy. He turned to watch the kender performers with an absent look on his face, almost as if he was reliving a pleasant memory or perhaps imagining something pleasant to come.

"Sir Knight, what happened to the Kagonesti?" I turned my gaze toward Alla. Her large, dark eyes were still shimmering with threatened tears. "Do any live still?"

"I believe so, milady. Some have fled to Cristyne, but others continue to resist the White. The Kagonesti most definitely still live."

Tears finally spilled over her cheeks. "I didn't have the courage to stay. May the Blue Phoenix forgive me, but I could not bear the destruction any longer. But they live still?" she asked, struggling to keep her voice steady.

"By my honor, milady, the Kagonesti continue to bear arms against those who would take their ancestral lands from them."

"Good." She lowered her head, continuing to weep silently, her tears flowing freely. My eyes drifted to Leth. The young Qualinesti put his arm around her and leaned close. He whispered something in her ear. She nodded and swiftly wiped the tears from her eyes. She stood and with an obvious effort of will steadied her voice to say, "Sir Liam, I appreciate your gracious hospitality . . . but I have grown tired. I bid you good night."

Sir Liam rose to his feet. "I shall have a Knight escort you—"

"No need, Sir Liam," Leth said. "I shall see Alla safely to her chamber. Allow your Knights to continue to enjoy themselves."

Liam nodded. "As you wish."

"Are you all right?" Gilthanas asked, genuine concern in his voice.

"Yes," Alla said, another tear trickling down her cheek. She swiftly wiped it away. "I am tired. That's all. Just tired."

Leth took her arm. Although he was trying to hide it, I saw in his face a pain at her sorrow. As they left the table, Willam came into view. My young charge was watching them as they left—watching *her* to be specific. And he made no effort to hide the pain he was feeling. The damn boy was smitten and every tear that she had just shed at the table had probably felt like a dagger in his heart.

I swear that the gods made elven women the way they did to torment young men.

The next night, Willam and I again stood at our post in White-stone Glade. We had been on watch for mere minutes when the topic I knew he would broach came up.

"You spent time on Southern Ergoth, didn't you Gavin?"

"Yes, Willam. I served under Lady Riva for three years before returning to Sancrist. At the time, the White was expanding his domain. We helped many elves flee the island to Crystine."

"So, you've seen many elves?"

"Yes, lad. And before you even ask, I have seen some that rival Alla in beauty."

"But none as graceful, I am certain." His face took on a distant expression. "When she moves . . . it's as though the wind itself has taken mortal form."

I grunted. "She's taken, boy."

He snapped back to reality. "What?"

"She's taken. Did you see the way Leth looks at her?"

"No," he said, his tone guarded.

"Well, when you're around them tomorrow, take a closer look. It's more than just chivalry for him, and she returns his feelings. Spare yourself embarrassment and heartbreak." He looked so crestfallen that I had to laugh. "Consider yourself lucky, boy. You know what happened the last time an upstanding Knight got involved with an elf-maid, don't you?"

"He died a heroic death, defending the Tower of the High Clerist against the forces of Evil."

"All right. I forgot about Sturm Brightblade. I was thinking of Lord Soth, Willam. Don't let lust override your sense of honor."

"I think you insult me, Sir."

"No, Willam, I'm just imparting to you the benefit of my years. Elven women are beautiful, exotic creatures. The first few times a young man encounters them, they set his head spinning. I know, because I've been there. And I know that you should put her out of your mind because she and Leth are already in love with one another."

A silence fell between us. For several long minutes, the only sound was the wind snapping at our cloaks.

"I can't get her out of mind, Gavin."

I looked at him, trying not to laugh. "You'll never become a Knight of the Sword with that kind of willpower, Willam."

A miserable expression crossed his face. "I've gotten past the gender of Lady Sheryl and Lady Hannah—I view them now just as fellow Knights—but how can I ever reclaim my heart from Alla?"

"She doesn't have your heart, you young fool! And I suspect that Lady Sheryl wouldn't mind if you were to acknowledge that she's a woman as well as Knight."

"Now you mock me. She belittles my abilities as a swordsman every chance she gets."

"And she also offers to train with you every chance she gets! Why do you think that is?"

Willam blinked. Then a startled expression appeared on his face. "But she turned me down when I asked to escort her to the Autumn's Twilight festival."

"Of course she did. She was leaving for Gwynned the day of the festival, escorting Lady Crysania and her party to the emperor's court for an audience."

"She never said that."

"No, because you scurried out the hall so fast she didn't have a chance to explain. Lady Crysania was traveling to Ergoth to see if the emperor's daughter was ill or strong in the mystic arts—the child was claiming that spirits spoke to her. Sir Liam wanted the Revered Daughter to have extra escort while away from Sancrist."

Willam looked like he was about to say something, but then closed his mouth and turned his gaze up at the moon.

"Talk to Lady Sheryl tomorrow, Willam. Her you might be able to win, but Alla is as unreachable for you as the moon."

"Lady Sheryl is a beautiful and intelligent woman indeed, but she is to Alla as the moon is to the sun—she pales by comparison."

I sighed. "I've done what I can for you in this matter. This conversation is at an end."

The rest of the watch passed in silence, with Willam deep in thought. After we had been relieved and were walking back to sleeping Castle Uth Wistan, he said, "I'm not sure I can accept your estimation of Lady Sheryl."

"My advice is that you seek out Lady Sheryl to at least clarify her feelings toward you," I said. "Don't be surprised if she laughs at you initially and challenges you to a sparring match. If she does, I am right. If she instead gets serious and apologizes to you, then I am wrong." One of the tales of Gilthanas and Silvara came to mind—the version where he doesn't discover what he has lost until it is too late. "I have given you my best advice already, but I want to add this: I truly believe you should seek out Lady Sheryl and talk to her, man to woman. If you don't, you may find it's too late and then you'll regret it for the rest of your life."

As I spoke, we climbed the steps to the battlement, intending to enter our quarters from there. Alla, in her cloak, appeared at the top of the stairs, starting down them without really looking ahead. After a few steps, she noticed us, a startled look on her narrow face. She began to apologize and to retreat up the stairs.

"No, milady, please, you go first," Willam said, moving back down the stairs, pushing me behind him. "We would not think of impeding your progress."

The elf lowered her eyes demurely, a slight smile on her face. I got the sense that she was embarrassed by Willam's chivalry.

"Why are you up at this late hour?" Willam asked. "Is there something you need assistance with?"

"No, kind sir. I just found myself unable to sleep, so I decided to visit with the griffins."

"Allow me to escort you, milady."

She lowered her eyes again. "I don't want to be a bother, Sir Knight. I will be fine. You need not concern yourself."

"Nonsense. It is no bother. Further, I would be fascinated to hear of your travels with Gilthanas of Qualinesti. I have heard many tales of his deeds in the years during the War of the Lance, and I would like to hear some more."

"Okay," she said with a sweet, bright smile. He offered her his arm and she took it.

I caught Willam's eye and frowned at him. "We have an early morning tomorrow, Sir Willam."

"You've no need to concern yourself, Sir Gavin. I will go straight to bed once Lady Alla has checked on the griffins."

"Please, Sir Knight! I am not of noble blood!"

"But your beauty alone makes you deserving nonetheless of the honorific," he said, smiling at her. She dropped her eyes again, blushing and smiling slightly. He then looked back at me, an imploring look on his face.

"Very well," I said. "On your honor, you will rest this evening. And you will uphold the Measure in every way."

"Of course, Sir Gavin!" He sounded startled. Yet, there he was, arm in arm with another man's woman. "My honor is my life!"

I frowned at him again, unsure as to whether he understood how serious I was taking this matter . . . but if I brought it up, I would have embarrassed young Alla. I felt that if I were to berate Willam in front of her, I would be dishonoring myself, as I feared he was about to dishonor both her and himself.

Instead, I merely said, "I know, Sir Willam. Escort Alla back to her chamber when she is done inspecting the griffins. I will see you at sunrise tomorrow." I headed up the stairs without looking back.

As I entered my quarters, a page was returning the bedwarmer to its stand. "Good evening, Sir Gavin," the boy said. "How was your watch?"

"Cold," I replied, dismissing him with a gesture. My thoughts revolved around Willam as I removed my weapons belt. Greater Knights than he had fallen victim to the temptation of an elven woman. In my youth, I myself had done so. She hadn't been involved with another man, however. As I started to remove my armor, a pounding on the door and shouts in the hallway interrupted my thoughts. I swiftly grabbed my sword and threw the door open. The page was outside, white as a sheet.

"Monsters!" he shouted. "There are monsters on the castle walls! Sir Willam is fighting them!"

I pushed the boy aside and stormed down the hallway. "Sound the alarm!" I shouted. From beyond the reinforced door that led to the battlement of the castle came a strange screech, a sound that could only have been uttered by a creature from the Abyss, I thought. I hesitated briefly, but then my courage rose again and I flung open the door.

Hovering above the wall was one of the griffins. Willam clung to its side, his arms wrapped around the waist of a black-clad person—I could not tell if it was a man or woman, for a billowing cloak obscured his or her form and hid the face in the shadows of a drawn hood.

Willam looked over his shoulder as I rushed forward. "Gavin! Thank the gods!"

Then I saw a flash of steel amidst the folds of the cloak. The rider twisted in Willam's grasp and drove a short sword through the crack where his breastplate and back armor met. Willam let out a strangled cry and released his grip. The griffin soared upward, Willam's weight pulled him free of the blade, and he clattered to the hard stones of the battlement.

I leapt over his prone figure and onto the crenellation. I swung wide with my sword, hoping to strike the griffin before it was too far away, but all I achieved was to almost lose my balance and plunge into the icy moat forty feet below. Against the bright disk of the moon, I could see all three griffins that Gilthanas, Leth, and Alla had arrived on. The one I had witnessed on the wall was lagging significantly behind the others. A single cloaked figure sat upon each of the two trailing griffins—but I could see two figures upon the lead one . . . and one of the people had long hair that fluttered in the wind. It was Alla!

I jumped off the wall and strode to Willam's side. Blood was streaming from the wound and the page stood over him, looking confused and frightened. The boy was actually wringing his hands.

"Fetch one of the mystics," I barked. "And make sure it's one who knows how to heal!"

The page blinked at me, then rushed into the castle, leaving the door open behind him. I put my sword aside and kneeled next to Willam. I pulled him into my arms and said, "It'll be all right, Willam. Just relax."

He looked at me, his face twisted with pain. Then he coughed, and blood spilled forth from his mouth as he trembled in my arms. I'd seen enough good men die to know that he didn't have much time.

"Get a healer to the northern battlements," I shouted. "To the Abyss with the damn mystics, just bring me a healer!" Elsewhere in the castle, someone finally sounded the alarm.

Willam clutched at my cloak. His breath hissed over his lips, forming bubbles in the blood. "Alla," he moaned, his eyes locking with mine. "Alla."

"You did your best, Willam. There is no dishonor in failing, only in not trying to perform your duty. You and I shall hunt down the villains that abducted her when you have healed. They will pay for what they've done with their lives, and we shall mete out justice together."

His eyes widened and a strange look passed over his face, a look the meaning of which I could not determine—it almost seemed like desperation. He drew a shuddering breath and spoke her name again. "Alla."

Then his eyes went blank. His final breath bubbled across his lips as life fled his body.

"By Mishakal!" I heard someone cry. It was the young girl who served as the Revered Daughter's assistant and the page I had dispatched. She was wearing only a dressing gown and ran across the icy flagstones of the battlement in bare feet. "I will help him, Sir Knight. Goldmoon has instructed me in healing magic!"

She kneeled at our side and placed her hands on Willam's bloody chest. She closed her eyes and prepared to use the final gift of the gods, but then her eyes flew open and she drew back her hands as though she had been burned.

"It's too late," I said, regretting the words even as they left my lips. It had been an unbidden phrase, said without consideration. They were not the words this child needed to hear.

She raised her hands and looked at the blood upon them. They were trembling. Her doelike eyes drifted to Willam's body, and she burst into tears. "I'm sorry," she sobbed. "I'm so sorry I didn't get here in time. I was sleeping. I'm sorry!"

"It's not your fault," I said, forcing back tears of my own, struggling to keep my voice steady. I lowered Willam to the cold stones and covered him with my cloak. I then helped the girl to her feet. She put her arms around me and sobbed against my armor. I lifted my eyes to sky, to where I had seen the three griffins pass by the moon. "It's not your fault, milady. They killed Willam, not you. And, by my honor, they will pay."

The battlement exploded with activity. Squires and a healer arrived. Knights in varying states of dress with their swords drawn suddenly seemed to be everywhere. Somewhere, I heard Leth calling the name of his beloved. That odd, desperate expression in Willam's eyes flashed in my mind. I wondered if the boy had died with a burning passion for a woman with another man in her life—died afraid that he would never see her again.

Then I heard Gilthanas's voice. "What happened?" the elf asked.

I turned to him after passing the sobbing girl off to the page. As he led her away, I said, "The castle was infiltrated. Someone has abducted Alla, stolen your griffins, and used them in their escape. Sir Willam was slain trying to stop them."

The elf-lord's brow furrowed in a frown. "That's not possible."

"You saw the blood on that girl's hands, did you not?" I said, anger welling up inside me. "Do you see the body here on the ground before us? If you check the courtyard, you will see that your mounts are indeed gone. It is possible, Lord Gilthanas, and it has happened."

"Yes, Sir Knight, I understand, but what you are suggesting has happened here is impossible."

"Are you saying I am lying? Are you calling my honor into question?"

"No, Sir Gavin," he replied softly. "I was thinking about the griffins. They won't obey anyone but Leth. How could they have taken the griffins with him still here?" As if to prove Gilthanas's point, Leth howled Alla's name. Someone had told him the news.

"They could have taken the griffins if they used dark mysticism to usurp the bond that Leth has nurtured with them." Lady Sheryl emerged from the chaos of Knights that were streaming back and forth along the battlement. She was dressed in her nightgown and steel-toed boots. In one hand, she carried her sword. In the other, she held a piece of parchment she had picked up from the flagstones. She offered it to me, her eyes drifting to the shrouded form on the ground. Blood was starting to seep from beneath the cloak.

I examined the parchment. On it was a crude representation of the Seal of the Emperor of Ergoth with a black spot at the center.

"What do you mean, dark mysticism usurped Leth's bond with the griffins?" Gilthanas asked.

"I went through my trials on Schallsea with a Knight who spent part of her childhood at the Citadel of Light. She could communicate with animals through the powers of the heart, and I once saw her convince a hunter's loyal hound to abandon the scent of a deer she wanted to go free. If she can do it, so can mystics who are of a darker spirit."

"And this symbol relates to them?" I passed the parchment to Gilthanas who studied it intently.

"Yes," Lady Sheryl replied. "While at the Ergothian court earlier this year, the emperor's daughter said that the spirits that speak to her warned her of an Evil that is represented by this symbol. When the librarians researched it, they discovered that it stands for a movement that rose during the War of the Lance—a movement devoted to the service of Sargonnas and the destruction of the Empire of Ergoth."

"But why abduct Alla?" Gilthanas asked.

"I don't know," Lady Sheryl said. She shivered violently as she looked at Willam's body again. "The Revered Daughter would know. We should go ask her."

"Yes," I said. "Let us go. You'll catch your death, Sheryl."

"He should be brought in from the cold as well," she said, her eyes still on the body. "He's going to be much colder than I."

"Go, Sheryl. Ask the Revered Daughter to prepare herself for an audience with myself and Prince Gilthanas."

"Yes, Sir Gavin." Her eyes fluttered to my face. Her lower lip trembled, but her voice remained steady as she said, "I kept asking him to let me teach him how to use his sword better."

I barked at a couple of squires who were gawking openmouthed at my fallen charge. "Take him to the crypt, you lazy dogs. Start preparing the body for its time in state!"

"Were they close?" Gilthanas nodded toward Sheryl who was walking down the hall, too slowly and with her shoulders slumping. The blade of her sword was barely off the floor.

"No," I replied. "But they should have been."

Sir Liam, Gilthanas, Leth, and I stood in the Revered Daughter's audience room, listening as Sheryl—now more appropriately dressed in a tunic and trousers—explained what she knew of the cult. I confess that I barely heard a word she said. The sight of Willam dying in my arms hovered before my eyes and the echo of his final word reverberated with deafening intensity in my head.

The events that brought Willam and the kidnappers to the battlements of the castle were shrouded in mystery, but for some reason, he had left his weapons belt in the courtyard below. Perhaps the villains had threatened to harm Alla unless he dropped his blades. They then took to the air and he leapt up and grabbed hold of one of the riders. Perhaps it was something else. We will never know, for although a Rose Knight with the ability to communicate with the spirits of the recently dead attempted to speak with Willam, he had already gone to join Paladine in the Beyond. Only those who had flown off on the griffins could now tell us what had transpired.

"I will hunt these animals to the very edge of the Abyss," Leth cried, shaking with rage. "And if they have harmed her, I will kill each and every one of them!"

Gilthanas put a hand on his shoulder and gave him a stern look. "Be calm, my friend. We will hunt these villains together . . . but first we must allow Lady Sheryl and the Revered Daughter tell us what they know about these cultists."

"There isn't much more to tell," Lady Sheryl said. "They have their lair somewhere in the mountains along the border between the Ergothian Empire and the goblin kingdom of Sikk'et Hul. They are rumored to perform some manner of rites on the Winter Solstice at a place called Raekel's Pit, so it is quite possible that they kidnapped Alla to sacrifice her in some foul ritual."

"But why her?!" Leth wailed. "Why her?!"

"Few places in Ansalon have such a concentration of men and women who are valiant and pure in body and soul as Sancrist," Crysania said softly, her sightless eyes turning toward us. "Perhaps they abducted Alla over one of the

Knights because of the reputed bond that the Kagonesti share with the land. The very fact that they subverted Leth's bond with his griffins show that they are powerful dark mystics. Perhaps they intend to tap into her energies."

"Is such a thing possible?" Sheryl asked.

"The dragons absorbed the life energies of their slain foes during the Dragon Purge. Perhaps these followers of Sargonnas at Raekel's Pit are engaged in similar activities."

"Or perhaps they are merely honoring their god," Gilthanas muttered. He looked around the room with a pained expression. "Several years ago, I encountered people who I now believe to be members of this cult on the island of Elian, off Ansalon's eastern coast. Almost a decade later, in Solamnia I met a man I thought I had befriended back then but he was bent on killing me.

"Alla's predicament is my fault, for I believe she was abducted as part of an attempt to gain revenge upon me. For what, I'm not sure, but it could be as straightforward as them wishing to avenge the death of a comrade. It could be bigger than that. But that is why she was chosen, I am certain of it." He placed a hand on Leth's shoulder. The other elf looked at him with smoldering eyes. "If Lord Liam will provide us with a fast ship, we will travel to Northern Ergoth together . . . and I shall see that you are reunited with the woman you love, or I will die in the attempt."

"You will not go alone," I said, a knot of anger clenching in my breast. "I will join you to avenge my friend. He was murdered most foully, and I will be the one to destroy these followers of Dark Vengeance."

"It won't be an easy task," Sheryl muttered, a look of deep sorrow appearing on her face. "I should be there at your side. But I can't. I have a duty here. I have to stay and protect the Revered Daughter. For all we know, she was their intended target, and may still be."

Crysania held out a hand and Sheryl took it. The aged priestess said, "I appreciate your devotion to duty even if your heart cries out to avenge Willam. The gods will reward your sacrifice some day, dear Sheryl, because you are putting Good above the need to expunge your pain."

"My thanks, Revered Daughter," Sheryl replied so softly that it was almost inaudible. "That is small comfort, as I don't think the gods have ever heard a single one of my prayers."

"You may take my ship," Crysania said after a slight pause. "Sheryl, would you please go wake the crew and tell them to prepare to depart with the tide?"

"I will fetch my gear," I said to Gilthanas. "I will meet you at the ship."

$$\textit{\ding{43} \ding{43} \ding{43} \ding{43} \ding{43}}$$

I chose to travel light: a cloak, my broadsword, two daggers, a crossbow and ten quarrels, and a rucksack containing extra clothes, a spare pair of boots, oil for my weapons and armor, and my armor. These evil priests were going to know that they were meeting their end at the hands of a Knight of the Sword.

I returned to the Whitestone Glade before heading to the harbor. The Knights posted there realized with a single glance at my grim visage that they should not speak to me. They retreated deeper into the forest as I kneeled in front of the cracked and broken Whitestone.

The wind rushed through the glade, biting at my cheeks as I looked up into the heavens where the mad swirl of stars left in Chaos's wake glimmered dimly.

Do you think they still watch over us?

I pushed the sound of Willam's voice out of my mind. I cleared my mind and whispered a prayer to Kiri-Jolith, the patron of my Order. I kept my face turned skyward, my eyes scanning the stars. Kiri-Jolith would guide me in this quest. Kiri-Jolith would ensure that I conducted myself honorably, as a man devoted to his service should. I didn't want to be sent to a different age. I just wanted strength to comport myself with honor.

Do you think they still watch over us?

I stopped praying. "No," I whispered to the echo of the dead man. " I do not. If Linsha Majere found anything in this grove, it was the memory of the gods but not their presence."

I went to the docks.

SOTHI NUINQUA TSALARIOTH

Rackel's Pit, 298c

Gilthanas slashed hard on the back swing and the goblin's head flew from its skinny shoulders, trailing blood and freezing the creature's horrified grimace into a death mask. The head tumbled away like a misshapen ball, and by the time the prince looked around to seek his next target, the rest of the runts were scattering into the night.

Nearby Sir Gavin was already cleaning his sword on a rag he'd ripped from a dead goblin's cloak. Lethagas was panting, with his bloody blade still raised. Nervously the young elf spun about, hearing an imaginary threat behind him.

Perhaps two dozen goblins sprawled around the trio in various postures of grievous injury or death. A few moaned, or gasped for breath, but for the most part the loathsome creatures remained still. The rest of the tribe had run away, vanishing into the cracks and crevices of their mountain home, and Gilthanas felt that there was little chance they would be back.

"Are either of you hurt?" he asked his companions.

"I'm fine . . . a few nicks, that's all," replied the young elf.

"Quite untouched, thank you," stated the Knight.

Gilthanas looked at the old man with fresh appraisal. He had wielded his great sword like it was a twig, carving away at goblins to all sides. In the end, his full-throated battle cry— "For the Oath and the Measure"—had put the panic into the attacking goblins.

"They must have been watching us for the last few miles," Sir Gavin suggested. "That gave them time to make their attack in numbers."

"And this was the last place they could get close to us without being seen—at least, the last place on this side of the pass." Gilthanas looked at the sharp ridge etched against the skyline before them. From this valley, their path would take them onto the broad mountainside, where the trail was steep, but visibility was clear for miles in any direction.

"Perhaps the superstitious buggers feared to cross over and get too close to the Pit," suggested Sir Gavin.

"Do you think the gully dwarves knew what they were talking about when they told us to come here?" asked Lethagas, hesitantly. "There could be more than one 'Black Mountain' along here."

Gilthanas shrugged. "They're all we have to go on . . . and I've known gully dwarves to be helpful a time or two in the past. I think we should take their word."

"You're right—we don't have any other choice," Leth said. "And if they can help us find Alla—and whoever took her away—then I couldn't be more grateful."

Grimly the three travelers started onto the steep slope. Breathing hard, they leaned into the climb and plodded resolutely up the trail. Gilthanas thought of the task that had brought them here, to Northern Ergoth—of the stormy crossing from Sancrist, the trek through village after village of barbarians or gully dwarves, finally the ambush by a hundred goblins. He was relieved at the thought that they were almost done. Then, finally, he would go seek the silver dragon that just might be the one he loved.

These thoughts carried him all the way to the crest, where he stood with his companions just before dusk and looked into a barren, rock-strewn valley. In the center of the vale the ground plunged away to form a deep hole—a gap in which mists writhed and strange winds moaned.

"We've found it!" Leth declared. "That has to be Raekel's Pit!" He started down the slope at a trot. "This is where the cult worships and where those bastards must have brought Alla!"

"Wait!" hissed Gilthanas, still taking in the rest of the surroundings. "If this is their ceremonial center, they'll have guards!" Hundreds of small caves, rough knolls, and little ravines could conceal an enemy. And the mouth of the pit was at the bottom of the hill, in clear view from all directions.

"Hurry!" was Leth's only reply.

The Knight and the elven prince did the best they could, gasping for breath as they joined their companion at the very lip of the pit.

"Mark my words—it's a hole straight to the Abyss," declared Sir Gavin grimly. Indeed, the bottom could not be seen because of the mist and smoke that curled through the air below them. Even so, they could see far enough to realize that the hole descended a hundred feet or more without reaching bottom.

"There's a trail, with steps leading down," said Leth, pointing.

"We know that the cult worshiped around Raekel's Pit. We don't know that they went inside it," Gilthanas argued.

"Where else?" demanded the young elf, almost contemptuously taking in the barren valley with a gesture. "I'm going down there. That's where we'll find Alla!"

"We're going with you, lad," said Sir Gavin, and Gilthanas nodded curtly in exasperated approval. "Just go slow enough that we can stay together."

The trio of travelers started down the narrow stairs, which were black stone steps that had been carved directly into the steep wall of the pit. Lethagas took the lead, followed by Gilthanas and then Sir Gavin. After two dozen steps, the route led to a small platform, like a balcony overlooking the obscure depths of the pit. More stairs led down from there, and they passed a succession of such platforms, dropping deeper and deeper into the cylindrical cavity. They couldn't see the bottom, but they began to make out outcrops of rock below them.

"There she is—Alla!" cried Leth, abruptly racing down a dozen stairs to come to another platform. Here no further steps led down deeper into the pit, but as he arrived at his companion's side Gilthanas, too, saw the elf maid.

Alla was sprawled upon the top of an obelisk of rock thirty or forty feet below. She lay spread-eagled, on her back. Her eyes were closed, but she did not have any visible wounds.

"By all the gods—if's she's hurt I'll kill every cultist in this hole!" Lethagas cried.

"Too late, I'm afraid . . . we already did the job for you."

The three companions whirled to confront a tall Dark Knight standing on one of the platforms just above them. The man was dressed in black armor, even to the grotesque mask that fully concealed his face. Other Knights, the armor less elaborate in decoration but just as complete in coverage, flanked their leader and glared impassively down at the two elves and the Solamnic Knight.

Lethagas choked out a strangled curse but Gilthanas spoke loudly, before the younger elf could do anything rash.

"Whom did you kill?" he asked.

"Three of them, the cultists of Raekel's Pit. They were little more than children, really. They lived like savages in that valley up above. Still, the wench among them was a handsome thing—too bad she fought so hard that we had to kill her."

"You butchers! What have you done to Alla?" cried Leth.

"Why, nothing at all." The Knight raised his voice, shouting down into the pit. "Isn't that right, my dear?"

"Of course." Alla's voice was as firm, as strong as ever.

When Gilthanas looked back, he saw that the elf maid had risen to stand easily atop her obelisk of rock. She waved mockingly to the speechless trio as one of the Knights threw down a rope. She scampered up the line like an acrobat, some distance away from the platform where Leth, Gilthanas, and Sir Gavin watched in shock.

"She's mad . . . under some dark spell!" gasped the young elf, finally, before calling out to her. "Alla—beware sorcery!"

She only laughed, and let go of the rope as several Knights assisted her to stand next to their captain. "Oh, Lethagas," she chided. "You're such a child. Still, it was fun to toy with you for awhile." Touching the captain on his broad shoulder, she struck a coy pose beside the burly human. "But it's here, with the Dark Knights, that the future lies—mine, Qualinesti's, and all Krynn's. I have made my choice, and my master is called Khellendros now. You should have made yours, as well . . . though it will be up to Fate to see where it carries you."

With a groan the young elf covered his eyes and dropped to his knees.

"Why?" Gilthanas demanded. "Why did you do it?"

"Why, she did it to bring you to us, of course," said the Knight commander. "She was an important part of a scheme that has been in place for many years. Perhaps you will be interested to know that she is the stalker who accompanied the assassins you encountered earlier in your journeys."

"Why do you want me?" asked the prince.

"It's not us," said the Knight, "But someone who will pay a good price for you. Still, our own Order will rest more comfortably in Qualinesti, knowing that you are safely out of the way."

"Vile treachery!" shouted Sir Gavin. "You shall not have us!"

Before Gilthanas could stop him, the elder Knight drew his sword and charged up the stairs. Two much younger warriors clad in black armor, each with a great blade raised, met him. Sir Gavin hacked at the first one, knocking him off the stairs. With a hysterical scream, the Dark Knight toppled into the depths of Raekel's Pit.

But the other Knight was ready. His blade cleaved down, cutting deeply into the elder warrior's shoulder. Sir Gavin fell face first, slipping back down the stairs, leaving a trail of fresh blood.

"We can fight them!" Lethagas hissed, rising and stepping to Gilthanas's side. "Take them down—or die trying!"

The prince sighed. He gestured to the array of Knights glaring down at them, easily two score blocking their route out of the pit. And how many more were lurking in the valley without?

"We have been captured." Gilthanas glared at Alla. "Betrayed, true, but only captured. Now is not the time to die."

Leth grimaced in reluctance, but made no move to advance.

"I surrender to you," declared Gilthanas, drawing the sword of Purstal and holding it, hilt first, before him. "Though if the dungeons of Silvanesti couldn't hold me, I doubt that yours will do any better."

Alla laughed, while the Dark Knight took Gilthanas's sword with a good-natured shrug. "It's only for a short time," he said. "And then the blue dragon will decide what to do with you."

"As to Silvara," teased the elf maid, as a rope was secured around Gilthanas's wrists. "It seems that she will just have to wait."

D. CRAMER

Silver Hearts

Castle Eastwatch, 28SC

Castle Eastwatch is an ugly place. It is a drab and gray building of stone, unimaginative in its construction. Built from the stones of a fortress that rebels cast down during the civil war that gave birth to Solamnia, it was constructed with very little else but functionality in mind.

The one flourish it has is a balcony outside of what was intended to be the Lord's quarters. After I expressed an appreciation for the view it afforded of the harbor and the sea beyond it, Lady Riva had given it to me as my quarters, despite my protestations.

"I want to be treated as just another Knight," I had said.

"You are not 'just another Knight,'" she had responded.

"And while not everyone serving at Castle Eastwatch knows this, Sir Francis and I do. That is why he is stepping aside as the ranking Rose Knight and why you will take his place. It is also why you will have these quarters."

When a Knight of Solamnia has made up her mind, one can do nothing to change it. Riva even showed me, both in the revised Measure and in the one that was in effect in my youth, why taking her quarters was in accordance with the Code that we both upheld.

My eyes drifted to the windows and the balcony beyond them. I had felt his presence stronger than I had in years. He was out there.

The bond silver dragons share with mortals is not something I can ever fully explain to someone who isn't one of us. Many decades ago, I had an opportunity to have civil dealings with a blue dragon who called himself Cobalt. I tried to explain it to him, but it was impossible. Even gold dragons find the concept unfathomable, although they acknowledge intellectually that the bond exists. Blue dragons like Cobalt, of course, furiously insist that we merely possess weak spirits and that we imagine our bond with mortals because we wish to be like them.

Only other silver dragons know that we feel the emotions that we inspire in mortals as surely as others might feel a gentle caress or the harsh blow of a fist. Those sensations are increased dramatically should we ever be fortunate—or unfortunate, depending on your point of view— enough to meet that one single mortal with whom our spirit is in complete harmony. Most silver dragons live their entire lives and never experience such bliss and torment, but those who do must pursue this relationship or wither and die. Some would say that the brood that gave birth to me was cursed, for both my sister and I met that one mortal. For her, it was Huma. For me, it is Gilthanas.

I wanted him to love me as I loved him. I *needed* him to love me. For a time, it seemed I had his love as we battled together against the forces of the dragonarmy and risked our lives for the good of all. But after we settled in Kalaman that changed. He started to ignore me, to lose himself in "work" created for the sole purpose of allowing him to avoid me. Only when the city was in crisis had he seemed to acknowledge the bond between our souls. At other times, he refused to listen to all my attempts to explain how his disregard of me wounded me at other times.

As I called upon him to understand that the bond we shared was not a casual thing for me, we had occasional arguments. During one of them, he told me that he could never forgive me for not revealing my true nature as we lay in each other's arms on the shore of the Thon-Sorpon in Southern Ergoth. He refused to see that I had been frightened at the idea that he might reject me. He never could have understood the pain his fear and horror would have inflicted upon me, just as he couldn't comprehend the pain his indifference was putting me through in Kalaman. No matter how hard I tried to explain it to him, he failed to understand the nature of a silver dragon's soul, and so he refused to let his resentment fade. He simply could not accept that Silvara, the elf maid who he loved, did not truly exist.

I finally decided that the only way to make him understand my suffering was for me to put him through the same pain. I had no choice but to leave Kalaman behind. Once he realized that my absence was as painful to him as his indifference had been to me, he would come for me, I thought. I left Kalaman and drifted through the nearby hills for several months, longing desperately to have him near, expecting him to come searching for me. But he never did.

Finally, the pain became too much to bear. I had to retreat to the Dragon Isles and the comfort of my own kind.

But even there, I found no solace. My longing for Gilthanas was too great. I eventually returned to Ansalon, where I struggled with my pain for many months, hoping and praying that he would finally recognize that he needed me as much as I needed him.

But he didn't. I eventually came to face the fact that my mortal soulmate had rejected me and that the pain of his rejection would kill me. But then I found a way to be as free of him as he had made himself of me: by abandoning the form of Silvara. I found a way back to the life of contentment I had once known, and I threw myself into that life with abandon.

But now, decades later, I felt as though I had woken up from a dreamless sleep, my soul again singing with the love that Gilthanas had for me . . . or the love that he had for Silvara, to be more specific.

I rose and put on a robe. I called for a page and asked him to bring me a ranking scribe and all the dispatches about Dark Knights, elves, and any ships that were expected to arrive on Southern Ergoth. The page tried to argue with me. He suggested that it could wait until morning. Further, he said, he was afraid that he might be whipped if he were to awaken a senior scribe at this early hour. I proved to him that I was a far greater threat than a scribe's leather belt. I displayed the strength I possess even in the apparently frail human form I have adopted and with one hand lifted him up under the ceiling. "You will fetch a scribe," I snarled at him, allowing my human form to waver, permitting him to look into my eyes as they truly are. I dropped him to the floor. He fled in terror, a dark stain spreading down his trouser leg. The scribe arrived less than fifteen minutes later.

I stood on the balcony, that one touch of beauty on the castle, letting the wind wash over my skin as the portly man entered, with what few hairs he still possessed standing on end from his pillow. He went on about Dark Knights threatening the stability of Ergoth, about more thanoi arriving in Southern Ergoth, about nothing that I had any interest in hearing and nothing that brought to mind the sensations I had felt when Gilthanas touched me in my sleep.

I eventually realized that the man's teeth were chattering, as the icy wind from the sea—which merely slid across my skin as pleasantly as silk slides across a mortal's body—was rushing into my quarters and chilling him to bone. I dismissed him.

"Y-y-yes, L-lady Arlena," he said, shivering violently. "I h-h-hope the inf-formation was of use."

"Yes, Dolan. You have been very helpful."

I remained on the balcony for another few minutes after he departed, looking in the direction from which I had sensed Gilthanas. I saw the snow-shrouded hills of Eastwatch glittering under the pale moon. Beyond them, I could barely make out the night-black sea.

This was not the first time in recent months that I had sensed Gilthanas in my sleep. On other nights, I had awoken unsure whether it had merely been a dream. But tonight . . . tonight, I was certain. I had dreamt about Gilthanas in the past months. I had sensed him on other nights, but the sensations had never been as strong as they had been this night. Somewhere, nearby, Gilthanas was thinking of me. I could go to him. The dream was still strong enough in my memory that I could find him. I spread my arms and stepped closer the railing, preparing to take on my true form and to soar into the sky.

No. I would not do this.

Gilthanas never loved me. He loved Silvara, a Kagonesti elf. And she no longer exists.

I turned from the balcony and returned to the comfortable surroundings of my quarters. I caught sight of myself in the full-length mirror in the dressing area. I paused to study the form of Lady Arlena Plata, Knight of the Rose.

In recent years, I've found that I cannot adopt a form that isn't pleasing to the eyes of the species I am trying to emulate. In the years immediately following my return to Ansalon from the Dragon Isles, I made several attempts to do so—I found myself longing to be among humans, but I did not want to attract attention, so I endeavored to make myself plain. I failed. I made one last attempt a few months after I had returned to Castle Eastwatch, but settled on the form I wear to this very day.

I let the robe slip from my body and studied myself carefully. I appeared thinner than what I've come to know that most human males find attractive. As Sir Francis once put it, I appeared like the kind of female who "dies trying to bring a baby into the world, but who kin dance circles 'round most Dark Knights while carvin' 'em to bits." The bridge of the nose was too straight. The lips were too thin. The hair with its plain straw color would never inspire bards to write songs. Nonetheless, everything was in perfect proportion; I was as beautiful as the average woman, and more than many—and that after an attempt to not be attractive.

Still, this form was no Silvara. With that thought, my form changed, almost unbidden. My shoulders narrowed as my body grew shorter and slimmer, my skin darkened, and my eyes grew larger and more slanted. My hair turned a silvery-white. The image looking back at me in the mirror was Silvara, a female who was the very pinnacle of what the Kagonesti considered beauty.

"We want your guidance," Lady Riva had said when I first came to Castle Eastwatch with the intent of aiding the Knights here. Naturally, I wore the form of Silvara. "Your experience, wisdom, and insights will be an invaluable aid as we gather strength to oppose Gellidus the White and his minions. But I cannot tolerate you appearing in that fashion. My Knights will find it difficult, and the mercenaries will find it impossible to take you seriously when you appear like that. They will either view you as a fantasy come to life, or they will treat you as a barbarian savage. I need you to be a Knight of Solamnia, not an elf whom my troops might look down upon."

This form had inspired bards to write songs. This form had set the heart of my beloved Gilthanas aflame. This form had brought me much pain and suffering.

It was also the body of a woman who was dead as far as I was concerned. And with her, the bond I had shared with

Gilthanas had died. The day I became Lady Arlena was the day the pain ceased.

With a thought, I resumed the appearance of Lady Arlena. She was respected by her peers and feared by those who would do evil both in Southern Ergoth and in the goblin nation of Sikk'et Hul. She was a warrior whom other Knights trusted and whom they knew would always come to their aid no matter how impossible a battle might seem.

Lady Arlena is a woman who has no need for love. The Knighthood is both her husband and child. She has many friends and enjoys their company, but she never brooks any suggestion of romance between herself and anyone else. She is married to the Order of the Rose, and she has no room for anything else in her heart. Silvara loved a mortal and now she is dead. Lady Arlena now exists where once Silvara had been, and Lady Arlena loves only the Solamnic Orders.

I am Lady Arlena now. The dreams of a dead woman mean nothing . . . and Lady Arlena will not cry over such trifles. The heat from the fireplace is causing her eyes—my eyes—to water.

Lady Arlena does not cry over the lost love of a different life.

I do not cry over the lost love of a different life.

I do not feel Gilthanas's love burning my soul. I feel nothing. I feel nothing.

🍂 🍂 🍂 🍂 🍂

The creaking of the hull timbers was a steady rhythm, reminding the prisoner that he was in fact still alive. The manacles, soaked with saltwater, had long since chafed his wrists raw. His tongue was swollen with thirst, but Knights gave their prisoners only enough water to keep them alive.

Though he was barely conscious, Gilthanas knew that Lethagas was here, as were Banatharl, Carranias, and the other elves. The Knights had told them something of their fate: They sailed toward the mainland—toward a destiny with a monstrous blue dragon called Khellendros. He had plans for the prisoners . . . plans that were unknown, but clearly horrifying, to the Dark Knights.

Gilthanas leaned his head against the hull and closed his eyes. When he squinted hard, turning his imagination back to a full remembrance of his past, he saw just a glimmer of silver scales.

"She's out there still," he whispered, making no sound but drawing comfort from shaping the words with his lips. "And she waits for me . . . I know she does."

Appendix

Using the Appendix

Each entry (or site) contains several sections, which contain information similar to that found within the *Leaves from the Inn of the Last Home* book. All entries have an introduction, a history, and an adventure seed. Each one also contains a section either on secrets or on present-day information, or both:

- **Introduction:** A brief paragraph or two describes a particular site, region, or phenomenon visited by Gilthanas in this book. These descriptions provide cursory information that anyone on Ansalon might know about the place.
- **History:** This section contains information known to people living near the site but not those from other regions. The information in the history often sheds some light on events you read about earlier.
- **Secrets:** This section contains knowledge that very few (if indeed any) people in Ansalon are aware of. Sometimes it includes specific game characteristics so that Narrators or Dungeon Masters (those who mediate the game and directs the storyline for the players) can immediately use the secrets in a roleplaying game.
- **Present Day:** This section describes the present-day condition of the site.
- **Adventure Seed:** This section contains the essential nugget of an adventure that might take place at the site in question. Not all of these seeds take place in the present day.

If the information in this appendix piques your curiosity about adventure games, but you don't know how to get started, ask for the *DRAGONLANCE: FIFTH AGE Dramatic Adventure Game* or DUNGEONS & DRAGONS Game at your local book or hobby store.

The Hill of Sol-Fallon

Silvanesti is a lush, rolling land with a forest that covers hundreds of acres of gently sloped countryside. Some hillocks lie buried by the cultivated oaks and pines, with a leafy canopy above so thick that it never seems brighter than dusk even when the sun shines directly overhead. Waving grass covers other bluffs, allowing visitors to gaze out over the rest of Silvanesti. Such places are quite popular among the elves for stargazing.

No hill in all of Silvanesti, however, offers a view as wondrous as the one from Sol-Fallon.

A History of the Hill of Sol-Fallon

The view from Sol-Fallon has, for as long as any elf can remember, been considered the most breathtakingly beautiful in all of Silvanesti. Those who have visited this site say that the stars seem close enough to reach out and pluck from the sky. Perhaps that explains why Silvanos, the first leader among elves, chose this hill as the site for the first Sinthal-Elish (the Silvanesti elf Council of High Ones) in the year 4000PC.

It was on the Hill of Sol-Fallon that representatives of the most powerful elf families met. There they struck an accord to form the first elven nation and made preparations to defend their new nation from dragon attack. They met here again some seven-hundred-fifty years later, after the dragons were defeated and the elves' sovereignty secured, to elect Silvanos the first Speaker of the Stars.

From that time forward, the Silvanesti elves have revered and honored the Hill of Sol-Fallon. Elves have crafted great works of song and poetry here, and Silvanesti leaders of every generation have come here to consider matters of grave importance. They say that the view from the hill inspires one's mind, and the souls of all those who have come before bolster one's spirit. Also, in the wake of the Chaos War, a new quality has been attributed to the hill.

While the view from Sol-Fallon has always been majestic, in the dead of night it now transforms into something that can be described only as miraculous. At the stroke of midnight, the now-familiar sky with its one pale moon disappears and is replaced by a vision from the past. Three moons once again ride high in the sky, lighting up the countryside as they did before the gods' departure: one white, one red, and one black—though only those who have been trained in the art of dark magic can see the black Nuitari.

This sight, though, is witnessed only from the summit of the hill. Those standing anywhere else, at the foot or even halfway up the Hill of Sol-Fallon, notice nothing strange (other than the look of wonder on the faces of those atop the hill). One must be atop the hill at the stroke of midnight in order to see the display; climbing it later reveals nothing, even if others are still in the midst of their revelation. The vision lasts for as long as the viewer remains on top of Sol-Fallon or until dawn brightens the eastern sky.

Former practitioners of High Sorcery flocked to Sol-Fallon in hopes that the light of the moons would restore their abilities to cast spells. While some of them claimed to feel a sense of euphoria, none ever exhibited a return of their old powers, leading scholars to conclude that the vision is merely an illusion rather than some gods-created miracle (though they have reached no agreement as to the source of the illusion).

Since the raising of the Silvanesti Shield, no one can enter Silvanesti to examine the site. The more paranoid members of the academic community fear that the elves raised the shield for the express purpose of keeping the Hill of Sol-Fallon to themselves. They claim that the moons give off an infinitesimal amount of magical power, which the Silvanesti plan to use to expand their forest home to cover all of eastern Ansalon (an assertion which is belied by the fact that the forest behind the shield seems to be shrinking at an alarming rate).

The Secret of the Hill of Sol-Fallon

While the nightly vision is a well-known mystery of the hill, there is another less-publicized enigma. Some visitors to Sol-Fallon have reported hearing distant, pain-wracked moans that coincide with the vision of the moons.

The truth of the matter is that these sounds have nothing to do with the nightly illusion. Rather, they come from a secret facility built into the base of the hill. In the years after he seized control of Silvanesti, General Konnal needed a cell in which to detain prisoners whose capture, should it become public knowledge, would cause his regime trouble. Konnal's men hollowed out a small cave in the hill and fitted it with bars, making a perfect dungeon into which any dissident could be thrown. As it turned out, shortly after its completion, the cell became home to Gilthanas Solostaran. For twelve years the Qualinesti prince rotted beneath the hill and was certainly the source of every rumor of ghostly moaning.

Gilthanas escaped on the day before the Silvanesti Shield sealed the forest nation from the prying eyes of the outside world. No one knows whom, if anyone, Konnal has imprisoned in the cell since Gilthanas's flight.

Adventure Seed

Though it has been proven that the illusion of the three moons provides no return of High Sorcery or clerical powers, stories circulate within Silvanesti that the vision does have an effect on practitioners of the new magic. Both sorcerers and mystics who have recently visited the Hill of Sol-Fallon report that their spellcasting abilities were severely impaired (and in some cases completely eradicated) after viewing the illusion. The effects have lasted from a few days to nearly an entire month, but so far it has not caused any permanent losses.

One sect of priests of E'li (the elven name for Paladine) claim that this is the punishment the gods of magic inflict on those who would practice the new magic (which these priests consider to be blasphemous). Dissidents whisper that the effect is part of some great scheme by General Konnal to eradicate the practice of magic by anyone who has not sworn allegiance to him. Still others say that Sol-Fallon's illusion is a sorcerous working powered by the magical energy of the forest itself. Since the Silvanesti Shield has been draining the forest of life, the hill has had to find an alternative source of power—spellcasters who visit the site.

Does the illusion actually impair the use of sorcery and mysticism? If so, why is this just being discovered now? If not, what is causing this effect? The gods? General Konnal? To what end? Or is the hill actually a natural energy sponge that soaks up the magical abilities of its visitors?

The Missing City

In the realm of Brass Dragon Overlord Iyesta stands as odd a place as there is in all of Ansalon. Those who travel along the Courrain coastline in this realm eventually see a medium-sized city on the horizon. The city shimmers in the desert heat, occasionally seeming transparent or even blinking out of existence. Many people assume it is merely a mirage. As they draw closer, though, it becomes clear that at least some of the buildings are solid. This is the Missing City.

On the one hand, the city is a spectral town with buildings of the style that the Silvanesti elves built in the years before the first Cataclysm. But that's not all—ghostly figures inhabit the city; these spirits seem to live normal lives completely unaware of the real world around them.

The Missing City is more than a magical curiosity, though. The Legion of Steel, an organization devoted to championing the cause of justice in Ansalon, has built an outpost here, constructing solid buildings that look exactly like the mirage beneath the translucent images. They also have built structures outside the spectral walls (for those whose nerves cannot handle living in the midst of ghostly activity) and constructed a pier so that they can engage in sea trade (since the nearest city is more than one hundred miles away).

A History of the Missing City

Scholars agree that the mirage of the Missing City represents the ancient Silvanesti town of Gal Tra'kalas. A Silvanesti tome records that in the months following the Cataclysm, griffin riders traveled to check on all the elves' settlements. One rider reported that not only was Gal Tra'kalas destroyed, but also noted the following: "The city was haunted by fiends, who took the forms of our brothers and sisters in order to entice us to lower our guard. The city too is reborn in an unholy mockery of life, for though rubble litters the place, the likeness of every building and barn still is visible." From that day forward, Gal Tra'kalas became a shunned place. No Silvanesti was to visit there on pain of death.

So, the site stood empty for centuries. Certainly, nomads and travelers visited occasionally (scholars presume that several plains barbarian folktales regarding "the city of the dead" actually tell of real excursions to the ruins), but no organized group of civilized people set foot on the site until after the Second Cataclysm.

Shortly after the Legion's founding, members of the Legion of Steel scoured the continent for places to build enclaves away from the influence of either the Knights of Solamnia or those of Takhisis. The Missing City seemed an ideal location and symbolically well suited to the Legion's task. They meant themselves to be an invisible order, living among the people and fighting for neither Good nor Evil, but instead for truth and fairness. To build a headquarters under the cover of an existing (if insubstantial) city was perfect.

Today, this Legion cell operates under the leadership of Falaius Taneek, a giant of a barbarian whose reputation of being "tough but fair" has won him the respect of nearly everyone in town. Falaius uses the Missing City as a place to coordinate the actions of their operatives in neighboring

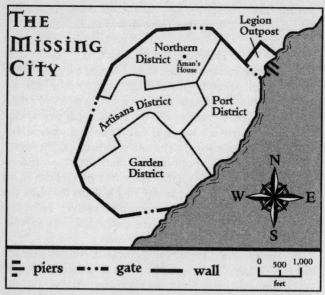

THE
MISSING
CITY

Legion
Outpost

Northern
District
•Aman's
House

Artisans District

Port
District

Garden
District

N
W   E
S

≡ piers   ▪▪•▪ gate   ▬ wall

0   500   1,000
feet

dragon realms, as well as a safe haven for any Legionnaires on Ansalon's eastern coast whose activities make it impossible for them to move about at large.

Residents of the Missing City draw a strong distinction between their home and Gal Tra'kalas. Any solid item belongs to the Missing City, while anything spectral or immaterial is from Gal Tra'kalas. Nearly everyone who visits the city remarks about the unsettling feeling of watching the ghostly residents of Gal Tra'kalas move about their very ordinary lives.

Oddly enough, the residents of the mirage city change in the same way anyone in the real world would. They age, bear and raise offspring, and eventually die. Some occasionally move out of the city. Despite the fact that the population of Gal Tra'kalas was, at the time of its destruction, almost wholly Silvanesti, the ghostly residents of today come from a variety of races and regions.

Many scholars believe the city represents an alternate reality—some tributary of the River of Time in which neither the First nor Second Cataclysm occurred. The Missing City is a window, they say, into a more perfect world than modern-day Krynn. Other scholars believe the mirage is a magical illusion with an unknowable purpose, created by one of the gods (either Majere or Hiddukel, depending on the scholar's bias) before departing Krynn at the time of the first Cataclysm.

Secrets of the Missing City

The Missing City is one immense set of ruins. None of the original buildings still stand (though here and there a section of a wall has survived two cataclysms and several centuries). While the Legion has removed most of the rubble from the sections of town it inhabits, visitors to the rest of the city should move about cautiously: One never knows when an apparently clear doorway might lead to a pit full of jagged boulders.

The city of Gal Tra'kalas was (and still is) divided into four districts. The eastern quarter, known as the Port District, was where most of the city's commerce took place. Small open-air markets dotted the district, and shops of all varieties lined its streets. This district is where the Legion constructed most of their buildings. The hustle and bustle of Gal Tra'kalas is nearly matched by the goings on in this section of the Missing City. Visitors must be wary, lest they mistake a real person for a phantom and walk headlong into him or her.

The other three sections of the ancient city were the Garden District (filled with the ornate and opulent homes of the richest and most powerful families), the Artisans District (where masters of various creative arts made works of unsurpassed beauty), and the Northern District (the only place for those without money, breeding, or skills to live).

In recent years, the Missing City has grown beyond the borders of Gal Tra'kalas (so that people might have a place to go when they tired of walking among the "ghosts"). Falaius Taneek has his base here, and it is the only place a person may build without keeping within the style of Silvanesti architecture.

Adventure Seed

While staying at an inn within the confines of the mirage city, one might awaken in the morning to find that one or more of his or her belongings have become incorporeal. At the same time, one of the items in the room (of roughly the same size as the affected article) that had been ghostly the night before has now turned completely solid. While one ponders what to do, a ghostly figure you've never seen before enters the room, picks up the incorporeal item, and walks out of the room. Before he does, though, he looks directly at him or her and winks mischievously.

What is happening? Who is the old man? If he is from Gal Tra'kalas, why can he see the "real" person when no one else from the mirage city can? How did he switch the articles, and is there a way to reverse the process? Is it possible to bring people back and forth in the same manner?

Ruined Purstal

Stretching across the eastern Plains of Dust like the shattered spine of a long-dead giant is the King's Road. Prior to the Cataclysm, the Silvanesti nobles and merchants traveled in marvelous carriages on this elevated highway. Trade cities lay along its length, the greatest of these being Purstal. Once the pride and joy of the nation of Kharolis, the city became another victim of the circumstances that led to the Cataclysm.

A History of Purstal

As the Empire of Ergoth entered its Golden Age, some two thousand years before the Cataclysm, one of its ancient enemies became an ally: the nation of Kharolis. Founded when scattered tribes united to stand against the conquering hordes of Ackal Ergot, the Kharolish inscribed the name of their nation alongside the other signatures of the original Swordsheath Scroll, despite irreconcilable cultural differences with their Ergothian neighbors. (The Kharolish, named for the warrior woman who united them, were ruled by a matrilineal monarchy while the Ergothians were patriarchal in all things.)

Following the signing of the Swordsheath Scroll, trade between all the civilized nations greatly increased, and the border town of Purstal was in a perfect location to benefit. Located where the borders of Ergoth, Silvanesti, and Kharolis met, the city became a hub of overland trade between the three nations. As it grew in size and importance, the elves of House Mason constructed one of the wonders of pre-Cataclysmic Ansalon: the King's Road. Molded rather than carved from stone, this marvel ran thirty feet above the ground and was supported by great pillars for some six hundred miles, starting from the western shore of the River Thon-Thalas in Silvanesti and terminating in Purstal. The city was never widely recognized for anything—such as the fabled ships of Tarsis, the Tower of High Sorcery in Palanthas, or the golden domes of the Imperial Palace in Daltigoth—but in the space of two hundred years it nonetheless became very important.

When the provinces that would eventually become Solamnia declared their independence from Ergoth, Purstal's importance only grew. The newly established nation was hungry for trade goods, and its leaders anxiously wished to remain on good terms with the Silvanesti Speaker of the Stars because of the nation's well-crafted elven goods. The Kharolish people were more than happy to oblige and performed a balancing act between Solamnia and the Empire of Ergoth, trading with both nations without offending either side.

As Istar became increasingly powerful in the wake of the Third Dragon War, however, Kharolis's balancing act came to an end. With Solamnia and Istar taking hostile stances toward Ergoth, the nation of Kharolis joined them; Solamnia was dominant militarily and Istar was increasingly powerful as a trade nation, so there seemed little point to appease Kharolis—a nation in shambles. When Istar began imposing and aggressively enforcing trade standards upon other realms, Kharolis willingly adopted them. The political stance of the nation lessened Purstal's importance somewhat, as the Silvanesti remained allies of the Empire of Ergoth, but elven merchants continued nonetheless to come to Purstal even after they had stopped trading with Istar proper.

In 280PC, with the installation of the first Kingpriest, Kharolis saw a glimmering of what the future was to bring. In his first address to the people of Istar, the Kingpriest stated that mortal women were to be subservient to mortal men, as Mishakal was subservient to Paladine. Although Istar's ambassadors quickly apologized to the outraged Queen of Kharolis, a succession of Kingpriests carried this viewpoint forward. When Istar finally implemented the Proclamation of Manifest Virtue, with its lists of "evils" the nation was devoted to combating, a passage appeared to be directed squarely at Kharolis: "It is a sin for Woman to elevate herself above Man. As Paladine rules over the gods of Good, so shall Man rule over righteous mortals. Any Woman who elevates herself above Man is doing the will of the Dark Queen."

Kharolis expelled all of Istar's priests from within its borders, triggering several uprisings among the people. Many of them had accepted Istar's position that the Kingpriest was the chosen intermediary between Krynn and the gods. As the nation descended into chaos, Istar's legions invaded. Purstal was the first major city besieged. The legions swiftly took control of the eastern province of the nation, as well as the western portions of Silvanesti that Speaker Lorac left uninhabited (he had ordered his people to the far side of the River Thon-Thalas after the Proclamation of Manifest Virtue).

The siege of Purstal lasted from 89PC to 82PC. Kharolis had not made much effort to muster an army, trusting instead in the might of Solamnia to protect them against the only potential enemy they had feared: Ergoth. While the Solamnic Knights were initially happy to help the Kharolish army subdue the armed uprisings in various parts of the nation, in 83PC, the Kingpriest ordered the Grand Master to withdraw all Knights and troops from Kharolis, except for those serving in the garrison in Tarsis. While the pretense was one of reinforcing the legions fighting the goblin and ogre uprisings in the Khalkist Mountains, it was clear to all observers that the objective was to weaken the Kharolish government's ability to control its countryside. The Grand Master, however, withdrew only half the number of troops that the Kingpriest had requested, and the Silvanesti House Advocate had been covertly supporting Purstal ever since Istar's legions marched on it. Nevertheles, Kharolis no longer had the resources to both fight Istar for control over its eastern lands and keep the uprisings from spreading like wildfire.

In the fall of 82PC, the legions of Istar broke down the gates of Purstal. The streets ran red with the blood of both its defenders and civilian citizens. The city's last mayor is said to have called upon the darkest of magics to raise the spirits of the slain citizens and turn them upon the legions.

Whether the tale is true or not, Purstal's defenders inflicted terrible casualties upon Istar's legions as their city fell. The city was then set ablaze, the earth around it salted, and it was never resettled. The legions left the bodies of the slain citizens for scavengers to consume, but they carried all of Purstal's riches back to Istar. Within the next fifty years, the wealth of most of Kharolis followed; the last queen is said to have been reduced to a personal concubine of the Kingpriest. When the Cataclysm destroyed Istar, the resulting quakes around Purstal toppled the remaining few buildings left standing.

Secrets of Purstal

Five centuries after its destruction, Purstal remains in ruins. The harsh desert climate around the city has discouraged any civilized folk to resettle the site. Additionally, the rumors of the curse imposed by its last Lord Mayor keep most nomads away from it.

Still, such locations are to adventurers as honey is to flies. By all reports, several types of undead inhabit the city. Some say they are the citizens of Purstal and the legionnaires of Istar still fighting for control of the city. Others say the place has become a magnet for the spirits of Evil dead from all across Ansalon, and that these creatures attack anyone who enters the ruins. Yet others claim the undead go through everyday routines and remain oblivious to the living when they enter their realm. (This last rumor is largely discounted as coming from ignorant folks confusing Purstal with Missing City to the south.) Despite this threat, many brave bands have ventured into Purstal and had varying experiences, though by all accounts nobody has any forgotten hoards.

Adventure Seeds

While visiting Tarsis, the heroes meet Davin Luckwand, the eldest son of Sharina Luckwand, the Lady of Tarsis. While working to catalog the long-neglected records of the city, he came across a missive that dates from four years before the Cataclysm. One of these was a letter to Queen Kharolis XII, the young monarch who was reputed to have been enslaved in Istar. In it, an unnamed agent stated that he had confirmed that the bulk of the Purstal City Treasury was still concealed in the secret vault. Part of the letter contains directions to that vault and a warning about the many new traps that the agent has built around it. He says that he will await the queen's arrival in Elial, and that they will then go with a force to Purstal to collect the wealth and use some of it to buy safe passage to Ergoth. "The spies of the Kingpriest will never suspect that you are fleeing in that direction," the message ends. The scholarly young man knows this to be wrong—Istar's priests supposedly took the queen captive the year the letter is dated.

Davin wants the heroes to help him find the treasure hidden in Purstal. He believes that some of the references in the letter will help them succeed where no one else has. He wants to use the bulk of the money to hire mercenaries or to help the Legion of Steel in Tarsis muster a large armed force and liberate its people from the oppressive rule of Beryl the Green Wyrm and her Dark Knight minions.

A bitter twist in this tale may be that Davin is actually an agent of Beryl. He betrays the heroes after they have helped him get through the dangers of the city

Is there hidden treasure in Purstal? Is the city truly infested with thousands of undead? That's up to you to decide. (In the case of Davin the Betrayer, here's a suggestion: A trio of adventurers looted the treasury of Purstal decades ago. All that remains are sacks of copper pieces and a couple of dented gold crowns. The total value of the treasure in this betrayal scenario is 230 steel pieces.)

The Town of Stone Rose

As towns go, Stone Rose is small. Home to about two hundred hardy souls, it is one of only three permanent settlements along the Run in the Plains of Dust. Unlike the other two (Duntol and Willik), Stone Rose is not a trading post, though centaur and human barbarian tribes occasionally use it as a convenient meeting spot. In fact, the town seems to serve no purpose other than as a navigation point, and it likely would have become deserted long ago if not for the garden from which Stone Rose draws its name.

A History of Stone Rose

The settlement that later became Stone Rose was founded during the Age of Dreams, when the plains were still fertile, farmable land. In fact, the town began as a marketplace where farmers and artisans from the region could sell their goods.

Little or nothing of interest is known to have happened in the town, until roughly one hundred years before the First

Cataclysm, when a Solamnic Knight brought tales of a town with "a garden of stone roses" to Vingaard Keep. It soon became fashionable, and later expected, for Knights to make a pilgrimage to Stone Rose within five years of passing the Knight's Trial; the Knighthood encouraged members of the Order of the Rose to make the journey at least once every decade. This tradition faded in the wake of the Cataclysm.

No reliable data exists on the creation of the Garden in Stone Rose, but two legends have survived to the present day. The first concerns a Black-Robed mage who laid a curse upon an existing rose garden (scholars are in agreement that, if this tale is true, the spell must have been cast around the time of the Kinslayer War). The other tale centers around a Kharolish princess named Kojen who defied the dictates of the Proclamation of Manifest Virtue. Many folktales of the time center on similar figures, and there is no reason to give one particular story credence over any of the others.

Following the first Cataclysm, Stone Rose remained one of the most intriguing places in southern Ansalon, and anyone brave enough to travel made it a point to visit. However, due to its now remote location, the town drew fewer and fewer travelers until it nearly stopped appearing on maps.

A community still lived within the town, though. Many of the folk who, in years past, provided lodging and amenities to the journeying Knights remained in Stone Rose. They adjusted their way of life, irrigating and farming where possible. After all, they reasoned, the Garden is still here—eventually people will start visiting again. This, however, turned out to be far from true.

Today, the only people who regularly visit Stone Rose are merchants taking their caravans along the Run (the road that follows the borders of the modern realm of Duntollik), nomadic tribes of humans or centaurs looking for trading partners, and travelers who have lost their way. None of them, as a rule, have any clue that the Garden of Stone Rose (and occasionally, even the town itself) exist.

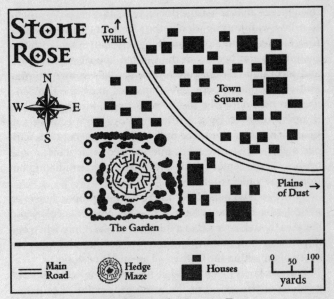

Stone Rose in the Present Day

The modern town of Stone Rose is nothing more than a collection of aging buildings. The town square is the remnant of the town's once popular open-air market. Now, the only merchants who visit the square are those who bed their horses or camels down there for the night.

Although the desert has taken a severe toll on nearly every building in town, several impressive mansions from Stone Rose's heyday still stand. The most noteworthy edifice in town, though, is the arched marble doorway and crumbling tower that locals call "the Castle."

Although these structures seem as though they might once have belonged to a great palace or manor, nobody can find evidence that any such building stood on the site. Historians believe the locals built faux ruins as an added attraction to the Garden, which lies directly behind the archway.

The Castle stands at the top of a low hill. After walking

through the arched marble doorway, visitors step directly up to a low wall that overlooks the Garden of Stone Rose. At first, one might not notice anything unusual; from a distance, the bushes and hedges in the Garden appear quite natural and seem quite reminiscent of rose gardens in many typical affluent neighborhoods. Five topiaries mark the Garden's western boundary (the southernmost sculpture is of a silver dragon, followed by a griffin, gold dragon, pegasus, and finally a brass dragon). The bulk of the Garden contains various styles of hanging roses interspersed with short, round bushes. At the center stands a low hedge maze radiating out from a tiny vallenwood tree.

A visitor who gets closer to the Garden proper, however, notices that the plants have a strange, off-white color, and shine as though covered in a thin film of wax. Only when one draws very near is it evident the roses, stems, and leaves of every plant within the Garden all are made of stone.

No one knows exactly what type of stone composes the garden—it has many of the same properties of polished marble, but scholars insist it does not resemble any natural rock found in Ansalon. Geomancers who came to study the Garden found that, even with their magical control over rocks of all sorts, they could not affect the stone roses. In fact, as far back as anyone can recall, no weapon, spell, or force of nature has so much as scratched any of the "plants" here.

The Garden is generally a quiet and solemn place where people are left alone with their thoughts. The caretaker, a kindly man in his mid-fifties named Tam Granger, has quite a keen eye for assessing people's moods. When he sees someone who needs a body to talk to, he ambles up with a friendly smile on his face and lends them his ear.

Adventure Seed

One day a party of heroes are summoned to investigate reports that the stone roses in the Garden are actually growing. In fact, anyone who has been to the Garden before notices that all the hedges are larger and more disheveled than they appeared on the last visit. This has Tam Granger in a snit, because the plants remain impervious to all his gardening tools. To make matters worse, stone seedlings are springing up all over the city. One woman became trapped in her home when several stone plants grew across the only door to the building.

Why have the stone roses suddenly begun to grow after so many centuries of lifelessness? Is there an outside force at work, or is this merely part of the Garden's curse? Can the heroes find a way to stop the growth, or at the very least, an effective method of trimming the plants? What will happen if these petrified plants begin to spread across the continent?

Frozen Past

Millennia ago, a bizarre race of diminutive creatures known as the huldrefolk dwelled in distant corners of Krynn. Their origins remain a mystery and all that remains of them are ancient ruins of their cities and sacred sites. Without fail, these sites remain virtual sinkholes of magical energy even to the present day.

A History of Frozen Past

Untold centuries ago, the huldrefolk built one of their mightiest cities on the storm-tossed waters of the Courrain Ocean. Their skill with elemental magic has yet to be matched by any save the gods, and it was a fusion of earth, water, and air magic that allowed them to create a city the size of Palanthas that hovered above the waves.

The earliest records of this city are found in Silvanost. They tell of elven sailors trading with the huldre and learning elemental magic from them. Only the bravest or greediest of seafarers would trade with the huldrefolk, as the strange race was just as likely to destroy the vessel and enslave the crew as offer them favorable trade terms and insights into their magical secrets.

The accounts indicate that the city was a tangle of spires, streets, bridges, twisting alleys, and tremendous statues of beings that no elf had ever witnessed. The most amazing of these was, according to Daralthanias Farsailer, one of the founders of House Mariner, a levitating statue of a spherical creature whose face consisted of a single huge eye and a wide mouth filled with terribly sharp teeth. Upon its top writhed sculpted stalks, at the end of which ogled a dozen additional stone eyes. The huldrefolk said it was a terrible beast from beyond the stars. Daralthanias didn't press for more information, but his brief account of this encounter gave rise to a variety of dramatic bard tales where foolish wizards cast spells that bring the toothy-mawed monsters down upon Silvanesti by the dozens.

The huldrefolk city's name sounded vaguely like "Frozen Past" pronounced in the huldre tongue. Since the huldre just repeated the name when asked "What does it mean?" that's how the elves started referring to the city.

Although the huldrefolk abandoned Frozen Past many centuries later, the city seemed oddly unaffected by the passage of time. Although the huldre had left the city with food remaining in their pantries and, in some cases, even forges still burning in workshops, the food never spoiled, dust never gathered, and flames never flickered out. It was as though time no longer mattered in the city—nothing decayed, fire burned but didn't consume any fuel, and those who spent time in the city never got tired or hungry. If they tried to eat, they felt sick and bloated. Sleep was impossible.

However, as soon as someone left the city, hunger and fatigue would overtake them. One report tells of an elven scholar who spent three weeks searching the city in the hopes of finding a way to translate the bizarre huldrefolk written language. Whether he did will never be known, because the moment he stepped from the city's wide dock and onto the gangplank leading to his ship, he dropped dead from starvation and dehydration.

After making this discovery, the elves avoided the city, believing it dangerous, pointless, and impractical to attempt to unlock the secrets of the huldrefolk. They did discover that a large arch in the city's southwestern quarter actually functioned as a teleportal. It allowed those who figured out how to activate it to cross hundreds of miles to another abandoned huldrefolk city that hovered above the waves of the Turbidus Ocean, off the southern shores of Kharolis. Unfortunately the elves could never activate this wondrous teleportal the same way twice, so soon they abandoned it as well.

After the Cataclysm, the southern glacier rapidly moved northward. Although its advance crushed islands and southern coastal cities, the huldrefolk cities south of Ansalon remained immovable and indestructible; soon they were completely encased in the ice . . . all but two massive arches that rose over the glaciers. These arches are the focus of the teleportals that allow instant passage between the two cities, and they have reportedly remained functional even in the wake of the gods' departure.

So encased, the name Frozen Past seems even more appropriate for the mysterious huldrefolk city than ever before.

Frozen Past in the Present Day

Despite the efforts of the white dragons living in this area, the southern glacier is slowly starting to retreat from this part of Ansalon. In contrast with the incredible speed at which it expanded from the south pole in the centuries following the Cataclysm, it is pulling back very slowly, moving only a fraction of an inch each year.

Still, despite the fact that Frozen Past and its sister city lay buried under tons of ice, the teleportals remain visible. They appear like giant stone arches surrounded by irregular bumps in the ice. Drawing closer, explorers who look down can see the hazy forms of the buried city beneath their feet. As in ages past, it is virtually impossible to figure out how the teleportals function or when they will activate. Rumors about these miraculous devices aren't hard to come by—including stories of adventurers who have stepped through an active arch never to be seen again.

As the glacier has started to retreat, another legendary area of Frozen Past has been freed from the ice. Warmer winds may have caused the glacier that had engulfed it to melt quicker than other parts of the ice, or perhaps the city's magic caused it to retreat more quickly.

Shortly before the Silvanesti decided that Frozen Past was too dangerous to explore, a young elf named Eli Brightsun found a finely crafted, enchanted boat. According to the stories he told, this magical boat took him to whatever destination his heart desired; his father had been taken captive by human pirates a few weeks earlier, and while Eli sat in the boat wishing he could sail it to where they might have taken him, the boat suddenly moved. It delivered the young elf unfailingly to a secret coastal village on the shores of what someday would become the mighty merchant nation of Istar.

The story was written down, but ultimately was lost in the dusty archives of the Imperial University in Ergoth and the Royal Archives in Silvanesti. When Emperor Mercadior Redic VI of Ergoth ordered the Imperial library refurbished, the story resurfaced. Recognizing the potential of a boat that could transport passengers unfailingly to whatever destination they desire, the emperor dispatched adventurers to Icewall to look for the huldrefolk city and the boat. Several returned to Ergoth, some even brought a boat along with them, but it was never the correct boat. Many other groups simply vanished without trace.

Secrets of the Huldreboat

The huldreboat is an artifact created by the huldrefolk, and like most of their other creations, it functions in a way that seems bizarre and impractical to other beings.

The boat is twenty-five feet in length and it appears as new as though its creators had just hammered the final nail into its hull. The planks are smooth and the hull always remains polished to a high sheen. The boat and its passengers are never subject to the elements no matter how severe. The boat is also immune to the passage of time, although its passengers aren't. Therefore, at the aft end there is a cask of water and a crate containing loaves of bread. Upon inspection, the passengers can see that the provisions would last a single person for an entire month.

Carved upon the ship's transom is elaborate scrollwork. The words are written in the huldre language—a script which no mortal is ever known to have mastered. Appropriate divinatory magic allows passengers of the boat to decipher the writing:

> *I gift this vessel to my people*
> *So that we can travel safely where we will*
> *Trading Meaningless Time for Precious Life.*
> *You who would pilot, touch these words*
> *Speak of the place or person you seek*
> *And you shall arrive safely and without fail at your destination*
> *So long as it stands by the Element of my birth—Eternal Water*

If someone touches the writing and focuses on a destination (or person) after launching the boat into open water, it starts to head away from the shore. After some three hundred yards of travel, a fogbank mysteriously rolls in and rapidly engulfs the boat. The riders then find themselves in a fog-shrouded environment where all sounds, except the lapping of the waves against the boat's hull, seem strangely subdued—the sound of the water in contrast is somehow amplified.

For those riding in the boat, twenty-five hours pass for every one hundred miles of distance between the destination and the point of origin; if the trip is less than one hundred miles, a full twenty-five hours pass anyway. The distance is calculated in a straight line, regardless of whatever terrain might exist between the point of origin and the destination. The boat can even carry its controller and passengers to unconnected bodies of water. The destination must have enough water for the boat to sail upon, though.

However, no matter how many days the trip seems to take for the passengers in the boat, five years pass in the world beyond the fog bank. It doesn't matter whether the distance covered is ten miles or on thousand miles—five years always pass between the moment the boat enters the fog bank to the point it emerges at its destination.

Once engulfed in the fog, it is possible for the controller to change the destination by touching the transom again and expressing his or her new desire. However, the distance to the new destination is calculated from the point of origin. No actual time is added to the journey.

The exact properties of the boat cannot be immediately discerned by any group of heroes should they find it. For example, only experience will tell them of the effect that causes five years to pass whenever a journey is undertaken. (Narrators should think carefully before introducing this boat into their campaigns unless they *want* time to pass without the heroes being able to affect events.)

Finally, the huldreboat always returns to Frozen Past after use. If left for more than three days in a port other than one within fifty miles of Frozen Past, the boat vanishes without warning or trace. In truth, it is magically transported back to Frozen Past, appearing there instantly. Anyone who is on-board at the time of this transport travels with it.

Adventure Seed

The Emperor of Ergoth commissions a party of heroes to find Frozen Past and the magical boat that is mentioned in the ancient Silvanesti text. Should the heroes successfully reach Frozen Past, they may have to face thanoi, other adventurers, or perhaps even some huldrefolk who have returned from wherever they disappeared to so long ago.

Perhaps the heroes accidentally activate the huldre portal while there. The portal might take them to other abandoned cities, or it may take them to an inhabited place where they can learn the secrets of the huldrefolk.

Claren Elian

Located east of the Goodlund Peninsula, Claren Elian has been the object of legends since the days when Silvanesti merchant vessels were common sights in Istar's harbors. A heavily forested island, it has nonetheless not been plundered by minotaurs for lumber and virtually no known exploration of it has been undertaken—even by kender.

Most people in eastern Ansalon believe the tales that powerful forest spirits dwell on the island. The fact that those known to have embarked on expeditions to Claren Elian have failed to return, or have returned with tales of terrible beasts lurking in the forests, reinforce the perception that the stories of the island are anything but kender tales.

In truth, the island is home to beings who are at once much less and much more than the legends claim.

A History of Claren Elian

Claren Elian is inhabited by the Ran-Eli, a little known culture that has lived in isolation for many centuries. They were once peaceful philosophers, but after being enslaved by magic-using dwarves, called scions, to help build the city of Claren Elian, they sought to master every form of combat so they would never be enslaved again.

Their society is strongly patriarchal, and the measure of a man equals his skill at arms. The greatest honor for a male of the Ran-Eli is to become a Master of Rank. These are the greatest warriors among them, and one reaches this stage only by surviving a grueling series of tests. The highest honor for a woman is to bear the children of a Master of Rank.

Before the Cataclysm, the Ran-Eli dwelled high in the eastern mountains of Istar, interacting with others only when they were sought out. More than once, they served as assassins for the Kingpriest, but mostly they kept to themselves. When the Cataclysm struck, the vast majority of the Ran-Eli warriors were killed, leaving only women, children, and the elders—the master philosophers of the fighting orders. Only the highest of the mountain villages and the city of Claren Elian survived. Claren Elian itself is now known as the Forbidden City, for only the Masters of Rank go there or can give permission to visit it.

From this base, they rebuilt. They continued to hone their fighting abilities and became the greatest of all warriors and assassins in Ansalon, despite the fact that they rarely used their skills beyond the confines to their island. (Many explorers, however, met their end on an Elian blade.)

Claren Elian in the Present Day

Only skilled sailors can approach Claren Elian safely. The waters around it are fraught with reefs, and both the winds and currents are unpredictable, making the waters dangerous even for expert crews.

The eastern, southern, and most of the northern shores of the island rise steeply from the Southern Courrain Ocean. These sheer cliffs and the local currents can pound ships with unwary crews to tinder. Dark, forbidding forests stand atop the cliffs.

The western and part of the northern coasts are lined with narrow beaches of black sand. However, reaching these beaches can be very dangerous. The waters are shallow and rife with reefs, making it dangerous to bring even small boats close to the island. As the shore continues north, cliffs start to rise about fifteen to twenty feet from the beaches.

Larger vessels can approach the island at only one well-known place. In the decades before the Second Cataclysm, Illtide Bay emerged as a regular portage for the vessels under the command of the notorious Gad Maccaby. He charted a safe course through the reefs, reportedly at the cost of two

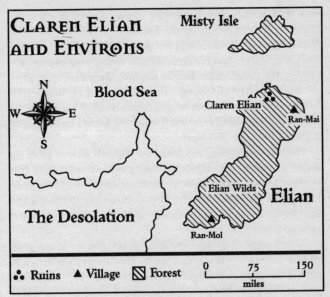

CLAREN ELIAN AND ENVIRONS

Misty Isle

Blood Sea

Claren Elian

Ran-Mai

N W E S

The Desolation

Elian Wilds   Elian

Ran-Mol

⠿ Ruins   ▲ Village   ◩ Forest |0   75   150|
                                        miles

ships. His raiders could anchor in a well-sheltered natural harbor and replenish their water supplies from the falls of pure, sweet-tasting water that tumbled over the fifteen-foot cliff onto the beach.

Although Maccaby's grandson, Scarrel Maccaby, continues to plague shipping in the Blood Sea, he does not make use of Claren Elian. When Malystryx, the great red dragon, seized control of the Goodlund Peninsula in 3SC, she almost failed to notice the Ran-Eli.

Almost.

Upon transforming the Goodlund Peninsula into a volcanic wasteland, she turned to the islands off the coast. She realized that the skilled killers on the island could be of use, and she set about to intimidate them. After burning a swath across the island and destroying the entire population of a village, she realized they would die rather than submit. She tried a different approach and sent an emissary to learn how she might earn their submission. The leader of the Masters of Rank, the Superior Master, said that the Emissary would have to best him in combat. She did, and the people of Ran-Eil swore allegiance to Malys. As a result, Scarrel does not want to draw too close to the shores controlled by the Red Marauder.

The majority of Claren Elian is covered by lush green forests, and even though Malys demonstrated her power by scorching the island's center, the hearty forests have already started to reclaim that land.

No obvious paths lead from the island's shores to its interior, and would-be explorers must cut their own trails. This is slow going, with a party covering only one mile in an hour. Once away from the shore, however, they start to encounter overgrown blocks of stone and toppled pillars here and there.

These signs of ancient civilization become more common as one moves northward. Finally, the forest falls away to reveal the crystal ruins of a once glorious city, now overgrown and resembling a gigantic garden. Pillared courtyards vie for attention with many tiered buildings that tower as high as sixty feet. Friezes of serpents and flowers decorate everything. Ornate statues stand everywhere, representing idealized dwarves, and many walls are carved with scenes of dwarves being served by human slaves. At the heart of the city is a one-hundred-fifty-foot building. Slender crystal towers capture and focus the light onto the center palace, which sparkles like a thousand stars.

Claren Elian enjoys a mild climate for most of the year, thanks to warm southern currents from the Blood Sea. Summer lasts for nine months of the year, and winter is only a dulling of the ever-present heat.

Adventure Seed

Mysterious assassins are stalking Palin Majere and several of the students at the Academy of Sorcery. Palin believes these are the same group of assassins who attempted to kill

Goldmoon a few months prior. Is there a connection? Is someone trying to stop the resurgence of magic in Ansalon? If so, who?

Heroes can become involved and find themselves targeted for assassination themselves. Eventually, they find clues that lead them to Claren Elian. Here, the Superior Master directs them to the city of living crystal, explaining that many of his people have fallen victim to the sorcerous control of an insane scion who has recently reappeared within the city. He says that unless the heroes slay this evil being, the scion will continue to force the Ran-Eli to destroy those working to unlock the foundations of Krynn's magic.

The heroes must brave a maze of fantastic creatures and living plants before coming face to face with one of the most powerful magical beings the world has ever known.

Dragon's Graveyard

On the northeastern coast of Ansalon is a secret graveyard for the Good dragons. Dragons too sick or too severely injured to reach the Dragon Isles come to this secluded area where they can enter the sea and disappear. For centuries, adventurers who heard the legend of the Dragon's Graveyard have sought for this place where dragon bones and treasure are piled higher than a kender's head.

A History of the Dragon's Graveyard

Although the Dragon's Graveyard has been popularized through stories that are told and retold in taverns, few people, save Ergothian bards and a handful of scholars, know the true origin of the tales. Fewer still realize that the stories actually have basis in fact.

In one of the compilations of works credited to Quivalen Soth, a brief song tells the story of a silver dragon who cried out to the gods for protection after the body of his mate was seized by humans and used for food, clothes, and tools. Although Paladine seemed deaf to the dragon's fears,

Habbakuk and Branchala answered, creating a place to which dying metallic dragons could retreat and where their physical forms would be protected from desecration by mortals. The gods combined their powers and raised a tiny island from the sea, a few miles off the northern shore of Ansalon. Here, if a Good dragon raised his or her voice in song, a grave would open. The dragon would lie down and when the might creature expired, the earth would bury them body in a grave that no one would ever find.

For once, the legends are completely accurate. Although the island itself sank beneath the Turbidus Ocean when the lands of Nordmaar rose from the depths during the Cataclysm, the Dragon's Graveyard still exists as a place where Good dragons can magically inter their bodies at death. Where before the dragons would either have to fly or swim roughly thirty miles from the coast, they need now only walk to a secluded cove on the northern shore of Estwilde. There the waves open up to swallow them after they sing a song that is holy to Branchala and Habbakuk.

The Dragon's Graveyard in the Present Day

The Dragon's Graveyard remains a key site to metallic dragons. Parents are considered derelict in their duty to educate their offspring properly if they fail to tell their young about the Dragon's Graveyard. Despite the departure of the gods from Ansalon, the site retains its magic and continues to render the corpses of Good dragons inaccessible to those who want to desecrate them.

The cove that allows access to the Dragon's Graveyard can be reached by boat or through a narrow pass that leads through the hills and granite cliffs that make up Estwilde's northern shore.

Although apparently free of dragon domination, members of the normally peaceful Lor-Tai tribe of Estwilde have taken an oddly militant posture recently against those who enter their territory, which includes the hills and cliffs around the

Dragon's Graveyard. In ages past, the Lor-Tai were simple shepherds, but with the advent of the Age of Mortals, they seem to have been transformed into fierce warriors—perhaps a natural reaction to the perpetual twilight that has descended to the west and the dragon overlords that have seized territory to the east of them. Further, they have been seen constructing idols of dragons, before which they perform some ceremonies. Few outsiders have witnessed these ceremonies and escaped with their lives.

Adventure Seed

An Aesthetic from the Library of the Ages might hire a group of heroes to escort him safely to the Isle of Schallsea. Iryl Songbrook, long retired from the life of an adventurer, operates the Cozy Hearth Inn in the town of Schallsea and writes histories of the Citadel of Light and its members for the Great Library. The Aesthetic claims to have been sent to the isle by Bertrem to gather more details about the Dragon's Graveyard, as well as directions on how to get there. (Iryl's histories consist mostly of her own observations and thoughts and pay little attention to trivialities like where the events she talks about took place.)

As the heroes and the scholar meet with Iryl, a group of men from Claren Elian attempt to kidnap her. If the heroes take any of the attackers alive, the heroes can force them to reveal that Malys has been tracking the scholar's progress and is determined to find the location of the Dragon's Graveyard herself. They don't know her plans or what aroused her interest in the site.

The City of Kalaman

Kalaman is a key port on the northern shore of Ansalon. The city sits on the estuary of the Vingaard River, and its harbor is deep enough to accomodate all but the largest of merchant ships.

A History of Kalaman

Grown from a fishing village by ambitious Istar merchants three centuries before the Cataclysm, Kalaman has been the center of trade in Nightlund for well over half a millennium. The city's population remained constant from the Cataclysm to the Chaos War, though Palanthas eclipsed its status as the chief northern port after the destruction of Istar.

Almost since its foundation, the people of Kalaman were, generally speaking, happy and prosperous. The poor inhabited a small section of the city, but even they lived better off than the poor of other cities did. The lords of Kalaman descended from a line of Solamnic Knights who, after the Cataclysm, swore off that heritage for political reasons. Still, these lords still held to the ideals of the Knighthood. For generations, Kalaman kept its walls in good repair, trained its defenders to be vigilant and competent, and even maintained a small fleet of four war barges to assist in the defense of the harbor.

In the early stages of the dragonarmies' western offensive, Kalaman fell through treachery rather than siege or honest battle. Dragonarmy agents infiltrated the city and murdered most of its defenders, the lord Knight, and his family as they slept. Only one member of the ruling family was spared— Calof, the third and youngest son of the lord. Dragonarmy galleys sailed into the harbor uncontested and defeated Kalaman's war barges with little resistance. When the new day broke over the city, the citizens awoke to find themselves with new masters.

Just as the city was the first to fall to the dragonarmies, so was it the first to be liberated by the Whitestone Army under the command of Laurana, the Golden General. Around the time Gilthanas assumed the position of military governor, elements of the Blue Dragonarmy made several attempts to retake the city, each of which failed due to the expert military leadership of Gilthanas and Silvara.

As the threat of the dragonarmies waned, Gilthanas involved himself more and more with the politics of Kalaman. During these years, citizens reported seeing Silvara wandering listlessly through the streets in her guise as a Kagonesti. Occasionally, her spirits would seem to lift when someone needed her help in settling a dispute or when a merchant or mapmaker invited her on an expedition. More often than not, however, the citizens felt uncomfortable about approaching her.

Eventually, Silvara was seen no more. Some claim she left the city after a cabal of corrupt merchants and shipbuilders tried to trick her into eliminating their competition. Others claim she left because Gilthanas had grown to hate her since she was not truly an elf. Whatever the truth, several people last saw her flying north along the coast, the setting sun glinting off her magnificent silver scales.

When the Dark Knights invaded Ansalon during the Summer of Chaos, the citizens of Kalaman found themselves wishing for the dragon and the elf who had led them through the dark years. Those men the Dark Knights didn't kill were relocated to Neraka to serve as slaves.

In the wake of the Chaos War, the strange twilight that spread from Dargaard Keep to encompass all of Nightlund seeped across Kalaman and the estuary. For more than two decades, the city has seen neither night nor day, leaving the local vegetation weak and sickly. A steady migration of people away from the darkness has drained the population even further.

Kalaman in the Present Day

From its earliest days, the harbor of Kalaman served large merchant vessels. The docks are wide, making it easy to load cargo to or from more than one ship at a time. The lords of the city consistently built and maintained warehouses along the waterfront rather than the taverns and houses of ill repute so many other cities display next to their ports. This arrange-

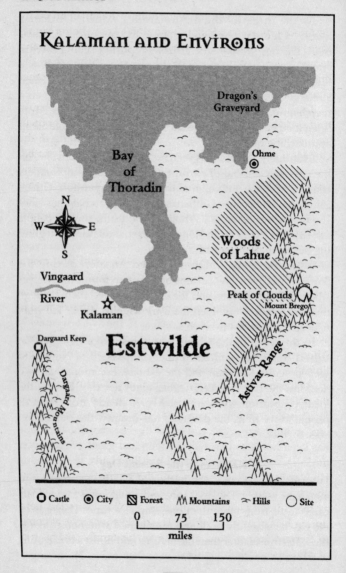

KALAMAN AND ENVIRONS

Dragon's
Graveyard

Bay
of
Thoradin

Ohme

N
W   E
S

Woods
of
Lahue

Vingaard

River

Peak of Clouds
Mount Brego

Kalaman

Dargaard Keep

Estwilde

Dargaard Mountains

Astivar Range

O Castle   ◉ City   ◪ Forest   ⋀⋀ Mountains   ⌢ Hills   ◯ Site

0   75   150
miles

ment always has given the waterfront of Kalaman an oddly deserted appearance. Sailors who don't know better sometimes feel their hearts sink when they put into the port and see only rows of austere gray buildings, rather than the hustle and bustle of welcoming inns they experience in other cities.

The only structures along the docks not intended to house trade goods and other cargo are the harbormaster's offices and the facilities of the single shipbuilder remaining in the city. Most of the warehouses now stand empty and deserted, while a handful of others have been converted into living space by people hoping to leave Kalaman on the next ship that puts into port.

In centuries past, the heart and soul of Kalaman's business district was the famous open-air market. Once, the open-air market held virtually every kind of good from almost every part of Ansalon. In the many stalls, one could find maps, exotic foods, livestock, and even curious artifacts from the ruins in nearby mountain ranges. Now, the market stands like a deserted clearing in the crumbling city. Citizens tend to avoid the area, and if forced to cross it, they rush as quickly as they can to get back to the safety between the buildings. Almost all trade now occurs along the waterfront, as very little overland travel reaches the city anymore.

At the center of the city stands Castle Kalaman. Despite the pall that drapes the land, the city's lords have maintained the structure, which remains one of the most beautiful buildings in northern Ansalon. Within the last century, the castle has been home to two women who had great impact upon the modern history of Ansalon—the Blue Lady, the infamous Highlord of the Blue Dragonarmy during the Solamnia offensive; and Lauranalanthalasa, the Qualinesti princess known as the Golden General. Gilthanas also kept quarters here during his tenure as governor. The castle now serves as home to Tierrel Rychner, Lord of Kalaman; his family; and his trio of advisors and their families.

Adventure Seed

While sailing along the northern coast of Ansalon, a storm forces a group of heroes into port at Kalaman. Gilthanas has returned to the city and is recruiting skilled warriors to investigate the strange disappearances of ships that have been occurring along the Vingaard River. The heroes are to join the crew of *Myrella's Heart*, a vessel commanded by the river pirate half-elf twins Myrelana and Leana. The journey is supposed to go from Kalaman to Jahsburg in the south.

The river pirates aren't exactly accepting of people from outside of their culture. It's an uneasy journey—unless the heroes impress the rough-and-tumble pirates, they spend the whole voyage subject to abuse. There should be plenty of opportunities for adventure, though . . . there is not one reason, but several, behind the disappearing vessels. First, the Dark Knights have established a base in the swamp at the Knight's Spur delta, and they have been seizing vessels carrying cargo that spies in Kalaman tell them is valuable. Second, a new breed of undead has started to appear along the river . . . undead river pirates. These creatures also have been seizing vessels. Unless the heroes discover the secret behind their origins, over the next few years, the numbers of the undead will grow enought to block all travel along the Vingaard. Such a tragedy would finally bring about the death of Kalaman as a city, not to mention ending the thriving river pirate culture based in the city of Vingaard. (For more information on the Vingaard River, the river pirates, and the Dark Knights at Knights' Spur, see the *Heroes of Defiance* game supplement.)

Peak of Clouds and Mount Brego

The Peak of Clouds, the highest point in the Astivar Mountains, and its companion peak Mount Brego have been a center of mystical and otherworldly activities since the Cataclysm. Few beings are aware of the area's significance, but those who are know that it is a place that is best avoided.

Lorrinar, a reclusive green dragon who claims the Astivar Mountains and the Forest of Lahue as his realm, however, is very familiar with the mystical properties of the Peak of Clouds and is presently working to find a way to take advantage of them.

A History of the Peak of Clouds and Mount Brego

The Astivar Mountains are a towering wall of stone that was pushed up from the depths of Krynn during the Cataclysm. Their peaks range mostly from four thousand to ten thousand feet above sea level, but the Peak of Clouds soars to fourteen thousand feet with Mount Brego reaching twelve thousand feet. While the foothills are not particularly treacherous, the higher peaks of this young mountain range feature severe slopes and near-vertical cliffs. The mountains have yet to be softened by the effects of wind and weather and stand like a giant row of jagged teeth.

To the west of mountains sprawls a dense forest of wiry trees that has been home to the Tribe of Lahue for as long as anyone can remember. Reputed cannibals, they found themselves the target of the legions of Istar's failed attempt to commit genocide in the decades prior to the Cataclysm. Even the upheavals that turned their peninsula into the border between Nordmaar and Estwilde and which threw the Astivar Mountains skyward did not destroy them.

Presently, the Tribe of Lahue continues to live in scattered woodland villages while diligently defending their ancestral lands from invaders. Although still fiercely independent, survival has forced them to acknowledge Lorrinar (or "Fume" as they call him) as the lord of their forest. This is not an arrangement that bothers them, however, as Lorrinar makes no demands of them—other than to be left alone.

Small communities of ogres and dwarves dwell within valleys hidden within the Astivar range. They acknowledge Lorrinar's power, but, as with the Lahutians, he mostly leaves them alone. The green dragon only occasionally calls upon them to help with research into the properties of the reputedly magical peaks.

Secrets of the Peak of Clouds and Mount Brego

The Cataclysm did more than just alter the face of Ansalon. It was a disaster of such magnitude that the very fabric of reality tore in several locations. Although Mount Brego has always been charged with magical energy, when the Peak of Clouds jutted up, it became a place where the boundaries between Krynn and the vast Abyss beyond the world were particularly weak.

Between the Cataclysm and the Chaos War, the Peak of Clouds became an intersection point between the Abyss and plane of Krynn. When Lunitari and Solinari were full and in alignment, the chaos of the Abyss could be laid bare to those knowledgeable in the ways of magic and powerful enough to withstand the draw upon the body and soul that the forces of other realities place on a person.

As the Peak of Clouds could permit access to worlds and places beyond Krynn, tunnels and caves riddled Mount Brego and emerged elsewhere in Ansalon entirely. Few written records describe where these magical caverns lead. One of these records, the writings of Iryl Songbrook, a Silvanesti elf who donated her journals to the Great Library of the Ages, includes an account of how she and her companions used one of the caves to travel instantly from the Mount Brego region to the Isle of Schallsea.

After the Chaos War, much of the magic was drained from both the Peak of Clouds and Mount Brego. Sorcerers and mystics who have visited the Peak of Clouds indicate that the portal to the Abyss that once existed there can no longer be found, while those who have braved the caves of the ogres who dwell below Mount Brego nowadays have found no magical portals. Further, in centuries past, Mount Brego was reputed to cast no shadow, nor did any shadows fall upon its faces, which is a phenomenon that Iryl Songbrook herself witnessed and wrote about. Since the Chaos War, however, Mount Brego has been as susceptible to light and shadow as any other object.

The dwarves and the ogres living at the peaks represent communities that are less than a century old. The dwarves dwell in a village named Hearthhome at the foot of the Peak of Clouds. They consist of soldiers from the War of the Lance and their descendents who chose to establish their own community rather than return home to Thorbardin. Their leader, Krun Silverchisel, was a young officer in the warband during the War of the Lance and, although he has started to slow down a bit, the dwarves still look to him for leadership. Silverchisel also serves as the go-between for the dwarves and ogres and the dragon overlord.

The ogres are the remnants of the Bloody Fist tribe. After unsuccessfully trying to defend their lands from the dragon known as Cinder, they fled north and resettled in the caves of Mount Brego. When Lorrinar arrived, they thought it best to submit rather than fight—and were pleasantly surprised when they discovered that the dragon was interested in working with them rather than subjugating or destroying them. The ogres are busily engaged in mapping the tunnels that honeycomb Mount Brego and looking for magical gates that lead to other places on Krynn; any treasures the ogres find, Lorrinar allows them to keep. All the dragon wants are the maps the ogres create.

The tribe's chieftain, Hrench, makes sure that Lorrinar gets what he wants in short order. As soon as search parties return to the main settlement, Hrench collects the new maps, checks them against any areas that overlap with others, and then makes copies for Lorrinar. He has a friendly relationship with the leader of the dwarven community, Krun Silverchisel, and lets the dwarf deliver all the maps the Bloody Fist search parties produce. This way, Hrench can better keep his chaotic tribe focused on their task.

Adventure Seeds

Magic has left the world . . . no priest or wizard has been able to cast a traditional spell since Chaos walked the land and the gods fled fifteen years ago. However, a party of heroes have learned of a wise man dwelling atop Mount Brego who reportedly still knows the secrets of magic. No one has found his dwelling, however, and the locals are getting increasingly nervous about searching the area as word has reached them that a green dragon has been spotted in the Woods of Lahue in 16SC.

If the heroes brave the rumors of dragons, cannibals, and marauding ogres, and if they survive the climb up Mount Brego, they find an eccentric kyrie and a silver-tressed Kagonesti maiden. He tells the heroes that he already has a student—the Kagonesti elf—but if they retrieve the Iron Staff of Kharda, a mighty artifact that once belonged to the consort of the demigoddess Artha, he will consider teaching them how to wield magic in "the new world."

Alternatively, the heroes could hear another rumor about the wise man on Mount Brego: While in the town of Ohme to the north, they hear that he will reveal secret techniques of magic to those who are willing to pay him one thousand steel pieces and a single enchanted item. The heroes' source even tells them exactly where he can be located. However, if they seek out the wise man, bandits attack them, intending to steal their money and magic items and sell them to the Dark Knights as slaves attack them.

Once the heroes return to Ohme (or another nearby town), they learn that the daughter of a merchant (she was also a former Wizard of the Red Robes) went in search of the wise man, but didn't return. The merchant had believed that she had become a student, but now it seems she was sold into slavery. The heroes are asked to locate and rescue her from her slave masters.

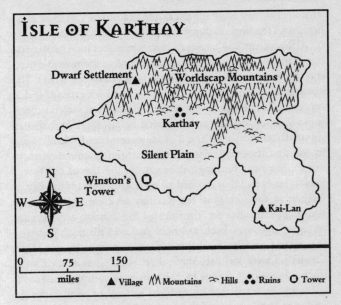

ISLE OF KARTHAY

Dwarf Settlement ▲ Worldscap Mountains

Karthay

Silent Plain

Winston's Tower ○

▲ Kai-Lan

N
W E
S

0   75   150
miles
▲ Village ᴧᴧᴧ Mountains ～ Hills •• Ruins ○ Tower

Winston's Tower

Rising from the ruins of an ancient fort, Winston's Tower is a one-hundred-thirty-foot, six-sided structure of gnome construction. It was once a beacon established to mark the harbor of Karthay. Now, it stands on the southern edge of the Silent Plains, a remnant of a long-gone age and the center of tinker gnome activity in eastern Ansalon.

A History of Winston's Tower

In the wake of the Great Trade War between Ergoth, Silvanesti, and Istar, which lasted from 673PC to 649PC, the Istar government undertook massive construction projects geared toward fortifying main trade centers and harbors. One harbor that was reinforced was Karthay, a port at the edge of the minotaur lands. These fortifications took place centuries before the formulation of the Proclamation of Manifest

Virtue, and they were the products of a mixture of Istar ingenuity and the best nonhuman architects had to offer.

Although many masterpieces were created during the one-hundred-fifty years it took to complete the massive projects, the most noteworthy of these was Winston's Tower. The structure was named for the governor of Karthay, and it served both as a lighthouse and a fortress from which vessels seeking enter the Bay of Istar could be attacked. Its ballistas reputedly could fire at ships as far as one hundred miles out to sea, and they used magically enhanced gnome devices to target. Further, the magical beacon at the top of the tower was so powerful that it could be seen anywhere on the Bay of Istar or in the forests of the Karthay on clear nights, and it could cut through even the thickest fog. Finally, any number of secret defenses, both technological and magical, guarded the tower and harbor. Records discovered in the High Clerist's Tower indicate that when High Clerist uth Blevin visited Winston's Tower in 213PC he was so impressed with some of the traps that he ordered several of similar design added to the defenses of the great tower in Solamnia.

The mighty Winston's Tower came into being because Governor Winston had an open-minded outlook that was rare even among his Istar contemporaries and which would only become rarer as Istar grew in strength. He brought gnome, minotaur, and Istar engineers to an unprecedented meeting of minds, bringing out the best in all their outlooks and likewise eliminating the worst of their tendencies.

From the gnomes came all manner of innovation in defensive technology as well as a vast improvement in the working of lighthouse beacons. The practical eyes of the minotaur engineers curbed the gnome tendency to create overwrought and self-defeating devices while devising great offensive weaponry for the fortress—which the gnomes then enhanced in their own unique fashions. The Istar engineers were responsible for the design of the fortress itself, applying the gnome and minotaur innovations within the context of superior Istar architecture. The Istar mentality infused the fortress complex with the kind of grandeur that Istar's government felt their nation embodied. During the early stages of the construction, Governor Winston stood at the center and made sure that all the disparate parts of the process came together into a greater whole. And, although Winston's Tower was not completed in his lifetime, his successors were loyal enough to his vision to see that it was carried through to the end.

As the nation of Istar grew increasingly intolerant toward nonhumans, the few minotaurs who remained free of slavery at the hands of Istar retreated into the mountains of Karthay, leaving the forests and coasts to the humans. The descendants of the gnomes who had helped engineer the defenses of Winston's Tower remained in the fortification where they continued to maintain the devices and implement occasional improvements under the watchful eyes of Istar's commanders. In keeping with one of the provisions of the Proclamation of Manifest Virtue (that gnomes were creatures of chaos who should be isolated from the glorious order created by the Kingpriest), the gnome enclave found itself restricted to Winston's Tower.

In the final decade before the Cataclysm, as Istar's legions stationed in Karthay were committed to exterminating the minotaurs, Winston's Tower was left almost entirely for the gnomes to manage. The legions and commanders had mostly moved into the mountains by order of the Kingpriest, who had declared that the last vestiges of an independent minotaur civilization had to be wiped from the face of Ansalon in order to fulfill the tenants of the Proclamation of Manifest Virtue.

When the Cataclysm struck, the ensuing earthquakes reduced the fortress around Winston's Tower to ruin, but the tower itself remained intact. The disaster that spelled the doom of Istar became the salvation of the minotaur nation, as the Karthay province was drowned beneath the Blood Sea of Istar, except for the islands of modern Karthay, Mithas, and Kothas. Here, the minotaurs rebuilt from centuries of oppression and genocidal policies. The minotaurs on Karthay, however, remained in a state of barbarism, dwelling for the most part in their mountain caves. The single tribe who descended southward established the village of Kai-Lan, where they occasionally trade with sailors from Mithas. This is a rare occurrence, however, as these savage minotaurs have a reputation of being cannibals.

As the minotaurs rose from the wreckage of Istar, the gnomes became an entrenched settlement in the area around Winston's Tower. Both savage and civilized minotaurs shunned the place because the gnomes were viewed as dangerous and annoying if disturbed. So, in the centuries since the Cataclysm, the gnome clans of Winston's Tower have been running wild, implementing all kinds of "improvements" to the tower's defenses.

Winston's Tower in the Present Day

The structure towers above the overgrown ruins of the Istaran fort, a grim spire amid the discarded remnants of a dead civilization. The harbor it once protected was swept away by the Cataclysm, and the sandy beach and rocky peninsula upon which the ruins stand do not appear to provide any place for ships to drop anchor safely. However, a series of sandbars and a narrow reef near the shore do indeed make good and fairly sheltered anchorage for those interested in exploring the island.

Upon drawing near, explorers see little evidence of the gnome chaos that exists within the tower. The only external evidence can be seen at the tower's top, where the gnomes have "improved" upon the massive beacon by adding a dozen more focusing lenses and curved metal plates to the ones that were already mounted there. The net effect is one that causes the top of the tower to appear almost like an open rosebud that shines and glints in the sunlight—the gnomes are very dedicated about keeping them polished even though their "improvements" have long made it so the beacon no longer functions.

A ramp spirals upward from the ruins, around the tower to a parapet eighty feet above the ground. Several doorways stand open, allowing access to the tower's interior. However, the parapet also sports the first sample of the gnome's innovations. They have converted the parapet into a treadmill that activates as soon as someone steps on it. Although the intent was to carry a person from door to door, the treadmill moves so fast that only the most nimble heroes can remain standing or even get off the contraption once it has been started.

The interior of the tower is a series of stairs, ladders, catwalks, and platforms at various levels. Dark shafts fall away to dizzying depths. There is very little evidence of the practical design that the Istar and minotaur engineers imposed upon the gnomes. Now, not even the gnome clans can safely navigate through the tower's interior, trying instead to keep to their respective portions of the tower while using a variety of methods to scale the outside of the tower when they need to venture into the outside world.

The tower is a dangerous maze that is filled with whatever hazards the Narrator cares to dream up. Those that are known to exist include the following:

- A gargoyle automaton. (Use stahnk statistics.)
- Rubber walls and floors that make falling characters bounce until somehow rescued.
- Trapdoors to slides and shafts.
- Mechanical tendrils that pull victims into grinding gears. (Use wyndlass statistics.)
- Vats of strange gnome chemicals that may spill over at any time.
- Mechanical spiders and electrified webs. (Use giant spider statistics.)

To the north of Winston's Tower, the Silent Plains stretch toward the Worldscap Mountains where barbaric tribes of minotaurs continue to dwell in caves as they did before the destruction of Istaran. Ruins of Istar roads and villages litter the desolate, sandy plain, the greatest of these being the city of Karthay. Like the fortress guarding the port, earthquakes shattered Karthay. The few citizens who survived were butchered when vengeful minotaurs descended upon them, emboldened by what they saw as the gods rewarding their perseverance by punishing Istar.

In addition to the minotaurs and gnomes, a small clan of dwarves dwells upon Karthay, the descendants of dwarven explorers who became shipwrecked when their vessel was smashed to tinder against the jagged northern coast of the island. After encountering the savage minotaurs, the dwarves retreated high into the Worldscap Mountains, where they now dwell in caves above the snowline. After two hundred years, they still remain deeply afraid of the minotaurs, and the approach to their dwellings is guarded by all manner of deadly traps. The dwarves sustain themselves with the help of a magical artifact that both produces food and cures all illnesses.

Also high in Worldscap Mountains are a series of abandoned kyrie aeries. In the decade before the War of the Lance, a minotaur priest of Sargonnas came to Karthay with many of his followers with the intent of performing certain rituals. These rituals might have led the chief minotaur god to return to full strength in Ansalon after the Cataclysm (before Mishakal). The priest's efforts were thwarted by a group of heroes and the kyrie. Afterwards, the kyrie relocated to parts unknown to avoid the wrath of the minotaurs. They may still be living elsewhere in an even less accessible portion of the Worldscap Mountains, or they have perhaps left Karthay for a place where they can be safe from the minotaurs.

Adventure Seed

After being captured by minotaurs while sailing on the Blood Sea, a party of heroes is brought before Emperor Chot himself.

Here they learn that his heir has gone missing while exploring the ruins of Karthay and Winston's Tower. Further, the search party that was sent to locate him has gone missing too. The heroes are given a choice: They can entertain the royal court in the Arena, or they can join the second search party to search Winston's Tower for Chot's chosen heir.

Should the heroes make it safely past the gnome contraptions, they find Chot's heir hopelessly insane. He thinks everyone and everything are machines. However, he cooperates with whatever the heroes want. Unfortunately, once they bring him back to Emperor Chot, the minotaur leader insists they find a cure for his son.

The Valley of Crystal

Just south of the dwarven kingdom of Zhakar is a bone-dry valley of the Khalkist Mountains, which recently has become known as the Valley of Crystal. The valley is one of the more spectacular legacies Chaos left on the surface of Krynn.

History of the Valley of Crystal

In the summer of 383PC—which is treated as Year 0 by the scholars at the Library of the Ages in their new reckoning. The sun stopped moving in the sky, the oceans boiled, and new breeds of monsters swarmed across Ansalon, destroying even the memories of every living thing in their path.

Then came Chaos, a being who claimed to be both the beginning and the end of all life on Krynn, including the gods themselves. According to stories told by bards all across Ansalon, only by facing Chaos in the Abyss could the combined forces of the Knights of Takhisis, Knights of Solamnia, and the Good and Evil dragons defeat him. However, in addition to the death of virtually every being who went to face Chaos, victory came at a price: The gods had to leave Krynn to its fate, ushering in the Age of Mortals.

Chaos left many marks upon Ansalon. Some speculate the farthest reaching of these was the new sorcerous magic Palin

Majere and others discovered in the decades after the Summer of Chaos, although there is no proof of this. Chaos's most spectacular creation in this time, however, undoubtedly is the Valley of Crystal.

No one can say for sure why Chaos did the things he did, but one tale told is that after Chaos had caused all the Lords of Doom to erupt as they had never erupted before, he decided to reflect their hellish glare into the heavenly domain of Paladine himself. To accomplish this, he created the Valley of Crystal, a dazzling collection of crystals, the like of which Ansalon had never seen. For as long as the volcanoes erupted, the tale says, a beam of red light reflected from the valley into the heavens.

Although someone who never actually saw the Valley of Crystal and who has no sense of geography concocted this story—the valley is hundreds of miles from Lords of Doom—it has become quite popular.

The fact remains that no one knows why the Valley of Crystal was created or what purpose it serves, if any. That is perhaps no surprise—how can any being truly fathom the mind of Chaos incarnate?

The Valley of Crystal in the Present Day

This dry vale brims with a bewildering array of stones. They line the cliff sides and cover the valley floor; heroes who enter it must wear hard-soled boots, as the jagged crystalline protrusions quickly slash soft-soled footwear to ribbons. Even characters in hard boots must be careful, as someone who trips and falls may, at best, gain terrible scars, and at worst, suffer fatal wounds.

The Valley of Crystal lies within the territory claimed by the ogre nation of Blöde. Within recent years, the ogres started collecting the crystals here, and that harvest is gradually becoming a fixture of the nation's economy. The ogres trade most of the crystals to Blöde's Dark Knight neighbors in exchange for weapons and armor.

Moreover, several units of Dark Knights garrison in south-ern Blöde, where they keep a watch over the domain of Sable the Black. Unlike many other dragon overlords, Sable has no interest in forming alliances with the Dark Knights. Her curi-ous interest in magical experiments and the creation of new and bizarre life forms concerns the Dark Knight leadership; they feel it beneficial for all involved parties to accept pay-ment from Chieftain Donnag, the current warlord of the tribes of Blöde, in order to strengthen their southern borders. The ogres have not established any permanent camps near the valley—water is too scarce in the region for that. Further-more, the dwarves of Thoradin, whose kingdom borders on the Valley of Crystal, have access to an exit that leads from their hidden underground realm into the valley. Dwarven war bands typically swarm and kill any ambitious ogres arro-gant enough to try establishing a permanent outpost.

The dazzling reflections of sunlight off the thousands of crystals make it so impossible to see that it is difficult to enter the valley during the day. Humans, ogres, and other beings who don't have sensitive vision can move carefully through the valley, so long as they make an effort to shield their eyes with veils; even then, they must squint against the painful brightness. Elves, goblins, dwarves, and others whose eyes are highly sensitive to light risk permanent blindness should they enter the valley during the day; the glare is so sharp and their eyes so sensitive that it may even burn through closed eyelids.

Heroes who come to the valley can collect 1 to 100 crystals for each hour each individual spends searching. The leaders of Neraka and Sanction are collecting the crystals and will pay 100 to 1,000 steel pieces per crystal. In both cases, how-ever, they pay such high prices only if the heroes assure them the crystals were not touched by living, bare hands during collection—otherwise, they only pay ten to one hundred steel per crystal. Neither the Dark Knights nor the agents of Hogan Bight, the lord of Sanction, will explain why they want to know if the crystals have been touched. However, they will use magic to verify the truthfulness of the heroes regarding the crystals for sale.

Secrets of the Valley of Crystal

Although the ogres of Blöde have yet to discover the true importance of the crystals found in the Valley of Crystal, the Dark Knights and agents of the mysterious lord of Sanction, Hogan Bight, have come to realize that some of them are a type of magical battery.

When carried by a person with the ability to use mystic magic, certain crystals can boost his or her spellcasting ability by a significant margin. Roughly one in one hundred crystals has this ability. (The Narrator should draw from the Fate Deck or roll 1d10 to determine if a crystal harvested by a hero is thus enchanted. If the result of 1 comes up twice in a row, the crystal is magically charged.) It is impossible to tell a magically charged crystal from the others until the hero actually uses it—and it can be used only if a character is carrying it and attempts to cast a spell after he or she feels completely drained of magical abilities.

SAGA rules: The charged crystals of the valley each provide from 10 to 100 additional spell points. Once a charged crystal touches the bare skin of a hero or character, it automatically attunes to him or her; no other person can ever gain the benefit of the spell points stored within them. (Even if a being has no capacity for using mysticism, the crystal still attunes to him or her—no one else will ever gain the benefit after it touches living skin.)

A person with mystical abilities who carries a charged crystal can draw upon the extra spell points once the reservoir of magical energies within him or her as been expended. The crystal must be touching bare skin in order to be effective. The spell points are expended as per normal rules, but they never recharge. If the hero keeps drawing spell points from the crystal, it eventually becomes nonmagical. (The Narrator should secretly keep track of how many spell points are in a crystal.)

AD&D rules: The charged crystals hold 1d10+5 spell levels each, only usable for the casting of priest spells. Once a charged crystal touches the bare skin of a hero or character, it automatically attunes to him or her; no other person can ever gain the benefit of the spell levels stored within it. (Even if a being has no capacity for using priestly magic, the crystal still attunes to him or her as described above.)

If a being with the ability to use priestly magic carries a charged crystal, he or she can recast spells of his or her choice, using the crystal to do so. The crystal must be touching bare skin in order to be effective. If the bearer of the crystal tries to cast a spell even after he or she has expended all spells prayed for that day, the spell is drawn from the crystal. When stored spell levels are expended, they do not regenerate. If the hero keeps drawing spells from the crystal, it eventually becomes nonmagical. (The Dungeon Master should secretly keep track of how many spell levels a crystal contains.)

Adventure Seed

A Daewar dwarf from the Kingdom of Thorbardin approaches a group of heroes. The dwarf's name is Rohar Hammerflint, and he introduces himself a follower of Severus Stonehand, Prophet of Reorx. If given the opportunity, the dwarf explains that Severus and his followers believe Reorx is testing the faith of the dwarves in these dark times and that it is the duty of all to prepare for the eventual return of the gods.

Severus has charged Rohar with a mission he believes is sacred to Reorx. Severus believes the Daewar and Hylar dwarves must reclaim the ancient city of Kal-Thax, which has been inhabited by the "accursed, foul Zhakar" since the Cataclysm. He asks the heroes to serve as his extra swordarms and comrades. He promises them vast riches, as he has heard that Reorx brought a bounty of precious stones to the surface of Krynn as his final gift to its people before departing. These treasures lie before what Severus believes to be long-forgotten accessways to the city, which Rohar expects will allow him and the heroes to sneak into Kal-Thax—or "Thoradin," as it once again will be called when its rightful inhabitants reclaim it—and gain an estimate of how many Zhakar dwarves live there.

Nothing is ever this easy, of course. The heroes first have to travel through ogre territory, fight dangerous creatures near the Valley of Crystal, and then find the hidden entrance to the city without being slashed by their supposed payments. Once within kingdom of Zhakar, they must avoid capture by the hideously misshapen dwarves infected with a terrible fungal disease. Should the heroes interact with the Zhakar dwarves, they claim they are keeping a deadly evil from escaping into the depths of the city and that if Severus and his followers invade, it will break free and spell doom for possibly all of Krynn. If the heroes voluntarily depart Zhakar, they will make enemies out of Severus's cult.

Note: The future of Severus Stonehand and the outcome of his quest to drive the Zhakar from Thoradin is described in the DRAGONLANCE: FIFTH AGE Dramatic Adventure Game.

Godshome

In ages past, "Godshome" referred to two locations. First, there was the widely known City of Godshome, a place with temples devoted to most of Ansalon's gods. Second, there was a hidden valley that only those chosen by the gods could find.

Located within the Khalkist Mountains near the heart of the Dark Knight-controlled lands of Neraka, both Godshomes are mystic sites all but forgotten by the peoples of modern-day Ansalon.

A History of the City of Godshome

For many centuries before Istar became powerful and corrupt, pilgrims from all across Ansalon made the city of Godshome their prime destination. In ages past, every devoted worshiper hoped to make such a pilgrimage at least once in his or her lifetime.

Godshome could be described more accurately as many cities within a single city. The city's layout resembles a great wheel, with its districts radiating outward from the Great Temple of the Stars, which is a grand structure containing cathedrals devoted to all twenty-one major gods of the Krynnish pantheon. The city had fifteen different districts, which pilgrims and inhabitants could gain access to only from a single gate in the city's outer wall. The followers of some deities did not get along with the followers of other deities, so limited access helped prevent hostilities. Each district was completely self-contained, with inns, shops, residences, and all other features that one might expect to find in a city.

Lesser temples and churches dotted the different districts, each devoted to a different aspect of the god or operated by a different sect devoted to honoring the deity in their own way. While travel from district to district was also possible theoretically through the Great Temple of the Stars, only high-ranking priests or those granted special dispensation by the Worshipful Master of the Stars, the higest-ranking priest and lord of the city, could use such passage.

Clearly, with twenty-one gods in the pantheon and only fifteen districts in the city, not all the gods maintained temples at Godshome outside the Great Temple of the Stars. The three gods of nature—Habbakuk, Chislev, and Zeboim—and their followers could not abide the relatively close quarters of Godshome, and therefore had holy sites elsewhere. Similarly, the three gods of magic did not have temples in Godshome, as their followers typically made the equivalent of a pilgrimage every time they visited one of the Towers of High Sorcery.

As Istar and its Kingpriests grew in power, the importance of Godshome waned. The Kingpriests encouraged the centralization of worship in their own seat of power. They implemented steps on many levels to discourage the traditional pilgrimages. These included included leveling outrageously high taxes against the inns on the roads to Godshome, *not* providing regular patrols—while discouraging local lords from doing the same—along the roads so they became a hotbed of banditry, and funding the construction of a great temple in Istar that supposedly superceded all those in Godshome.

As the final century before the Cataclysm dawned, the efforts of Istar had effectively caused many of Ansalon's peoples to view Godshome as a corrupt and seedy place where hucksters sold false cures and blessings, tricksters performed fraudulent miracles, and blasphemers espoused hypocritical modes of worship that offended the gods. Eventually, the Kingpriest and his clergy grew so powerful that they commanded their legions to attack Godshome and raze it. The priests and holy warriors who still remained there settled their differences and valiantly defended their city and temples. For almost two decades prior to the Cataclysm, the citizens of Godshome defended their city and temples from an overwhelming and implacable foe—until one night, the entire populace vanished without trace.

The commanders of the Istaran legions marched their troops into the abandoned city, intent on solving the mystery of its emptiness, but within hours, the Cataclysm struck. Distant Istar was destroyed without trace, struck by a fiery mountain and swept away by tidal waves. Earthquakes wracked Godshome, causing the temples to collapse. Only a handful of the thousands of soldiers that had laid siege to the city survived to tell of its fate.

Secrets of the City of Godshome

Godshome has lain abandoned since the Cataclysm, the roads that once led to it shattered by earthquakes and disintegrated by lava flows. The ogres and nomadic herders who moved onto the arid plains in the ensuing centuries believed the foothills in which it stood to be haunted, and adventurers who visited the region confirmed this: Ghostly soldiers still roam the shattered city and hills surrounding it, looking for the vanished priests and holy warriors. Few adventurers have survived excursions into Godshome, but those who have return with great treasures. So far, none of the many sacred artifacts that are rumored to have once been located there have been recovered.

A History of Godshome Vale

Although Godshome was the end destination for most ancient pilgrims, a select few would continue onward to one of the most holy sites on all of Krynn. If the priests in the city determined that a person was worthy of the direct attention of the gods, they would tell him or her of a secret trail that led into the mountains to the true Godshome.

Secrets of Godshome Vale

In ages past, none could find their way to Godshome Vale unless the gods themselves permitted it. If the gods did not wish to assist the petitioner, the trail would wind its way through the mountains and eventually deposit those following it back in the foothills near the City of Godshome. However, if a worthy person (or persons, as such pilgrimages could be undertaken by questing parties of heroes as well as individuals) traveled this trail, the god whose guidance he or she sought would subject the petitioner to tests intended to verify devotion to the ideals the god held dear. Few records of these tests have survived to Ansalon's present day, but they each maintain that the tests often proved lethal to those who undertook them, causing those who were unworthy of the god's attentions to perish during the experience.

After the tests, the successful petitioners would emerge in a bowl-shaped valley. Its steeply rising, evergreen-lined slopes offered no apparent exits from the valley, although one always presented itself after the petitioner had reached the center of the valley. However, the means through which he or she entered the valley would be swallowed by the cliffs, as well.

At the center of the valley was a depression in the shape of a perfect circle. It was surrounded by twenty-one shapeless boulders, which represented the major gods. The bottom of the depression consisted of black rock polished to such a sheen that it appeared to be a pool of water at first glance. Regardless of the time of day or weather conditions, the constellations and moons of Krynn's sky reflected in the black surface. An avatar of the god would appear on the constellation that represented him or her, and provide the petitioner with guidance. Invariably, the god's message would be short and cryptic, and once it had been delivered, a pass would open elsewhere in the cliffs to allow departure from the valley.

In the wake of the Chaos War, the valley has become a little-known passage through the Khalkists. Narrow trails that cannot accommodate wagons or even horses wind their way along ledges and through crevices until they converge on a single narrow pass that leads either northwest or southwest, depending on which side of the mountain range a person is coming from. The passes open into Godshome Vale, which is now barren and devoid of life. The evergreen trees are now blackened, toppled stumps and the mosses that once grew among them are fine ash that sweeps across the stony ground in the breeze.

The boulders that once surrounded the black pool have vanished, as absent as the gods. The shiny black surface has cracked, now taking on the appearance of a mirror that someone struck dead-center with a fist. There is still some mystical quality to the site, as a distorted reflection of the moon that appeared in Krynn's sky after the gods departed can be seen in the cracked surface.

Adventure Seed

Shortly after the founding of the Citadel of Light, a group of heroes are approached by Iryl Songbrook and Jasper Fireforge, two of that mystical organization's leaders. They wish to seek Godshome and find evidence of the gods' presence on Krynn. Before they leave, however, they ask the heroes to join them in their quest. Using a map recovered from Tasslehoff's belongings following his death, the mystics and the heroes head into the Khalkists in search of Godshome.

After braving many dangers—including marauding hobgoblin hunting parties and ogres—they find the valley, and its appearance almost breaks Jasper's spirit. As they depart the valley, they encounter a group of Knights of Takhisis under the leadership of an aging Knight of the Skull. The Dark Knight, as distraught as Jasper and driven partially mad by the loss of his goddess, challenges him (or a hero who still follows the true gods) to a duel to the death. The Dark Knight is convinced that if he kills a priest of a Good god in honorable combat, the Dark Queen will once again whisper her plan in his ear and bestow her blessings upon him.

River of Healing

Located in a secluded valley in the Vingaard Mountains, the River of Healing first appears in text in the epic poem "The Serpent and the Knight." The verses relate the story of a maiden who saves a blinded Crown Knight from certain death. Later, she is revealed as a gorgon. Although the epic is largely believed to be the product of a Palanthian bard's imagination, this place is indeed very real, and its powerful healing properties persist even into the Age of Mortals.

A History of the River of Healing

The River of Healing is located in an almost inaccessible valley in the Vingaard Mountains. Only one known way exists to reach the River of Healing. An ancient, mostly washed-out road leads from the village of Korval and through a pass that is blocked by snow for five months of the year.

Although the reputed properties of the river are well known to many citizens of Korval, even the bravest or most desperate person among them has not dared travel through the pass for many decades. The pass is oddly barren, and all locals who attempt to travel through it invariably turn back well before reaching the summit. All report sensations of being watched by some sinister force, although no living beings are anywhere to be seen.

The sinister force felt in the pass are the spirits of a tribe of kyrie who once protected travelers from harm as they journeyed through the pass. They all devoutly followed Mishakal, but in the dark years following the Cataclysm, bandits in the employ of a Black-Robed wizard killed them. The wizard wanted their corpses for his efforts to create a flying golem. The spirits of the kyrie still haunt the air around their aeries along the top of the cliffs of the pass, angrily gazing down upon those who travel toward the river. They cannot attack beings who are touching the ground, but they set upon any flying creature immediately.

Once the pass has been traversed, explorers emerge in a drop-shaped valley that is ringed by steep mountains. A trail leads from the mouth of the pass to a shimmering lake of crystal clear water. On the far shore, almost directly across from the mouth of the pass, stands a dilapidated structure.

Although few living beings remember, this body of water is named the Lake of Light. The River of Healing feeds it from the north. The building on the far shore of the lake is a small temple that was once devoted to Mishakal, a goddess of fertility and healing, who was widely worshiped in Solamnia. Within the temple, on the walls of the chambers containing its Holy Circles, explorers can see a mural portraying Mishakal bathing in the lake outside the temple. The priests believed the healing properties of the both the lake and the river came from Mishakal's blessing. The temple is home to

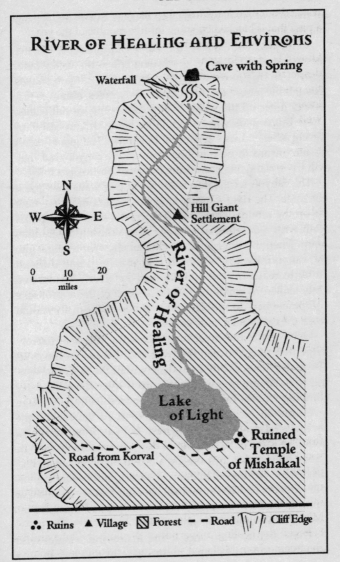

RIVER OF HEALING AND ENVIRONS

Waterfall

Cave with Spring

River Of Healing

Hill Giant Settlement

N W E S

0 10 20
miles

Lake of Light

Ruined Temple of Mishakal

Road from Korval

∴ Ruins ▲ Village ▨ Forest - - Road ⑂ Cliff Edge

all manner of small animals and vermin, but nothing there can threaten the heroes lives.

To the north of the lake, the valley climbs steeply to meet the mountains. The River of Healing enters the valley here, flowing from a narrow, fertile canyon. The canyon snakes through the mountains for roughly sixty miles, although just twenty miles up the valley lives a community of hill giants. These humanoids moved here after being driven eastward during Khellendros's seizure of Solamnia. The giants aren't hostile toward those traveling through the canyon, but they will try to claim one horse from mounted parties as a toll.

The canyon terminates as the sheer cliff walls that line it converge. The river's headwaters are located in a cave high up on the mountainous wall. The crystal clear water pours forth with a dazzling of rainbow colors during the midday hours when the sun is at an angle that allows it to shine into the canyon. Explorers should find it a steep and difficult climb to reach the cave containing the river's headwater. Only skilled mountaineers in possession of the appropriate equipment can do so. Naturally, heroes who can fly should reach the cave much more easily.

Once inside the cave, the heroes can follow a narrow ledge that runs between the river and the wall of the cave. The water flows swiftly from deep within the cave, threatening to wash anyone who gets into it over the cliff. After climbing steeply for almost two hundred feet, the passage levels out and widens into a large cave. At the back of the cave, crystal clear water pours forth from a spring, forming a pool. The River of Healing flows down the mountain from it.

Scattered about the cave are a dozen highly detailed, life-sized stone carvings of humans, dwarves, and kender, mountain climbers or adventurers all. An examination reveals that a few of the faces are calm, but the majority of them appear startled while others appear horrified.

These statues were once living males and females who have been turned to stone by the gaze of the gorgon who lived here at one point. A careful search of the cave reveals a small tunnel in the most distant corner. In order to explore it, heroes have to get down on their hands and knees. The tunnel terminates in a small cave. The dried and withered corpse of a creature that was part snake and part human lies in the rotted remains of furs and blankets. Shriveled remains of snakes cover the top of its skull. These are the earthly remains of a gorgon, perhaps proof that the epic poem "The Serpent and Knight" is based in fact.

The river's healing properties are strongest at its origin. The waters here can cause lost limbs to regrow, make the old young, and even bring the dead back to life. As the river flows southward, its magical effects are diluted. The waters of the lake have refreshing qualities and have been known to instantly cure colds, but little else. Beings submerged in the river find themselves cured of more serious ailments and diseases, including life-threatening wounds and fatal poisonings. Drinking the water has no effect.

Secrets of the River of Healing

Although Mishakal may never have literally bathed in the River of Healing, its waters are sacred to her and they continue to grant her healing gifts even in the Age of Mortals.

Another part of the valley where her presence may still be felt is the temple on the shore of the Lake of Light. Before the Cataclysm, it was home to some of her most devout priests, and a vestige of Mishakal's power still remains here. Spellcasting heroes who meditate or pray within the walls of the temple find that spells cast with the intent of healing injuries or curing diseases have maximum effectiveness for a period of twenty-one hours afterward (one hour for each of the gods of Krynn).

The spirit of the deceased gorgon still lingers in the cave where she lived, waiting for the Crown Knight whom she rescued to return. (He left to resign his rank with the Orders, but when he reached the High Clerist's Tower, other Knights convinced him he had been under the influence of mind-effecting magic—love for a gorgon was not natural!) The gorgon, however, waited for him, pining away until she finally died of a broken heart. Heroes who are attuned to the spirit world will feel great sorrow when they enter the cave. The spirit is invisible and insubstantial and the living can communicate with her only through the use of proper magical spells or abilities.

The only danger this undead gorgon poses is that it will attempt to force anyone who enters the cave wearing the armor of a Knight of Solamnia to stay—her undead state has caused her perception to become confused. She will release the Knight if someone explains the reality of the situation—that she has been dead for hundreds of years, and so has the Knight she loved.

The water of the River of Healing has the following game effects:

Location	AD&D rules	SAGA rules
In the lake	Restores subdual damage	Restores 1 card
Lower river	Restores 1d6 hp or cures poison	Restores 3 cards or cures poison
Midriver	Restores 3d10 hp or cures blindness	Restores 6 cards or cures blindness
Upper river	Restores 3d20 hp or regenerates limbs	Restores 9 cards or regenerates limbs
Headwater	Heals all injuries and ailments, raises the dead*	Heals all injuries and ailments, raises the dead

* Characters and heroes who are raised from the dead, or who regrow limbs are subject to the system shock rules under the AD&D rules.

The spirit of the gorgon has all the abilities and properties of a haunt. (See the AD&D MONSTROUS MANUAL™ tome or DRAGONLANCE dramatic supplement *The Bestiary* for details.)

Adventure Seed

A party of heroes are in Korval when a child falls deathly ill. The healers can do nothing for the child, but a sage who retired from the Great Library of the Ages in Palanthas to live among the simple peasants of Korval is familiar with the River of Healing. He and the child's family approach the heroes and ask them to accompany them to the pass between Korval and the river. Unfortunately for the heroes, a bandit lord who heard Pehter's tale of the river (see the short story) has decided to use it as a source of income. His men have sealed off the pass and have turned the old temple into a fortification to guard the lake.

The Footprint of Chaos

The terrain north of Thelgaard is as close to uninhabitable as one will find in Solamnia. The soil is fertile, and the land rises and falls in a series of foothills leading up to the Vingaard Mountains. Great pine trees grow in copses here and there, but that is about the only life one will find in the region.

Travelers who do make the arduous trek into the mountains, though, may crest one of the hills to find themselves staring down at what appears to be a canyon in the shape of a gigantic three-toed foot. This is the Footprint of Chaos.

A History of the Footprint

The Footprint serves as a reminder of the Summer of Chaos, when all of reality was nearly destroyed. When one first sees the Footprint, the canyon floor seems to be covered by a thick haze. As one draws close, it becomes clear that the bottom of the Footprint is filled with smoke, as though something in the canyon was burning. It is only about as thick as a light fog, and it does not impede travel. Those who have explored the site say that they found no fires or any other logical source for the smoke inside the Footprint. They note, though, that the smoke smells like brimstone, and it stings both eyes and lungs. Also, they discovered while standing in the bottom of the footprint that the smoke rises about fifteen feet above them.

Although no settlements exist in the area, woodcutters and hunters frequent this region. Game is plentiful and, by all accounts, of very high quality. Deer, rabbits, boars, and squirrels can be found here in amazing numbers, quite probably because the only predators in the area are eagles who nest in the Vingaard Mountains.

Since this beautiful and verdant region is fairly unpopulated, the Footprint has remained a remote curiosity that most people have heard of, but very few ever visit.

Secrets of the Footprint of Chaos

Although the canyon is in the approximate shape and size of his foot, the Chaos god never trod on this section of Ansalon. Rather, this phenomenon is the result of a wing of fire dragons (children of Chaos), who flew low over the land and scoured it with their flaming breath. When they were done, the fire dragons disappeared, leaving only the Footprint of Chaos. No one will ever know if the shape of the canyon was intentional or just another happenstance associated with that turbulent summer.

Nothing lives at the bottom of the canyon. This is not terribly surprising considering the fact that the Footprint was created by dragon breath, but since the rest of the region quickly rebounds after a fire or other natural disaster, it is curious that the canyon remains lifeless even thirty years later.

Adventure Seeds

Rumors circulate that the smoke in the Footprint of Chaos has amazing recuperative powers. People from all over Solamnia begin flocking to the canyon as a way to heal everything from aching joints to blindness. Someone claims know someone who has a friend who had a severed arm regrown by the smoke. However, as heroes ask around, it becomes clear that while everyone has heard these rumors, no one

they can find has actu-
ally been to the can-
yon. In fact, anyone in
town who did go has
never returned. Are the
rumors of the smoke's
restorative properties
true? In either case, who
started the rumors?
And why? What hap-
pened to the people

who went to the Footprint and never returned? Are they still
living up in the wilderness, or did they simply vanish into
the smoke?

Another adventure can begin when a group of heroes
encounter a trapper who begs for their help. He and his partner were hunting in the region of the Footprint of Chaos
when they heard a terrible wailing coming from the canyon.
They could see nothing through the smoke, so his partner
walked down into the canyon to see if someone there needed
help. As soon as the smoke swallowed him up, the man
began screaming that he was being attacked. The man's cries
were silenced almost immediately, and the trapper heard the
sounds of a wild animal (perhaps two or three) growling and
chewing. What animal (or animals) could be living in the
Footprint? Why does it lie in wait for people to walk into the
smoke? If there is no creature in the canyon, is this man delu-
sional or is he purposely lying to the heroes? Why?

Çhe Grove of Anaya's Çree

Since the founding of Qualinesti, a grove of oak trees has
been held as a place of memorial to which elves travel to
meditate on the difficulties of relating not only to other elves
but also to other races. Qualinesti woodshapers—elves who
share a particularly strong bond with nature—view the site
as sacred.

A History of the Grove of Anaya's Tree

Among the recordings of Kagonesti oral histories set down by the great elven bard Quevalin Soth is that of the Keeper of the Forest. Mithranhana, the forest that later came to be called Qualinesti, once had a long line of protectors charged with ensuring that no one despoiled it in any way. Although one can only speculate that the first Keeper came about when the elves were created, the oral histories of the Kagonesti contain hints that the Keeper was always there—until the last one died in Kith-Kanan's arms.

The first Keeper was named Ziatia. Kagonesti claim that a unicorn came among an elf family long ago and stood silently before young Ziatia. In the moments that passed between them, the girl seemed to hear something that no one else could. Then, with a farewell wave, Ziatia climbed onto the unicorn's back and was never seen by her family again. Rumors that she had become the Keeper eventually reached their ears as the tale spread throughout the wild elf tribes.

The second Keeper, Delarin, was taken from a wild elf family generations later. Ziatia apparently trained her well before becoming one of the great oaks that dot Mithranhana. Apparently, Delarin died after driving a dragon out of the forest. Her successor, young Ulyante, took her place, followed by Camirene. Sadly, Quevalin Soth could not find any stories about these two Keepers, so they remain but names in his records. Finally, Camirene took the last Keeper, Anaya, as her successor.

As scholars of elven history know, Anaya was the first love of Kith-Kanan, the founder of Qualinesti. The two pledged themselves to each other while Kith-Kanan was living in the forest. She showed him the sacred cave of the Keepers before giving her life and that of her unborn child's to save him.

Legends among the Qualinesti and the Kagonesti state that as Anaya died, she (like Keepers before her) became one with the forest, transforming into an oak tree. Years later, that tree split open, and Silveran Greenhands, Anaya's unborn child emerged fully grown. He went on to become the second Speaker of the Sun and is also reported to have been a powerful woodshaper.

This enchanted grove has held an important place in the rites of passage that bind together the Shapers of Destiny, as the Qualinesti woodshapers are formally known. Once a young elf with the natural inclination to become a woodshaper decides to follow the Path of the Shaper, he or she must spend three days and three nights in meditation within the grove. During this time, the young woodshaper has a vision that reaffirms the elf's bond to the forest and sometimes gives the woodshaper a glimpse into his or her future.

In ages past, the Shapers of Destiny believed that Chislev herself reached out to them during their time of meditation. In the wake of the gods' departure from Krynn, many still believe that they feel the touch of the goddess—that she grants them insight into what she knows their life's purpose to be—but many others believe that it is merely Chislev's child, Nature, that is calling out to them.

Should a young woodshaper fail to experience anything but hunger and fatigue during the three days, elder woodshapers deem the candidate unready for the responsibilities of a Shaper and tell the elf to try again the following year.

Although now well over 2,000 years in age, Anaya's Tree still stands at the center of the grove where Anaya merged with the forest. Despite its vast age and despite being split down the middle, showing the hollow where Silveran Greenhands matured, it remains vibrant and healthy. The same is true of the eighteen similarly ancient and immense oak trees that surround Anaya's Tree. Legends state that they originated from splinters that were driven into the ground when Anaya's Tree gave birth to Silveran. Qualinesti woodshapers and priests believe that each of these oaks represents one of the Krynnish gods—except the three gods of magic whom the Qualinesti believe have no desire to be represented in the natural world—and that for as long as these trees remain healthy and hearty, Qualinesti too will survive, no matter the hardships. The simple fact that the grove survived the burning of the forest during the War of the Lance by Dragon Highlord Verminaard's troops entirely unscathed seems to prove this theory's verity.

The Grove of Anaya's Tree in the Present Day

The Grove of Anaya's Tree continues to be an important part of the rites of passage of young woodshapers. However, far fewer formally follow the path of the Shapers of Destiny, as Beryl, the dragon tyrant who has seized control of the Qualinesti Forest, and her Dark Knight minions have declared the grove off-limits. Qualinesti turncoats informed Beryl that the Shapers were among the most fiercely patriotic of the elves and that steps had to be taken to weaken them if the intermittent rebellions were to ever be quelled. Further, just as the grove remained untouched by the raging inferno unleashed upon the forest by the Red Dragonarmy, so has Beryl been unable to affect it with her mighty woodshaping abilities— she can neither coax the vegetation to grow faster within the grove, nor can she destroy it. The grove has also resisted her attempts to unlock the secrets of its magic; in retaliation, she has ordered the Dark Knights to put to death any elf who is found within its boundaries.

Still, every year, a brave woodshaper or two uses his or her close relationship with nature to sneak past the Dark Knight cordon that surrounds the Grove at all times and to remain there for at least three nights and three days. Stories abound that these woodshapers have found their abilities greatly enhanced from the visit. Whether there is any truth to these stories, no one can say for sure.

Adventure Seed

Allorran of Qualinesti is a woodshaper who has resided on the Isle of Schallsea for the past decade, serving as an instructor in the powers of the heart at the Citadel of Light. One morning he awoke from a particularly lucid dream that he firmly believes was sent to him by the spirit of Anaya.

In the dream, a beautiful, green-skinned maiden whose face was painted in the style of a Kagonesti shaman told him to journey to Qualinesti and to cut a live branch from the split oak. Then, she said, he was to plant it in the Dryad Grove near the Citadel. There it would take root and come to be a new site to which all woodshapers—Qualinesti, Kagonesti, and Silvanesti—could journey to commune with nature, irrespective of their cultural backgrounds. "A new day is dawning for all elves," she said just as he awoke.

Allorran approaches a group of heroes either at the Citadel of Light, in the Port of Schallsea, or at a port along the Abanasinian Coast. The Narrator should present him of an old and trusted friend as one or more of the heroes (perhaps even having him appear in an adventure previous to this one in order to establish him as part of the campaign). He asks them to help him undertake his mission into the depths of Beryl's domain and to be part of something that will unify all woodshapers.

If the heroes join in the mission, they must avoid numerous Dark Knight patrols and outsmart a group of brutes, draconians, or one of Beryl's lesser green dragon minions. Helping Allorran secure the branch will be most challenging, as some of the most dutiful and vigilant Dark Knights stationed in the Qualinesti Forest have been charged with guarding the grove.

Should they and Allorran be successful, it remains up to the Narrator to decide if the woodshaper truly was inspired by a higher power or if he was merely possessed by hopeful fantasies. His woodshaping talent and the magic inherent in the branch will cause it to take root in the Dryad's Grove and the dryads will certainly welcome the addition to their forest, but is it truly the momentous event he believes it to be? If it is, maybe the branch matures into a massive oak overnight.

Whitestone Glade

Whitestone Glade was one of the most revered sites of the Knights of Solamnia for over two millennia. In present-day Ansalon, Whitestone Glade continues to hold significance, even if its importance has waned as a result of developments during the War of the Lance and following the Chaos War.

The History of Whitestone Glade

In the decades after Solamnia broke from the Ergothian Empire, Vinas Solamnus grew concerned that the nations he had led to freedom from the corrupt Ergothian Empire would eventually slide into corruption themselves. Therefore, as the twilight years of his life approached, Solamnus undertook his fabled Quest of Honor, a search for insight, wisdom, and guidance.

After many weeks spent in the mountainous wilderness around Palanthas, Solamnus sailed to Sancrist Isle. Upon his landfall, he forged into the forested wilderness west of Mount Nevermind. In time, he found a glade where a black stone of granite, twice as tall as a person, stood as though thrust into the ground by great force. He instantly sensed there was something special about it, so he fasted and prayed to the gods of Good.

After three days and three nights, Paladine, Kiri-Jolith, and Habbakuk revealed themselves to him. As their constellations shone brightly in the sky overhead, ethereal music filled Solamnus's head—Paladine's grand justice represented by well-ordered chords, Kiri-Jolith's courage by enduring themes, and Habbakuk's temperance in balanced counterpoint. With the music came visions and wisdom—the framework within which Solamnus could create a knighthood that would carry forward not only his own legacy of truth and honor but would uphold the high ideals of the three gods for generations to come.

In a flash, Solamnus knew that three orders would be established, and that their members would embody honor and live it day by day. The highest order would be devoted to

Paladine, championing justice. The second would uphold the high standards of courage and self-sacrifice embodied by Kiri-Jolith. The third would be devoted to Habbakuk, forever personifying loyalty and obedience.

As Solamnus's vision ended, the heavens blazed with a divine light so strong it blinded him. When his vision cleared, the black rock had transformed into a gracefully twisting pillar of white crystal so brilliant it appeared as if a piece of a star had fallen from the heavens and lodged itself in the ground on Sancrist.

Solamnus returned to the mainland and founded the Solamnic Knighthood, penning the original Measure—the standards to which all Solamnic Knights hold themselves—and the Oath. "My Honor is My Life" are the words they continue to live by.

As the Orders grew in size, settlements appeared in the wilds of Sancrist. Whitestone Glade served for centuries as the place where the heads of the Orders would meet to discuss changes to Measure and pass judgment on Knights who had committed gross infractions against the Oath and the Measure. The Uth Wistan family was charged with protecting the island and the sacred glade. Over the centuries, the Whitestone came to hold meaning for the rest of the peoples of Ansalon, becoming a symbol around which the forces of Good could rally. One of the first Kingpriests of Istar even offered a blessing at the stone, declaring it sacred to the gods and forbidding mortals to touch it.

The Knights of Solamnia have stood proudly against Evil for over 2,600 years. Although the spiritual center of the Orders fell victim to corruption in the years following the first Cataclysm, they have been revitalized by the efforts of two exceptional Grand Masters within the past century, Gunthar uth Wistan and Liam Ehrling. The Knights remain a strong force for Good in present-day Ansalon . . . a union of men and women willing to sacrifice their lives in battle for truth and justice if called upon to do so.

However, there are those who call these the final days of the Knighthood, despite the resurgence it has enjoyed in recent decades, and such doomsayers seem to have more evidence for such predictions than they had even during the darkest times following the first Cataclysm. This evidence is found in Whitestone Glade.

One of the more powerful legends that surrounds the Whitestone is that it is a symbol of the divine support and blessing for the Knighthood. The nature of the stone and the glade seemed to bear this out. Regardless of the time of year, the climate in the glade was one of late spring . . . always mild and pleasant, even while the rest of the surrounding forest was baking in summer heat or shivering in the depths of winter frost. However, during the War of the Lance, the stone was split in two when the blacksmith Theros Ironfeld threw a dragonlance into it. Although the Knights of Solamnia were instrumental in defeating the Dark Queen's forces during the War of the Lance, some philosophers took the destruction of the Whitestone to mean that, despite the fact the gods once again bestowed their gift of priestly magic to their followers, they had withdrawn their blessing from the Knighthoods.

For a time following the War of the Lance, the Knights of Solamnia appeared to prosper, but then the Knights of Takhisis swept across the continent in an unstoppable wave during the Summer of Chaos. The Knights of Solamnia were virtually wiped out and even the mighty High Clerist's Tower fell to the forces of Evil. Further, when all magic ceased to function in the wake of the Summer of Chaos, the glade's pleasant weather ceased. Although fragments of the Whitestone remained in the Glade, still as white as the stars in the heavens, its magic—and the blessings of the gods—appeared to have departed entirely.

Whitestone Glade in the Present Day

With the magic of Whitestone Glade apparently absent, even some members of the Knighthood itself consider this loss of magic a symbol that their days are being numbered. The Whitestone is shattered, the eternal spring of the Glade is no more, and the Knightly Orders have been in retreat for the last decades, surviving only by abandoning several of their traditions in favor of stealth, and, some would claim, dishonorable conduct.

Sword Knights and Rose Knights who have traveled to the Whitestone Glade to follow in Vinas Solamnus's footsteps, however, tell a different story. The most widely retold tale is that of Linsha Majere, the first non-Solamnian woman—and one of the youngest at that—to ever earn rank in the Order of the Rose. Only days after Linsha's acceptance into the ranks of the Rose Knights, the Order asked her to become part of a clandestine circle of Knights somewhere in east. She became deeply troubled. Wanting not only to live up to the examples set by her grandfather and father—the famous Caramon Majere and Palin Majere—but also to the grand traditions of the Order of the Rose, she feared such a mission was wrong and dishonorable. In 23SC Linsha embarked on her own Quest of Honor, hoping to find a resolution to the moral dilemma she faced.

Travelling to Whitestone Glade, she spent two days in prayer to the gods. On the third day, she used the mystic magic she had mastered as a girl at the Citadel of Light to reach out to any spirits that might be present in the Glade. By the end of the third day, she felt drained, both physically and spiritually, but as she looked to the heavens, no stars blazed at her—all she saw were clouds drifting in the pale light of the moon.

Suddenly, she was attacked. Another Knight, a member of the Order of the Sword named Wandyll, had followed her to Sancrist. He felt jealous of her accomplishments and that he had been ignored for advancement to Rose Knight in favor of her. Linsha fumbled for a weapon as the corrupt Knight attempted to strangle her. Her life was slipping away when her hand fell upon a rock. She felt energy surge through her as she used the fragment to strike the man's skull. She struck him two more times and he tumbled aside, now shouting in pain instead of fury. Then, almost instinctively, she called upon the powers of the heart and commanded nearby vines to lash out and grab hold of him—where she had been spiritually drained, she now felt completely rejuvenated. She looked at the blood-smeared rock she had used to fight off her attacker. It was a fragment of the Whitestone, somehow missed by scavengers and relic hunters. But it shone with a soft white light that faded even as she noticed it.

The gods still watched over Krynn, Linsha decided, and then and there resolved to serve the Knights of Solamnia in whatever way the Grand Master saw fit. If she had been meant to die there, the magic of the Whitestone Glade would not have come to her assistance. Upon delivering her attacker to Castle Uth Wistan and the justice that the Measure demanded, she returned to her parents' home in Solace and from there vanished into the obscurity of a clandestine circle.

Recently, other Knights of the Rose and even mystics who are not part of the Orders have reported strange flashes of rejuvenation while in or near the Glade. Skeptics say that the so-called magic of the Glade is merely an illusion brought about by desperation or wishful thinking on the part of those who experience it.

Nonetheless, Whitestone Glade is gradually returning to importance as a site that more and more Knights of Solamnia once again wish to visit. The Grand Master of the Orders has made his position clear on the matter by reinstating the honor guard in the Glade: If the power of the gods still resides there, the Knighthood keep any minions of Evil from despoiling it.

Secrets of the Whitestone Glade

There is indeed magic present in Whitestone Glade, but whether it is part of the primordial magic that was infused into the world of Krynn at its creation or the product of a god's watchful eye is unclear. Heroes must discover the properties of the Glade through play.

ЅAGA rules: Heroes whose natures are derived from cards with White or Red auras from the Shield, Sword, or Crown suits receive additional spell points while in Whitestone Glade. The points can be used to create only spells of the alteration, animism, and channeling spheres. The number of points received varies and is determined by drawing a card from the Fate Deck and doubling the number on the card. Once used, the points do not regenerate, but each time the hero returns to the Glade, he or she can gain its benefit. (The extra points remain with the hero until they are cast, even after he or she leaves the Glade.)

AD&D rules: Heroes of Lawful Good or Lawful Neutral alignments and the ability to cast priest spells receive the curious ability to retain spells in memory even after they have been cast. Whenever the priest casts spells from the Animal, Plant, or Protection spheres while within one mile of the Glade, he or she can roll a successful Wisdom check to retain the spell in memory. For each additional casting beyond the first, a cumulative +2 penalty is added to the roll.

Adventure Seed

A party of heroes is hired to escort an old Rose Knight, who is sick and dying, to Whitestone Glade. He has heard that a young Knight says the gods touched her while she prayed there, and now he wants to visit Sancrist one last time to see if Paladine will reveal himself to him as well. However, a long-time enemy of the Knight, a former Knight of Takhisis, opposes the heroes and their charge during their travels. This foul-tempered individual fell away from the Orders after the gods left Krynn and doesn't believe the Dark Queen has returned as some claim. The heroes must escort the Rose Knight safely to Sancrist, or at least keep the Dark Knights' minions from interfering as the two old enemies have their final duel.

Raekel's Pit

Raekel's Pit is a terrible mark left upon Krynn by one of her most Evil priests. Even in the Age of Mortals, it continues to fester like an open sore. Located in the southern part of the Sentinel Mountains, its true origins are shrouded in legend, but little doubt exists that it is rank with Evil.

A History of Raekel's Pit

As Ackal Ergot was conquering the lands that would some day become the Ergothian Empire, legend has it that a priest known as Raekel plotted against him. Although Raekel claimed to be a priest of Manthus (an Ergothian god of industry and dreams, known as Majere elsewhere in Ansalon), he in fact served a triumvirate of Evil gods—the Dragon Queen (Takhisis); Aeleth, a god of death and disease (Chemosh); and Argon, the god of Dark Vengeance (Sargonnas). The deities had promised him Ergot's fledgling empire if he would perform certain rituals that would grant them ultimate power over Ansalon. Somehow, three gods of Good—Manthus the Mighty, Corij the Blade (Kiri-Jolith), and the Blue Phoenix (Habbakuk) uncovered the plot and sent their own champion against Raekel. The identity of the champion varies from story to story—some cast Ackal Ergot in the role of champion (these are the most popular versions in the Empire of Ergoth), while others cast the elven leader Silvanos or a lowly kender or gnome as the chosen one. (A highly ahistorical variant popular in Solamnia states that Vinus Solamnus was the one who defeated Raekel.) In all versions, the hero arrives too late to stop Raekel from performing the sacrifices that begin the ritual, but instead throws him into the gap he has opened to the Abyss while the three gods of Good combat the three gods of Evil.

A chilling Ergothian song tells of a day when a cabal of thirty-three dark mystics will raise their voices in a dirge that will bring Raekel back from beyond the Veil. He will finally complete the ritual he started almost three thousand years ago and assume dominion over the empire, turning it into a charnel house. Few Ergothian bards ever use the song as part of their active repertoire, but virtually none of them ever forget the names of the thirty-three mystics.

Raekel's Pit in the Present Day

The gods have withdrawn from Krynn in the Fifth Age, but Raekel's Pit still yawns up, a two-hundred-foot diameter shaft which is filled with boiling mists and howling shadows. The hunters from the nearby barbarian village of Ker-Manth rarely come within twenty miles of the place—and those brave hunters who have dared to search for game closer say that they have not seen any animals once they are within ten miles of the Pit.

Since the Chaos War, stories have circulated that on the darkest, longest night of each year, a ten-year old child has crawled from Raekel's Pit. Many doubt the truth of these tales, as their origins have been traced back to a kender who in 19SC claimed to have been taken captive by a group of young humans who called themselves the Children of the Pit. He also supposedly witnessed one of their number being born. He died shortly after stumbling into Thisway in southern Kenderhome, wounded and suffering from a disease that none of the kender healers could cure. To further discredit the tale, when Belladonna Juniper, the afflicted kender who rules of Hylo, dispatched parties to search for these mystics, they came back empty-handed.

Nonetheless, tales abound of a hidden group of mystics living somewhere in the southern Sentinel Mountains. It reportedly consists entirely of exceedingly handsome humans ranging in age from ten to about thirty. Some tales claim a bent, ancient man leads them. The more detailed versions of the rumor claim that he wears a holy symbol of Argon, although he also has the symbol of Manthus branded on his face.

Secrets of Raekel's Pit

There is indeed a tiny group of mystics living in the Sentinel Mountains not far from the pit—and only one of them is of Krynnish origin, the old and decrepit Dolan Rak-Mahl.

As the War of the Lance raged across Ansalon, Dolan Rak-Mahl was getting by as an alley-basher. He kept a low enough profile so that neither the Thief Guild chapter in Gwynned nor the authorities noticed his activities. However, his luck ran out when he attempted to rob a priest of Manthus. Unfortunately for Dolan, this priest had been part of the Ergothian delegation to the recent gathering of the Whitestone Council on Sancrist. There the priest had met Elistan, one of the first generation of priests to wield the magic of the gods since the Cataclysm, and had gained knowledge of the proper ways to honor Manthus, who granted him priestly magic. This magic took Dolan completely by surprise, causing him to stiffen so that he couldn't move a muscle, which allowed the priest to drag him through the town to the City Watch.

When Dolan went on trial, he begged for his life. The judge said that normally he ordered violent criminals like Dolan hanged, but that the thief was so pathetic that it was hardly worth it. Instead, the judge turned to an ancient law that seemed appropriate now that the gods were returning to Ansalon: He ordered Dolan's face branded with the symbol of Manthus so that all could see that he had transgressed against the divine powers. Even though the priest, the victim of Dolan's attack, objected, the judge upheld his ruling.

A brand that had not been used for over four hundred years marked Dolan's face. Still sobbing from the pain, he was dragged through Gwynned and thrown out of the city's front gates. Here, he cooled his sizzling face in the mud by the road. As he lay there, he screamed at the gray city walls, swearing that all of Gwynned would suffer at his hands some day. The guards on the walls laughed.

Suddenly, a silky voice asked if Dolan was truly interested in revenge. The thief looked in the direction of the voice and saw a red condor sitting in a nearby tree. The condor continued to speak to him, and Dolan discovered that it was a messenger from one of the true gods and that only he could see it. The condor offered him the opportunity to serve the god of vengeance, Argon, and told him to journey to the ruins of Fav in the south, where he would discover the ways to honor Argon, if he survived the trials he would have to undergo.

Dolan succeeded, and thus became the first priest of Argon in Ergoth since the Cataclysm. He worked to further the dark will of his god and to expand his worship for the next three decades. During the Summer of Chaos, as the gods prepared to depart from Ansalon once again, Argon's messenger came to Dolan to tell him what was happening. He commanded the priest to journey to Raekel's Pit to perform a ritual to start a process that would eventually bring about the final destruction of the Empire of Ergoth.

Dolan obeyed the commands of his god. As he performed the ritual on the edge of the smoking pit, he felt the presence of Argon, which had been a constant part of his being for thirty years, fade. A sharp red flash sparked from the pit's smoky depths and in the heavens the very constellations changed. Dolan held his breath as he awaited a tide of destructive forces to vomit forth from the pit—but nothing happened. Unsure of what do to next, Dolan took up residence in a nearby cave and waited for an additional sign from his god.

A few months later, on the winter solstice, the sign Dolan had been waiting for came in the form of a young boy of unearthly beauty. "I am a child of the pit," he said. "I will teach you the ways of magic, and you will teach me the ways of revenge. With your help, my brothers and sisters will eventually consume this land."

The child showed Dolan how to master spiritual magic, the final gift of the gods before they left Krynn. Dolan taught the child the proper ways to honor Argon. A year later to the day, the child took Dolan to the pit. Here, they witnessed another beautiful child crawled out of its depths.

Each winter solstice since then, another child has emerged from the pit. Dolan has learned that a ritual that started three thousand years ago is finally reaching its fruition. This will continue until they number thirty-three. Then, the final days of Ergoth will be at hand, and its demise unavoidable.

Dolan hopes that he will live long enough to see this demise. He has already started using the foul magics taught to him by the children to extend his life. He hopes that Ergoth will die with him—in fact, he has grown to hope that all of Ansalon dies with him!

When a small force of Dark Knights came to Raekel's Pit in 27sc, three of the oldest pit-born were slain when the Knights came upon them unexpectedly. The remaining pit-born have assured Dolan that they will return, emerging from the pit as they had once before. "No living being can stop us," one of them said. "Only he who slew Raekel, the one known as Julius Har-Retal, can harm us—and he is long dead."

The knowledge that an unavoidable doom awaits Ergoth in the not-too-distant future keeps Dolan clinging to life.

Adventure Seed

A pair of teenaged kender vanish from their homes east of the mountains that hide Raekel's Pit. Heroes in the area listen to the kender parents plead with them to find their lost children. Some afflicted kender locals tell the heroes they are convinced the two missing kids were abducted by Evil cultists dwelling near Raekel's Pit. One of the afflicted kender can lead the heroes there, but she refuses to expose herself to any danger.

After a battle with some of the cultists—all of whom are very powerful in the mystic arts—the heroes are almost overwhelmed, until a pair of young kender show up and turn the tide of battle in their favor. These are the missing teenagers.

They had not been abducted but had merely run away from home because their parents had said they were too young to get married. Before the in-all-likelihood quite irritated heroes can bring the pair home for a happy ending, Dolan Rak-Mahl casts a deadly curse upon the heroes that causes a rotting disease. He reveals—possibly as his dying words—that the heroes have seven weeks to find a place known as the River of Healing. Only there can the curse be lifted and the disease cured. They will die if it takes longer than that.

Dragon Wars™ Card Game

A card game for 2 to 4 players
Revised rules by Steve Miller

DRAGON WARS™ is a card game that has gained widespread popularity throughout Ansalon over the past few decades. Those who play it claim that it was conceived by regulars of the Broken Horn, a tavern in Sanction, shortly after the War of the Lance. In those days, each player "played" a Dragon Highlord battling for a piece of the crumbling Dragon Empire; to win, each Highlord had to destroy the Dragons serving the other Highlord. With the advent of the Age of Mortals, players thought of themselves as dragon overlords fighting to destroy the dragon minions of other overlords. The people of Krynn play the game both purely for the fun of it as well as for money.

Although the people of Krynn play it using a TALIS™ deck (a Krynnish deck of cards used for everything from fortune telling to games of chance), this game can be played with a standard deck of playing cards, like the ones used for Poker or Bridge. In addition to the deck of cards, each player at the table needs thirteen counters (coins, scraps of paper, pieces of candy, or other small objects). A piece of paper and something to write with may be useful as well.

The Object of the Game
Each player must protect his or her loyal Dragons from harm and try to slay Dragons in the service of other players.

The Rules
Each suit in the deck represents a specific element of the game. The suits of Clubs, Hearts, and Diamonds represent *attack values* or *defense values*, the mighty weapons and defensive

fortifications of the opposing forces as well as the battle prowess of the mighty Dragons. Clubs are attack cards, Hearts are defense cards, while Diamonds can be used either for attack or defense. Defense values are played to protect a player's Dragon, while attack values are applied in attempts to eliminate the Dragons controlled by other players. The value of each card equals the number printed on its face. Each face card in the deck also has a point value. Jacks have a value of 11, Queens of 12, and Kings of 13. Aces are worth 1 point.

The suit of Spades represents the Dragons that are recruited into service by the players. The numbers on the Dragons represent *health points*. Each Dragon has a number of health points equal to its value. If a Dragon suffers damage from an attack that exceeds its health points, it is slain and placed in the *Trophy Hall* of the player who slew it.

Getting Started

In preparation for play, remove all cards from the suit of Spades and the Jokers from the deck. The Jokers are not used in this game and should be set aside.

Shuffle the thirteen Spades and place them face down in the center of the playing surface. This area is called the *Dragon Nest*. Each Spade represents a Dragon of different strength and ability, with the Ace being the weakest Dragon

Each player should count out thirteen counters and keep them ready. These keep track of the current health levels of the Dragon under the player's control and will be referred to as *health counters*.

Each player draws one Dragon from the Nest, with the youngest player drawing first, and places it face up on the play surface in front of him or her. Each player should place a number of health counters on his or her Dragon equal to its health (at this point, the same as the card's face value). Shuffle the rest of the deck and deal each player a hand of five cards.

The game can now commence. The player controlling the most powerful Dragon goes first.

Playing the Game

1. At the beginning of each turn, the player refills his or her hand to a maximum of five cards (players already holding five cards skip this step). When a player draws the last card of the deck, simply shuffle the discard pile and start again.
2. Flip the top card of the deck. The suit of this card is the *trump* suit for the turn.
3. The player can choose either to attack one opposing Dragon, or discard his or her complete hand and draw a new one. If the player discards, his or her turn ends when the new hand is drawn. If the player launches an attack (see "Attacking and Defending Dragons"), the turn ends after one attack.
4. When the turn ends, play passes to the left.

Attacking and Defending Dragons: When a card is played, the attacking player does not reveal the card he or she has played until after the controlling the Dragon being attacked has chosen to defend and has selected the specific card he or she wishes to play. The initial attack and defense cards are revealed simultaneously.

Attack: To launch an attack, the player chooses an attack card from his or her hand and initiates a battle against an opponent's Dragon. The face value of the attack card indicates how many *damage points* the attack can cause. If the card used in the attack is trump, flip the top card of the deck. If it is an attack card (Club or Diamond), the face value is added to the attack. If the new card is also trump, repeat this process until the flipped card is not trump, adding each subsequent attack card's face value to the damage point total. Defense cards do not count toward anything.

Defend: The player under attack can attempt to fend off the assault. Once the total attack score has been calculated, he or she applies the value of the defense card from his or her hand to block all or part of the damage inflicted upon the Dragon. If a card he or she used for defense is trump, he or she flips the top card of the deck and adds its face value to the total defense score if it is a defense card (Heart or Diamond). If the new card is also trump, repeat this process until the flipped card is not trump, adding each subsequent defense card face value to the total. Attack cards do not count toward anything.

Press the Attack: If the attacking player has another attack card from the same suit as the first one played, it can be used to press the attack. The card's value is added to the attack total. For example, if a Club was used to initiate the assault, in order to press the attack the player must use another Club; if the player cannot play another Club, he or she cannot press the attack.

The defender may then choose to add to his or her defense. However, he or she is free to use any defense cards in his or her hand (Heart or Diamond). The attacking player may, in turn, choose to further press the attack. This sequence continues until the attack cannot be pressed any further.

Assess Damage: To determine the outcome of the attack, subtract the total defense from the total attack. If the remainder is positive, the targeted Dragon suffers that many damage points.

For every damage point a Dragon suffers, the controller must remove one health counter from it. If any health counters remain, the Dragon survived and play passes to the left. If all the health counters are removed from a Dragon, that Dragon has been slain! It is removed from the game (see "New Dragons and Despoilers") and placed face down behind the attacker's Dragon. It is now in that player's Trophy Hall.

All cards used in attack or defense are discarded and placed, face up, next to the deck.

New Dragons and Despoilers: When a Dragon is removed from play, its controller must immediately draw a new one from the Nest, put the appropriate number of health counters on it, and refill his or her hand to five cards before play passes to the next player. If no Dragons remain in the Nest, the player is still in the game, but he or she is a *despoiler* rather than the warlord he or she has been up to this point.

A despoiler has no Dragon to protect; he or she fights only to kill other players' Dragons. A despoiler is at something of a disadvantage. While the player continues to refill his or her hand at the beginning of each turn, all defense cards drawn are useless since the player no longer has a Dragon to defend. They can be disposed of only by discarding the whole hand, preventing any attacks that turn.

Winning the Game

The game ends when every player has had one final turn after the Nest is empty or the last Dragon dies.

When the game is over, each player adds up the health point value of the Dragons in their Trophy Hall. The resulting number is the player's *victory points*.

If any Dragons remain face up on the table at the end of the game, they have survived the Dragon war! Their players receive five additional victory points for successfully protecting the Dragon until the end of the war. The player with the highest victory point total wins the game.